WE CAN
REPORT THEM

WE CAN REPORT THEM

by Michael Brodsky

Four Walls Eight Windows

New York/London

Published in the United States by:
Four Walls Eight Windows
39 West 14th Street, room 503
New York, N.Y., 10011

U.K. offices:
Four Walls Eight Windows/Turnaround
Unit 3, Olympia Trading Estate
Coburg Road, Wood Green
London N22 6TZ, England

Visit our website at http://www.fourwallseightwindows.com

First printing October 1999.

Library of Congress Cataloging-in-Publication Data:

p. cm.
ISBN 1-56858-144-0
I. Title.
PS3552.R6233W38   1999
813'.54--dc 21   99-36040

                                                             CIP

10 9 8 7 6 5 4 3 2 1

Printed in Canada
Typeset by Precision Typographers, Inc.

Chapter One

Bert and Belle were that rarity among rarities, a truly happy pair, barring one or two flies in the ointment. But aside from these, things were flowing along as smoothly as they should, under the circumstances.

They lived in a suburb where the dwellings were as placid as saplings. Next door to the screech of the birds, a little river (unnamed, to this day) ran unabashedly amuck over splinters and stones.

Getting out of the convertible at the airport where he was picking up Belle's mother (mom, nowadays), he noted the sky was unusually purulent, jowlly even, for this time of year. Joyce, the mother-in-law, interrupted to point out that the V.I.P. lounge was clearly not what it used to be, the attendants nothing less than staunchly indifferent to client needs (she'd already punched out a fax of complaint to Fred, her current lawyer and one of her ex-husbands). In spite of everything, she took her time, Bert noted, stirring her aperitif, as if to say: What the hell is life anyway, will you tell me, without its recreational cozy nooks and crannies?

Leonard, her present spouse, was trying to comfort Joyce, promising that of course they'd follow up with a call once semi-settled in Manhattan. Remembering Bert's father (dad) had been terminally ill for going on several years now (which fact might account for his get's lean and hungry look), Joyce took it as her duty to ask whether it mightn't be a good idea for him—an obviously inarticulate slob eschewing all legitimate outlets for the feelings he didn't even know he had (if anything, woman, they were too clear-cut for comfort and by no means simple loving ones)—to pour out his heart to an old, trusted friend. (And, in any event, wasn't she even the least bit aware yielding but once to this need to disburden would only generate an infinite sequence of instances of such need?)

But he tried to remind himself that without hindrances like Joyce, and Leonard, littering his path, there'd be no path. For the path was the sum of its changes in direction and such changes subsisted by virtue of the obliteration of stumbling blocks. Back at the house, just as Joyce was about to light yet another cigarette from Leonard's butt (her seventh, at least), Belle saw fit to remind Bert he had to pick up his boss at the Armory heliport. Before sticking it in her holder, Joyce said, I'd have thought at this stage of the game you were no longer on twenty-four-hour call as America's favorite yes-man. Leonard went on looking straight ahead, as if waiting for a bird—any old bird—to fly into the bay window-framed paulownia tree and become a leaf. Bert looked at his wife, but Belle's smile was not quite throwing in its lot with his own.

Leonard said, I've been ailing myself. So I know what it must mean for your pop. Father, Bert said. Father, said Leonard: One doctor says Yes, the other No. Leonard tends to exaggerate, for comic effect, I presume, Joyce remarked. The tests show nothing. Belle took Leonard's hand and patted it adroitly. Saying, I'm not a monster, Belle, if that's what your gesture is trying to say, Joyce stood up and allowed the paulownia, still framed by the big bay, to become more than a backdrop: it was now her sidekick-in-residence. How many times have I forgiven him for ordering me to his bedside in the middle of the night to announce the end was near. So if I don't get busy stroking his paws at every whimper, you can understand why not. In any case, when you get to the ripe old age of Bert's pappy (Albert, isn't it?) you should stop the hammy self-indulgent meeching and get on with the business of croaking. You are afraid, mother, Belle cried. One concessionary stroke, so you thought—think—and one simply binds oneself to the concession for all eternity. But what she doesn't realize, said Belle to Leonard or Leonard to Belle—Bert was too dazed by all the tasks before him to be able to distinguish—is that holding back can be far more provoking of whimpering insatiability in the matter of such concessions.

But there are moments, said Joyce, turning away in grimacing acknowledgment, when indeed I do want to rub my nose comfortingly in his prickly old hide. But it's so damned hard, ladies and gents of the hung jury, to isolate a specimen of authentic feeling-cum-doing in all this hash of oughts and shoulds. So hard (the repetition seemed more for effect, however) to swoop down on some rare bird of unprompted unselfishness at a moment's notice.

Bert looked surreptitiously at his watch (it needed an overhaul) though surely there was no shame in being a busy man. As he got his coat from the hall closet, one of his daughters, crouched on the staircase, eyed him with some interest. He waved as if back at her, not knowing himself why. Belle, her back turned on his exit, went on conferring with Joyce about the subject of dinner, whether in or out, introduced minutes before. Leonard looked over—discerningly, as at an old print—the provokingly bare wall above the open baby grand.

Bert works himself too hard, said Leonard, as if the hard worker were already well out of earshot. To the very bone, Joyce subjoined expressionlessly. Then, with tone at last matching words: Don't you worry your prissy little head about Bert. He's damn lucky to have the job he has—any job at all—and in times like these! (I hope I don't have to remind you: do I? how many billions are out of work world-wide. I have the statistics in one of my Gladstones.) If he's so upset about his sire's state that he can't—won't—toe the line and bring home the bacon, she pursued, trying hard not to sneer, he should, as I've told you I don't know how many times already until I was blue in the face, talk to an old friend. Or better yet, a professional. That's what my third husband—a. k. a. your father, Belle—used to do every chance he got (I have him to thank for this here cigarette holder, though not for much else). The truculence of the remarks hobbling the pretense of their having been spun—right before their very eyes—out of a one hundred per cent rancor-free woolgathering, Joyce seemed to think it best to quit while she was ahead with: We were never without our dearest friends, professional or otherwise. Belle said outright: Well, Bert hates friends, dearest or otherwise, in defiance for once of her need to be always convincing Joyce of somebody's right to be different, that is, to just be. But the deep sigh that came after said she already knew only too well her efforts to convince attested to one thing and nothing but that thing, namely the wounded craving still for a mother's authorization. Joyce declared: Anyway, old Albert's a burden on Bert and, more to the point, on Bert's capacity to provide for his growing family. He should have bowed out long ago.

He reached the FDR Drive, or rather, the 60TH Street (in any case, not the Armory) Heliport just as what had to be the airship in question was making its way out of a multi-pinnacled cumulus cloud, lording it over the skyline like the cream of the cream of some heavenly jest, the significant thing about this beast being, as far as Bert could see, its continuing to grow right before his very eyes and with every new excrescence, however overinvaginated in its rococo charm, clamoring to be regarded as the single most crucial building block and so organic to the final structure, no matter if a mere hodgepodge of outpouchings and likely to remain so, that said structure must be not just incomplete but pretty much unthinkable without it. Maybe this had something to do with the fact that every such appendage automatically managed to suggest that it had been extruded through a nothing less than ruinous—no, self-annihilating—albeit haphazard, expenditure of all remaining inner force.

His chief, B. Austin Samuels, of the Turing Advertising Agency, descended the gangway with a ceremoniousness of the distinctly chilly sort, evidently vexed at being held once again at bay by lurking autograph hounds about to pounce. Right off the bat Bert reminded Samuels that his father, his stepfather rather, was as ever gravely ill and might therefore at any moment have to be rushed to the chronic emergency care unit way off somewhere in the wilds of the Bronx. Samuels shook his head gravely, revealing no thoughts, much less feelings, on the matter other than those Bert could, if he so chose, determine to have been squelched by the headshake itself.

After shaking hands, the two men proceeded to the taxi bank (Belle would retrieve the jalopy after the endodontist). As their cab negotiated a steep curve out of the blue Samuels said: This may turn out to be the most crossroads-like pow wow of your career, and laughing heartily, that is, with the sort of effusiveness Bert thought he recognized only too well as forced by a bad conscience, added, We're meeting with a client who's heard of you and, better yet, your work. He's positively loco about your last commercial: you know, "The Reflection Principle". I sort of thought so, Bert answered, feeling suddenly as sick as if he were entering Bangor (Maine), say, under its notorious freezing autumn rains and not a single motel in sight. I mean (to Sam's quizzical and not altogether amiable look), I sort of surmised that somehow today of all days we'd be meeting with the Client of Clients. They were at this very moment descending the gravelly drive of what looked like a trendy inn: that is to say, in spalike annexes it vividly abounded, but of the flagship there was nowhere a trace. Samuels murmured: A veritable paradise enow for the bushed chief exec. And on the cutting edge of nowhere to boot.

With cocktail in hand, Samuels, as if resuming an interrupted conversation, said: In short, with this client on board things are beginning to open up, wider and wider, so don't be surprised if the same nobodies peeling pencils in their ventless cubicles today aren't giving some flunkey directions on how to oil their very own monogrammed large-bore electric sharpener the day after tomorrow. Bert didn't want to look as brightly expectant as he knew he must but out here, on a stamen-studded suite-connecting verandah, with its shamefully direct vantage on not-so-distant pool friskers (the poker-faced stewards be hanged), it was simply impossible to look, much less feel, combative, especially with Samuels now drawing forth from his attaché case an impressively thick ream of what looked like abstracts, all branded with the same vaguely familiar heraldic figure in the upper right hand corner of their cover sheet. And wait, here was Samuels yet again, extending a pen—and to Bert, of all people—for use, presumably, on those dotted lines he'd already heard so much about and never seen (all prior contract signings having been pretty shabby apprenticeship affairs).

The pen dropped at Bert's feet, still shod. Turning distastefully from the younger man's sneakers (sold to him under the name of walking shoes), Samuels, halfheartedly eyeing one of the lovelies at halfhearted play, noted that he seemed a wee bit nervous. Bert (as if taking note of a flaw in the landscape): I guess it's my moment to feel overwhelmed and to want, frankly, out. Having spoken, he immediately dreaded Samuels' dread that this modest admission would immediately debouch on a semihysterical confession demanding in its turn the sociably sympathetic upheave of a homolog casting plenty of self-glamorizing aspersions on some specimen from the boss's own (all-too-human) past. In fact, he didn't like Samuels' all-too-human side, a sideline at best, and nothing would give him less pleasure than to have the old fart trot it out for an airing. But there was something in the moment (Samuels was lifting one of the contracts or abstracts—who's to say what they were? did Samuels himself know?— that had fallen along with the pen) big with the imminence of somebody's feeling in duty bound to pour out his heart. Especially now that the waders were making the splashes preliminary to a showy exodus from unbriny shoals. This "something in the moment" was of course just the pain-event he'd been dreading ever since Joyce cast doubt on his breadwinning abilities but how frame it before it framed him, before he became a mere stillborn depending from its udder.

You see, every time I hint at a change of direction Belle—that's the wife—feels obliged to point out that Joyce (the mother-in-law) or somebody intimately connected with Joyce has undergone *the very same crisis* and at the exact same time of life, thereby robbing the rite of passage and me in tandem of all uniqueness.

In other words, Samuels said, removing his sunglasses, she makes a frame for the terrifying unknown so as to soothe herself all the while peddling her ploy as a sop to you. And the proofs she brings forward to affirm that she would never abandon you no matter how hard you fell on your face (after yet another misguided venture into the unknown, but that's none of her business) no doubt only capsize what little credibility her protestations of undying support have managed to muster. Eh, my boy? Am I warm or am I just plain warm?

She and her mother think I'm a bit unhinged.

Sounds like she's the one who's unhinged. They, I mean.

So, Mr. Samuels—Bob—won't you please forget what I just said about wanting out (something he'd—Mr. Samuels'd—Bob'd—just said—what was it? excoriation of the mother-and-daughter act?—had acted as a tonic) and…reconsider…hiring me. This could be my big break.

I'd like to—hire you back, I mean. Even if you didn't make the Flowers Best-dressed this time around.

Bert chose not to address the Flowers issue just yet.

Please, Bert said, though with far less conviction, not at all because he was losing hope (he'd never had much to begin with), but rather because now that he'd tried on for size this none-too-deft impersonation of the eager beaver and played it—as constituting (at least from outside the impersonation itself, looking amateurishly in) the royal road to manly potency—to the hilt, he was discovering he'd done just enough to demystify such a role forever. In short, impersonation as handselling the infinitely enviable all-that-was-not-Bert both in and out of the workplace was already contaminated by the stenchy tailings of all-that (inescapably)-was. For no other reason than the impersonation's having itself required the services of the very one who was to be done definitively away with, compliments of impersonation.

Better do something about The Joyce, Samuels acknowledged, rising to go, for he had espadrilles and sunglasses in hand.

Belle.

What?

Belle. The name's Belle. Joyce is the in-law. I mean, the by-law. I mean, the byword. For a second—longer, however, than Samuels' shrug depreciating such hairsplitting—Bert noted he himself was having some trouble distinguishing between the two or, more to the point, needing or wanting to so distinguish. Before we get started, Samuels roared from the door to his suite (though the distance by no means warranted the racket he was so proud to be making), now might be a very good time to get a visit or two to your old pop out of the way, and with this, more command than suggestion, Samuels disappeared waddling, though he was by no means overweight—on the contrary, there couldn't be a trimmer CEO on the face of the earth—behind a potted palm.

Chapter Two

The road to the rehabilitation wing—indeed the world itself—
looked much different now that he knew he was to be getting his third
(or was it in fact his tenth?—at any rate, his biggest) shot at directing
a commercial, and the road being absolutely silent, Bert began living
(as so often before) the silence, positively pulsatile with well-being, so
what if not his own, as long overdue guarantee of his stepfather's take-
off to the next world, yet here was the old boy (as so often before) wav-
ing to him from his window (the one with the dirty blinds expertly
tripped), though not in greeting: clearly something dire (a near-miss
fractured hip? two, then, in the space of a little more than a week?)
once again required immediate attention. While parking Bert had to
resituate—resurrect—himself in a world where events clearly refused to keep pace with his wishful thinking. Here he was faced with
the old problem, then, of aching to make his indifference visible without however making it too much so, especially now that he, Albert,

was being obliging enough to be dying. Though in the case of Albert dying appeared to be just another form of life, perhaps the most reinvigorating form known to man as Turing machine. And/or was he in fact dying: this was the question, and the question's being a hanging one was what made Bert fragile, immunologically speaking, so that at the end of every encounter, not so much with Albert as with the assorted well-wishers and helpmates multiplying faster than spirochetes with whom he surrounded himself, more than ever did Bert feel the need for a long hot shower to disinfect himself of their assurances of a quick and permanent recovery.

For they assumed he loved Albert more than words could tell and wanted nothing more than for the operation on his anus or his crop, scheduled to take place any year now, to be a smashing success. As he advanced on the sickroom unlike any other (or was he just thinking in TV commercialese) his discomfort (Albert was, after all, not his father) again became so great the only remedy, short of that far-off shower, was to, as usual, direct a grim and thoroughgoing attention to what needed immediate doing [not his father, though, least of all owing to genetic unaffiliation but rather because the old guy simply did not like (no)—love (even less pertinent)—believe (there!) for according to the latest accredited definition wasn't a Father he who believes at all cost, that is, whose belief is in direct proportion to the ever-expanding sum of cogencies already superabundant thereagainst (still, no denying Al's non-belief might be the only sensible course where Bert's doings were concerned)]. But first he had to call home. It was Leonard who answered, saying: I know how Albie's illness must make him so— a bit—difficult, and Bert could only fume at this inept effort to partition the stages of the other's life as if he'd been any less trying in the old—the very best of health—days. Didn't Leonard the Kindhearted know Bert's unease was deserving of something far better than this smarmily downplaying transformation of its cause, Albert's careerist hypochondria, into mere old age-specific semi-helplessness? Don't think I'm not appreciating your heroic efforts to cheer me up, Len, Bert murmured, striving for virile neutrality. It's just that in the long run it's far easier to be dealing with the old boy as an invariant quantity rather than have you try to perspectivize his gripes and groans. On a lighter note, I hope you're having loads of fun with the girls and can you please put Belle on? But Leonard stuck to his guns so Bert gave up and asked, How was the damn barbecue? to be pleasant or, rather, to underline how much of an effort he was willing to make—host even in absentia and despite prevailing circumstances—to sound so, at which point Joyce saw fit to take the law into her own hands by snatching up the phone and once again excoriating the errant stepfather's shameless refusal to step into his coffin and allow Bert to at last get on with the business of making his name in whatever numbskull company might still be willing to clock him in and out.

Entering ready to confront him in his unchanging, what was Bert's astonishment (albeit an astonishment he allowed for from time to time and one that did nothing to mitigate the doomed sense of such unchanging) to find the thing he was nevertheless always least prepared for: a slight change. Evidently exhausted by what appeared to have been an unusually strenuous series of tests, Albert was now discovering as he rattled on that in point of fact he was home at last, better yet, safe and sound in his bed, with nothing more taxing than the evening's snack and the evening's TV shows to look forward to. So here, once again, was Albert exertionlessly staying more than a step ahead of him, Bert, the—his—disease(s) doing all the strategizing required and that strategizing a maddeningly ever-elusive entity forever beyond his latest coming to terms with it.

You know, Albert said, licking his lips after what must have been a copious dinner but positively de rigueur for one about to undergo the intricacies of resection (the traces thereof, including overbed table and papboat, had all been cleared away: Albert demanded prompt service from his staff, and the featheriest flair for continental courtesy, if you please), you can go on vacation after my—Bert thought he was going to say *passing* (detestable, intriguing euphemism) but no such luck. He shook his head and replied: Belle and the kids might go (with Joyce and Len, he's her consort of the moment: a goodhearted guy) but I can't be thinking along those lines just now. He realized after he'd spoken that Albert would take this to be a homage to his monumental frailty and hated giving him cause for such presumption, for in actual fact he'd been thinking of the commercial he was scheduled to shoot if all went as planned. But it was clearly the appropriate—the only conceivable—response, for here was Albert, right on cue, and maybe even a little beforehand, insisting, with a singularly self-satisfied lack of conviction, that he didn't want to stand in the way. Or maybe he was insisting that he didn't want to be a burden, or to have a hard-on, but whatever the gist Bert was incapable of receiving it with suspended disbelief, much less compassionating gratitude, for Albert was not the typical aging parent, or rather, indeed he was along, alas, with being supplementarily propped on the stilts of a lifetime's valetudinarian cunning for the most part unmotivated by the exigencies of old age. The very fact that he was speaking of Bert's vacation at all was especially enraging inasmuch as a further longevity was thereby posited for the old boy, in this case determined by whatever time it took for Bert to drag his (presumably tanned and toned) ass back to where it belonged. The future Albert was kind enough to be stretching out to Bert was also being stretched out for him, Albert, in animated cartoon-vivid tandem. In fact, the future remaining (when hadn't it been?) Albert's sole property and invention, Bert was being vouchsafed leave once again to make use of it almost as he so chose, within certain clearly defined limits, of course.

He said nothing, hating himself for striving through sheer poker-facedness to will the old bastard into insensibility, to annihilate him through abstention from even the merest sign of life. So there would no longer be any hospital visits to interfere with his shoots. The doctor—an altogether new one—entered, already in his streetclothes, in sign that he had to get going pretty soon, what with the raw wind rattling the snowy pipes and more to the point (though here he stayed decisively mum) the flakes of honey locust enchanter-fleeing the Macks over on First, Third and Eighth whose stampeding sideline is, as everybody knows, to close-shave the jaundiced pinnae right off their—First's, Third's and Eighth's—tarry, rutted skulls. He and Bert shook hands, the doctor (one Frank Q. Pratt, if his name-tag was to be trusted) exuding a no-nonsense, no-frills deference for the presumed agonies of the next-of-kin. This, the most familiar whiff of his kind, at least according to Bert's extensive experience of medicos, did not offend, didn't even unnerve, because it bore no connection to the case at hand. Was it the fear of being forgotten amid all these preliminaries that spurred Albert to extend the remains of a banana still in its skin which he'd evidently been hiding under the sheets (the very crime for which he routinely, albeit timidly, excoriated his roommate and father-confessor when the latter was safely, at least from Al's perspective, out of earshot). Here, doc, he said smarmily, I can't take one bite more. Accepting it with a conspiratorially reproachful smile, Pratt wrapped it in the plastic sandwich bag he'd already managed to remove from the left inner pocket of his sport jacket and held it behind his back, prestidigitator style. So, if such interplay was any barometer, over his relatively brief stay in this, the diagnostics wing, Albert had become quite the favorite of the staff, even its mascot, but, come to think of it, hadn't preferment to that subprofessional post been in no small measure contingent on flashing forth symptoms from every nook and cranny in such a way as to tax collective ingenuity to the utmost without, of course, denying it a jubilating final accession to decipherment. This was what, in the domain of viscera, must be known as ready wit. With a geniality that bordered on fulsomeness, Dr. Pratt proclaimed, He's quite a magical concoction, your pop is. He overturns, by his very being, rather by his flagrant—some might say pornographic—persistence in that being, all our textbook notions of wear-and-tear. But Bert was now no longer listening for what all the chitchat pointed to was the following: Henceforth in the presence of this healer and his flunkeys, he, Bert, would be obliged to traffic in—have truck with—a new Albert, plundered of all the familiar—nay, his signature—excesses, and so the doc's obvious infatuation with this contraption made him dread any further intercourse with it, for that intercourse must now be overshadowed by amphitheatre-size flummery of a particularly intricate sort. How he loathed (and dreaded) making his way back to Albert still beside him through such a tunnel of forbearing fondness as had just been dug by the good doctor.

But once Albert had been wheeled off for his own good, the doctor, good or otherwise, put Bert's self-hate temporarily to rest by stating with a kindness that surprised him—drove him wild with gratitude—as kindness always did, All kids go through this with their folks. Hearing the remark in the key of ultimate recovery he could of course only bristle. But once he began heeding it in the way it positively cried out to be heeded, as not-so-latent felicitation for all the freedom to come should Albert finally have the good grace to go the way of all flesh, he found he could also heed it as intimating a bit, but only just a wee bit, more, something along the lines of, say, a tempered plea for compassion (however burdensome the body in question may have been or might for that matter still be), it being well-understood of course that even the threadbarest deference to said plea would involve no diminution whatsoever (this was clear, wasn't it? from the way old Pratt crinkled up hitherto unsuspected crow's-feet around eyes, nose and mouth) of its gist: disinterested commiseration for Bert's center-stage arctic plight.

Arriving back at the temporary headquarters of the Agency (and before he even could don his trunks for a dip in the pool), he noticed there was already a fax in the machine set up (by whom?) adjacent to the walk-in shower. Was Samuels having second thoughts about Bert's being the man for the job? If so, why not simply walk his dubieties over in person or slip them under the door? Before he could read the communication, however, there was a call from Dr. Pratt's office: his right-hand man—he's an intern, but no matter, and he goes by the name of Dr. Frank Grass (so said what sounded like a receptionist highly unsatisfied—rightly, Bert was sure—with her current pay scale)—wanted to speak to him: Please hold please for Dr. Grass. Although he had to restrain himself from crumpling up the piece of paper in his hand, he managed nonetheless to listen carefully as Pratt explained that Albert was coming along splendidly—blood pressure, heartbeat, penile discharges (as to color and consistency), rectal diameter, all were well within the perinormal range for one in his age group—and could be expected, in time and with the proper attention, to become only more so, splendid, that is, as the cutting and splicing, the butchering and suturing (to quote his mentor), proceeded apace. The music that had been piped non-stop into the theater of operations had certainly contributed to the turn from the expected turn for the worst and, needless to say, of course the nursing squad deserved highest marks for esprit de corps, even if it had been relatively easy to muster owing to the fact that Albert was well-liked, positively everybody without exception having taken to him from the minute he flashed his toothless gums in their general direction. Unfortunately, there were a few matters—noticeable pause (as Grass signalled to somebody to not mind waiting and he'd be with them in just one moment?)—that needed to be discussed immediately.

So he had no choice but to hurry back to the hospital, leaving the still unread (yet still uncrumpled) fax under his favorite coffee mug (it followed him everywhere: a gift, not at all atypical, from Joyce who, as it so happened, had also been visiting when he'd received his first promotion not too many years ago).

He was met in the visitors' waiting room by Pratt, swinging a stethoscope and sipping, from a styrofoam cup, what smelled like unsweetened herbal tea. He spoke breathlessly though it didn't look in the least as if he'd been on the run: The first stage of the maneuver has yielded a forty-to-sixty per cent good-response rate, one far more impressive in fact than we had any right to expect. We hope to have the patient—your dad, I mean, your stepdad—ready for the second exploratory stage as soon as they've managed to scrub down recovery room B according to management specifications (they're real sticklers, these M.B.A. administrators, about everything except what really matters but enough about me and my one-man campaign for bedpan justice). He could hear Albert groaning, presumably in recovery room A. As he might have predicted, the groans did not disturb him in the least. Indeed, he couldn't help giving all his attention to this fact, outshone only by its obverse, to wit, that he was even less disturbed by the long (and to anyone with recognizable human feelings, patently ominous) silences in between. What did, on the other hand, affect Bert and to the point of panic was the fact that the waiting room was filling up at an alarming rate. I think I'll go get some coffee, one waiter said briskly to another, presumably his better half of going on for what had to be at least fifty-five-odd years, all golden. When he came back, she impatiently disregarded the stains on the receipt, not to mention the coffee itself, and tallied with avidity so as to make sure he, that is to say, the two of them, had not been gulled. The counter girl's a real crook, groaned said better half: I remember her from the time mom had her first liver transplant only they didn't call it a transplant in those days. Come to think of it even in those days—maybe as far back as Arnie's girlfriend's double mastectomy (what was her name again?)—she was always sticking her grubby little hands—don't let those cheap rings fool you—in the cashbox. The coffee retriever shrugged, stung or completely indifferent or perhaps slightly relieved that reminiscence was depriving him of her company, that is, disembarrassing him of her unceasing scrutiny. But of course, Pratt went on, this will depend on many, one might even go so far as to say too many, factors, not least significant among which is your overall attitude as next of kin. At this point, not quite a juncture, a young man in a business suit charged in.

I was just telling Albert's stepson here, Pratt intoned, that we are confused (vigorous assenting headshakes from the intern) and our confusion (basilisk look to squelch such lickspittle assent) takes the following form: Why should the symptoms stop dead in their tracks the minute they enter our wards? In short, he may have to remain under observation here for quite some time. Oh my God, Bert, super-conscientious to a fault, murmured involuntarily for he was already envisaging all the arrangements to be made in such an eventuality: the rerouting of correspondence, invoices, bank statements, the selling of furniture, the closing out of each and every retirement account for the sake of a little ready cash, the cashing-in of preferred stocks or whatever they were called, worst of all the inevitability of having to throw himself on the goodwill of the very neighbors Albert had spent a lifetime and then some alienating with his complaints (about their noise,

uncleanliness, low morals) however mousily conveyed and who therefore doubtless harbored not-so-secret and completely justified ante-
diluvian grudges. He must beg them nonetheless to keep an eye out
for burglars, landlords, fans, terrorists. What we are attempting to do
right now, resumed Dr. Pratt in a tone suggesting he'd already read
Bert's racing thoughts and was hereby striving in the name of all that
was humanly decent and professionally sound to forestall any premature frenzies of adaptation, is to stabilize a rapidly worsening condition. This means getting him to show some consistency, however ominous, however . . . fatal, in his symptomal life, not only in but also out
of hospital. And I know for a fact that he wants to go home: a man's
home is his castle, after all: I myself hate these places myself, God
knows: always have. Bert sensed this was neither the time nor the
place to explain that *more than anything* Albert hated to be rushed out of
a sickbed, would defend to the death—that is, anybody's but his
own—the God-given right to go on occupying it. Of course he's become an asset—a most tangible one—and not just to the staff (to
who else then? Bert dully wondered) and we don't look forward to losing him. Why, the avenues of investigation opened up through the
auspices of his everchanging clinical picture are virtually limitless, for
the fact of the matter is he seems, your sweet old step-pappy does, to
embody so much of what plagues and inflames the modern world. The
modern world, echoed young Dr. Grass, though without the slightest
trace of irony. He manages (how does the old boy do it?) to provide a
habitat, and a most viable one, for what we up to now took—mistakenly, as is every day being dramatically demonstrated to our top
men—to be highly incompatible body-, that is, pain-events. Why, he's
singlehandedly rewriting our whole lexicon of aberrations, and not
just of the cocktail party chitchat sort. He's a fucking genius, intoned
Grass, for whom slick hyperbole evidently entailed no diminution

whatsoever of self-worth, no reared ugly head of compromised professional integrity.

But, Bert saw quickly enough (did Grass see too?), though he wasn't quite sure he could say, unequivocally, that he was happy about the seeing, there simply had been no catching the eye of his mentor with so pop a pronouncement. You see, proceeded Pratt without missing more than this one beat, old Al is something of an entrepreneur: he is constantly effecting new combinations of the means of production of the very symptoms that are our stock in trade, lifeblood, meal ticket, what have you, which is not to say he can expect to leave here making this function his cash cow—sorry, vocation: it can only and will ever emerge mixed up with other, far less essential activities. And it is more than a mistake—it is a downright crime—to think Al's entrepreneurship would have been best studied in the days just before he first became a patient, that is, a symptom-generating Turing machine, and, stark naked (except for lime stick, lime box, pubic apron and rectal bib), paraded his slit gongs up and down the roof of some Iatmul ceremonial house. For in those days, a headhunting permutator like Al simply had too many malfunctions to perpetrate ("far less essential activities", Bert told himself) and so his characteristic specialty—lost in the shuffle, so to speak—could hardly be expected to stand out diacritically in adequate relief. But now that he has you and your wife (Belle, isn't it?) not to mention a primal horde of loving neighbors to assume the buying-and-selling, managerial and legal responsibilities that once absorbed so much of his apparently limitless energy, he can give himself up wholeheartedly to the command of his discharges. Mind you—and Grass, you back me up here—he hasn't so much created any daringly original symptoms as (exploiting whatever means of production were lying unused in his hairless old trunk to his own sly Schumpeterian advantage) brought forth some pretty challenging new combinations of the old. What can you do, his orenda elects to participate only in phenomena that are at heart permutational. So until he exhausts all conceivable variants of one symptom-cluster, it refuses to move him on to another. Having still sought once again (in vain) to deliver himself of a supplicating look capable of capturing his mentor's eye, Dr. Grass, sore bestead, finally gave up saying, as if to revenge himself: You can see him now, but just for a moment before they sponge him down: do speak softly and only of things light-hearted. The fact is, Pratt added, as if the last remark was an unsightly clot of dust and his tone the whisk broom, papa's downhill course may have something to do with the staff's being at this very moment not a little displeased with Our Mr. Al. You see, our madly theorizing diagnosticians whose job it is to think him through are feeling a bit dwarfed—obliterated—by all this permutational propagation of ostensibly incompatible events on the part of one who should have the decency, at least part of the time, to just lie still and be grateful. They feel (am I right, gentlemen, wherever you may be?) there has to be a happy medium between such unstoppable multiplication of pathemes (body-events positively reeking of morbid process) as completely hobbles the operation of their mind-stuff and the kind of stark dearth of events that causes said stuff to atrophy from want of target-oriented stimulation. In short, though they depend utterly on your pappy for thinkable things, the actual thinking is being submerged, devalued, through the sheer unthinking proliferation of the things themselves. But go see him—hurry! most patients find it very comforting. Very very comforting.

The recovery room, as large as but in no way resembling the billiard hall of an Edwardian country house, in fact was far more akin to a madly pulsating shroud. Entering he could only marvel (as in the case of Albert's previous groaning) at his total insusceptibility to the despair he'd heard tell was appropriate in such places. Was this because he was managing (once again? at long last?) to burrow into the tiniest of intervals, both in time and in space, whence all that might otherwise be expected to lacerate was necessarily excluded? What mattered in any event was that he was no longer undergoing (for the first time? for the thousandth?) Albert's dying, if dying it was, as a process triggered and unfolding inside him, Bert, as just punishment for insufficient vigilance. At long last, in this gurney coop, he was allowing himself (for the first time? for the millionth?) to stand back and take note of its— the process's—sheer exteriority, that of a tramp steamer afloat on the horizon with no clear-cut itinerary. Just for the hell of it he whispered, Before you take one step further, Albert, will you do me a favor and tell me just this much: Have you ever been the least bit proud of me as your son if not as your son-and-heir? It's true I devolved on you as another man's waste product. Not even a gurgle in response: time to go. The fax, if nothing else, clamored for his immediate attention.

But then he remembered. He was here to proffer comfort. Don't worry, Albert, he said. No response. Don't worry about anything. Still none. Don't worry about a blessed thing. More of same. But just when he was about to give up on the comfort Pratt had almost gotten him to believe he was capable of administering and Albert of greedily accepting and it looked like the latter was to be wheeled into another part of the forest of gurneys by a low-level white-coat looming half-in half-out of a broom-closet, Albert murmur-muttered, I wonder what they've found. No response. Very curious about what they're going to find. Still none. Aren't you? More of same for Bert was simply stunned. Hell, he could understand (surrendering wanly at last to smiling assent) *some* chatty-scientistic curiosity about clinical entities (the essence Albert had been all his life struggling to situate as if it were that very *neshamah* cooked up by Ike Luria and his crowd?) but—Yet what if the

utterance was not about curiosity at all but rather about the form stoicism takes in the self-importantly unheroic or rather about, simply,
babbly nerves? But whatever the utterance was or wasn't about and
granted it was Bert's comfort and Bert's comfort alone that had made
such purgation possible, for all that he couldn't help missing an old-
fashioned sorrowful, quasi-repentant admission of the primordial
dread that alone constitutes explicit recognition of the comforter
which, in this case, was the comforter's overarching objective. So, as
white-coat (her lapels needed starching) came forward to claim her
passenger there was, maddeningly, no getting *I'm very curious about what
they're going to find*'s implausibility (for at such a juncture nobody—not
even a virtuoso somatizer like Albert—experiences the perfect
schoolboy's eagerness to learn expressed thereby) out of his head. [Un-
less it was because his superannuated schoolboy's body—for so long
an insatiably rotten thing hence taboo—had, under the sign of rotting
certified and accredited, become an admissible, even commendable
(because institutionalized), subject of learning.] And even more mad-
dening was his certainty that Albert himself didn't hold the key to the
key in which the real words behind the implausible ones had really
been sung. The gurneyed patient acted, then, without knowing that
he acted—effortlessly, flawlessly; and if he didn't end up axed by the
fax, Bert must get his recruits to do the same.

Chapter Three

When he finally got to the fax (after barely two hours sleep and that bogy-racked) it was in the kidney-shaped ad hoc executive conference room (transferred, no doubt, by a quick-thinking chambermaid) the following morning. The Urgent now stamped in red across the top almost cancelled both letterhead and logo. Skimming as Samuels introduced the topics in the agenda of the meeting, Bert gathered with great difficulty (he was experiencing the beginnings of one of his migraine toothaches) that following a just appraisal of his previous advertising-related theatrical and video work for the firm he had once again been denied entry into the environs of eternity via the just-published Best-dressed list of the right honorable Professor Floyd Flowers.

In short, he did not qualify as canon-fodder. By the way, would this affect Samuels' decision (had it been one?) to let him direct the pivotal production (a commercial about serial killers, wasn't it?) of the firm's career? The fax, quoting very much to the point from the Herr Professor's preface to the latest edition of his List, reminded him that the workings of said eternity had been determined by the good doctor to within a very small margin for error and thus if Bert had been denied participation it was all on the basis not only of good clean fun but also, and of course more to the point, of sound metamathematical thinking. They were all looking at him, waiting to ingest, like a second breakfast egg, his self-defense so as to be able to jeer, he was sure, at its lameness later on, in, say, the recesses of the executive washroom. He merely said: So, no point in permitting me to go on whittling and carving for the firm. Everything's already been decided well in advance of any future member of the sequence of my productions. But maybe next year, that is to say, on the basis of my good work this year— GreenHurstWood, one of Samuels' most dedicated lieutenants, shook his head primly: Professor Flowers has miraculously managed to do far more than merely forecast the future of men such as you: he has done what no man has done before—telescoped the process whereby the authentic masterworks in our domain succeed in carving out a niche for themselves . . . in eternity. What GreenHurstWood means, said Samuels (it was unclear, however—ordinarily a stickler for lightning clarification for once Bert blessed its non-emergence and was almost ready to beg for more of same—whether he was exasperated by his sergeant-major's pill-sweetening bombast or embarrassed by its adjacent brutality), is that our Professor Flowers is immune to oversight. No charge of same is ever, and never will be, layable at his doorstep. He is capable as no other of determining immediately what is eternal since he's mastered all the misassessments of the past. But how, Bert cried, in spite of himself and in spite of the fact that he knew he was about to make a spectacle of himself before almost-strangers, to wit, his coworkers or (as they referred to each other among themselves) his esteemed colleagues, how could they talk about having mastered the past, that is, the errors of the past, when the same appetites and consequently the same atrocity-sanctioning blindness engineered by those appetites as facilitator of their satisfaction went on upwelling as long as man was man. As much talk about schooling oneself in not getting hungry, in this case, for the blood of one's fellow creatures. Instinctual needs, that is, rapacities, would forever clamor for satiation—in this case, for the unjustifiable abasement of as many of Flowers' betters as were required to stifle his own self-loathing and maximize the impact of the naming of the chosen all-too-few whose instant apotheosis became his very own.

All the same, Bert couldn't pretend the Flowers list wasn't the promised land, like the towers of Christminster for that unfortunate on whom he'd been modelling himself for most of his life, Jude Fawley. He looked around him, at those of his coworkers—no, colleagues—whose names had achieved inclusion therein. He could almost lick his chops with vicarious delectation as, almost by a reflex, he mimicked what must be the solemn self-satisfaction of this year's victors as well as those of yesteryear (indeed, the bloom was never off the rose when that rose was a genuine Flowers)—the chosen in and out of season—clearly dead—and why shouldn't they be?—to the possibility that there was something just a wee bit degrading about having one's messy artisanal strifes already baptized (and in a font of fonts coyly planted right smack in the groves of academe), all prettily dressed for posterity's gourmandizing, or was this just his honest-to-God envy talking.

Bert: Then there is no appeal? GHW shouted No as Samuels shook his head discreetly, trying to mute the gesture. We've already told you: Flowers has managed to factor every conceivable and bothersome contingency of process into his speculations on the Stock Exchange of

Eternity. He, unlike the obsolete critics of yesterday, has been trained—has trained himself—never to take artworkerly best shots (swoon-worthy anthology pieces all maimable to the same sameness) at face value. Any such concoction—nay, the very act of creation—is now recognized to be nothing more (thanks solely to his efforts) than the warning symptom of an artworker's need—his banal compulsion—to seduce and must be diagnosed-analyzed out of existence accordingly. [Which Flowery diagnosis-analysis, Bert muttered under his breath (or maybe he just *thought* it under his breath), then rushes right in to become itself *The* (supremely seducing) Artwork of Our Time.] Or of any time, GHW hisssed. None better than he knows all about workers (and a worker's evolution) and the traffic in futures. Why no one better than he, asked Bert with a lump in the pit of his stomach. (Everyone, not just GHW, was at the steam table so he now found himself competing for their attention, divided even at the very best of times, with croissants and Scotch broth.) His question went unanswered since GHW's eventual *Because already knowing into what each work will evolve (or fail to evolve) over centuries, over epochs, he has absolutely no trouble smelling out the magnum o. sure to be still mag millennia and millennia hence from the snooty little period piece,* coming far too late for lump-emulsification, acid-test of any true-blue answer, could not qualify as one. Still Bert had to admit that as Flowers' pro bono press agent, GreenHurstWood was making one hell of a case for his Boy. But didn't they all see that he needed His boys merely as proof of their airy expendability in the name of a phenomenon that would turn out to be far more lasting—that would reverberate across ice ages to come as the only true art work—namely, his own incomparable discernment, his uncannily unerring ability to separate the men from the boys, and the demiurges from mere men, so what if the demiurges so deemed were in actual fact least likely to pass muster as such, much less as men, for first and foremost weren't they Flowers' boys? He was the true celebrity (no denying, however, that to those he fancied F. Gave Good Blurb) and these winners the mere raw material—the canon fodder—of his campaign. Mere dungs they'd been before he saw fit [as chief executive officer of the world-class, state-of-the-fart, cutting-edge (though not necessarily in that order) public relations firm Acuity, Unlimited] to alchemize them into perennial blooms of worth and glory (which once so deemed meekly crumbled back into the very dung whence they'd had the audacity to spring, dungier than ever). It was Flowers, then, and Flowers alone who, simply by assigning them such a destiny, brought assorted false-works and workpieces and parerga to a fruition with which they could never in a million years have hoped to have the least truck if left in the hands, to the devices, of their so-called—their mere—creator. Without a definitive naming cum destiny as perpetrated by Flowers these works would still be so much dung. Though, from the Herr's perspective, in essence raw material still, now they were raw material with a difference, a rack focus, that focus being on canon-conscious (as others are said to be diet-conscious) Flowers.

Looking down at what appeared to be his own annotated copy of the fatal fax GHW said: Too bad you're so visible, Bert, and always in a negative way, what with your step-pop at death's door so I hear, for—how long has it been going on now?—five years give or take a decade or two. Bert, you've lived too much, far too much, amid the stench of death and I frankly don't know—correct me if I'm wrong, counsellor (to the company attorney, one Hal Dane)—if such a bedfellow, however strange, does the company any good: it sure as hell can't do that commercial you're slated to direct starting tomorrow any good. Even if, Bert murmured, no simpered—for he knew he was scoring a point—it deals with the serial killer as an American folk hero on the order of—In short, your familiarity with matters deathly, GHW went

on, a little winded but from all indications (for one thing, he'd managed to don an intimidating pair of tinted bifocals somewhere down
the pike) undaunted, cannot help but alienate the very constituency
we've worked so hard to build. Bert remarked: I don't recall your having exactly been in on all the building from scratch, Sy. If my memory
serves me right you managed to materialize much later, and hardly at
ground-floor level.

Discounting Bert, bifocaled Sy pushed on with: What I mean is,
you're too familiar with death—Dietz's Great Unknown—in the
wrong way. I hear tell you're quite the virtuoso in staving off the demands (or is it the advances: come clean) of near-stiffs—that your
specialty is getting all recognizable human feelings out of the way so as
to proceed with those illegible hijinks on the waves of woe your
kind—though (alas, bub) it's one of a kind—confuses with bigger and
better things. But let's face it, we need somebody who can make his
hams depict exactly what joe blow or your average Joesephine would
feel in his/her bones when told mom or sonny boy's been hacked to
bits and steer him/her through the sewer of *those* feelings step by step.
So, assuming we gave you carte blanche, what happens? Instead of
buying back in to Serial Kill as an unjustly maligned popcorn subgenre, the public our clients are out to net now spends all of our time
bemoaning its failure to keep up with your evasions.

Sheepishly, Samuels said, Bert, Up to now I'd had every intention
of passing on that account we talked about earlier, on the verandah.
Really I did. But, also really, I don't know too much about tumors in
general, much less your pop's in particular, but I've been led to have a
sneaking suspicion that somehow you'll end up handling the assignment we hand you in the same way your pop has handled—that is,
manhandled—his disease (I have, you see, a few connections down at
Met General: isn't that where he got himself diagnosed?). It'll start off

as something to oppose to the tumor—the weapon with which he strafes the world—but will end up only mimicking it.

GreenHurstWood interposed: To sum up (that is, if you want me to, Boss? To Samuels' credit, he didn't respond, just went on staring straight ahead.), you won't be able to enter into the assignment because you'll be too caught up in using it—in your hands, the clankiest of implements—to remedy your exclusion from the Flowers best-of-the-dressed (among other things), in other words, to bludgeon Flowers as your stepdad (Albert, isn't it?) or Albert as Flowers or Flowers and Al as everybody else into a drooling insensibility infinitely more reassuring than tumorous death.

Your obvious trepidation over the assignment—over being at the mercy of everybody and his brother's potential for hate-fuelled ridicule once you set foot in it—betrays a self-hate consequential to your hatred of Albert who is after all, from what I can make out, so very much you. [This last from the company medico, an overweight but extremely competent-looking fellow sporting a pick between his teeth and a cornflower in his buttonhole. (But Bert took heart. For the diagnosis had been made without conviction, as if the utterer were merely keeping his hand—rather, his tongue—in lest, in the unlikely event of there being a for once truly unselfish urge to shed light, too-long abstention should discover him without the means.)]

Interposing without begging leave to do so (but not—Bert at this moment oh so desperately needed to believe—just to flaunt his prerogative as chief), Samuels mournfully intoned: So if you could only try loving Al, your aged and aging parent, after all, it might reduce your work-obstructive self-hate by more than half and go a long way towards engendering a stance more compatible with (forgive me for rearing their ugly head. Though, come to think of it, why should I be forgiven?) market-place values.

So there was no choice (though he'd never be caught dead admitting as much to the likes of GHW, much less Samuels—or to the likes of Samuels, much less GHW—or to the likes of the medico, much less the medico) but to get back to Albert as fast as he could and love him according to company specifications, which, when you got right down to it, were by no stretch of the imagination all that different from Flowers canon-fodder-type specifs. And as it turned out it was indeed lucky he had elected to rush right to the hospital when he did for on whom should he first lay eyes but Albert himself already well on his way to the operating room from recovery room C.

But before he could make up his mind about how to start loving Albert the latter was gone, to his rendezvous with the butcher-and-suture men. So he decided to return to the patient's room and amid the sodden familiarity of his few possessions come to some decision. Just as he was becoming deeply—almost snoringly—absorbed in weighing himself on the scale in the adjacent nurses' lounge (unobserved so he thought) he felt an arm underneath his own—the one adjusting the weights: Dr. Pratt was taking him aside without preamble, a bit rebukingly, Bert thought, like a child caught, once again and after repeated warnings, playing off limits. Patting him on (and by some fluke at the same time restoratively kneading) his shoulder, right off the bat he announced: There are things that need to be kicked out into the open, the sooner the better. Bert suggested they might be better—best— aired in the patient's own room. Pratt concurred, adding, But they don't concern the patient—at this moment, the very least of my worries. Sitting himself down in a chair opposite the bed and under the pay-TV (had Bert remembered to take care of this week's leasing fee?), he said: From the way you lurk about like a lost soul, one could only assume you believed his ailments were the result of some ghastly dereliction on your part. No, that's not it at all, what I meant to say was something redolent less of your idiosyncrasy than of your status as universal man: Being (some clearing of phlegm)—a penny ante chiseler if ever there was one—no, I mean a scalpel-wielding artist of middling gifts—incises in its own time. So don't you be sitting around (Bert was still, adamantly, standing) waiting for the announcement of his death, for the only time you can rightfully expect such news is when you are too deep in the proliferating tasks connected with his dying to be on the lookout, partner. Then, and only then, the news will indeed come, overheard, the way poetry is supposed to be, and you won't really take it all in, busy as you'll be cashing checks right and left to cover last-minute emergencies like the need for a new night nurse (her surly predecessor having been given the boot, on no uncertain terms) or having the pipes declogged on the home front in preparation for the beloved's return. In short, being—sorry, Being—nosocomial artist-in-residence thanks to some foundation celebrated for subsidizing geniuses, will make it her business to have you learn of Albert's death when it no longer seems that you need him to die in order to be free, for by then you will have accepted your unfreedom— which is not to say that once apprised of the blessed event you will be free—that, my friend, you'll never be: who the hell do you think you are anyway, Manny's noumenon, the toast of Coney Island? One thing is certain, however, Bert began, not sure if he was concurring or contesting (and not caring particularly one way or the other for as far as he was concerned he was still on the lounge scale, poised for flight), there is a trajectory—a process—in—through—all this and, like it or not, I am nowhere near the end.

No, no, no, said the doc, that's not what I meant. Hell, I wouldn't expect such drivel from my intern. Simply, you're still far too entranced by the servitude Albert sees fit, even en route to the operating room, to shovel your way not to be more than willing to undergo it as your unquestionable self-defining lot. Why, you positively lap up the drudgeries by way of distraction, I suspect, from your deeper troubles: business-related, perhaps, although you don't strike me as one having too much entrepreneurial savvy. What line are you in anyway? It's true, Bert keened with a shiver, things might be much worse without them. There was the faintest edge of supplication in his voice, which he tried to suppress, even if there'd just been something in Pratt's tone that definitively hinted at sympathetic susceptibility. In other words, if Albert's mad intestines weren't strangulating you, your own might be and you yourself dead and buried, or so you've been taught to think. And by whom—Albert himself? your boss? the little woman?

He thought of explaining his plight at greater length but opted against trying to. If there was any justice and he got to direct the serial-killer commercial, as Samuels had seemed in his own way to promise, there'd be no more plights, ever—would that he could finally for-swear such glibnesses but words were always so far in advance of his very best intentions of turning into a man of few—of no words at all. He looked up: The surgeon was gone, and out: Rosy rooftop fumes slanted toward the horizon, on whose book-of-hours vellum budless, birdless maple-, oak- and poplar-prints were now (in keeping with this institution's too-intrusive theme?) commemoratively inscribed. Sud-denly Pratt—no, Grass—was in the room, informing him breath-lessly—no, quite calmly: it was Bert who was breathless—that Albert had just died, ironically enough, following the success, no less than staggering (We could report it), of an unanticipated tonsillectomy.

Chapter Four

But you've got to go on, you've got to go on, go on you absolutely must, Joyce cried, at the very moment they were all trying to squeeze into the white stretch limo that was to take them to the chapel. Being spared the sight of her through a just-in-the-nick-of-time relegation to the rumble seat emboldened him to say, while bypassing the passing sidestreets (dominated, oddly enough, and everywhere he turned—he saw without seeing—the ever more menacing reluctance of stockboys to halt their hosing down around areaways for the rush-hour foot traffic), I read the headlines and the small print and my heart always goes out to those who, butchered by events or by serial killers (elected or otherwise), just can't find it in their hearts, to say nothing of their stumps, to get a move on and go with the flow inasmuch as the Powers That Be have at last decreed the End of Atrocity and the beginning of Peace in Our Time. In short, dearest Joyce (still refusing to look her in the eye), my heart is with the dead and dis-

membered who, accursed rabble, are simply incapable of letting bygones be bygones with the speed that is demanded of them by the media so as finally to be getting on with the airy, lighthearted and long
overdue business of sharing, caring and healing. And so they—and
their sympathizers, scum like me—are rightly deemed refractory,
worse, irrelevant, to progress—defined as this lighthearted ability to
be getting on with it, stumps or no stumps—and therefore expendable. They—the dismembered—whether in Sarajevo, Kigali or
Crown Heights—the very key to the meaning of Event in Our Time
insofar as Event in Our Time, a.k.a. destruction in all shapes and sizes,
has a meaning—end up being marginal to the Event that wouldn't exist without 'em. Of course, as well I know, it's an obscenity for me, who
never endured a wound bigger than the hole in my penis (Belle, in a
stage whisper: Bertie, please!), an overrated organ if ever there was one,
to be speaking about being marginal. It certainly is, Joyce remarked to
Leonard who was dozing or pretending—wisely—to do so.

However, just when—why, almost as if he'd decided to follow her
advice to the letter!—he found himself coming back to life what with
Albert's sudden death and the small though not insubstantial legacy
(it would take care of the kiddies' chess and piano lessons for the next
several years) left to his two daughters, and Samuels' overriding of the
majority of GreenHurstWood's objections so as to put him in charge
after all of Serial Kill on the little screen, Joyce was taken seriously ill.
The depth of Belle's attachment to her mother, vastly underrated,
Bert now saw, by everyone, especially him, incapacitating her for the
assumption in a pinch of her responsibilities, Bert found himself once
again running the show. In short, Belle went almost to pieces. In short,
here was a chance—a second chance—to rectify his mistreatment of
Albert and emerge therefrom with all essential muniments of the
showman who at long last knows how to want—or to look like he

wants—what his mass public wants. In this case there was a much larger supporting cast, as was demonstrated by the instantaneous presence at the hospital (the same as before, though Joyce's wing was almost perpendicular to the dead man's) of Leonard and Fred as well as a few other ex-husbands. At any rate here was a Joyce altogether different, or so it appeared as he first entered the room, from the creature who had exited blooming and beaming from the VIP lounge at the airport several months, or was it just days, earlier? on the well-padded arm of her husband of the moment, the gentle Len. She looked, as the saying goes, considerably older. But at the same time, or maybe a little later, she hastened to assure him and whoever else happened to be present or cared to listen that she had every intention of returning home, however long it took—there was no rush, for when a man was sick to his stomach and then some said home (the babble of ill-assorted well-wishers notwithstanding) was definitely not his castle—massively, monumentally restructured.

And at the same time that she vindictively proclaimed her intention of recovering completely, she was not forgetting to do her duty of apprising him, and loudly—a little preview, it was—of the ordeals sure to come yoked to that recovery, thereby whetting his appetite for the tasks about to devolve on him.

One of her neighbors had just cablegrammed a lavish bouquet of zinnias for the sole purpose, so it would now appear, of allowing Joyce to make heavy weather of her zealous deprecation of such tokens, since the flowers in the bouquet (she explained) always died (thereby paying homage to the world's most tenderhearted soul). Only today—her very first day in ordinary, so to speak—why shouldn't the grosser implications of the sermon be cut from the program: hence the blooms were prominently phototropic on the narrow sill and Joyce herself had taken to wearing a few in the improvised buttonhole of her pink-and-blue peignoir, as if saluting the new lease on life she might just take it into her head to secure compliments, needless to say, solely of her own wily fortitude. He consequently could save face by complimenting her on the grand-hotel nattiness of her attire and was then able to ease into explaining that he had to be getting back to rehearsals: he'd already lost quite a lot of time owing to Albert's death and burial, to say nothing of having had singlehandedly (no other sibs) to put things in order long before the funeral baked meats could even be thought of. Joyce looked skeptical, as if the rehearsals, whatever they consisted in, would be a pretext for keeping away from her as much as possible. Bert told himself not to take her doubting personally: it was a universal strategy for fending off connectedness and of punishing him for highlighting her unavowable sense that, from the word go, she was unworthy of the attention she insatiably craved. But given the existence of such doubts he might as well feed them (and secure thereby a much larger freedom of movement), by warning her, for example, as he now proceeded to do, that these rehearsals were going to be lasting all night, tonight and every night. Only he was averse to lying because he was sure he would ultimately be denied what he was claiming for himself in and through the lie. Or because it was simply too painful to be reminded how far he (still) was from what the lie painted in such awful colors (to lie, my boy, is to whiplash oneself with the reminder of one's still insurmountable distance from the promised land sketched by the lie). To lie was to reawaken what he'd hoped until a minute ago was a dead craving—the craving to succeed with the actors, in/on the world's terms—dead no longer: to lie was in fact to be reawakened to craving, period. To lie to Joyce (to anyone, for that matter—No! stick to Joyce) was to relinquish the indecipherability he'd managed to half-master with Albert.

Chapter Five

The downtown converted warehouse in which they met the following night (Billy Meister Street, between Ludlow and Essex) left much to be desired in terms of aeration and basic sanitation but little, even he had to grant (though was he really the stickler others made him out to be?), as regards boundless working space. The stage manager, Samuels' new mistress (well over the hill but in comparison with her protector, a bona fide bobby-soxer), dutifully trudged off for coffee and doughnuts and champagne well before everybody was accounted for. Bert was deeply moved by their mere presence on the scene into which he read nothing less than a nakedness of measureless expectation. He tried to connect names with faces as quickly as possible, willingly forgoing his doughnuts in order to study them more carefully, particularly while they were eating.

May I step in here? Samuels asked. I can say—without of course letting you know the precise nature of the commercial—I myself don't know its precise nature, and why should I?—that it will, within the traditional thirty-second slot, convey the message that Crime does not pay. But at the same time it will hopefully resurrect the serial killer as a major mass-entertainment figure since, believe it or not, his or her popularity is dwindling; and with so many projects built around such a figure about to be released in time for the holidays, to say nothing of the multitude on the back burner that simply cannot be shelved any longer, much less trashed, it is our obligation as the small proud promotional voice of our client to ensure the self-perpetuating impact of those projects. Within the requisite time-frame, our product will manage to do what no other product on the same subject has done before, namely, cover the rampaging encounter with a final victim, chosen not quite at random, of that unavowedly best-loved of all American folk heroes down through his inevitable incarceration and deathwatch.

Get comfortable, Bert suddenly announced (liking the self sketched by his paternal tone). Priscilla (Jamestown: Nona Vincent Agency referral), he noted, was keeping her distance from Gift (just Gift, and unreferred). Ralph, the freckle-faced redhead to whom he'd already taken an immediate liking, looked a little less on his guard.

Acting, Bert began, has much—too much—to do with lying, as we all know. Of course, I'm not talking about the kind of lies we tell our mothers-in-law, for example. Those lies are not even worth mentioning (though he somehow knew they were). For example, you, Priscilla, may be obsessed with becoming a star. But a funny thing happens when you're in the presence of, say, Ralph. You find yourself playfully chewing him out for the very same obsession, which all of a sudden, in Ralph-land, that is, has turned into the sort of malignancy (you know the kind) the scalpel of your being is able to circumnavigate with death-defying ease. And during the instant of transfer—of the onus of abject admiration for "the stars" from you to Ralph—you achieve transcendence, that is, rid at last of your most tell-tale and hobbling defect, you become another, but only for an instant. Seeing, however, that his purely hypothetical case was making her uneasy, he quickly subjoined with what he tried to make seem a superjovial catch in his throat:

Hey, did I ever tell you the story about my old pal, Marty Heidigger (sic), ex-Nazi extraordinaire but, in spite of one or two minor quasi-youthful indiscretions, all-around regular all-right guy. Anyway, me and Mart were—I mean, was—taking one of our usual postprandial walks through the F. A. O. Schwarz Wald at Coney (for all our willingness to sidestep its John Franklin Bardinish fleshpots in the name of so-called higher pursuits we nonetheless knew there was a limit to our capacity for self-denial and at some point we'd just break down and have "to eat baloney/On a roll": God, how I love the way Lee Wiley enunciates those words, penned I might add by another old pal—albeit not a mutual one—Larry Hart) and out of the blue Mart turns to me and with a look straight out of William Irish says, You're looking around, eh, Bert? You think you're perceiving—grasping— taking it all in. I can tell, because you've got the fidgets: You want nothing so much as to get right back on the IRT and head directly home to sketch in every last detail so you won't forget. But as your old pal Larry would say (though there he was shamelessly plagiarizing old Plato's old pal Phaedrus)—Marty begrudged me my friendship with Larry—It's so easy to remember/And so hard to forget. You're afraid to forget because the consequential hankering to remember must force you to really undergo the given, that is, by having to recreate it from scratch and in far greater detail than can be confirmed by, much less copied from, its mere reality out here on the sands. But more of that later. Right this minute you want to break camp and get back home because you think you've been abandoning your inner sphere by too much standing beside the given, too much yielding yourself up to the given. In fact, you're wondering if you still have an inner sphere left and one halfway capable of annotating its facets. But if you've been really perceiving—which you very well may have been, for all I know, and, more important, for all you know—you were still deep inside that hallowed sphere all the time you were also alongside the thing in question—the trophy of your peregrinations—this Coney Island fecalith cum ventifact qua shitheap on the half shell. So far, so good, Bert remarked to Priscilla and Co. But then he came at me with a real whopper, right below the belt, can you imagine?—Marty, my best friend from kindergarten days, as lovable a guy as ever you'll meet (all right, except for that brief unspeakable stint as librettist to the Storm Troupers). What did he say that was so terrible? Gift asked sneeringly, as if whatever it was somebody like Bert had clearly deserved far worse.

How could Bert continue his story without (as was now inevitable) seeming to be hastening to satisfy Gift's morbid and exasperated curiosity?

The roller coaster was right above us, the air quite reeked of caramel popcorn and hot fudge sun—What did he say? He said, said Bert taking a deep breath and not just for effect, that the real perceiver, such as I took myself wrongly to be, never hurried back, with his booty stuffed up his ass, to the musty cabinet of consciousness in order to inventory his rakings-in. In the case of the real perceiver, the real man of the theater, Grasping, raking in, preserving, all took place both inside and outside at the very same moment so there was never a need to be scurrying back, ratlike, to some tome-lined outhouse for the purpose of completing a process that, if properly undergone, was instantaneously complete. The true explorer never needed to worry about hurrying back, armed with his booty, to confirm the intactness—nay, the continuing existence—of his insides for they were always there beside him helping to procure this or that ort of boards magic. But can you imagine? He referred to my perceptions as booty; to him my mind was about as capacious as a musty old outhouse. But I knew better than to take him to task for he was simply struggling—like our hypothetical Priscilla with her hypothetical Ralph—to disinfect himself of what he took to be his very worst tendencies, metastasizing fast— those that must, if unscuttled, condemn him to the lifelong status of a second-rate thinker, a "dealer" in entities, by arranging to have them, the second-rate tendencies, devolve upon me. For he, you see, was the one demonically possessed by a miser's rage to treat perceptions as so much swag, so much contraband to be gotten out of harm's way—out of the way, that is, of his own rabidly envying appropriative machinations eagerly ascribable to others—at the very earliest opportunity. In other words, whatever it was Mart did that chilly day at the beach riddled with sunbursts that never amounted to anything penetrating and sustained (but whose wavelets, on the other hand, no matter how puny-slapdash their initial momentum always achieved one hundred per cent infiltration of the dulse-clogged shoals for which Coney's—justly or not—world-famous) is what I'll expect each of you to be doing non-stop, and with the same monolithic—dare I say, bratwurst-laden—conviction, during our brief stint together, namely becoming yourself only in a hated other, that awful, irreplaceable other guy (or gal) you were (whether you know it or not: better if you don't know it just yet) "born to play".

So according to you, said Gift, we lie from a perverse need to be the other guy—we fart our perversity in defiance of what we are condemned to be here and now? You don't agree, said Bert, looking at his watch the way he did when in the presence of Joyce. The walls of the loft were greenish, he noticed now for the first time all evening, or maybe they were just greenish for the very first time. You're damned right I don't agree and if the others had any guts they'd admit they don't agree one bit either. I act to tell a story—my story—from my unique and undislodgeable point of view. I act so that other people can put themselves in the place of me and my struggles to make something of myself in this hardscrabble world. But this horse's ass's telling me (to the company at large who immediately responded by skewing themselves at various angles of embarrassment) the story—the point of view—'s of no importance whatsoever as long as it's not a self-detesting one—one I've routinely rushed to dump ('cause it did nothing to blunt my premonition—per h's ass, that is—of what deepish down I know I am) on some poor slob en route to work. He has the gall to announce POV doesn't count as long as it's not the autolytic one I secretly share with poor folks who'll never become the toast of, say, Soho or Noho or the Berlin Film Festival.

To shepherd the discussion into more neutral territory(?), Ralph asked, What about the lie we tell when somebody catches us napping on the job, say, or farting? What about it? Gift countered, belching his by-now-signature sneer. Such a common lie, said Bert, is in no way akin to the type we've just been analyzing for it reflects a different relation between talk and world. When Gift—*pace* his protestations—adopts a diametrical point of view to his own as his own he is still—more than ever—affirming his belief that talk mirrors, is reciprocally intertwined with, world. He hopes his new point of view, perversely preconized, will not only make him over (such being the power of talk over world) but also keep the keepers of the contrary point of view (the one he in effect shares but hungers to disavow so revolted is he by his fellow-sharers) from transforming him into them warts and all (such being once again the power of talk over world). But when somebody—not necessarily Gift, certainly not Priscilla (she blushed pret-

tily)——nods off or farts and then, caught outright in the act, belligerently denies having nodded off or farted, then he or she is lying the
way politicians lie, with a straight face and without anguish. That is to
say, he or she does not regard his talk as a lie because, no matter what
he or she says, the fart remains a fart in the far off, inaccessible plane
of farting and the nod likewise in the adjacent though non-intersect-
ing one of nodding off, and the talk, in a plane neither parallel to nor
intersecting the others, remains just talk. And the liar——the farter
and/or napper——justly punishes talk for daring to think it may en-
croach on planes whose events it can never hope to have anything in
the world to do with contextualizing, or rather he——the liar——punishes those slow learners who, all the voluminous counter-evidence
notwithstanding, think nothing of insisting that talk and world are to
be made one——joined cryosurgically at the hip——by denying outright
what said slow learners take, at the mere moment of this sigh, this fart,
this moan, to be their truth everlasting. So if you, in your little lives,
are constantly being confronted with a scandalous discrepancy between words and events, between talk and world, made all too palpa-
ble through the good auspices of news commentators, politicians,
heads of state or government, non-profit organization treasurers,
murderers, their attorneys and of course farters and nodders, then
know the excruciation is very much a self-inflicted and gratuitous one
for there can never be a discrepancy between realms completely incommensurate: one cannot lie in the one about what is or is not happening in the other for there is no point of correspondence, ever. But
even if the realms/planes are in one-to-one correspondence which of
course they are not, in any case the nod's past and gone, that is, non-
existent, so how does one become a liar simply by denying what exis-
teth not? So do our most illustrious politicos repudiate the counts
against them via this all-too-American contempt for words——for

talk—as a vile vial, a toad's toady instrument, the feather boa constrictor of a much higher truth, that of the only reality worth trolling: movement, thrust, event. For the liars—the lawyers, the politicians, the power-brokers, the hucksters, the compulsive seducers—there is never such a thing as lying in the face of the boundless minute-to-minute self-cancelling fluidity that is their native element. In other words, talk does not lie: at best or at worst it only anticipates and embodies (even if in fact it cannot embody any element in a realm with which it is incommensurate) the imminent cancellation of some youthful indiscretion like, say, Marty's brash infatuation with that high point of innovation in twentieth-century pop choreography, the goose step, and you'll be practicing that kind of lie too: a lie that's not so much a falsification of a move just made as the truest depiction you'll ever find of a move that's just about to be made.

But what about the good old-fashioned asslickers who lie, so they think, to save their own skins? Take you, Bert, for example—you must have had your share of CEOs to suck up in order to get where you are now, wherever that is. Well, what is your question, Gift, Bert asked, looking pointedly at Priscilla, who turned discreetly away. My question is, maestro, Will we have to play asslickers in the course of this commercial? Of course, you will, or rather, of course you might: Who knows. The dramatis personae are still being developed by the . . . CEOs. In any event, as an actor you must learn to obey. In any event, as any halfwit would confirm, asslicking is not always in the service of seedy self-preservation or advancement. As an actor, you should be alert to nuance. For asslickers of a certain stripe, the contempt of those they flatter—that is, make the receptacle of their lies—becomes a distraction from an even greater torment: the overpowering anxiety connected with persistence in their own being. The contempt of the sucked-up-to—the lied-to—other palliates and postpones the most solitary of all excruciations: the realization of their own destiny. So, Gift, for ass kissers of this stripe and asslicked both, such contempt and the intermittent clowning (asslicker) that foments and mitigates it, comprise the towey rope-strands, however frayed, of connectedness to another being, and offer each party to the covenant hereby an escape from that most gnawing of all fatalities, a failed selfhood. When all else fails—and if those asslicked I have known are in any way typical, all else always does fail—the clowning can reinvigorate the host's flagging conviction of impregnable superiority (to such abjection as the way of the world).

Last, there are those who, though they begin by being terrified of lying as a violation of the sacred bond between talk and world (and you may be called upon—you, Prissie, and you, Gift, and you too, Ralph—to impersonate them), must nonetheless lie to save their ass in some endlessly recurring painful situation within that world, one involving, for example, a hated relative who has fallen ill. To avoid paying too many sickroom visits to said relative (because said sickroom refuses to become a death chamber) our liar in this case feels compelled to invent imperatives, the kind that may govern the life of an artist, no less, but the invented routine (sorry, got to run: my fans are anxiously awaiting my return to the podium) only serves to incessantly re-establish the radical gap between what in fact he is and what he says he is as a pretext for the self-bashing widening—if any further widening is still possible—of that gap. Even worse, by its very upwell the lie induces and betrays a craving for what it proclaims him to be, thus calling into question the conviction (sole remaining prop of his self-respect) that he is free for all time of craving. Furthermore, knowing, for instance, that the sickroom occupant might go on being sick forever, the vigil-keeper is rightly afraid of depleting his stock of such lies: He tells himself he should have saved this particular lie, about the podium and the screaming fans, for some more appropriate (virulently needy) occasion. Yet—and here's where a brighter side rears its ugly head—for days—weeks—years after the utterance of the lie he finds himself in his wanderings steering prophylactically clear of podiums, rostrums, lecterns and daises, and anybody even remotely resembling what he might, in a moment of conspicuous madness, take to be a bona fide fan of his likes—not of he himself, but of his likes—in other words, he ends up steering clear of what he takes to be the byways of this invented—this fictive—being whose triumphs, however (growing more stupendous by the millisecond), are by no stretch of the imagination to be regarded as fictive. So he, the unfortunate, has managed (unfortunate no more) to reorder the world after all, to modify it through the intervention (parasurgical) of his massive lie, and if there is some price to be exacted for such potency—a continuous pain, say, along the gut-balls axis and/or within the sacred space between penis and anus—it surely cannot be considered anything but a scandalously small one. In plying now as his singular and all-consuming trade the keeping out of the way of the tyrant he himself invented to be able to steer clear of a sickroom's unreasonable demands, our slob is experiencing a prodigious, if belated and undesired, triumph after all: Compliments of his lie about being an artist simply too much in demand he has indeed become one, an artist, that is, though hardly in demand, having through world-transforming talk added to the world's denizens a new, even luckier stiff than he himself whose every step he is sorely tempted but must on no account dare to dog. But maybe there just isn't a way to steer clear either of tyrant or of invalid who are, in fact, pooling their resources to conspire against him and for whom he has, also in fact, made his ensnarement and enervation all too easy. The lie has serendipitously gone much further than intended and created a loathsomely enviable tyrant double whose triumphant footsteps dog liar's every cringing plunge into this or that alleyway of last night's trash. And this is how actors—good actors like you—create the characters they become. Via progenitive envy of their rivals.

Chapter Six

So, there's nothing left to do now except distribute draft copies of the script and fill you all in (especially Gift) about your characters. When we first meet you, Gift, you're a down-home family man leaving your rent-controlled apartment, ostensibly to go to work. You notice, to the extent that you're capable of noticing anything besides the ebb and flow—mostly the flow—of your own grievances, that your older son, a post-adolescent, has a new way of eating. He wolfs down his vittles with a grim, sexualized urgency, his arm protectively surrounding the plate lest some stranger's semen or saliva pollute the precious ration. He does not acknowledge your feeble head- or handshake of farewell. He of course doesn't suspect that you might never be returning to the fold after today's serial kill.

Outside it feels like—though clearly it is not—dawn. Dodging the streetlamps reflected deep in the asphalt's quim, you turn scowling away from one of your fellow creatures, a beggar, possibly homeless, but you want—on this, your last day as a free man for you know somehow you're going to be cornered and caught—the turning scowling to encompass not just irritation but outrage—yea, righteous outrage—that the world could connive at such abjection without turning a hair. In other words, you are attempting to convince the unseeing street (it is dawn, remember) that your turning scowling is more . . . far more . . . than a mere knee-jerking panic at some possible pull on your pocketbook. So the outrage is all an act, Gift said.

All an act, Bert repeated, but it was unclear whether he was merely musing or conceding the point. Only time will tell. We've first got to know your character better. Our serial killer—our living prime time proof that Crime does not pay—is a gut-crunching intricacy on second-hand stilts, so let him be for the time being. Let's just say he knows that today is his last day as a free man because today's the last day he's willing to play a certain game. Until today, his unspeakable acts served in his own eyes to englobe all chaos, all hard-hearted and gratuitously malicious rejection, all misery. After a murder everything unconnected with the act that had had the capacity to revolt or unsettle him, like his son's newborn guttling at the breakfast table, got itself completely rectified doublequick, turned picture-perfect, and so when he—I mean you, Gift—returned home to the little woman (you, Priscilla, in one of your many incarnations but more of that later) all the toxicity associated with the home front had been belched away, vacuumed into the act itself—left far behind, in the belly of some alleyway on the Lower East Side or the Upper West Side or out in the wilds of Jersey—leaving room only for applause at the master's return. Since you, Priscilla (you're the wife in this first scene, remember), live in constant fear of losing him forever, understandably during the first few instants of his eternal return you are always so beside yourself with relief (exquisitely, you mistake it for joy) that of course you are more than willing to accord him the applause he thinks he craves. In point of fact, he can tolerate it for only minutes at a time, that is, until its lustre is blurred by the old self-hate.

As is your wont, you must first drop off some videocassettes containing films . . . of a certain sort at your vendor's. The same shrew as yesterday and the day before and the day before that stands guard in the front of the store. You hand them over, box after box after box, indifferent to her possible reaction to the lurid pictures on the cover with their, worse, too-straightforward titles. You do not send them flying over the counter like all those careless yuppies you see growing alarmingly in number all around you, pre-empting your space, sniffing your ozone. In other words, Gift, you make sure your hands and hers (however horny and overpainted) interlock on the not-so-neutral terrain of each object as if it were the Field of the Cloth of Gold. They needn't touch but their alignment must be direct enough to allow for the transmission of shock waves from you to her and back again. For the shock waves assure you that the object is indeed returned, archived, no longer associable with you and your . . . proclivities. For in addition to murder, you are addicted—but never mind all that for now. Still you are afraid that, as you re-emerge into the sunlight, she will pursue you like Morgan le Fay (her wilting perm as electric as a banshee's frizz), having suddenly uncovered some proof of failure on your part to abide by the terms of the rental agreement. Or is it, Gift suggested slyly, looking in the direction of Priscilla (who'd never looked lovelier), that my reluctance to relinquish the product in question has engineered a slip-up for which I anticipate connection-prolonging rebuke, so that the process of return will never be complete and the object in question never out of my hands for good? But you want to relinquish the object, Bert answered, exasperated in spite of himself. Nothing obsesses you more than to be rid of it forever. The whole morning has been organized around making sure all borrowed goods are in perfect order so return can proceed without let. Remember, there are more important things to do: You have to pick your victim. And once your decision is made you have to stick to him/her no matter what. You've learned to be hard-hearted: on too many occasions, just before the final stab or throttle, you listened to them cry out in protest against having been chosen for no reason at all—against the violation or the disregard of their uniqueness, their precious little uniqueness. They just don't understand that their very emptiness, their falling short of all you imagined a true victim should be, constitutes their sole claim to genius—a positive (as opposed to negative) genius, if you will, for infinite pliability. They don't understand why you should applaud their nothingness (it allows for intersection, fusion, with other nothingnessses so that from so much fusing of nothingness the Perfect Victim may emerge). They don't understand that a guy like you—a Serial Killer—needs to do in a quite sizeable number of folks before the composite portrait of the Perfect Victim can precipitate out of the too muddy solution of their frantic plea bargaining. For Perfect Victim is Serial's meaning—it is the Perfect Victim who tells him What It Was All For. And if the Perfect Victim is to emerge—not necessarily as anything more real than a celluloid concept—something to be worked out in a Hollywood sequel to his life—then as many potential versions of that Victim as possible must be recruited to incessant overlap and reciprocal deformation of contour. But you can talk or stab until you, or they, are blue in the face—they won't understand that it is the very falling short of what your desire willed them to be that is their saving grace. The falling short renders them susceptible to agglomeration with other fallings short to a point where suddenly it is no longer a question of falling short but of far too much for any one soul to bear. But when said plenitude finally decides to make its presence known you of course will be at least six feet under and so it will be the prerogative of your wiliest disciple or your Hollywood simulation to gorge himself on all of its Perfectly Victimizable members. But try to be understanding if your victims, always less than perfect, just don't get it—refuse to get the fact that they are all in the service of something greater—vaster—than their own puny deaths, namely, the totalizing symptoms their falling short breeds in you.

Surprisingly, Gift said, I'll try to be understanding. I promise. Priscilla giggled a little, from nervousness not from malice, of that Bert was sure. But isn't it true, this youngish actor suddenly said in the old sneering tone (though, strictly speaking, it wasn't that old: it hadn't even lasted out the night), that as a Serial Killer I'm always savvily on the lookout for a certain kind of victim—one who promises to collude with my hunger for mass media coverage. (The Serial has got to know he's nothing without the Right Victim.) For me, becoming a media hero is a matter of life and death, ain't it? What's more, I know for a fact—I, Serial Killer, not I, Gift—that the public—especially the American public but then again is there any other kind of public nowadays?: the whole damn world is the American public, bub—has a soft spot for the travails of a nobody struggling for all he's worth— especially if that all doesn't amount to very much—to turn himself into just such a contraption (that's what Louise Brooks called Dietrich: a contraption). There is, my fellow Americans, a tacit, infinitely indulgent understanding subsisting between nobody and crowd, which is at the same time as ironclad as the protocol to an international convention on cruel or unusual punishment, to the effect that satisfying some fussy prerequisite of mass murder is indeed a small price to pay, albeit a non-negotiable one, for contraption status. So, once the threshold is overleaped the crowd, now rhizomed to its TV sets, dutifully forgets the atrocious intricacies of said prerequisite, as they dutifully forget the leader before the tape, the raster before the image, the borborygmi before the massive and manumitting shit, which is all as it should be. The mass media naturalize, domesticate, the prerequisite, am I right, Bert?

Though smashing his hoarded imago to bits thereby, Bert could not refrain from blurting, almost like a little girl whose bladder contents are simply too much for her bloomers to bear: We're not here to beat up the media. The media pay our way, and don't you forget it. As if he hadn't heard, Gift continued: The public—the crowd—the masses can be depended on to be sovereignly forgiving of whatever sum of stunts is required to mount the depolarizing spike ultimately indistinguishable in their Argus eye from an eternal blaze of synapse-shredded glory. The acts, Bert—the acts you want me—I mean, my character—to be capable of (and if my character is capable of perpetrating them then I, Gift, am capable of—even worse—thinking the perpetration), however unimaginable in their brutality are, for our Mass Public, generic and narcotizing, even babyish, with respect to the main design, that is. Take it from me, I know. Though in fact committed by our Folk Hero of the Moment, Bobb Q. Pudd, for Mass P. such acts have absolutely nothing to do with him in his essence, much less with the truly riveting virtues—the tour guide-friendly points of interest—that are now foregrounded compliments of all this shrewd-cookie but fundamentally venial attention-grabbing. The Serial Kills constitute the successful bid for attention that everybody else never gets beyond dream-farting about—the only successful—the only conceivable—bid for same and once successful are of course immediately discarded as irrelevant to the real order of business: manifestations of Our Hero in his Pearly Essence. In the view of your Masses, Bert, and in my view, too—I might as well admit it—the Serial Killer has no choice but to perpetrate so as to render himself—first things first—localizable within the historical continuum and then capable thereby of going on to reveal his truest—noblest—self (which of course would never dream of having any truck with atrocities much less with the nonentities who go out of their way to serve as the fomenters thereof) for without such a ploy the nobility in question—and not just of bearing—would otherwise not stand the ghost of a chance of attracting the attention it so richly deserved.

Bert said: Don't glorify your character's horrors as, like Marty's H's, a mere youthful indiscretion or you'll never get anywhere as an actor. The courageous actor knows shit when he smells it. Just remember what makes him an authentic scourge is the euphoric conviction that every kill constitutes a perfectionist's protest against the surrounding horror (be it a homeless cry for small change, a near-child's shielding his breakfast eggs against lethal irradiation or a part-time shrew's having, on her last legs yet! to inventory trafficked video smut) along the lines of spending money to make it. That he knows he's a connoisseur of horror and can stink it out even in places where, unthinkable but true, it doesn't exist (sheer dissimulation hence infinitely worse) galvanizes him every now and then into reproclaiming his perfection the only way he knows how—by multiplying said horror at least a thousandfold.

Not hearing, thus Gift: What makes me pick a victim? What makes me pick this victim over that? There was no discernible rancor in Gift's tone as he asked. For one rare moment he was bundled into the sack-cloth of a true professional. Bert cleared his throat and said: Sometimes you will pick a particular victim simply because he or she seems to mute or even cancel your rage at fellow Serials who have made it into the headlines and are consequently known everywhere. And sometimes you will pick a victim because the particular rage generated by that particular victim does not render you refractory to other rages (for example, the aforementioned rage at not being a household word like some of your spiritual buddies). At other times (and it is these times that constitute the majority of your times) you pick a particular victim (something about his or her odor or body type or hair color or texture suddenly makes it quirkily imperative that you trust your instincts and hang on for dear life) to prove that, even if you are not a nationally feted mass murderer, you still have a right to go on murdering. You pick such victims to convince yourself that you are not responsible for the world's indifference—nor, even more direly—for the consequences of that indifference (mainly to world: world is the loser). Good soul that I am, Gift remarked, my first concern has always been the good of the world, specifically, the dire repercussions on its flora and fauna of this witless refusal to avail itself of my talents, is that it? So, there seems to be a bedrock hunger to pick and slaughter independent of any given conditions, whether they be enhancing or suppressive. Bert: What do you say, Priscilla? And what about you, Ralph? At first Priscilla fidgeted and said nothing. But just when Bert had given up all hope of a response she murmured, Once Gift manages to put aside his preposterous sense of guilt for the world's failure to misjudge him into celebrity, he will be able to get on with the business of picking and slaughtering, or whatever it is he does best. With what looked to (slightly jealous) Bert like love in her hazel eyes, Priscilla turned to Gift and murmured: You worry too much about the world, Gift. World's non-recognition will not, contrary to what you may have been thinking, destroy it—meaning world. Though the world is an unloving monster capable of a new monstrosity every second yet easily—monstrously—shocked by the slightest breach of etiquette, it will never overdose on the toxins it harbors in its Kleinian (Felix, not Melanie) bad breast. Your failure to get your slaughters touted in all the right places will not destroy the world as the sum of such places. In short, Gift, you are not responsible for the world's self-deprivation and so you have the right to get on with your business.

Clearing his throat, Bert resumed: So after the object is returned and the harridan is done shouting after you from her post at the door, whence issues an odor of kasha knishes and air-conditioning [the vendor is next door to a delicatessen (Kaplan's) that takes in most of its considerable profit from the lunch trade], you choose your victim and stick to him thereafter: a tall fellow, too bony in the knees (for he is wearing shorts). He sports a baseball cap (blue felt) back to front as is the fashion nowadays in all age groups. A little, this tracking, like love or like the fidelity that all too rarely informs love. A certain movement confirms the adequacy of your victim—adequate for your purposes precisely insofar as he manifests inadequacy, by not quite managing to negotiate, for example, the curb puddles resulting from the most recent snowstorm's thaw. This is now a bond between you two: his doing, your seeing. Gift said: Couldn't this very bond subsist between us—i.e., lead me on—indefinitely without recompense. I could go on following him forever, not knowing when to stop. Bert replied: All that goes on—and you must repeat this to yourself all the time—is in anticipation of the precise final moment. Gift: But what, after all, would constitute the precise final moment? Some event out there or a mere feeling deep within—having no connection whatsoever with the world of events? By a law of economy elegant as a mathematical proof of which you are not in the least aware but to which your whole being attests, your choice (of victim) has already transported you into the world of event and not just any old event but event that makes a difference. It is already evening: late winter. Gift said, As a matter of fact I do remember an evening just like the one you're describing, specifically, the moment when the serrated edge of the rooftops was as sharp and clear against the horizon as it'd ever be. So, Gift, when, inspired by the beauty of just such a wintry night, you collar the chosen one and put a knife to his throat (for, as I just indicated, you're already deep within the very heart of event), he surprises you (but not greatly) by saying, Take it, for I've come to look upon my life as an experiment that never quite validated all the hypotheses put forth to justify it. I have absolutely no stake in it. Despite his initial resignation or indifference, he begins to whinny like a pig, right there between First and Second, with night falling. How dare you, you—Bobb T. Pudd—cry out. How dare you start whinnying like a pig in the middle of nowhere with nobody to hear you. It would be bad enough with a leering crowd about, or threatening to collect, like scum on the rim of a tub-in-kitchen (as the classifieds for East Village walk-ups used to say, and still do, for all I know). And so rheumily incensed do you become by his insistence on perpetrating it unconfirmed by the presence of bystanders, much less of media folk, that you fail to take note of his getaway until he is completely out of sight.

How ungrateful is our little Gift! Or rather, our not-so-little Bobb T. Pudd. For in your victim's escape, his temporary vanishment, you were being handed an event: the very sort of event over which, when reported, you cream in your pants but in the flesh it is of course another matter. Bref, an old master style event (cigar box and all). To wit, loss of the beloved. And what do you do? You refuse the delectation of being true to its form and one with its content. You choose instead to fart your whines that your target, your little victim, your passport to immortality, is proving to be insufferably elusive. But just to show how deep your ingratitude runs you are completely blind to it as ingratitude. Of course there is always an enormous gap between the event lived vicariously in print or on the silver screen and that event undergone at last. But the authentic Serial knows when adversity is being dumped in his lap as an opportunity to grow spiritually by leaps and bounds. For you, however, the adversity of seemingly irrevocable

loss is not a springboard toward self-enlargement but a pretext for sim-
pering vagrancy.

Gift said: But surely I must catch up with him again. Bert said: You
do [at this very moment he is flitting past the rear window of a particularly flashy sports car parked in front of a fast-food cafe (corner of
Second and Sixty-third) and about to step into its (window's) out-of-
frame world of wonders] and through your gazes the two of you agree:
Since contact at this moment is going to be so fugitive and unrepeat-
able and confined to the eyeballs, why not be shamelessly exploitative
of their encounter and invest it with as much goitrous (Tex) Averyian
veracity of voracity as possible? But for all the rush, he does leave a
trace, a spoor—almost a kerf—in the thick, not quite smoked glass.
In short, he incises the moment with the speed of his panic, and its
(panic's) kerf remains and you, also remaining, are pained, by the stark
gap between what the eye of reason tells you he is and what your imagination shrieks he must turn out to be, that is, if the media moguls are
to assure you your fifteen seconds in the sun. And the kerf, asked Gift.
Yes. Do I see it with the eye of reason or via the swollen gland of imagination? Bert replied: It's imagination's gland not reason's eye that's
overwhelmed by kerf's size in the by now smoked-over glass. Surely
anybody who leaves a kerf so chasmic is too mighty to be hackable to
bits and, as eye at once sadly notes, there's no convincing gland otherwise. In fact, at this very moment she is trembling as before an erupt-
ing volcano. Thus, with gland epileptically a-tremble and with so
much pain leaking out of the patent disaccord subsisting between reason's eye and imagination's gland, how is said reason to reasonably get
on with the reasonable business of mass media-potable hacking? (For
anything that is your true vocation is by definition reasonable.) Neither Gift nor Priscilla nor Ralph ventured a guess. But make no mistake about it: He will be getting on for if there is pain leaking out of the

eye-gland rift there is pleasure too, namely eye's pleasure at acknowledging, however reluctantly (they brethren are, after all), the inadequacy of gland's assessment of size. For eye's discerning acknowledgment of gland's inadequacy constitutes a ringing affirmation, albeit a deprivation-laden one, of the unlimited purposiveness of a something bigger than both but vitalized only by their rift.

So (compliments of eye's ineluctable propensity for catching in the act but never nipping in the bud every upswell of gland-motored intimidation at the hands of nature and chalking up such hairtrigger discernment as yet another specimen of eye-orchestrated purposiveness without purpose) you are able to dismember the myth of your victim's phantom might (whatever the size of the kerf hacked by his ignoble flight in the jalopy's backside glass) into useful ideas about his capture, untimely demise and posthumous transfiguration by the media. But always remember, Gift, whatever violence is being done to you by kerf, compliments of gland's ability to exaggerate its might and majesty, ultimately redounds to the credit of (a far mightier and more majestic) eye.

The sidestreets are not at all as you remember them from your last exploit. But what irks especially are not the too-gentrified airs of the pocket parks, or the callary pear trees shedding shamelessly against the blue, or the snaky chain-up of pizza parlor areaways, but rather the fact (it comes to you, like all your thoughts, at least the good ones, the ones worth writing out if ever it comes down to competing bids for your memoirs) that whatever you might have to say about anything on those sidestreets (excluding, of course, your prey) could be easily made to apply to anything else. But you are not alone in your predicament (though perhaps you prefer being alone—it is your bid for grandeur): Steinberg's Rodin, for one, was always grafting limbs onto the wrong body.

Stodgily you advance into the residential fens off Lex, no, Second, never having dreamt, though you're dreaming it now—in spades— shanties of such a just-barely-make-ends-meet dreariness could subsist in the trapdoor shadow of mullionless high-rises. You track him into a doorway (triple keystones with a vermiform pattern). You hide outside, under what in somebody else's time was called the stoop. You watch him open and close his mailbox. Yet every time he closes it as if for good he doesn't seem to be satisfied and has to reopen in order to repeat the process of closing, which new round only serves to breed its own skepticism-motored successor. As you watch, incongruously you feel an upsurge of hope the likes of which you haven't experienced since the—your—last murder and to celebrate the gift of such a moment you murmur, At last and at least I'm working again, even if the work is only low-profile stalking.

Fact is, you envy him, or rather the process that absorbs him totally. For all this verification, highly erotic in terms of the deft manipulation of holes and catches, is the pathway to production of an artifact, a postindustrial shard, an artwork nonpareil, and it is precisely your victim's refusal to take any preceding version as definitive, not any of the versions themselves (or combinations thereof), that constitutes the artwork in question. And the more he gives himself over to the working out of his obsessional verification (and what, I ask you, is more "highly personal" than obsession?)—of the ever-elusive fact that the mailbox is indeed closed for good but of course it will never be so, that is, from the point of view of verification—the more he finds himself, through infinite replication of the same shard (in this case, the moment of failed confirmation), all at once both at the very heart and on the cutting edge, to say nothing of the lunatic fringe, of the singular movement of our time that prizes, or makes like it prizes above all, such humorless mimicry of assembly-line rigor. It is your incorruptible victim alone who has found that the road in [toward the infinite replay of the most personal of all (obsession-motored) acts] is the road out (toward the mechanical reproduction of the most exquisitely impersonal of artif-acts). Private becomes public and vice-versa in the course of self-disablement as self-perpetuation. As you watch him he resembles not so much a specific victim—a specific body—as the just-so-much body needed to produce the photo-finish clarity of a given gesture. You can't quite decide, however—in so far as it depends on what stage he's reached in the endless cycle of reverifications and this is not always clear (and not just because of your partial-view seat): whether he's, for example, reopening the accursed box with his key or, being pretty sure he's closed it, inserting the nail of his forefinger into the slit between door- and jamblet to make triply sure—just how much body he lays claim to and is inhabiting at any given moment (and of course as his future murderer you want to be sure you are converging on an intact, flawless, eminently media-worthy corpse-to-be).

In any event, you are relieved to note (with just a hint of the sort of strangled sob that stems from blistering envy) that he is in no danger whatsoever of succumbing to that last refuge of scoundrels: finishing touches heralding the completion of a masterpiece (if he has his way, and he very well may—that is, until you arrive upon the scene—the process of confirmation will go on forever) for he is interested (this is clear from the way he licks the key before reinserting it for—you've been counting—the thirty-seventh time) in producing less a stably fixed and formulated end-product than an infinite sequence of such products. For more than a beautiful thing what interests him (you can tell from the way he runs his hand along the inner surfaces of the open box for—what is it now?—the thirty-third time) is the (Rodinian) ruin of a beautiful thing, that is, its bombardment by mishap, chance and accident for only chance and accident, unlimited, can call a halt to his doings as undoing. Thus inasmuch as there is simply no (so you are learning the hard way from your seat in the peanut gallery) definitive confirmation of the final shutting of a mailbox (every schoolboy knows that) it's no wonder he's not the least bit daunted by the intrusion of the ostensibly alien [a slow-moving and nosy tenant on the prowl, for example, or (to invoke the worst possible contingency and have done with it once and for all) the death of one of the two sixty-kilowatt bulbs illuminating his field of operations] for by opening wide its thighs to the thrust of such brute fact [as he seems to do, you pointedly observe from your now stage seat, when he opens the box for the seventieth time at the very moment his incontinent widowed neighbor from across the hall is clipclopping down the stairs in her stockinged feet (it's as if her dentures are coquettishly knocking about in his mouth)] he ensures that the ensuing supremely public flowering of the work through its collusion with fact (for what property is more public than fact?) becomes one with a supremely private confession of an abject infatuation with fact's wrecking crews. In short, you envy his loverly public surrender to the circumstantial as shortest pathway to commerce with his most unspeakable innermost demons. In shorter, you envy obsession's generation of an infinite sequence of doomed verificatory acts that smoothly assigns to each such act in the very private domain of verification a homolog in the very public range of postindustrial toys. All this you envy in your victim.

How you envy his removing, and not quite removing, his mail from the rusty old box. The walls are polyp-encrusted: they're true Bronx primitive. He does not seem to mind living in a first-floor apartment that is as dark as a goldbrick superintendent's sub-basement flat. But here I go again babbling about—of all things—apartments. Like my old friend Mike Monty (Marty Heidigger's half-brother, in fact) I'm always smothering my assigned theme in foreign matter. But remember that, as in the musings of old Mike (*Essais*, III: 5) (he never made it, poor guy, to Coney with Marty and me), it doesn't matter with what subject I begin: they are all connected and to the same old subject: your destiny.

So pay attention, Gift: He (Ralph) is advancing down the corridor. It stinks a little of urine and stir-fries past. You enter just in time to see him disappear on the landing of the floor above. Outside an old woman in a fur coat, a tough-looking younger woman emerging from a taxicab, a row of orderly ash cans and the light caustic bequeathed to the stoop—your stoop—from a passing local bus strengthen your disgust for things and events, but particularly for the human mechanism since it is people that run both. Or rather, you are already dishing up a hard-boiled snarl of disgust for the delectation of your media-generated audience-to-be. For artist that you are, you know the folks out there once they are in sight will be reading this disgust (without knowing they so read it) at events as in fact the rare and holy symptom of a commendable need to please, and be pleasing to the none-too-easily-pleased consumer. Your job where they are concerned is to put the everyday—the everyday in which they are steeped—into relief. You're here in fact not to murder and create but to cater to the public's hunger to aggress the world, hump every thing in sight, by proxy if at all possible—to reduce every being unlucky enough to have a soul to a thing that is humpable, in other words, known. So you hope, as they watch you penetrate the smelly corridor, that they'll be jolted to self-exalting identification with your manly inner recoil. If you are to achieve the status of a Serial Killer then you must become a skilled albeit at first highly reluctant reporter—in your signed confession and other facetiae—of your crimes, and of people and places (locales, as they call them in the world of TV commercials), and such reportage must be made to stand out from all the rest—from what all the others report when left to their own devices. As an aspiring Serial, you are in constant competition with and have an obligation to your fans to get "there" first—to places they don't quite have the guts to circumnavigate, much less ransack—and once there to unveil a there they never dreamed was there. The countless crimes are in fact secondary to this main design: to demonstrate mastery of, that is, unmasking disgust for, your little world that's got to seem like their world (the very ambition that will afflict the cop who takes you in, but more of that much later).

You put your good ear to the door of his apartment: This is a lot to remember in one session, Priscilla said, kindly, on Gift's behalf, so as to mitigate the effect of his incorruptible bad manners (he was rolling his eyes as he scratched his groin). Ralph remarked that it was almost dawn, at its most unmilky and menacing. In a soft tone (to show that he was not rudely discounting the observation), Bert said: Eleazar ben Pedath T. Jones, an esteemed if rarely visible colleague, once remarked during one of our celebrated round tables at the Kit and Kabbalah Klub (corner Delancey) (at first GreenHurstWood, that dear old curmudgeon, refused to listen to him) that for every Serial there was probably a uniquely correct order for the elimination of his victims, perfect or otherwise, but to realize perfectly that correct order would be equivalent to walking on water and waking the dead. In short, if you manage to eliminate your victims in the exact sequence in which they were meant to be eliminated you yourself won't live to enjoy the fruits of your labors, or your sex will change, or some other like disaster (or windfall) will befall you. Nor should you omit a single victim or add to your quarry bag one who was never meant to be a victim for if you do you will destroy the entire world thereby, as colleague Akiba reminded colleague Meir at another one of our round tables (once again, to GHW's chagrin). So all I'm saying, Gift, is be careful—and you two,

too—that is, if you don't want to find yourself sprawled on your gurney in a cramped side aisle of some fourth-rate teaching hospital
emergency room waspishly demanding (like so many old dames) to be
relocated to the main drag where there's always a far better chance of
being distracted by that most gripping of vaudevilles—the unfolding
calamities of others.

You carry a little pencil case with you, as protection through self-
definition. The smell of cooking mingles with that of rubbish and
dusty sunshine. When do we go home, mommy, says a little girl,
against the obligatory backdrop of choppy Czerny. When, indeed, said
Gift.

Chapter Seven

Before he could even begin to answer, he was called back to the hospital. Sat himself down, couldn't think of a thing to say (about the unforeseen complication solemnly revealed just minutes before—so she hissed through clenched, blanched fists—during a visit from—what was his name?—Prass!) that, however neutral, wouldn't burst the bladder of her ill will.

Yet just when it seemed there was not the slightest possibility of connectedness between him and Joyce, a woman in a nurse's uniform (Gottfriedina O. Jones, said the nametag deftly pinned to her breastbone) entered with a glass in one hand and a phial, colorless and empty, in the other. It was immediately obvious that she and Joyce hadn't hit it off and were not going to be making any further strides in the direction of reconciliation, the said Gottfriedina looking every inch the part for which she'd been cast, that of the stalwartly no-nonsense warrior, in the lists for nothing less than the golden mean of good health, who never permits derogation from that mean, however graphically life-threatening, to become a pretext for the gratuitous spewing of bile. So here she was not allowing the patient to take advantage of her inherent sweetness of disposition [as evidenced in the way she held the phial in one hand discreetly away from the glass (still half-empty) in the other] by answering in monosyllables only and sometimes, Bert saw [when, for example, Joyce began asking strictly out-of-line-type questions about the other's ethnosocial background, ancestry, level of schooling and, to judge from the subliminal spasm suddenly (but only fleetingly) mangling Gottfriedina's composure, hardly for the first time], not at all. But when electing to answer she seemed always to make it a point to be engaged in some work- (that is, vocation-) related, and therefore self-worth-bolstering activity, so that, for one thing, resistance would necessarily have to be attributed not to mulish insubordination but rather to the exigencies of sheer conscientiousness. Is it any wonder, then, that Bert took in the entire performance mesmerized by the hunger to recreate it down to its every last movement. He couldn't help thinking—knowing—she'd be perfect as the warden in the prison sequences. And (as if to confirm him in the aptness of his adoration), dusting off the night table, true to form—that is, to the form of her vocation as Bert had analyzed it—she did not reply when Joyce suggested it might be a good idea— but only when she got a chance, of course—to rinse out her soiled undies, with a little soap powder and lemon juice, in the bathroom slopsink. For insofar as Joyce patently was the kind of gal who needed, whether in sickness (as now) or in flawless health (over previous decades), always to be getting her money's worth and then some out of the anybodies employed in her service, she had long been skilled in the invention of just such finely honed stints for those unfortunates and in managing (even more important) to somehow multiply them exponentially whenever they, the stints that is, were in danger of running out, compliments of some old bugbear like unforeseen menial superefficiency.

While he and Gottfriedina (who whispered surprisingly—that is, given her previous taciturnity—that she liked to be called Friedinka, after her maternal great-grandmother) waited for Joyce to be gurneyed out (as, come to think of it, Albert had been not too long before), Bert said: It's hard to be waiting, thinking this remark sufficiently colorless to elicit some rancor-free concurrence on her part. (It was indeed a thrill, albeit a by-no-means pleasurable one, to have always to be titrating his utterances against her ever-readiness for rancid demur.) What he really wanted to say, but to Friedinka, was: Did you ever consider acting in a commercial (the hefty twinkle in one canthus assured him she would be just perfect)? Dare he ask her to audition at the next rehearsal.

Deciding to throw caution to the winds, Bert said with as much impishness as he could muster in the shadow of Joyce's avidly unnurturing scrutiny, I bet nursing isn't your true vocation—your first love, as it were. Not that you're not doing—as usual, I suspect—a hell of a good job ministering to the needs of this (stage whisper) termagant. What? Joyce rasped cloyingly, but was, fortunately for Bert, distracted by a housefly in the vicinity of the (blank) TV screen. Nonetheless I'm convinced it's no more (and no less) than the hated task, the execrated institution, in opposition to which you proceed on the sly to wrest and wrench parcels/morsels of your quintessence. Up to now, the only way for you to live that quintessence has involved resigning yourself to being caught at it—the true work—redhanded. This resignation necessitates the bovine placidity that so enrages those who employ you. No? But all that is going to change. He added quickly, as if anticipating her imminent rejoinder or the exposure of some flaw in his argument (in fact, Friedinka seemed as placidly uncontentious as ever, indeed, mightily pleased with the flow of his gab however inattentive she might be to the cruxes of its content), But of course you may not want things to change: you may welcome the constant threat to the true work incarnated by this, that or the other rent-paying stint of the moment, for when you are caught by the likes of Joyce, say, and made to feel shame (What, what? whimpered the employer in question, but she was once again too preoccupied, this time with the mole on her right elbow—Bert recalled it from her vampish sunbathing days—to proceed with a full investigation) you realize quickly enough that the shame, excruciating but only within the context of institutional protocol, conveniently blunts whatever far more excruciating—far more telling—shame accrues—and plenty does—from being stymied in the true work itself (and let's face it, Gottfriedina, if you are a true worker you are always being stymied with the agonized leaps from stumbling block to stumbling block). Call me Dinka, she murmured. This confusion of the boundaries—this overlap—of two kinds of shame of course soothes in the small but in the large—I assure you— it's another story entirely. But, never mind, or rather, more of that later. Dinka gently prompted, And in the large. So she was catching on! Soon, he intoned prissily (for he did not wish to appear to be responding to her prompt), you are routing and grubbing and scatologically rubbing your snout (though of course refusing to admit it, especially to yourself) in the cheesy duff of whatever stint business gets thrown your way, and loving it, and going home every night (or every dawn, if for the time being yours happens to be the graveyard shift) to your mate—as I have done and continue to do—for the sole purpose of venomously ranting and raving not because (though mate is cunningly made to think so) you loathe the stint business more than ever but rather because, *au contraire*, you're finding it easier and easier—far

easier than you could ever have imagined in the grainy-image and fil-
tered-lens Biograph days of your youth—to forget the so-called true
work entirely, and to drown (with your own carcass in tandem) the in-
adequacies vital thereto (nothing rots a true work as much as impecca-
ble credentials) in the small beer of a bywork. In a word, so much raging at the hapless mate is the repudiation of your discovery of the *most
horrible thing of all*—that deliciously Ibsenite most horrible thing of all—
namely that the true work is—no, has become—in fact a nothing. As
far as you are concerned, if the true work's elements—its very
progress—cannot be extracted illegally—on the sly—if the work
does not proclaim itself at every turn the embodiment of borrowed—
company—time—if the true work is not the vanishing point of the
daily grind—then it has no meaning. But, look, in any case all that
meaning has now been forfeited to the grind, the company stint. But all
this, Frinka, is subject to change, and to much more than just change.

He was recalled to the case at hand (the case being, as ever, Joyce)
by the fact that this time it—his titrated remark (*It's hard to be waiting . . .*)
—not only had not passed muster but was proving to be the straw that
breaks the camel's back: The waiting is the least of it, the patient au-
thoritatively sneered, as Gift, say, might sneer upon being asked to
measure his (diagonal) paces from one end of the rehearsal loft to the
other: it's what comes after the waiting, and she sneered again, this
time a full-blown guffaw at his heaven-sent obtuseness. Then she,
Dinka and the gurney were gone.

He woke up with a gasp. Surrendering at the open window to the
exhilarating stench of a long-deferred cigar [he half-listened to the
portable radio coming (presumably) from the lounge but in fact attended only to the small-print-voice codas of the announcers advertising everything from helicopter flight dismemberment insurance to
rectal bibs, wondering in spite of himself whether they'd indeed be able

to squeeze all that proviso-babble into the iota of airtime allotted] and noting there wasn't a single tree in sight below [to judge by all the clanking and squelching, Gottfriedina must be busy straightening up the bathroom, refusing still (then good for her!) to comply with the patient's lethal request regarding the steely undies]—no telling what time it was: the sky gave not even an approximate sign—he all of a sudden felt obliged to duck as the door opened twanging then closed with a bang (he was no longer ducking but trembling fingers strait-jacketed his chest cage): a tall man with a goatee strolling manfully in announced that *he* was Dr. Pratt (indeed it was: the goatee was new) and (something of an afterthought) that the operation had indeed been a complete success: they'd somehow managed to get it all (the speaker thereby making "them", him and Bert instant allies against "it", the big bad disease that had been robbing Joyce of her supremely well-deserved well-being and even more supremely deserving every-body else of Joyce herself). The rest of his team, minus Grass, hovered in the doorway. [So this was why Gottfriedina was being vouchsafed a (most uncharacteristic) temporary reprieve in respect of compliance with the undies ultimatum: all the time (of his uneasy napping) Joyce had been under the big knife.]

And within seconds Joyce herself was being wheeled right through the door: she was already sitting straight up and looking (at once frilly and despotically alert) healthier than a horse, extinguishing thereby the sense of well-being he hadn't even known he'd been en-joying for the all-too-brief interval when, as scalpel fodder, she was powerless to torment him, when (armed with cigar and portable radio) he'd been euphorically celebrating, again without even know-ing it, the little death of the gross importunity that was . . . the Joyce. He was recalled quickly enough from regret for such failed immersion by this, her suddenly flinging down the gauntlet of what looked like a standard hospital release form. Look at that! she cried, though strictly speaking all her utterances were cries, at the same time dismissing with a snap of her fingers the haggard-looking orderly behind the gurney: he stood his ground, however, either from dutifulness or from last-legs fatigue. I didn't know I was going to be operated on for a . . . tumor. Did you (spewed forth like a death sentence upon the world in the person of Bert)? He allowed himself to act (whatever he might in fact be feeling) more than a little surprised that at this stage of the game—and after so many extended consultations—she should be manifesting astonishment at what constituted, after all, ancient history, even if (especially because?) at the heart of the outrage, or rather, irritability aspiring unsuccessfully to the state of outrage, was what he and he alone perceived to be a certain characteristic crone-heavy yet wily amusement (at her own naivete? at its ability to make him or whoever happened to be near jump through hoops?).

At any event, there was definitely a point to be made, though preferably not by her (for didn't she have her hands full, what with the surprise tumor that might not be a tumor after all and the poker-faced gurney pusher and the lurking undies?), namely, that the time was approaching when it, the tumor or whatever it was, would be drawing to a close and then gone forever, so why be naming what was sure to be annihilated forthwith.

And he—as a director, after all—should be taking full advantage of Joyce's stage presence as an enriching source of fresh starts, if also at times false ones. So, if he knew what was good for him (out of the question: one had only to skim his curriculum vitae), or rather, for the troupe as a whole, he must let her go on railing, particularly against the stupid precipitancy of whatever doc had taken it into his over-medicated head to have this form hand-delivered at the very moment when she was being unceremoniously carted back from the recovery room. For so great was Joyce's power to convince—by George, wasn't that the mark of a great actress?—that is, to call in question and annul whatever fairly leaped to the eye in the modestly cut garb of the everyday, that for one rare moment—or was it only as usual?—Bert found himself beginning to wholeheartedly believe her campaigning against the tumor rather than the small, incontrovertible voice of the tumor itself. There would have been absolutely no tumor whatsoever—not the merest trace, not even now—especially now when, supposedly entirely wiped out on the operating table, it was far more menacing as the sign of its instantaneous regeneration—if only these meddling cretins had stopped their compulsive and pedantic naming, that is to say, their rampant misnaming, dead in its tracks before it got out of hand, that is to say, before it ever began. He must learn—for the sake of his actors—from Joyce's ability to punish the given by transforming it.

Of course, as he helped the orderly lift her back up on her throne, and as Gottfriedina went back about her business of straightening up the bathroom and setting the sills to rights, there did occur episodes of lucidity concerning the tumor and its much-contested right-to-life but these were quickly foreclosed—died as fast as they were stillborn—such foreclosure being her own self-vouchsafed reward for the merest sign, however blotched and fleeting, of compliance with the demands of any predicament. In any event, her guiding life principle seemed to be, as far as Bert could make out—and he needed to make it his troupe's own first chance he got 'cause it was grounded in magical thinking, and magical thinking was just a step away from magical effects, and magical effects made for Great Theater though was that what Samuels was requiring of him here and now—the following: The undergoing of any unpleasantness (of course unmerited by one as saintly as she) was already its obliteration, especially the obliteration of its name; thus, the momentary fulguration of that name—as now on a sheet of paper bearing the self-important and unimaginative letterhead (no logo in sight) of this institution in which she was so unfortunate as to find herself an inmate—should consequentially, that is, if there was any justice left in the world and even if there wasn't, encompass the death of the thing named, or better still, its definite storage in inactivated form, for who knew when Joyce might actually require its services as entitlement to yet another tantrum?

Although her belligerently wily look continued to ask why the (nonexistent) tumor was being treated as still very much a viable entity in the world outside, over and over she herself couldn't help resurrecting and revitalizing it, or rather, its notion, perhaps because this very notion most corresponded to her essence. For hadn't she singlehandedly from long before birth been elaborating this tumor (of loathing) for all things great and small? And now the mechanism of her essence cum tumor dared you to inform her of what she rightly refused to believe but already knew, for if she didn't already know all about it—tumor and co., that is—how could she and why else would she be directing so much rage at the bearer(s) of the tidings in question? So she knew, then, but the knowing, or rather, acknowledgment of the knowing, was to be suspended—the brute fact of the predicament was to be elided—indefinitely and until further notice, that is, until this particular truth, like all truths, in other words, all unpleasantness and all distastefulness, went away forever and she was left (permanently) in peace to get on with the business of robbing everybody else of theirs, which, however, was most definitely not to say that, from time to time and at her own discretion and just as she saw fit and to the extent warranted and so on and so forth, she wouldn't be making use of what finally had had the decency to disappear for once the disappearance was a fait accompli Bert for one was sure she'd feel

in duty bound to cultivate a respectful nostalgia for the thing disappeared, namely, the tumor that never was, invoking it at the drop of a
hat to justify her ill being even under the sunniest of circumstances:
How could she ever again be happy (so the implied jingle would go),
or rest on her laurels (or, more to the point, let anybody else rest on
theirs) now that she'd been mercilessly struck down and irrevocably
stigmatized by a tumor? How dare they, even Gottfriedina (she threw
the aide a withering searching glance), try to foist off on her what she
knew she didn't want to know she already knew, at least not until such
time as she could wield the truncheon of its concept with impunity,
and sow havoc everywhere guided by the ghost of its virulences past.

So it was but too understandable that later, with the monster definitively excised, she should be expecting to be able to play fast and
loose, torturing herself but most of all all others, with its magical resurrection. Bert was convinced that she was in fact beginning (or was he
jumping the gun?), despite herself and despite its projected use as the
mere bluntest of instruments with which to stun a well-wisher or two,
to believe in the tumor as a full-fledged event, particularly insofar as
for the white coats here assembled (still hovering in the doorway) it
had already become (a private poll targeting the collective puss of
these worthies immediately convinced him this was so) but an elusive
mangled shadow.

So Joyce was after all a kind of actress-hero: she would singlehandedly and against all nosocomial odds keep the tumor alive as
memory and as more than memory—as a staple of revival houses for
decades to come. There was grandeur in her hideous refusal either to
acknowledge the tumor or to surrender to it, and even more grandeur
in the isolation consequential to such hideousness. [If Gift could only
ape (on his ultimate gurney, for example, though they were nowhere
near that still point) her magical—and magisterial—rendering (as

she contrived to do this very minute) every would-be tonic onslaught of self-seduced institutional patter (for wasn't the photo ID-bearing creature suddenly holding forth, uniformed, out of the blue between papboat and bedpan a certified social worker?) infinitely less cogent than—via its smiling headshake and temple-cocked forefinger— Joyce's own weary deprecation thereof.] For some reason he was all of a sudden impelled to look Gottfriedina's way: she was able to smile a trifle sadly at—for—him without needing to catch his eye, as if managing to know (without in any way condemning him for that fact) that his thinking (about Joyce's imperishable grandeur) was all wet (or was it?). Right then and there he decided she must become part—and a vital part—of his troupe. For she'd caught a whiff of his infatuation with perversity and would not let him get away with it. He needed someone like her to cold-shoulder such freaks.

Bert began to pace, faster and faster: the idea that he might be infatuated with Joyce—more than infatuated—was making him nervous (preposterous: she was old, she was dying, she was his mother-in-law. No matter: she authorized the Real to be what her words declared It to be and such mana was enough to make anyone fall in love, albeit most unwillingly) and, presumably in response to that wild pacing, weren't the white coats now whispering among themselves—weren't a few even snorting behind cupped latex? And nobody could tell him he hadn't just heard the phrases *TV hack* and *Poverty row director* and *Amateur hour MC*, and worse, much much worse; no matter. He would let the entire team go on ascribing his jitters to pseudo-artistic mood swings (Pratt must have babbled something about his undertakings) and though such imputations were by no means easy to swallow—to service with a smile, as it were—Bert had no intention of protesting since, strange to say, these were far more innocuous than, for example, the insinuation Joyce was at this very moment capably elaborating like a bloody sputum to the effect that he didn't care in the least whether she lived or died: just look what his crazy *life style* (wretched term) was doing to her poor dysfunctional only daughter! Furthermore, mustn't the operative survival principle for any group centered on Joyce sick or healthy necessarily be some sort of almost snickering consensus *about anything other than Joyce*, said (entirely phantom) consensus thereby occluding the group's deep, dark, disavowed secret, to wit, that its members had no common ethos/eidos apart from whatever a deep, dark, disavowed loathing of Joyce herself might go, but only a tiny part of the way, towards underwriting. What matter, on the other hand, how they chose to think of him since who knew if such thinking so-called would ever wash up on the shores of—be cast (like—might as well admit it!—Joyce's irascible tumor-related flimflam-cum-speculation) in the perduring mold of—Thought. In any case he must remember to introduce the actor tribe to these medicasters' quirky—and in its own way definitive—take on El Deflection Principle, similar in certain ways to the one he'd recently permitted Gift to triturate. If the commercial was to be a success—even a pseudo-success—and it had to be, it just had to—then Gift and Co. must learn and quadruplequick how to win over their audience by singling out, neither on stage nor in the audience but somewhere way, way *out there*, just such a target as Bert embodied for the latex delegation (*its* audience being La Joyce) in here (and boy, was it ever stifling!). Exactly, come to think of it, like a late-night TV show host for was there anything, he—Bert—asked you, those SOBs didn't know about consensus, i.e., about allying themselves (against, in their case, some unsexable tattooed guest star in sequined hot pants simply too too shocking *for words*) with the universal constituency of the too too easily shocked, also *for words*, that is to say, the army of consumers, so as to get them, after a hosted orgasm, to commodify-eternalize it.

With Bert's pacing subsiding, however, there was no longer the pretense of a consensus—not even a phantom one—among the team of surgeons and assistant surgeons and aides who—like a veritable actor tribe or rather, like their own quirky take on what an actor tribe must be—were now entering her room in a flurry for each insisted on delivering his own peculiar variant of the proverbial glowing report on the patient's progress, glowing precisely insofar as his gruellingly diffi- cult choices had proved judicious and his highly specialized efforts en- tirely successful. But—since each artisan was so bound up in cau- tiously loving contemplation of the outcome in his domain only and so could hardly be expected to venture an opinion on what was to come after, or even laterally, for as far as each (having come to the end of the road in said domain) was concerned there was no here or after—of prognosis in the large, consensual or otherwise, there was none.

Pratt (maybe he didn't remember Bert and hence hadn't trashed Bert's falsework to his underlings) instructed the nurse on duty, who'd just entered with the dinner tray and seemed to take offense at the presence of the pensive Gottfriedina, to force fluids and take samples of the excretions and secretions arising therefrom. Turning to Joyce: You asked me, he said (she hadn't made a peep), just how long you have: I simply cannot give you an answer, and I assure you it is not from want of myself wanting to know, in every way possible trying to know. All Joyce could do was snort through the pink rubber tube, now completely inserted in, and madly polyfurcating like a beech trunk once it left the vicinity of, her mouth. Bert went back to the window, as he'd seen Gottfriedina do a short time before. Leonard and Fred (they were at the tail end of the health squad) continued to (prefer to) stare, hard, at this, the most unforgettable woman in their life. Out- side, an umbrella somersaulted wildly before closing up shop forever.

To Joyce, Leonard said (but a trifle too loudly, as if partial deafness had become one of the side effects of her spectacular recovery), We've been having tornado-like gusts, violent downpours. It's fortunate you've been able to sleep right through the worst of it. And now, when you awaken at last—when you come back to us safe and sound, dearest Joycie—look, the sky is a bright cobalt just for you.

Joyce shrugged at all this heavy weather being made of the weather, or rather at all this deference to its proposed effect on her. She of course couldn't bear not to be the center of attention yet once she was, as now, such attention was never enough nor of the right kind. Bert, if asked, would have been the first to admit he hadn't the least idea what the shrug was meant to mean but before he could even begin to think of deciding in favor of "indifference to all this defer-ence" over, say, "rabid contempt for all those abject enough to defer in the first place", Joyce had managed to spit out the tube, lie back and close her eyes to the world, the frugal sequence (or simultaneity) of gestures (this time clearly) meaning, I'm too tired (and, tired or not, much too forbearing by nature) to set all of you straight regarding this your simpleminded vision of—A diagonally upswelling odor of urine, vomit and liquid shit suddenly cancelled the good effects of what Bert had perceived only moments before to be a wafted gust of nascent springtime (though the windows were now sealed tight against life-threatening drafts). But forcing himself to look straight down and focus hard where before he'd merely been looking around seeing nothing he decided to refuse to let anything, Joyce included, interfere with what the deep focus was now bringing him, and in spades, to wit, definite confirmation of what he'd long suspected, namely, that there was nothing like the vision of a just-lit streetlamp, newtlike in its shrinkage through bare branches (gingko must do in a pinch but honey locust would have been better), to affirm both the inanity of any expectation and, in defiance of every contestable loophole, the certainty (prefiguring it in the totality of its stages) of the soul's ghat-like—bordered by all the crumbling tenements of such expectation—descent toward oblivion. But here, once again all too soon, were the nurses and their aides and the assistant surgeons and the floor captains and the interim surgeons-general, to say nothing of the collegium of husbands past and the syndicate of those present and to come, burrowing into—gnawing at—the pustule-scarred gooseflesh of his meditations. An assistant surgeon from the look of him (Pratt had managed to skedaddle) announced that the results of the last series of tests would be *made known to the family* (too prissy delivery of the phrase yet how else deliver such a phrase but prissily) within the next few days, just as soon, that is, as the laboratory finished analyzing the tissue samples in question and arranged (this being the most delicate, time-consuming stage of the procedure and the one most prey to slip-ups, sometimes life-threatening in their far-reaching implications) to have them notarized by a reputable clerk accredited by the complex (not too many made the grade). When Bert took a last look at Joyce (before saying goodnight to Leonard and Fred and Fred's current girl-friend, a modern-dance instructor—and a slightly more matronly version of Samuels' bobby-soxer), she was sleeping quite soundly. This gave him the courage to ask himself when he would begin to love her so as to have retroactively been loving Albert.

Chapter Eight

At the next rehearsal, which took place in GreenHurstWood's ex-wife's capacious duplex facing Union Square, he introduced Gottfriedina (as, simply, Dinka Grebbins) to the actors, already assembled. What's your background? he overheard Gift ask her (he'd just started flushing the toilet after a quick, too-long-deferred piss so couldn't catch the reply). From (upon quitting the toilet) the look of things, Gottfriedina, had, simply moving a respectable distance away, by no means considered it top priority that her new colleague's morbid curiosity should be satisfied according to his own time- or tantrum-table. To defuse the tension, Priscilla said: Don't mind Gift: he's just your friendly neighborhood rising star of the first magnitude paying his dues in the Off-Off underworld. Just as he was getting comfortable affirming to himself how much he liked Priscilla more and more, Gift stepped forward to challenge him. Yes, agreed Bert, long live our detractors and rivals, each and every one. Then (to the uncluttered, un-

littered space between Gift and Gottfriedina), think of our little experiment, isn't that what you call it? as an object, a second-hand piano,
say, or, better yet, the execution chamber wherein our hero, Pudd,
gasps his last or, better yet, the holding cell that precedes the chamber
or, if worse comes to worse, the typewriter of the clerk on duty taking
note of every one of your last movements as a live wire (there was in
fact a piano in the room—a baby grand—and it looked brand-new,
like everything else): we cannot let its defects, real or imagined, keep
us away from it. Self-unfolding could very well involve an active rehabilitation of the object in question. But you, Gift (reproach was moving in much faster than Bert had intended but now there was no stopping it), instead of regarding the repair of the object that lies before us
as consubstantial with such an unfolding, take the object itself to be an
ornament—not as an instrument with which you must fuse, defective
or not—and your outright recoil from its less-than-sheer-perfection
(loathing for your own flaws, real or hallucinated, displaced on- and
into it) becomes your peremptory gesture toward—the endpoint of
all—collaboration.

I can see from the way you sit or loiter, waiting for the rehearsal
to begin in earnest, that your eyes are thinking: If only this object—
this pianola—this lethal injection of laughing gas—this . . . rehearsal
situation—were defectless, as if (strangled guffaw) at this point in
time said pianola is the only sore spot on your horizon. Don't tell me
what I'm thinking, said Gift. Bert pretended not to hear the note of
menace and went bravely on, more to Dinka than to anyone else for it
was she who among all the others (Ralph and Prissie and the several
unfamiliar faces hovering in the shadows: was it possible they were
here as a result of having already heard some terribly good things
about this production from the various casting agents around town?)
looked least baffled. Priscilla, on the other hand, as well as the person

beside her (a tall blonde in a black leather miniskirt whom he thought he'd caught being addressed somewhere down the line as Annie), looked as if she wouldn't have minded in the least scalding somebody's dirty undies—even Joyce's—anything rather than endure this jaw, so of course he couldn't very well object to her suddenly going to the window and looking out even if she ended up luring (which was exactly what seemed to be happening) some—or rather, most—of the others toward a similar defection (Annie, oddly enough, stayed behind in order, apparently, to look him straight in the eye—so unnervingly straight he just had to turn away).

Bert cried, among other things to reestablish order: Gift, my boy (was he in fact that much older?), haven't you ever been young and in love with life? On your way here this evening did you even for a minute have the feeling that you—we—all together were about to usher in a new world? The purity of such an object is being marred by the experiment itself (these words were uttered haltingly—lingeringly—by what sounded like a much older voice than Gift's—a voice that was clearly used to being deferred to and not just deferred to but deferred to on no uncertain terms). In short, your pianola, my friend (it continued), like everything else you produce, is a wreck and not even an authentic one. [Bert now realized that the (portly but by no means obese) older man to whom the older voice belonged had all along been sitting, not quite in shadow, as far back in the loft space as he could get without seeming to be conspicuously seceding from the proceedings at hand. In his lap was heaped a featherless Stetson atop an elegantly finished topcoat as well as what looked like Gift's premeditatedly ragged black leather jacket.] Gift interrupted these observations with a well-timed and -turned sneer of support. Older man: The fact that you yourself were already riddled with defects was what led you to start your experiment in this defunct genre, to wit (or witlessness), the art commercial, which experiment has been assigned the impossible task of canceling those defects. Before Bert could point out that what had led him to the experiment was, among other things, the need to pay his rent and Belle's psychotherapy bills (she was still too ill even to pay her mother a visit), the speaker had gone on: Getting started was, I hate to say and contrary to what you may think, not so much a sign of the healthy desire to persist in your own being whether or not you ever made/make it onto my Dressed-best list (Yes! Gift's sudden smile seemed to say: He is none other than Herr Professor Flowers), as you sacrilegiously persist in calling it, as a strictly pathological denial of past failure (signified most pertinently and specifically by the failure time and time again to live up to my criteria—in other words, the criteria of the ages). Your great—your too great—torment over the failure has produced a corresponding too great, that is, too hysterical, will to go through with some act of experiment—any act, in actual fact—that will make the world—that is, the Canonizing World—repent. Only what do you find at the end of experiment (for the experiment is already over before it began) but . . . yourself, once again gizzard-deep in the same heap of defects, your most cutting-edge to date. Wiping his designer bifocals to punctuate the least flashy of codas he murmured (patently proud of this ability to end with a whimper), So tell me. Tell me what, Bert said, searching out Dinka—anybody—with his red-rimmed eyes. Precisely this, hissed Flowers, unintimidated by Bert's calculated obtuseness: Does the presence of this additional defect make the others less conspicuous?

Flowers—for Flowers it indeed was without a doubt (Bert recognized him from his frequent newspaper, radio, television and Internet appearances)—now turned towards Gift (the sheer physicality of the gesture required that he bypass all the other actors) as if to say, Are you proud of me? Gift adjusted the folds of his trousers and smiled enig-

matically. The smile froze his blood. He was afraid to lose consciousness right then and there and right smack in front of all the actors, so
challenged in his very vitals did the smile make him feel. Too much of
his own always-unfrozen self-hate was ready to collaborate with that
smile.

Gift, emboldened by Flowers, would clearly proceed to do everything in his power to obstruct the rehearsal process by calling into
question at every turn what he now referred to as the abstractness of
the work in progress, not, however, or so Bert thought or needed to
think, because truly he did not understand (when reading whatever
lines there were to be read or making whatever gestures those lines or,
more tellingly, their total absence, demanded he seemed to understand better than anybody the role he had obviously been born to play:
that of the Serial Killer) but owing rather to an obligation, especially
to Professor Flowers who would not let him out of his sight for a
minute, not to understand, at least not before an archetypal struggle
had been satisfactorily, that is, exhaustively, enacted with the work-
man-culprit for the benefit of . . . persons known and unknown.

But, if as the minutes wore on Gift was patently finding it more
and more difficult to participate in Bert's plans for his future which
was clearly the future of the whole troupe, perhaps of the whole television industry, the others were in contrast manifesting a greater and
greater protectiveness toward their leader, the news of his latest failure
to get himself included in the Flowers Best-dressed/Dressed-best having made the rounds. So as far as Bert himself was concerned, the only
conceivable response both to the alliance of Gift and Flowers whose
unshakable basis surely must be the desire to see him fail and fall, and
to the bright-eyed hunger of the others for expert guidance, was to
clarify his intentions as frequently and as fully as possible. With a sympathetic smile to Mrs. Samuels, Bert remarked, clapping his hands (a

new speakerly ploy) for emphasis, The world misleads us, at all times and at all costs. So what I am trying to do in this commercial is, *inter alia*, to mislead the spectator or, rather, italicize his sense of being misled for future lifetime's (or maybe, depending on your religiosity, lifetimes') reference, so that he or she can at last wake up to the process of being misled as it works itself out in everyday life every minute of the livelong day. When at this point Flowers shrugged and Gift took his cue from him instinctively Bert felt he simply could no longer go on, not without the crucial guarantee that all his efforts would not be effaced in and through eternity, and only Flowers himself (not least of all because of the universal esteem in which his Best-dressed was held) could furnish such a guarantee.

Bert lifted a floor lamp from the vicinity of the breakfast nook and resituating it close to Ralph (who couldn't take his eyes off Priscilla), directed its unsteady beam a little to the left of Gift. I want you (Bert shouted), as the Serial Killer about to enter the tenement apartment of your very last victim, to react to the beam as follows: At home, such a slant of light would flay you alive with all it dimly or brutishly evoked but here, in this foreign place, the very same slant reassures because it reminds you of home, even if the reminding per se is of a flaying. Here the beam cuts a friendly albeit motey kerf whereas home, sweet home the same beam is mad-dog, ax-to-grind merciless in its kerf-making. Here the content of the home-evocation is overridden—cancelled— by the evocation of that evocation. In a word, the evocation afield of a home-evocation, however inimical the latter may be, is not itself inimical. The things around us—I mean, around you, Pudd—the chair, the floor lamp of course, the potted palm, the whatnot piled high with state-of-the-art condoms, the name-brand car to be sold, the folding bedstead, the strawberry blonde—are here to attract your thoughts on the matter and to lay bare their bones. And what, asked Flowers

clearing his throat, is the matter to which you refer? Strong in the
surge of his thoughts about thoughts Bert did not feel obliged to answer. Remember: if the mind of the Serial Killer is to be attuned to his
act then it must be susceptible to thoughts that drive him inexorably
toward that act. What matters is not the content but the contour of
the thought laid bare by the potted palm, for example, or, better yet,
the stolen car in granny's garage (where Pudd's next crime was to—
but did not—occur). If you are to perpetrate your act successfully,
Gift-Pudd, you need triggering thoughts (not necessarily about the act
itself) and such thoughts can be called forth only by the things nailed
in/at your base of operations. So, Samuels butted in (reminding Bert
suddenly of GreenHurstWood at his most tipsily cantankerous), these
things—these beautiful things—that my staff worked so hard to procure for your use exist merely to trigger thoughts. Are being recruited
not to evoke a sense of place with which our public can plausibly identify as the very one wherein any self-respecting serial killer would
most naturally live and work (a touch of the exotic) and whence, even
more naturally, all his incurabilities could be expected to have sprung
(but not too close, this exotical touch, for comfort), but rather to stimulate thoughts that may never be translated, through stage business,
into light-of-day reinforcements of that sense of place (this commercial, like other commercials worth their pillar of salt, is also a trave-
logue, after all—a privileged glimpse at out-of-the-way eyesores that
must be made to seem reassuringly faraway). Thoughts about the car,
Bert said, will ultimately sell the car. Thoughts about the gurney will
sell gurneys. (I can already hear the hospital administrators braying:
They're selling like hotcakes.) Thoughts about—anything but the Act
will sell the impossibility-through-sheer-hideousness of the Act.
Watching Gift move so deftly around the floor lamp (in fact he hadn't
taken one step thus far) I've come to see that it is in fact your beauti-

ful things, whether sold or left unsold—establishment of those things in their home ground—that is the key concern and goal for the likes of us. And what are our likes like, said Flowers looking at Gift who for once (perhaps it was the example of the floor lamp, morally towering and invincible in its proximity) elected not to skid with his mentor into the home ground of their shared guffaw cum sneer. Bert pretended not to, or perhaps really did not, hear so absorbed had he become in more and more daring plans for the troupe: The goal—the (purposiveness without) purpose is to make things subsist in this cross-section of hell, really subsist, for which thoughts about things are desperately needed (whether they are ever uttered in the light of day is another story). And (with all due respect to your interior decorators—sorry, designers) it doesn't matter of course what those things are—they don't need to be the constituents of a plausible serial locale (better if they aren't for plausibility breeds complacency, in actor and spectator)—as long as they trigger desperate thoughts that get you going plotwise. So all of you have my permission to collide with whatever items take your fancy and need not, *pace* Samuels, limit yourselves to Samuelsiana.

How do we go about producing thoughts about the few things—whether potted palm or gurney (what's a gurney, by the way?) or strawberry blonde—you've situated here among us, Priscilla asked shyly, sweetly, looking Giftwards (for fear he might skid, with or without Flowers' help, into another sneer?). Bert tried to murmur What did you say, my dear, with equivalent shyness and sweetness (since the tint of her cheeks recalled Belle's postcoital flush of bygone days)—but he knew immediately he was failing miserably and so had to get right to the point: You mean, how do you make chairs and condoms and floor lamps generate thoughts that, although—or rather, precisely because—they have nothing to do with your assigned functions in this commercial (whether it's to serial kill or egg on, apprehend, convert, forgive or finish off the killer), are sufficiently charged to trigger the very gestures, movements, acts, unconscious and desperate, that have *everything* to do with those functions but of whose prosecution you would otherwise have been incapable: thoughts that, thanks to your frantic effort to escape their grossest implications, allow you to cover vast distances without remembering how or why or when you managed to get to what has now become your destination? *Voila.* To have such a thought (we've just seen how, with a little help from his friends plus a motey beam, Gift managed one so powerful it permitted him to cover the considerable distance between the video drop-off counter and the apartment of his next—his final—victim in a single bound) you simply take out of storage some prior thought unremarked and unremarkable in its prime (he was quickly warming to this French chef-type extemporization though a few of the others looked disgusted, albeit not the ones he would have suspected)—the more unremarkable the better, in fact (all of us can find a trunkful of such excreta if we put our minds to it)—and change its subject from, say, ex-lover who made a part-time job of ridiculing every last detail of your lovemaking before mutual friends and enemies alike, to gurney or floor lamp or toilet flush or motey kerf (no matter what, as long as, catching your eye, it's a recognizable prop of your histrionizing). But wait (seeing Gift go for the door), you're by no means done. You then link it pronto to some other thought (whose subject is also appropriately volatilized into the very same toilet flush or potted palm or fee grief or deadcat) at its—the some other's—most unremarkable point of attachment (indeed, such a point of attachment as nobody even at his/her wildest and wettest would ever have dreamed might serve as one). Not only is the yokage perpetrated, my friends, far more electrifying than any thought purported to be so by virtue of sheer *content* (which electrification non pareil then proceeds to propel you over your own version of considerable distance on behalf of getting the actorly job done) but far more, or just as, important it will compel our little old spectators, a.k.a. the prime-time billions, already up to their stiff-from-gawking necks in continuous revision, to yet another readjustment of their deductions about what a mere toilet flush, for example, or floor lamp or condom or gurney can do. And all the time they've been busy readjusting once again you've managed to get from A to B without their (or your, for that matter) having the slightest idea about how you advanced the plot thereby. For just when, compliments of thought 1, they were getting used to the alien vision of your friendly-neighborhood garden-variety toilet flush's encompassing a hitherto undreamed-of range of functions and feelings, along comes thought 2, or rather, yokage to thought 2, subjecting it—the vision— to a further and far more radical modification and at its unlikeliest point—a point that up until this very moment they never even suspected could *be* a point. Hence by being incessantly forced to give up all their misguided preconceptions about what a gurney or a condom or a goldbrick or a deadfall or a deadhead, potted or otherwise, may or may not be expected to do, they in tandem relinquish their most comfortable, least tension-inducing conception of themselves, that is, of their mighty powers of inference where life—the old harpy!—is concerned, and so, duly chastened and TV-landishly, they eagerly embrace the serial killer as the mythic personality most representative of this, their new, highly unstable self-image for by watching you, Pudd-Gift, career from thought to thought—I mean from prop to prop—all in a single galvanized bound and all in the service of advancing the thirty-second story-line—they've at last come to realize that there but for fortune goeth—anyway, you get the picture.

They may come to us, our prime-timers, believing that, for in-

stance, the model four-door sedan with its "irreproachable road manners" (nauseating genteel phrase) being hawked by one of our many
subsponsors and figuring semiprominently in the middle ground of
the commercial's penultimate shot—I forget the jalopy's brand name:
fancy cars have never been my forte—is inferior to a dune buggy but
by our, I mean, your—your—your—your (turning to the company
at large and pulling Houdiniform the right word straight out of the
tophat up his sleeve)—thoughts about it, or rather—or rather—or
rather—via your perpetration of those thoughts' unforeseeable yok-
ages (an act more antisocial, in fact, than any crime you might care to
commit on your own borrowed time) said sedan (having profited to
the hilt from being in another life amply thinkable as an embolomy-
cotic aneurysm, say, or even as "disqualification for artistic triumph
through addiction to the wrong kind of suffering" since in the world
of thinking, or rather, our kind of Off Off Broadway-type thinking,
anything gets transmogrified into anything else in the wink of a wall-
eye so what if, like "disqualification for . . .", strictly speaking initially it
ain't any *thing* at all) ends up going where and doing what no sedan has
ever gone and done before. In other words, allegory gone hog wild
whereby anything may easily supplant anything else as the bugaboo of
thought has proved beyond the shadow of a doubt just how truly superior to all its competitors, as the serial killer's means of escape from
clawing cloying fans, the unjustly trashed four-door sedan really is.
And all this compliments of the pseudoplausible yokage of such
thoughts—two, three, four or a billion—as hadn't, either in their
first incarnation or at any time thereafter, a thing in the world to do
with sedans, four-door or otherwise.

So, when you get right down to it, folks, there is no better way to
sell a product—whether it be rough diamond or jockstrap or law-
abiding citizenship or serial killer—than to highlight said product's

plausibility as at best an infinite sequence—a serial kill—of local phenomena—each jolted into being by a highly specific context and not
destined to survive for one instant beyond the nurturing constraints of
that context. Such jolts—entailing the transformation of ugly duck-
lings into even uglier swans—constitute the driving force of savvy
salesmanship and, even more important, end up themselves becoming
the product to be sold (at least in the plane of the language we will be
using here) with the result that [as if answering another (if for once an
unspoken) Gift sneer] the spectator-customer comes away from his
excursion into spectatorship/consumption immeasurably, ungauge-
ably, enriched, not necessarily because there is a brand-new diamond
or serial killer or sedan (this is rarely the case) wedged into the damp
and stenchy smoked-salmon-colored crotch of his armpit but rather
because all the jolts have managed to summate to something infinitely more precious: hard-won self-knowledge as the arduous knowledge of life as it is really—joltingly—lived.

Positing a look of disgust on Gift's face to account for his next remark, Bert went on: To our star, and whoever else fancies himself an
unbeliever, what I'm trying to begin to do here must seem completely
unlike life as we think we know it (that is, in our daydreams), yet the
procession of jolts I will be encouraging you to produce/induce—by
parasitizing ostensible thought trash [itself parasitic on thinkable
things (sedans, for example)]—said procession, I say, is nothing less
than the essence of the life process as we ought to be knowing it every
minute waking and otherwise. And if this doesn't convince you just remember from your experience at the movies (preferably, the Saturday
afternoon double-feature) just how much arduous artifice of preplan-
ning must have gone into producing the (for the huddled masses, at
least) exhilarating sense of real life—how much louder than in life the
urban cowboy power brokers must speak and how much longer the

hookers and their johns must stay sweat-glued to get straight across the reality effect of suckering and fuckering, disrespectively. (Without warning Bert turned mercilessly toward Dinka: she did not blush, even seemed a bit randily curious about sweat-glue and all that; Gift looked sad: he was refusing to return Flower's mentorly glare, at once beseeching and Torquemadish. Bert knew a thing or two about such sadness: he wanted to be free to come and go and at the same time keep this prepotent celebrity's tuition in reserve.) Just follow me, and on the level of saying as doing you will end up legislating in a new world.

Yet, Bert persisted, this invented world elsewhere—a better, a far far better world than the one out here—is not to be sought; rather, spurred on by our hatred of the known, the current, the available— worst, the dead-and-buried suddenly, from neglect, emerging as daz- zlingly novel—from such fare we uncover motives for our behaviors, our acts, our tiniest movements, that never existed before precisely be- cause we find said motives (on the level—in the plane—of the doing as telling) through instantaneous repudiation of, as irresistible pene- tration beyond, the ones we instinctively smell staring us in the face. Never again will you, Gift, and your goodly companions be forced to perform movements that have been recycled through the commer- cials hopper for eons. For your motives for movement will be com- pletely fresh thanks to the miraculous virtuosity of chance repudia- tion of every single motive that has already served and whose stodgy craving for sovereignty you'll quickly learn to whiff a hundred miles off. In short, Gift, Flowers simpered, he's here to save you from the al- ready done. Let's have a big hand for the little fellow. The new motives, Gift and Co., bleated Bert (Flower's sarcasm had managed, this time at least, to fine-hone and concentrate whatever there was left to expli- cate), exist not because one wishes them to exist or, more to the point, simply because one so wishes or because one feels them stirring directly and plausibly within but rather—*but rather*, simply the two most beautiful words in the language (let's face it, epanorthosis is my million-dollar baby)—because under no circumstances must the ones that already subsist—everywhere—be permitted to penetrate yet again and prove determining here. What you experience when you truly experience, in other words, when you are truly *motivated*, ladies and gents—that is, if your experience is worth a damn—is always an exorcising—an annihilation—of something else, something profoundly alien and anterior, something always blusteringly at the ready to impose itself as the only conceivable option—something bumblingly patchworked for all its apparent ease of upwell—something you were all along told you simply must feel the promptings of (if the planets were to remain in their orbits) without of course being told so outright. It was daintily left—the appropriation of the motivational horseshit in question—to that Scylla and Charybdis of the perimodern junkyard's self-help odyssey: your better judgment and your own initiative. So, just remember all this when I ask you to sidestep the floor lamps and walk straight across the room for reason or reasons temporarily unknown.

But if Gift's sidestepping of the floor lamp—or any act, for that matter—sidesteps its most—its only conceivable—motivation, what's left? asked Priscilla, still shy, still sweet, but from the flush of her cheeks (no longer postcoital) a wee bit appalled nonetheless. Left to whom? asked Bert, playing for time. Gift (getting closer and closer to the front door . . . once there, however, simply returning to his starting-point): To her. To me. As Gift. To me as Pudd. To Teutonic-looking health aides from central casting. To every one of us. To them, Flowers generously summed up—impaled beyond the footlights on the unmannerly stare-gasp of the prime-timers, as you've taken to calling them. Children (turning to the members of the troupe who suddenly, and to a man, did resemble children—Flowers' very own), when you get to be my age you realize in a flash all this sidestepping is nothing but tissue paper thin ingenuity [repudiation for its own sake of the blessed Goethean normal and natural on which I for one have staked my reputation—as a world-class (how Bert hated that smug-gutless honorific!) canonizer]. Bert: But as you yourself imply it's born of feeling most foul and unnatural and I'll stake *my* reputation (as what? as a non world class Mr. B.-style choreographer, of course!) on there being nothing less paper-thin than that.

So, Priscilla, just as you're about to sidestep the floor lamp for the usual—the normal and natural—motives you, or rather, your resisting sinews, must learn to cry out and rightly, rightly, Why bother if the sidestepping's not to be a vengeance on—a corrective to (and Goethean-norm/nat blessedness be damned!)—such motives but will only contribute more of same to the horseshit of sidesteppings immemorial? This, then (turning toward the windows for her ravishing forlornness was just too much to bear), is *what's left*—to maim the old sidestepping motives into ones so flagrantly new they utterly transform sidestepping itself. But enough about me: before we end I mustn't forget to prepare you—especially Gift—for the rigors of our next meeting.

Chapter Nine

Remember, you're the type of guy who's been crouching in door-ways every day of his life, waiting for not so much victims as signs (and alarms flitting across the skinny templum of service-entrance sky) that the right (and proper) victim is about to materialize. (Come to think of it, up to now all your victims have been murdered precisely and simply because they turned out to be the wrong victim, victim status being visited upon them in swift reaction against their inexcusable un-worthiness for promotion to such status.) But here you are facing a real victim at last—a real live authentic victim, plausibly clothed, or rather tattered, with an apartment all his own, a mailbox, neighbors, a job (you just saw him enter in his work clothes)—so what are you doing crouching on the staircase in the old way, the way of your salad-and dog-days, when the materialization of such a victim was still a long way off and you wouldn't have felt worthy of him in any case even if he'd been right around the corner and begging to be plugged.

You forget that your seniority as a Serial Kill places you well beyond the stage of not knowing how to pick or of not knowing what to do with what you've picked, and oh so astutely. The light in the corridor goes out. The tip of the match in your right hand burns the tip of your middle finger, gnawed to the bone. What do I do, what do I do, you hear your fingertips wailing. Warily you extinguish all avenues of thought. I entreat you, Gift—I mean, Pudd—to use the inspiration of the moment, such at it is, to blaze a new kerf, rather than revert to the old hoarded goods in the feeble hope they can be made to apply to and spur on—that is, pollute and disqualify—the occasion at hand.

For, to tell you the truth, or to tell us the truth, you've never trusted the actual moment (of stalking and, worse, finally having your victim in your clutches) to be forthcoming with the right directives, to get you going, homicidally speaking. You need your hoarded inspirations even if carrying them around with you is a burden and, worse, even if they no longer apply—can no longer be made to apply—to the situation at hand. So for you it's a perpetual war between the obligation to await the right and proper inspiration—the moment's spur—and resorting to surrender to the temptation of recruiting the old if not outworn properties. Do any of them apply? You'll have to titrate them against the receptivity of the context. But is there a context on that tenement staircase? What is the context at this very moment? You hold on tight—for dear life—to the vasiform balusters (as many as you can commandeer in a pinch) and suck in your belly. A cat meows (behind a closed door, it sounds like)—here, Priscilla, you be the cat—you *are* the cat!—and as scales are dutifully played, abominably, a female voice compliments the player on his or her progress, almost murderously. Never has praise sounded so let down. So the context is crystallizing. You try the door of the apartment of your victim. It gives, easily, wasn't locked, never will be again, at least with the present deadbolt. You enter. There is an odor of—smell it, Ralph? Ralph nodded. There is no odor, Flowers hissed. You move toward what must be the bedroom. The door is closed, or almost closed. A radio is playing, very low. You are happy to think that non-tempting surrender to such inspirations of the moment (the radio, the odor, the lock, the kerf in the dust made by your exhale)—the pantryful of cues yielded up by the moment—only indicts its incoercible poverty. There are radios, odors, locks, kerfs, Doctors Gradus ad Parnassum out in the world, sure, but no connections to be made among them here in the name of something vaster and unforeseen. You remain outside all this—right up your alley, I should think, Gift. Gift asked, eagerly for once, with a child's eagerness even: Is the radio continuing to play as I make my entrance?

You think (Bert continued): If only an old woman would emerge, for you have a lot to say about old women—some half-merry widow living off the proceeds of her honorable estate with a weighty dignity to which she is in no way entitled, but who are you to say? Only this time old women have nothing to say about the way space is being carved up between you and your victim, at least directly. Oh yes, your victim: a horse panting both to be led to water and to drink, deep. Your breath tastes of clotted blood. Not that you don't have a lot to say about old women, and not just about the happy few you pushed fatally down their basement stairs, having gained admittance as a fix-it man cum gas-meter snoop. But this is no moment to be resorting to old women. All you've been storing up against them (the more heinous your perpetrations, the more stalwart and ever-expanding your grievances), holding in reserve for the right (judiciary) moment, would quite simply disjoint the Spartan dynamics of this one, with its every right to fulfillment through collusion exclusively with the here and now. But let's for a minute play the devil's advocate and imagine ourselves vouchsafing you your old hag: far more liability than asset, she'd be forever displacing you from the straight and narrow of Serial Kill to a groping hagwards—towards the specifics of connection—in search of that supremely shameful thus omnisolving correlative in your own life invoked by her embodied passing (down a flight of stairs into the sub-basement? into the apartment of a neighbor, hated but exploitable for small favors and the analgesic of small talk?) since, Gift, there is a lot of the hag within you. For all this sporting of leather jackets and East Village chitchat you could easily pass for a middle-aged career gal undergoing her sixth hysterectomy in a fashionable Westchester clinic and, on or off her gurney, managing to denounce everybody in sight.

He—you, Ralph—are lying on the bed, a hand across your forehead, as if to shield yourself from the day's upwell of memories. You look genuinely afraid, Ralph. You don't say, What do you want? Worse, what have you come for? You, Gift, shut off the light, register surprise that the radio hasn't been turned off though who but you is the man for such a job? You look at him: Is he as disgusted with life as the hand across forehead declares him to be? In any event, the disgust is being tested, given a new slant on itself, titrated against the possibility of a way out. You move closer to the bed. He trembles violently. So he's going to be one of the ones who, the more eagerly they profess to be seeking death, the more they shit in their pants (already hopelessly besmirched) at its every instantiation. You begin by asking him (Ralph: victim, a.k.a. Hector Berlio) how he can live amid such a stench. He says, What stench. You refuse to look around, to justify your use of the word through appeal to the heaped junk amply justifying that use. You stand your ground. Your word is enough: no three-hundred-sixty-degree pan of the premises required. What stench, he repeats, because he must still want you to look around and, perhaps, alter your choice of terms. You tell him what stench: the stench of being, of these tabloids piled as high as the ceiling, these frying pans caked with beef curd, these mateless socks, these unsheathed, bone-dry ballpoint pens and, worst of all, these sunpatches marred by palsying petioles taking forever to disintegrate, no, swerve toward oblivion. They reassure me, he says.

Hearing this and melting at its touch, you, Pudd, don't know if you can go on with your work. But at the same time you remind yourself (or ought to) that it is a relief to be back (though you keep telling yourself you never left) in the domain of the work. The Killing work. For once back inside its beaten track you are no longer haunted, as you are when you stay away from the workplace, by the overarching conviction that everything could have been done differently. And so for the first time, and solely with this victim (though of course it is by no means for the first time: you've had the same fleeting sensation with everybody else in your gamebag), you are aware that just by following in the direction of your being's going you will start singing. And you do, start, I mean. And even if in the course of your going—around Hector Berlio's bedroom, say—you are assaulted by dismal memories only—what happened or rather, what failed to happen, three and a half years ago in some crowded airport urinal minutes before a runway hijacking—and even if memory is by definition hideous still there is one reliable little break in their clouds—one little piece of their real—that is never to be undervalued in so far as it single-mindedly proclaims all this, hideous or not, has constituted a life—yours—and there will be, and you need fear, no other. This was—is—your life and you need never fear the ousting of its elements (however hideous, they are still complete and intact) by others. It's inconceivable that anybody could—can—*do* you better than you yourself. For a moment, then, you allow yourself to scuttle the image of your life as undecantable lees

and sup on that of the lees' indisputable uniqueness. All the encounters are yours and yours alone, for better or worse. To have lived them
more consciously would be to have lived them less fully. To have been
more conscious of their every intricacy would have been to invent intricacies where none subsisted, would have defeated the purpose
which was to deposit you outside yourself, far far outside, while all the
time you of course remained very much within.

So, Gift, I want you (looking Ralph straight in the eye) to repeat
after me: Thank you, victim. Gift said: Thank you, victim. But, he
added with a mischievous nod to Flowers (who was himself nodding
off), shouldn't he be returning the favor with: Thank you, assassin?
Ralph did not appear to be listening. That's good, Bert said. We can use
that. Make a note of Ralph's inattention, won't you, Annie? She dutifully trotted off to the right, presumably for pen and paper. He—your
victim—doesn't seem to be listening to your grumblings of gratitude.

He just turns away, constant in his fear. And he has every reason
to be afraid, as do you, Pudd. I'm not forgetting you. All during the
days, weeks, months since the last Kill spent accumulating materi-
als—building blocks—strategies of reaction, let us call them, to the
incurables round about you've dreamed that once inside—of—the
event to come—the next and final Kill—the strategies would coming
into their own be cast in a new light. But now, in the event at last, you
are barred access to said building blocks and so barred you suffer for
what you take to be your depletion. In fact, it is not so much depletion
that causes you to suffer (the accumulated building blocks of strategy
you've dutifully dragged to the scene of the crime cannot be compelled to apply where clearly their term of applicability has already ex-
pired) as the slothful incapacity to transform into the moments of a
strategy—nay, a campaign—those bits and pieces of the ever-incur-
able life-sludge that are very much available to you at—in the—pres-

ent. So here you are, in situation, waiting for the world (now nothing more than what is taking place or refusing to take place in this tenement bedroom) as well as all its stupid little phrases and banal icons to be transformed into a malleable and marketable (your crime to be always has its eye on the camera) isomer of itself. But nothing comes. You wait, and nothing comes, as in a pay toilet. So you end up doing what all directors do when they die: you become a cinematographer. The room is like any other room. It has less of a view than your bedroom at home and must give on an alley. You find yourself paying particular attention to the pigeons bellowing. You are training yourself to be observant in the here and now so as to be able to use what you observe as armament. But there is nothing more to observe. Has he purposefully depopulated his digs of all thinkable, that is to say, strategizable bric-a-brac? It's clear: He's trying, Berlio, your victim, to unmask you as a failure and a fake. Yes, things are going on in neighboring apartments, many things, to judge from all the noise which threatens by the way to blot out for good the pigeon borborygmi. But you don't want to resort to them either. For this is what it comes down to: resorting to the extraneous to keep the unlocalizable, unspecifiable essential going.

So—Bert took a deep breath—you say to him, You're going to make me famous. Just like that. The sheets look unwashed. Somehow taking note of this detail just after an utterance that really matters is less painful than it—the taking note—would be following hard on nothing at all. Though nobody is holding a gun to your head to make you think, The sheets look unwashed. How do you know? Gift cried, who was looking more and more like a Pudd by the minute. You are free to think just what you like when you like, Bert said as quietly as possible. Gift, even more quietly, said: I confuse the burning consciousness of a desire to think, The sheets look unwashed, with easy access to thinking, The sheets looked washed. I confuse the urgency of an impulse that sweeps me off my feet with freedom—to be swept away by any old impulse I choose when I so choose. The necessity that determines my every impulse is so alien precisely because, being so welded to—so propulsive of—my every breath, it is impossible to localize, much less rope off. I'm more of a victim than my victims so how are you going to sell me to prime-timers? Precisely, Bert replied, as *more victim than your victims*. As if a gust-driven leaf should take it into its head to go on moving as a "highly personal" caprice. In short, Bert, I— Tomm Q. Pudd—am not in the least free to not take note of the fact that the sheets are unclean—from the minute, that is, I agree to be me.

Is it money you want, he asks, but you are both synchronized in immediately rejecting this as merest placeholder. It's the sort of phatic whimper each of you has come upon, albeit from opposite directions, too many times before. It would be so much easier if it were so, you— Pudd—reply. The thing is, I've come with other, though not necessarily bigger, fish to fry. You *are* after bigger game, he retorts. Or rather it's the closest he'll ever come to a retort. You are disappointed—in yourself. There's nothing to say and you so wanted to have so much to say. But it is nonetheless reassuring to know that as a consequence of all this fixation on dirty sheets (is that semen you smell?) your share of muniments looming or lurking at the ready (that is, of portable prefab building blocks) has dwindled appreciably.

You take the dwindling as a sign not of depletion but of relief, release, readiness for the real work, which entails thinking context-specific thoughts about the things here and now: the woodwork and as much blue sky as is accessible from the room. Why should the thinkable world be the storehouse only of your more successful rivals? Here is a guy then (turning fully to, on, Gift) who wishes either to rid him-

self of thoughts so as to be able to give himself to the story at hand or
to remain the pusher only of those sure to push it forward. For he
wants to be loved by people, even if he hates them—not that he is any
better than they. He wants to be loved and he knows there's no better
way to be loved, however fleetingly, than through a story.

But you need your prefab thoughts, no getting around that "fact",
and in fact you do have a muniment: a thought that could, with a little spit and polish, be made to apply. If only he would be kind enough
to give you an opening, and fast. For it is excruciating to have to wait
for the elements of a context to settle and become plausible. But wait,
any element would do—it doesn't have to settle, much less plausibilize, for don't all Serial Killers hold (taking their cue from a past master: one Mike O'Bakhtin, a.k.a. Citizen X, ultimately executed for
drowning a transfinite number of innocents in some fetid tributary of
the Volga) that if you take (*a*) a thought on a given theme and (*b*) a
thing within a specific context even remotely sympathetic/suitable to
the elaboration of said theme—and how can any old thought and any
old thing ever not be on the same theme for where stories are concerned, and not just stories about Serial Killers, there is always only
one theme—they cannot subsist side by side without intersecting,
nay, interpenetrating (whether they in fact confirm, complement or
contradict each other). Even ostensible agreement between a man-
thought and a maid-thing, billing and cooing to beat the band in mere
brute juxtaposition, is not free, then, of unforeseeable backlash.

But never fear, a thought-muniment is on its way. Something in
the way of not being able to help feeling for him, profoundly. Because
you know once they pick you up, and they will, he (either—
whether—dead or mutilated beyond recognition) will (already) be
(instantaneously) forgotten, worse than forgotten, contemned—and
not just by stalk-eyed bystanding shrews—even if he as much as you

will have been responsible for all the tabloid-cramming, something for straphangers to nibble on impenitently. Your pity is the muniment you've been waiting for. Neither a prefab imported muniment, though (whose subject in some anterior life was surely gurneys, potted palms or road manners, or the hopeless incompatibility thereof, but which is now forced into being about "pity towards one's victim"), nor, Johnny-on-the-spot, a knee-jerk rejoinder to the here-and-now. Rather a compromise formation, as is the case (or so our spinning yarn-embodyer needs desperately to believe) with most potboiler scraps. You haven't yet laid a finger on him but already your heart is very much with what is soon to be a new addition to the numberless dead and dismembered. In this way—beautiful soul that you are—you are completely unlike the media whores and their clients. Especially since his death and dismemberment will be immediately irrelevant—obstructive—to the flow and burst of the media commentary it adeptly triggers. Of course he deserves his fate for is there anything more shameful than to be so caught napping as to end up a bona fide victim whose unpleasant task it is to remind everybody else, as if everybody else should need reminding, bad luck—horrific luck—indeed exists and can't for the life of him be avoided, much less explained righteously away (only you as cool-headed torturer have a right to capture the public's fickle fancy for your act dutifully stimulates the hypersecretion of its perversity gland)? So/but/moreover/nonetheless, Pudd, you've got to make the spectators feel how much you're feeling for him, your victim, far more than your heart can express (you absolutely must express that wrenching *far more than your heart can express*), given that he must end up as so much detritus, so much dead-meaty impediment, in the media's way to glory. After all, Mr. Samuels' clients are depending on you. And insofar as it's the media that determine the length, the size of any event be it murder-in-the-courtroom or flawlessly fatal explosion over the Atlantic of 747 en route to Paris—and only the media have the right to determine how long we are to mourn for the victims—you feel yourself feeling for him more and more. He—Berlio—clearly misreads your throbs (as mere distress signals betraying the psycho's "fabled impatience" to be getting on with the official business of dismemberment) for he cries out, Why not get me over with and then move on. Your job, now that you've found me, is to find an infinite number just like me. One isn't enough. One is just the immediately expendable placeholder for—the breezily crossable threshold of—an infinite sequence of arti-facts, of giblets.

This remark enrages you—yes, indeed—for what you are struggling with almost to the exclusion of all else is precisely the need to stop adding, amnesiac, to your sum of conquests. You must go back and take stock. Yet taking stock means recognizing boundaries. Most of the time, however, you prefer to thrash about in the infinite set of your atrocities. If a set is the form of a possible thought then an infinite set is the form of an infinity of possible thoughts—in other words a charcoal sketch of your infinite variety. And if—as Cantor (Georg, not ol' Banjo Eyes), your favorite fellow chronic backslider at the Rucker Detox Center (est. 1883) out in San Darmstadt, CA, used to say—a set is also a Many that allows itself to be thought of as a One, naturally you've always been one to resist the cave-in. But of course you cannot say all this to Berlio: you're not even ready to say it to yourself. But don't get me wrong: you're still infinitely grateful for *Why not get me over with and then move on?* since it offers you an opening for some other muniment waiting in the wings. Only even before you can begin to think about choosing a tit for his tat, Berlio, that cagey little devil on no less than a roll (Kaiserly in its compass), is on (musingly) to (You see, Ralph, I haven't forgotten about you. You too seek an opening for *your* muniments and rightly so): I knew there wouldn't be much time.

And this is precisely what you, Gift-Pudd, have been waiting for, although you didn't know it until this very moment: a notation of resignation, that is, something to legitimate and vitalize—or rather, something you can wrench against all probability into a made-to-order legitimating and vitalizing of—your own. You suddenly realize your anxiety about getting in enough brutal slayings to justify your calling yourself a practitioner of the Serial has been for the sake of the world. All along you've been dreading the repercussions on the world should world end up shortchanged in respect of your slayings. So hearing Ralph-Berlio say, I knew there wouldn't be much time, fills you with relief, that is to say, with a craving to become him, or rather him insofar as *him* is a somebody able to give voice to the heretofore unsayable without fearing and in actual fact without perpetrating thereby destruction of self and, more to the point, world. Suddenly the fact of a mere lifespan's inadequacy with respect to accommodating any one individual's achievement can be made to pay. Simply by being honest about it. Though perhaps he isn't as invigorated by admitting to the inadequacy as you are by hearing about it. Who knows, invigoration on his part might have been definitive proof of the admission's inauthenticity. So (to make a long story short), you show your appreciation for this muniment-outpouring (*I knew there wouldn't be . . .*) donated to the cause of keeping the situation at hand alive, with a matching grant of your own: an ever-so-gently murmured Go fuck yourself.

Bound he listens intently even if you, Gift, are saying nothing or are not aware of overhearing yourself say anything. The side of a bus completely blocks out the pane. It's all so empty, you hear him whisper to the woodwork (not much of it to speak of, much less to). You know that you have strength enough to kill him but maybe not near enough to explain that the emptiness is not an occasion for panic. It's simply a matter of waiting, first, for the emptiness of which every violent encounter always seems to be the preeminent exemplar to somehow document itself through traces/slots/spoors/clues and, second, for the ensuing documents to interpenetrate so as to create the Big Red One. You try to assure him that you know for sure one day you'll be looking back and blessing all these seemingly failed encounters, for what you blithely took to be their hideous emptiness will have turned out to be in fact their susceptibility to resurrection as something far greater. You wonder at his blindness (after all, he is only bound). But you yourself, Pudd, are still very far from the old age home of salubrious retrospect so it's not very fair to be expecting much from your victim.

Ralph said: I'm beginning to feel, if not quite understand, that the event of murder, like my own, for example, is never doomed in itself (no matter how ineptly perpetrated), that is, in its emptiness, but only insofar as the parties concerned allow its aftermath to be brutalized by the never-say-die-like shadow cast by media decrees about what event should—must—be if it is to qualify as an enduring success, how events are supposed to be lived if I am to claim them as my own. Priscilla beamed at this uttered recognition, remaining blissfully indifferent to Annie's tugging at her brooch-lapel in sign of groggy impatience.

Bert tried not to sound pleading when he bleated: Just hang on a little longer: it's almost over and we're getting to a good part, though by no means the best: that comes much later, in the holding cell. He—Hector Berlio—tosses and turns: you feel, Gift—correct me Professor Flowers if I'm wrong—that you're fast becoming the madman his wild gestures proclaim you to be, and the more his gestures call you a madman the more of a madman you in fact become. You're losing control by leaps and bounds so conscientious are your efforts to enact more and more vividly what his panic accuses you of being. Even if you know beyond the shadow of a doubt that you are not—nor will you ever be—a madman, the uncontrollable perversity already set in motion by his suffering (with which—ah, there's the rub!—you are completely fused—with which you are more fused than is the sufferer himself, although this last may only go to show that, perversity being contagious, I've all too gladly caught the bug—I'm a showman after all) short-circuits your capacity to act otherwise for to act otherwise would be to begin to repair what you prefer to deem irreparable (or else, you'd indeed go mad: from moment to moment, madder and madder). You're simply unready, as the prison therapists put it, to acknowledge your defects and until you're ready to do the inevitable right thing (when will that be?) you have to somehow bide your time and clearly the very best way to do so where he's concerned (and, come to think of it, maybe not just where he's concerned) is to keep your distance via a perverse cruelty—a binding ever more tightly, say, until he is just barely able to breathe—for cruelty is not the real you, never the real you, and so to persist in such a course is simple perversity: such an advertisement of the deferral of your truest feelings as redounds to your own and nobody else's detriment. Ah, Gift, what a delicate soul you are, after all. In short, you are terrorized by the fragility of your victim and to somehow numb yourself to the terror (which would otherwise incapacitate you for even the simplest tasks—especially the simplest) you—kill.

Yes I am terrorized, Gift said, with what sounded like a sob in his throat—no, deeper, the chest. It is as if I am caught in the game of some half-assed deity—not that you, Bert, could ever be thought of as such, half-assed or otherwise. Game of some demiurge striving, since he has too much time on his hands—But not of the poignant Youmans stamp, Flowers sourly affirmed, beating on his pongee patella an off-key tattoo of what to Bert's ears sounded like the A section of the standard in question.—striving to test just how far I can make myself go in trampling on terror of Hector's complete and pathetic trust—he's supposed to some kind of hoofer, isn't he? A gifted art song writer, Ralph answered, already a bit role-proprietary. Gift: Exactly! an artist-type hence instantly dependent on any ill-looking stranger's ill will. No need to invoke a demiurge, though, to account for the fact that, statistically speaking, there just are infinitely more varieties of bad news than good to be had for the non-asking. Worse (Gift clearly hadn't, or was expertly making as if he hadn't, heard this, Flowers' latest pronunciamento) than a caged parakeet dying of an anal tumor, so is it any wonder I, a degenerate, am thrilled by the terror of betraying his frail trust into the next world at the drop of a hat? Merely by tossing and turning he names me, though he doesn't know it, as having already vilely betrayed him so I'm convinced that sooner or later I'll have to rub my snout in the tenement dust. Only the more convinced I get by the minute even surer do I become, though not necessarily by the minute, that such dusty apology must be delayed until further notice inasmuch as in annihilating all the vileness, it simply allows me—isn't that right, boss?—to go on (a further pull on the telephone cord around his neck here, a further slash with a grapefruit knife of his freckled wrist there) perpetrating in its total absence.

Under all the perversity, however, said Bert, is a desire to help your victim—to manage to help him before you are obliged to destroy him. I do want to help, I do, I do! Gift cried. Are you by any chance making a mockery of your character? Bert asked—Flowers more than Gift. Flowers shrugged uncomfortably, as if he was tired, oh so very tired indeed, of having his protégé's every enormity laid at his doorstep any hour of the day or night. It's just that our victims are like children, Gift added. How so, said Ralph. Thus so, punk (Ralph shivered slightly): Whatever efforts we decide to make on their behalf are always too late,

failing farcically to address the unforeseen (though, granted, unforeseeable) rebellious new direction of the moment, itself a reaction to our
last or next to last effort at making amends. And, God knows, we have
so much to atone for. Although who knows, Gift, perhaps the tantrum
of the moment has absolutely nothing to do with us.

In any event, you now tell him you've been standing outside his
window day after day, night after night, watching—deducing him
from his doings. And from the way he makes sure to get himself
plopped down before the TV at exactly the same time every evening
it's become clear to you he's been an addict for years. And you know
something, Hector (so you tell him), the more addicted you turn out
to be the more of a tantalizingly mimickable lifetime prescription for
invulnerabilization to the world outside the addiction becomes in my
starry eyes. Even if terrified (of being stabbed to death at any moment)
he—I mean you, Ralph—manages to acknowledge having in fact
been at it only for a few weeks—a few months at most—and now I
(you go on to say), a Polish immigrant (for the first time you, Gift—
look alive, for Chrissakes!—notice what is referred to in spy fiction as
"the trace of an accent"), am dying of myasthenia g. or AIDS, I'm not
quite sure. My memory is going fast. My doctor—the ass!—singsongs
something to the effect that it's merely becoming selective and pats
himself on the back (behind my own) for being so tactful. I assure him
I still have the same emotions [why at this stage of the game—or at
any other, for that matter (but we don't have time to go into all
that)—am I so intent on furnishing *him* with proof positive of what I
am not?]: it's just that I simply must rely on different (I mean: the
wrong, but I don't say so, not to the man in off-white) memories to
trigger and sustain them. Being who and what you are, Pudd—more
to the point, are to become—you quickly find you're not particularly
interested in his dealings with the man in off-white, and even less in

his disease per se. You mean (you say), all this comfy and cozy ensconcedness before the tube is not the schema for a lifetime but a mere interim, the hectic ploy of not-so-quiet desperation?

Is it a problem? he—Berlio—asks, with incongruous calm—a calm so unsettling you, Pudd, must transpose it to the off-key of irony. Is what a problem? The fact that it's all an interim. Well yes, you answer, almost playfully (or at least with an astonishing absence of rancor for, let's face it, he's caught you completely off guard), in that it painfully skews (in terms of my capacity to survive from moment to moment) my take on your life as supreme embodiment of the real— the everyday—and therefore the eternal. Your posited gluedness to the toothpaste tube of mass-market culture—is—was—an assurance that you were in the true way. But now I see all the semi-immersion hasn't gotten you very far. You're dying. Not very far at all. And the sitcoms on prime time survive you. Forgive me, boy, but I was enthralled by what I took to be your mediocrity—it intrigued—it fascinated me, for only mediocrity is capable of enhearsing duration—no, let me think seropositive for once—of bottling and airtighting it for future strictly rationed consumption by someone like me.

I can't believe in myself! you cry out, least of all in the authority of my suffering not even after all these murders, but I could believe in you, as long, that is, I was watching you seated before the tube, no longer (had you ever been?) trying to catch the eye of the public but very much part and parcel of its critical mass. At this point, Berlio would be stirring uneasily in his seat except that he is bound and semisprawled on the bed. Ralph/Berlio: You say you can't believe in yourself. But what about self cum sum of its marks on—all over—your victims—you know, those semiprecious objects never shown much in the way of quarter? Doesn't the starry spread of their gashes and wounds fix the constellation of a self—if not yours, then somebody's,

surely? The "inner turmoil" that led to such onslaughts was—is—
real. Gift/Pudd: I just can't get a grip on the killer role in which I'm
cast. (Here's where the commercial really begins to sell itself: Hey, the
serial killer has the same self-doubts as everybody else!) And I want to
get as far away from that role as I possibly can, believe it or not. Climbing the stairs to your apartment, for example, I felt completely outside
myself. I could have been—I was—anybody and everybody. And I
grieved heartily for anybody when he wept and exulted, equally
heartily, for everybody when she triumphed [Bert (fuming ster-
torously): Stop giggling, Gift, and don't look to Flowers for approval—in commercial-land serial killers *do* have sentiments just like
Pudd's and make it a point to express them exactly as he is doing]. But
then the old misery supervened as old misery so often—always—
does: at one's having ended up despite so much valiant effort as little
more than a fifth-rate Killer, a truncheon-wielding loser, a machete-
monger nobody's heard of, not to mention assorted failure (as family
man, business partner, community pillar, barroom live wire, Sunday
driver, Little League coach) in a wide range of allied disciplines—imposed from without and clamoring to be given a more clearly defined
and (like stationery) personalized shape. In short, I am (as I mount the
stairs) what I refuse to admit I've become, what I'm still becoming.

At which point you, Ralph a.k.a. Berlio—what a moniker!—rebuke him for not applauding what "he never dreamed in a million
years he'd become". All this failure—after having been voted most
promising member of the senior class—is a surplus granted by life.
Why, indeed (you say), should life be convicted only of realizing the
blueprint of our fantasies, no strings attached? What surprise, what
room to grow, is there in that? This—failure in its manifold and im-
previsible guises—is undreamed-of novelty—is life itself—at last. On
your behalf—simply because they respect the noble work you've been

doing over the centuries—circumstances have taken the trouble to step down from their pedestal to mold you in a manner that could never in a million years have been anticipated. Thus you are forced to stretch your sinews and become a man.

But remember, Berlio, in taking Pudd to task you are above all always gentle. And you, Pudd, become so overcome by the gentleness that you (just before you deal him the first semifatal blow) have to remind yourself gentleness is just one quirk among many, no better and no worse than, say, masturbation or addiction to asparagus tips. You begin to whimper again (still thinking of the gentleness of this creature you're about to murder), at the very moment you're about to place your massive hands (all your strength, all your hate is concentrated in your hands) around his emaciated throat. Fortunately for you, or rather for your project, Berlio manages to dispel the atmosphere of reconciliation the gentleness has cunningly evoked by misinterpreting your motive for moaning (in vain you cry out, It's a whimper not a moan): he ascribes it not to enthrallment with his ethical perfection but rather to the ever-renewed preoccupation with failure after so much effort in breaking new Serial ground. Here you are, says Berlio, forever putting Pudd's own interests before his own even quasi posthumously, living an event anybody in his right mind would give his right arm to be able to call his own, be it just for a little while: an event, I'm sure, you've been pining after your whole life long as long, that is, as it was part and parcel of somebody else's *curriculum vitae*. And now it's part and parcel of yours if only you'll let it be so: I'm talking about your fighting this your last losing battle with me as if your life depended on it which it does.

For it's obvious that once you're done *they*'ll catch up with you doublequick so as to be able to say they bequeathed you your fifteen seconds (and whatever residuals might accrue to your heirs—you do have heirs, don't you?—from image-reverberation in an infinity of consciousnesses Cantor-equivalent to a single one, five-fourths stewed and mine shaft sooty) and then it'll all be over. But instead of welcoming with open arms the losing battle—which you so swoon over when you undergo its groped perfecting by others (either in print or on screen or through hearsay) for you are a great fan of bios aren't you?—Saint Catherine (No more world), Georgie Trakl, Ulysses S. Grant replete with sugarloaf shako: admit it, they're all grist for your mill of ascension by proxy—you fart-whine at what you perceive to be the enormous gap between the event aspired to and the event lived. You keep forgetting—did you ever learn?—that to be lived at all this life of ours (take it from somebody about to be parted therefrom, and gladly) must do its very best to constitute a scratch sum of deviations from the wrinkle-free curve of the only ones deemed worth living (i.e., mimicking) because already lived. Bert turned to Flowers and said: Gift has to understand that at this point above all else he's compelled to try to justify himself in his victim's eyes. For his victim's making him feel like a victim. So he explains that when his models or his rivals or his betters or his inferiors play out an event—any event— the playing out always manages to confirm their idiosyncratic genius whereas in his case the same event only ends up attesting all over again to—to—the almost vengeful stamina of what might be (cautiously) diagnosed as "congenital disaffinity for event in any size or shape". You've got to make it clear to Berlio, Pudd, that your problem "stems from the fact that"—your problem *is* that you annex the event before you've lived it. Even before the arterial blood has begun to dry on the walls, you're already calculating whether this particular specimen— the corpse of the moment—is different enough from all the others to warrant your being finally hailed as a master chef who never repeats himself.

The fire escape tracery catches the last rays of the sun. Looking out at the oak buds against a blackish cloud stump which, straddling the street, seems to have wandered into the frame of your musing expressly to cushion its motherless greens, for a moment you imagine (without, maybe luckily, being able to *go into* details) how everything might have been so very different. The mattress sags as you pull him off: he offers no resistance.

He's strong enough to walk slightly in front of you with a gun pointed at his back in the direction of Schurz Park. The barges in the distance, etc. You want him to rot in the open air, as befits an artist. You take note of barbershops, locksmiths, bakeries (of the chain variety), notary-accountants, florists, and as you pass the friendly proprietors (since it's that time of day when proprietors, friendly or otherwise, take the air) you feel without catching their eye that they're all on the lookout still, and with the taut-as-a-string streetcorner amiability of folks who know they will survive, if they survive at all, only by the skin of the teeth of their merchant skills, and so they're busy sizing you up, getting you over and done with, vocationally speaking, commodifying you as a specific type with specific needs. The barber—You're the barber, Flowers, Bert said. (Look alive, make yourself useful, he wanted to add, ever so playfully.)—hands ausculating his paunch as if it's about to yean, focuses on your hair, rather on what's left of it, deciding instantaneously, that it will doubtless be requiring a scalding towel massage up and down, and including each (hairy) lobe. And while you (and your sidekick, Berlio, for that's what everybody around here takes him for, the proverbial irrepressibly good-humored sidekick) are trying to sidestep these demons, you're almost trampled by the home- and restaurant-going crowds. But *Esse est percipi*, buster, and since there's nobody around to spectate their rampageousness (the rampage, sweeping all before it, thereby annihilates the possibility of sidelines, observers, fans), it does not currently exist. And it certainly won't exist once all is said and done for these beings, these crowd-folk, subsist from moment to moment, with no inculpating, context-stiffening glue between. What they were *like* fourteen seconds ago, in a Ninth Avenue peepshow (do they exist anymore?), has nothing to do with what, tchin-tchinning with their boss at some overflowing-the-pavement corner bistro, they are *like* now.

But, never fear, Pudd, the quietude of the clearing in Schurz Park, framed by its leafy boughs, more than makes up for the indignities suffered en route. However, you insist, as usual, on indulging in a little self-intimidation by overestimating its incorruptibility (so that your own thirst for compromise can stink all the more? What compromise, though: You never budged an inch where the entreaties of your victims were concerned.) inasmuch as you've already managed to assume, and after just one little sparrowy glance straight up, that its domey sky wouldn't be caught dead submitting to so momentous a violation as cloud infiltration; *the thing is,* when you look up again [after having focused briefly—recreationally—on a few real sparrows (one with half a ruby-red earthworm in its beak) congregated around a corrugated muffin cup] it's gotten itself very much infiltrated, with helicopters and contrails and sooty wingbeats as well as clouds, although you do have to admit this self-betrayal does not in the least prevent its re-emerging, minutes later (like the stampeding men and women, of the crowd some way back), as opaline as ever. A lesson, then, in accommodation to the ways of the cosmos by those wishing to succeed and, more to the point, yet another laying bare of your compulsive misreading of such accommodation.

Berlio turns to you, though he's never been turned away, and, coughing, says (for he can read the writing on the wall of your kisser which broadcasts loud and clear that this clearing is to be his not-quite-final resting place), The fatal ambush is nothing compared with the ambush of me, Hector Berlio, by my own body. No matter what, I always end up with the same fulminating symptoms, then they fade, insidiously, so that when they return, and they always do, I'm almost glad because at least they're out in the open. In short, the ambush engineered by his body of the man who hates that body and its recurring outbreaks of need has it all over yours, chum, according to every criterion of slimy underhandedness. You think, as you strangle and stab him, that it's the word *chum* that's done him in—that's done the two of you in. If only he didn't give way to it. Like the shrubs in the clearing, like the clearing's skyey dome, *chum* informs—reminds—you he's just one more artifact in a long line of wrong victims (but how can you trade him in at this stage of the game?), one more ill-fitting shard in your tessera of atrocity which will never, no use kidding yourself, pass muster as hot ticket to even the tiniest, smelliest vestibule of immortality. But you really don't, or at least you shouldn't, want to scuttle his wrongnesses since it is (*a*) the very wrongnesses that, retroactively detached from their specific individual substrates, thereby agglomerate into the ideal victim and/or (*b*) the very sum of cancellations seriatim of one victim-set of wrongnesses by its successor (absolute value: zero) that after all constitutes the artwork craved.

After it's over (you're not absolutely sure it's all over), you waste no time trying to get away. But you don't want your getaway to succeed. Still you manage to make your way past York, First and Second to Third where (corner of Eighty-sixth) you dutifully board the first public bus gliding broadly toward the curb (even better if it were a Limited Stops Only, not to mention an express bus going Bronxwards, but it's not), deposit your tessera in the slot (you worked it all out the night before (you've always had to be your own detail man and, you know something? you like it much better that way), politely request your transfer and take a seat beside a woman, slightly overweight and large-pored, of unfazeable late middle age who's obviously spent her whole life doing menial chores to infinitesimal acclaim (no offers yet to appear on the cover of *Vanity Fear*, say, or *Bomb*). Much as you'd like to stay on and rest your weary bones attending to the sights and sounds of upper Manhattan, now the capital of the world, something drives you back to the clearing (but a few steps from the front steps of Gracie Mansion, come to think of it).

As you advance on what is by now almost surely a corpse well on the road to dry-rot, a unprepossessing-looking too-tall man with a microphone (almost a corpse himself) is already advancing on you, flanked by two adjuvants. [By our next rehearsal, we'll have recruited some other actors to take over these roles. For now, we'll just have to make do with what we have: Annie and Priss will play the adjuvants; I'(no giggling)ll be Mr. Media.] You don't need to look around to know the area is already crawling with coppers: there's even a patch of New York Finest blue (that is, if your eyes aren't deceiving you and they rarely do) atop Gracie Mansion itself.

The media and the force: inextricably and double-bound for glory. Just as he is on the verge of thrusting the mike in your face, you think you catch a glint of reproach in Mr. Media's eye, not so much for what you've done (his kind thrives on such doings) as for the way your story's been unfolding, over minutes, weeks, decades. Mr. Media and Co. don't have the time to make sense of your story so they blame you for its incoherence. And doesn't Mr. Media know he and his kind thrive on just the sort of shards you lavishly provide. Mr. Media's media are not sufficiently ductile to transmit anything but shards— image after image reverently accommodated to the limited attention span of the late-night viewer. The late-night viewer, just remember, doesn't want a story, doesn't want coherence: he/she's watching the news simply because as presented—in splintered fireworks of non-connection—it makes the transition to what's coming after—a favorite sitcom, say—much less impatient and/or the decompressive mourning for what's just ended—a big-budget premiere made-for-TV movie, for instance, with just the right amount of violence ensuring an equally right amount of coitus interruptus in just the right installments—much less painful. The purpose of the news briefs is (*a*) to reassure the viewer that he/she hasn't surrendered (as punishment for all the vicarious thrills just undergone) his/her franchise out in the real world and (*b*) to distract him/her from the fact that he/she is, until the next entertainment begins, very much in transit, very much a vagrant, very much . . . homeless. The news, then, is a homeless shelter sponsored by the major transnations out of the goodness of their hearts. Media Men, then, should be grateful to Serial Kill for furnishing so incoherent a series of episodes as stand-in for a life. Incoherence after all sanctions the non-making of connections. And the sponsors don't want connections made since such connections will inherently go out of their way to adumbrate another story—about government agencies, for example, playing footsie with big businesses—which may not prove a very palatable confection. Flowers (rolling his eyes): Oh stop the trendy posturing, for crying out loud! That Government agencies sacrifice needy parishioners to juicy contracts profiting their highest-ups is the only palatable confection: problem is, Hollywood has already done its palatability, that is, its shock-value, to death.

So sorry, so sorry for all the cant, Bert said (and he really was for he hated most of all to be convicted of trendiness): forget all the tripe about malfeasance in high places, now just a banal strategy of mass entertainment. What I really fear—so I should have come straight out with it—is that said media will group Pudd—who's fast becoming, thanks to our group effort, a bona fide exemplar of subspecies Serial

Killer—with its sleaziest simulacra of same contrapted merely to feed the public's newly revived interest. We speak of the cunning of the media but do all we can to ignore its exasperatingly naïve manipulability by those—its very own—simulacra.

Years ago (despite Samuels' *What's this I hear about my old friend the media?* Bert refused to quash, or even hurry, ruminative reminiscence) following the release of a certain mainstream flick, the Gigolo, like the Serial Killer thereafter, grew "hot" and so it became the duty of every self-respecting anchorperson qua sum of his gophers to track down the subspecies' bona fide expert practitioners in order to keep the fire going strong [and those that were, tracked down I mean, evidently deemed it their civic duty (though their fifteen minutes had come shamefully late) to hold forth before the cameras, albeit with no little truculence, on the trade they plied so selflessly]. But who were they, these expert gigolos, and where had the media gone—where could anybody go—to smoke them out (had the specimens in question been subject to comprehensive processing and if so was the resulting archive subject to reliable and continuous updates)? In such a case was it possible at all, in fact, to speak of experts, i.e., star fieldworkers duly certified by an accredited jury of their peers? No matter: whether or not EGs existed, or even if it made sense to posit their conceivability given the nature of the (two-backed) beast, the media desperately needed them—and fast.

I expect the women I serve to pay me well *for my time*, said one, mouthing this obviously picked-up phrase precisely because it transformed him on the spot into what he was claiming—what the media supposed him—to be. Only—and here's the fantastical kicker—this particular one's work in films of a certain subgenre (I immediately recalled, and recall still, his king-sized stamina) suggested he much preferred . . . serving his colleagues—for free, so what was he doing—or rather, what was Mother Media doing—setting him up as a Gigolo? But, never fear, presumably 99.9 per cent of all viewers knew absolutely nothing about this disqualifying other life: to them, he was Gigolo par excellence because prime-time had coopted him as such and the prime-time grand-Turing machine always gets its facts straight, doesn't it?

In their panicked hunger to have something to feed the public and thereby keep the ratings and their jobs, the media boys and girls, always hot on the trail, had once again come through with a hot subject but one whose very (wrong) hotness managed, at least as far as I (an informed consumer) was concerned, to melt away all contour crucial to its putative identity. (It wasn't—would never be—clear whether they were themselves dupes or, not caring one way or the other, had simply, as usual, knowingly, factored in the very high probability of their being so in order to get on as quickly as possible with the far more serious business of lucratively duping everybody else.)

Hence I couldn't stop wondering—based, that is, on the disastrous showing made by my triple-Xed friend—whether a connection would ever be proved to subsist between the name for this, the hot subject of the moment (and, come to think of it, for that of every other moment) and its conscripted incarnations. If indeed there was a subspecies Gig mightn't its members, in order to survive as gigolos, very well be caught up in a network of assignments so multitudinous and far-flung as to render them unnamable and unlocalizable qua practitioners of the calling under consideration or of any other calling for that matter. Or maybe the names for all callings having the misfortune, like Gigolohood or—dom, to catch the media eye were necessarily their own jokey epitaph on an immediate consequential implausibility.

Listening to this perfect specimen (known firsthand, as you may remember, to be an alumnus of male-male fuck films) discharge his salvos, I could only conclude (*a*) that Gigolo like all media hot spots was a concept—never a person; (*b*) that the word for the concept had been reinvented to squelch a surfeit of countertendencies—among others, those manifested in such films—which would otherwise have remained too dangerously afloat in the mainstream (so what if the one hour and forty-five minute major studio feature was the basest of rein-ventors: the gigolo existed, somewhat in the manner of an anti-parti-cle postulated by mathematical physics, because his already massive prurient big-bucks impact required him to); and (*c*) that some voca-tions were undocumentable except by televisable trains of thought better left to derail themselves.

But so what, Gift suddenly bellowed, if the anchors and their go-phers just went ahead and recruited anybody who declared himself to be a gigolo: who's to say that in the course of posing/pontificating each and every didn't actually turn into one at last—and a damned good one at that. In short, folks (thus Flowers, brushing up on his news-casterese), only by achieving a media plausibility does the ass-aspiring turn himself into the ass-authentic. Ralph (with very much the heart-breakingly irascible intonation of Berlio on his last legs): As you, Gift, will finally become an actor by calling yourself one right and left. Bert [giving Gift a two-shoulder shrug (to his infinite regret he saw that Ralph, and to a lesser extent Priscilla, got the brunt of it)]: I just don't want Pudd being taken for a slapdash media contraption when we all know he's ever so much more. As nobody rallied to reassure, or even challenge him, not even Flowers (was he dozing on his cane?), there was nothing for Bert to do but proceed.

In fact Berlio is not quite dead: competing with the glaze of the popped sclerae is a flush of pleasure for all the long overdue attention you're beginning to get, although there's something behind the flush that assures you he's not—he's never going to be—taken in by the

fawning of your captors. It's just that he wants you to get what's coming to you. Unlike you, Pudd, for since on some level your acts, that is
to say, you yourself, cannot survive without media collaboration, you
allow yourself to be taken in—to feel completely submerged by their
ability to rehabilitate you, reconstruct you from scratch as brand-new
and one hundred per cent improved. You need to believe in them as
your better—best—half because they—the media and their gadg-
etry—are your only conduit to the real world: the world of celebrities.
Celebrities, after all, are flawless.

You, Pudd, see the slight contempt in your almost-victim's eye,
for your—how shall we put it?—your susceptibility. You can't have
Berlio going to his grave or to his living glory thinking you're capable
of being undone by a wee bit of amateur publicity flaunting Gracie
Mansion as backdrop. He must be made to understand that you're
streetwise to the gyrations of Mr. Media advancing on you, much less
warily now, for you've been expertly handcuffed by the adjuvants. Bert
turned and snapped: the handcuffs. But shadows had gathered and
Samuels (clearly egged on by GHW) looked displeased: was it the too-
extended digression on gigololand fuck films or the prior, even seedier
business of Georg Cantor's going cold-turkey out in San Darm? did the
boss then (with or without GHW's help) deem all allusion not directly
related to stage directions rankest sabotage? Who cared: taking a deep
breath (which was, he noted, once over—no! while still going on—
more like a profound sigh) Bert would refuse to let it get him down.
So, Bert concluded, please take your scripts (Gottfriedina will hand
them to you on your way out).

Chapter Ten

The following night, finding himself once again in the tenth floor waiting room, Bert was told the delay in getting Joyce's final test results wouldn't be as long as they'd thought initially [the implication, if there was any, being Cheer up, we're going to lick this motherfucker (meaning the disease entity)]. Writhing, Bert tried at the same time proleptically to come at the moment of disclosure of the test results from every conceivable angle of rehearsal—apotropaic because, hopefully, simply too superdetailed to be reproducible by humbug Reality's Old Master majors-domo without on-the-spot arraignment for first-degree plagiarism—so as to get the inevitable good news (though of course not from his perspective) out of the way as an authentic possibility as soon as possible [for robbed through his foresuffering of its shock of novelty it—Reality—would—if it was anything like him and it had to be for doesn't everybody remake Reality in the form of his or her very own shrunken image, replete with idiosyncratic warts-

and-all?—necessarily back off, thereby making room for jubilation-free (lest he be punished for any overt and premature displays) preparation for the worst (once again, from any perspective but his own)]. He needed to get over the daunting hump of anticipating the exact form the good (though not for him) news about the test results must take—something to the effect that excision of the tumor had been spectacularly successful and Joyce consequently would be living forever and a day, burying everybody in sight and anybody else who dared to cross her path, yet in spite of that (enjoying the very best of both worlds, that of having her cake, and of gnawing it down to the bone too, all in a single refusing gulp) retaining all rights and reasons to complain of having undergone the shabbiest of treatment at the hands of the prosthetic gods, scalpel-wielding and otherwise, to say nothing of having still to endure the equally shabby persistence through thick and thin of the tumor itself and in a form now too vengefully occult and far too intricate to localize, for its supposed excision (a mere pretext, that, for boys-in-the-backroom-type self-congratulation!) didn't fool the likes of Joyce: the operation could very well constitute a groundbreaking coup for all the habibs in Christendom but not for the superastute guinea pig herself who divined rightly and righteously that her nemesis had simply gone underground, had managed, in other words, to assume a more unstraitjacketable identity—so as to ensure that such news (good, but not for him! and now irrevocably ditched through sheer force of premonition) never got itself announced in any form whatsoever. I've got to pay careful attention to these moments, Bert told himself, so I can properly guide Gift as to how to await Pudd's death sentence.

Of course, he knew better than anyone it might very well supervene anyway (this good news, but not for him), no matter how pointillistically accurate his prefiguration [for Mother Reality, unlike other great artists, did not mind in the least being convicted of plagiarism (in fact, it was good publicity for the old primitive, for any publicity, no matter how bad, was good publicity, at least that was what Joyce's fourth husband Murray used to say)]. For a minute he was buoyed up by the freshness of the evening air managing to perforate, here and there, even a barrier as thick as the waiting room's after-dinner stench, pungent still at almost nine p.m., and by the boldness of the setting sun's light as reflected off the fiddle moldings on a glass facade opposite (the Fritz Kreisler Building) and the even greater boldness of the wind-driven plane trees, also reflected in that same facade—then terrified that such exhilaration, for exhilaration it was, amounted to nothing more than the stupidity of allowing himself to be caught off guard before the inevitable kick in the teeth perpetrated by the announcement he dreaded most, namely, that Joyce's bout with and heroic trouncing of death and her equally heroic unequivocal recovery (as attested by those good-newsworthy Final Test Results which, by the way, were at this very moment being notarized preparatory to celebration of the entire case history in the next number of the most prestigious annals of oncology) had managed to render her stronger, healthier (her immune system was now as robust as a twenty-year-old athlete's) than ever before. In other words (so they would be announcing within milliseconds as if it must be a little water music to his virgin ears), *We can report her.* But then as pacing went about generating the old tumor of teeth-gritting loathing for Joyce and her kind, he suddenly felt sure he was on the verge of invoking the sort of news he himself wanted desperately to hear (in a word, the worst sort, but of course not for the likes of him) simply by having freely shown himself poised for the shattering reception of its opposite, that is, up until less than a minute ago when the consciousness (a pollutant at any speed) of this genuine dread of the inevitable (genuineness attested by the fleeting indifference that only uncontrollable rage at such inevitability can confer) began to entertain fancies of entitlement to something more.

So that, still pacing, it was clear he was back where he'd started from, and not merely—least of all in fact—in terms of his exact position on the tiled floor (just flooded over with disinfectant) for once again he'd managed to catch himself in the act (as if he were his own worst enemy—GreenHurstWood, say, or Flowers) of being absolutely convinced of what he nonetheless still knew to be hogwash, to wit, that his susceptibilities positively—insofar as they were pure of calculation—irrevocably determined the unshapely course of any event, that is to say, its ultimate form became the direct result of the direction whence he, or rather, his ultimately exorcising dread, bore down on it; in other words, that the event in question depended lock, stock and barrel (or was it hook, line and sinker?) on the tenor of inner being being cultivated as he set forth to meet it halfway. To be in the very foulest of humors, as he was now, consequential to having surrendered to the inevitability of bad news (in this case, bad for none but him) was somehow (or so he still believed, or needed to believe, proving of course indisputably thereby that he was not quite consumed by— since he still expected a substantial dividend from playing reluctant host to—that foulest of humors) to definitively foil such inevitability. Mother Reality would never dream of wasting the news in question on one already so well-prepared for its reception as to be completely done in—though not quite, for he had wits enough about him yet to get from one end of the room to the other (in spite of the pisspot fumes still rising from the tiles), or so he insisted on believing, or rather, so his being done in went on insisting on believing—for didn't the being already so done in foil all need for bad news of any kind? For the whole purpose of the bad news (albeit in this case—the Joyce case—bad,

bad, bad, to nobody but him) would be to do him in for having failed to love her disease and (as anybody with eyes to see must see) done in he already was, even if a-peeping from the very margin of being done in was the bloated expectation of reward for all the effort expended (which expectation of course only served to immediately invalidate being in every one of its guises, done in or otherwise).

At last the surgeon entered with an entourage of ill-dressed student types. He went to the window to escape them and more particularly the news they must be bringing and to think: Pudd awaiting news of a possible stay of execution and knowing it was hopeless. And what's more, the sky, never to be trusted, never to be counted on in an emergency, like now, with the prospect of Joyce's uncroakability hanging in the balance, sprawled, oozing like an egg, stranded on its foredunes, emitting no real light, much less succor, able or willing only to taint— for misery loves company—every available surface and seam with its gauziest equivocations. Turning back (after giving the situation such as it was what he considered to be enough time to transform itself into its exact opposite, whatever that might be), Bert saw, first, that Joyce was, alas, still very much alive if not quite kicking and, second, that amid all the postoperative well-wishing (nosocomial PR cum BS) she was making a point of maintaining a shrewdly provoking look, one of an almost-smiling, contemptuous skepticism which was infinitely beyond the solicitation not only of their chitchat but even of her own suffering in its most regal manifestations, greater of course, that suffering— that Joyce suffering—in and out of remission, than anybody else's, though was it still her own now that this gang saw fit to return it to her gift-wrapped and with the understanding that from here on in it was in escrow (that is, until such time as they were able, by expunging whatever shreds were still left of her assorted malignancies, to do away with it completely).

So, the news still was not out. More of same. In fact, Joyce saw fit to add (but a propos of what? he'd missed the lead-in, damn it), I'm going to lick this. Even if I have to fly all over the globe to get the right treatment (pep talk cum threat to her not-quite-handpicked personal team of medicos?). He had a sudden craving to write it all down as possibly useful filler, say, for one or another of the lines-starved actors (even if there was little enough of this "all") not (he realized) to not be forgetting but so as to have acquired something *against* the excruciation of swallowing such dark-beery self-affirmation completely undiluted and into whose barrel he was, to the bargain, clearly expected (she turned to him with imperious expectancy, clicking her tongue) to piss his two cents worth of collusive cheer. *The thing is*, with the day's light dying just above the airconditioner, Bert, out of the blue feeling he himself must be dying, was capable of colluding only with a desperate wish to get away, it didn't have to be far, just somewhere barely suitable for communion with his own symptoms, instantaneously infinite in number and in danger of proliferating if a survey of the situation wasn't taken at once. In fact, he could barely say goodnight to Joyce, much less to the team (insufferable in their good humor and still no sign of the news that was to determine Joyce's fate—more importantly, his own), for until absolutely sure the process was irreversible (he felt more aguish by the minute), as he suddenly was now, one felt tempted by all sorts of shifts: finding oneself, for example, all at once in the very best of health simply because of a momentary indifference to whether or not one was in fact ill; suddenly ill again, insofar as the most recent encounter with another human being had not been sufficiently replete with symptom-occluding innuendo. And what did all this show, but that he was too much of a creature in the small (topologically speaking), too susceptible to, too much on the squirrel-lookout for, the discontinuous individual collision with the power to make or break him. But, he must remember (was there any danger he might forget?) to contaminate the actors at every moment with the very same impressionability—to life as a series of discontinuous make-or-break encounters. Perhaps even Gift might succumb.

Down in the cafeteria, Belle sat at her supper, picking gingerly at what looked like barbecued chicken wings, and now that he too was eating, however little, she was spurred to unload her fears into the lap of his captivity. Like her old high school sorority pal Winnie Verlock, she was an old hand, when it came (as it so often did) to talking evenly at him the wifely talk. Looking up at her now and then, he found himself consistently begrudging what he saw—this, her inherent Belleness—Belleness intrinsicate—her very persistence in her being, as all along (he noted, in self-defense) he had been begrudged the corresponding very persistence in his own—lethally, somebody might add—by the Alberts and the Joyces and the Gifts and the Flowers and the GreenHurstWoods of the world, who, true to type, hated more than anything or anybody the persistence in being aforesaid of that thing or that body, insofar as it was (and by definition had to be) effected without their permission. So he was acting like Joyce, or was he merely acting apotropaically in anticipation of Joyce's raid on the always-unsuspecting Belle, who even in those rare instances when she foresaw and foresaw correctly never knew what to do with her foresightings. He had become Joyce, hideous transmogrification compliments of Belle's babbling and nibbling. How get Gift to impersonate Pudd as well as he knew himself to be impersonating Joyce? Belle's babbling and nibbling game him no choice but to become Joyce. How could he find Gift such a prop? But for all his compulsion to soil that innocuousness, deep down he was ever so proud of his little Belle's defiantly babbling away no matter what, persisting and then some in her own being, despite all that must be fomenting within, all that clearly loomed (a little caucus of horizon-bound clouds was waiting to swallow up the sun's exit) without. Thank you for taking care of Joyce for me, she said. I know she's—it's—not easy. If Joyce dies, he wanted to say, I'll no longer have to excrete her outrages through impersonation. Something in Belle's wan smile made him realize, however, that Joyce's death might fuse him with those outrages forever. So he must remain on his guard (forever) against making a cult of her memory.

Back in her mother's room Belle made straight, as was her wont, for the iceblink of the airconditioner. He dared not ask for news. The room was empty: it was obvious she was making a point of divulging nothing of what the departed team had doubtless laid before her. She did say, however: They want me to start on chemotherapy as an outpatient. Without seeking her out among the shadow-folk, Bert sensed that Belle had just turned away from this bald clinical fact of the case at hand to the somewhat more agreeable ones connected with mullions and moonshine. But how can I go home? Who'll take care of me? All my husbands—except one—are dead, or as good as dead. Just before you came in, Bert, one of the surgeons-in-training—and a real idiot, by the way, if ever there was one—leaning against the wall right where you're standing now and looking very busy reading my files (it was as thick as a textbook) had the gall to suggest that somebody— somebody!—could look in on me now and then, a neighbor, say. That's the stupidest suggestion I ever heard, she added, her tone managing at the same time to make it clear that under no circumstances would she take Bert's usual talking-to-the-wall silence to mean: What's so stupid about it? They could look in on me (it was clear she hated having to use the flunkey-surgeonoid's expression of choice) at 9:30 and I'd be fine and at 10:30, when they weren't . . . looking in on me, I could be in the throes of advanced . . .

Given her rage at the medical men (the news had quite possibly been bad though, if it had, not, of course, for the likes of him) all of a sudden it seemed opportune to note—mind you, merely note—the judiciousness of his or better yet Belle's—if only she'd be willing for once to shoulder, rather than shirk—procuring power of attorney at several—or all—of the banks where Joyce's alimonies had always enjoyed spectacular growth. Surely there could be none of that rage left to lavish on him for suggesting such a course of action, even if in the abstract it was all-over rife with possibilities for the fleecing of so defenseless an old broad as she'd become in a mere matter of hours. A flush, of snakelike suspiciousness, passed over her features, but before he could give himself over to ferreting out the target [idiot that he was, he'd plum forgot she could sustain snakelike arraignment of several targets at once (loathing the jackass surgicos did not incapacitate her for loathing him with equal, perhaps even with heightened, vehemence) or, if need be or if the fancy took her, amid a complete absence of targets] she, to buy time (she'd never give him the satisfaction of saying yes or no immediately: make him sweat, that was the ticket), asked (or so it sounded to him) if he wouldn't mind going and, please, getting her some of "those" mints (to countermand the too-oniony and -garlicky aftertaste of her tuna and sprouts snack—doctor's orders). So not only was she already experiencing the pleasure of ordering him around (in revenge for having been put on the spot about the P of A: so he'd found the courage to broach the subject, after all!), she was also quick enough to catch (and flush at: this time with unmistakable delight) the look of raging disgust as he braced himself (counting his coins for the slot machine in question) to do her bidding, which quickness enough proved beyond the shadow of a doubt she knew he knew she'd concocted the errand merely to be getting even, or be getting something in return for the granting of a permission now sensed to be inevitable under the circumstances.

Back on the scene after some feeble stage business with the mints and their wrappers, here she was, feistier than ever, asking him to call a few—make that all—of her several ex-husbands and (where applicable) their current spouses to find what *they* all thought. About what, he asked, though he knew damn well about what. This was but a symptom both of her suspiciousness with respect to his still waters and of her fear that those waters, however still, would never run deep enough to drown the powers that be. Though he might, he was sure she'd be willing to grant, be wily enough to dispossess her of her hard-chicaned swag, he was sure she was sure he'd be no match for such professionals as would be more than happy to dispossess him double-quick of his dispossessions.

He was within an inch of reminding—no, enlightening—her about just how unpopular she was among the members of this ad hoc cabinet when, as in a dream, he managed to remind himself that, indeed, such incontestable detestation must from her point of view be their very best recommendation, for someone like Joyce could trust—that is, begin to trust and then but tentatively—only somebody who convincingly hated her guts with a vengeance. So he braced himself to call them all which, he was sure, was nothing compared with the subsequent inevitable having to brace himself a wee bit more and then some to call her so as to communicate their confirmation, to a man, of the judiciousness of his hunch. Only every time he spoke of leaving to look up their numbers she interrupted, asking anxiously, What, what, for her wariness, stretched to the breaking point under the best of circumstances, was currently so hyperextended as to amount to a kind of deafness drowning out every discordance but her own. Driven as she most certainly was by the need to work him—nay, every interlocutor, i.e. exploiter—for all he was worth, any concession vouchsafed even if it was ultimately for her own good had to be earned the hard way.

When he returned (better, after all, to enlighten her face to face) with the news that all her relations had confirmed the soundness of his proposal, he knew better than to be kindly, self-satisfied and expansive (in short, he spoke brusquely) for Joyce would then have no choice but to react as to so much flayable carcass. Up at once on her high horse (though still unable to sit in bed), she began by remarking that all this calling, all this to-do over a P of A, had been completely unnecessary: she knew where to get funds when necessary: over the phone from headquarters, if need be, here in her room. He was barely able to contain the rage generated, as usual, by such freewheeling posturing—no loving her yet as Albert, according to Samuels, had deserved to be loved—and, then, only because the aide of the moment was nearby, in the bathroom to be exact, probably scouring Joyce's undies. But (aide or no aide), as Bert knew only too well, the art of dealing with Joyce's gassy swagger was the art of procuring a foothold somewhere along the isthmus between halves of an hourglass: rage served only to collapse the purchase, surely one always too dearly bought to piss away just like that into any old counter-tantrum. The trouble was that, even if he himself considered poker-facedness the highest good he could ever attain where Joyce was concerned, some moment corroded by Joyce's meechy appeal to his piety, worse, his filial devotion, worst, his undying in-law's love, was sure to come along quite obviously more than willing to do, or rather, more than willing to get him to do, the honors of overthrow of such a stance, given the fact that the poker-facedness, though self-defensively appropriate to their relation in the absolute sense, would now no longer be so on the microlevel created by said moment's meechiness [buttressed to boot by the appeal's construction of the appellant as one irreproachably worthy of all she craved (so what if she was only pretending to shyly solicit what she not so secretly laid claim to as her rightful due)]—

would in fact constitute an outrage—a violation of its essence (for where lay the essence of this moment, after all, but in its efforts to procure modest-minded Joyce the modest comfort she so justly deserved?). And such a moment had just come along: like a person blindfold he was running smack up against its post; like for a person seated calmly in the dark, the halogen lights had been suddenly turned on.

But cheer up (he didn't tell himself), at last he was getting a taste of what his long-lost pal Charley S. Peirce [who could never get a teaching job anywhere, no way, no how (how come?): en passant, where was old Charley hanging out now?] used to refer to as the something more than can be contained in a moment (he called it an instant) or the consciousness of the two sides of an instant. This here moment's meechy appeal to his better instincts was triggering the consciousness of an interruption into the field of consciousness, a sense of resistance, of an external fact, or another something; entailed a sense or sensation of polarity or reaction (all poor Charley's words, these). And how infinitely rich had said moment already become—even as he damned it, or rather, cheered on by his so damning it—through his refusing, resisting sense of there being indeed two sides to it (as unveiled by the meechiness of its appeal) and, indeed, probably, to any moment worth a damn: the side of the appropriateness of pokerfacedness and its yoked refusal to budge one inch as the only rational—the only healthy—the only conceivable defense against its barbarities latent or otherwise, and the side of the very same pokerfacedness's scandalous impropriety in the context of Joyce's—or rather, the moment in question's—meechy appeal to his undying love of her essence, tumors and all. At any rate, this experience of the multi-moment, what Charley (in a moment of all-too-characteristic lightheaded optimism) had dubbed Secondness, was if nothing else liberating him at last from the prison of Firstness (as also dubbed by Charley) wherein he had always been too much the slave of every moment lived, or even half-lived, so that there was never any real proceeding beyond the moment in the face of the moment's particular flavor since for there to be a proceeding beyond Firstness there had to be the locking horns with the moment's multiprongs that he—or rather, his pokerfacedness—was resisting for all it was worth. In short, the moment's meechy appeal was doing him a favor—graduating him from Firstness to Secondness on the way (hopefully) to a glorious Thirdness which would bind all these rawly, meechily malevolent moments of First feeling, and of Second feeling as resistance to feeling more than one feeling per moment, all together into an articulated complex and worked-over product that, as the idea, thought, sign, memory, retrospective creation of those feelings, would differ immeasurably from feeling qua feeling. And so differing would, this complex, perhaps be importable into the rehearsal arena for reprocessing as a Pudd- or a Berlio-thought about sedans or gurneys or potted palms or a stay of execution. Goodbye Charley.

And while he could of course forswear such an appeal within the bowels of its moment on the level of feeling, rather of feeling's absence, there was no avoiding collaboration on the level of language, for to make himself scarce on that level must entail nothing less than to admit outright he couldn't care less what tumors or bloomers Joyce saw fit to try on for size, nor would he ever be giving a damn, so help him. There were milliseconds, he had to admit (between the seizing and the swallowing of a mint, say), when Joyce seemed both to perceive Bert's indifference and hate and to accept them, or was it then merely her own she was proclaiming, loudly, too loudly for some ears though never for Bert's, testing their waters as the only possible survival medium for one so much sinned against as poor she, and for no good reason if you ask her (though of course nobody in his right mind ever did). No loving her yet. But right this minute—no, or rather, yes! there was no mistaking it: a new minute, instant, Peircean moment had clearly, or rather unlocalizably, just been born from the ashes of its predecessor—Joyce was burrowing (he couldn't quite map the burrowing onto any particular gesture or expression or utterance) for all she was worth toward Bert as . . . the favorite son. And for a minute, but a different minute—one uncontaminated by the brute (however unlocalizable) fact of her motions—Bert felt *something like pity* for all this self-suppression of her truest, vilest humors evidenced by the ungainly forthrightness of such motions. And surely someone like Joyce was to be pitied when prevented, as now, from remaining true to her vocation of sucking the blood of others right out through their marrow for what did all this mean but that she was in the grip for once of a force greater than her own vileness—and such a force had to be a very great—and a very terrifying—force indeed. For a millisecond she was regarding him with affection.

What a mess, he heard her moan. The moan was very much cut from the same cloth as her rancorless burrowing but even now, from behind the curtain of its cut-rate despair, peeped a wariness, a wiliness even, that of a child waiting, tantrum-true, to see how the big people are going to handle this particular demand. To someone passing by, presumably the floor nurse, for her coif rose higher than all the others that had already swum into Bert's ken, Joyce cried: Get the nurses' registry on the phone, please. I need someone for tonight. My son-in-law can't stay: his boss (how Bert hated that immitigable word) needs him. (And in a tone conveying that what was to come was meant only, or preponderantly, for Bert: I need to pour out my heart even if I have to pay through the nose for the privilege.) But before Joyce could finish with her moaning, her interlocutor (though not by choice) entered to say in effect that there would be no more nurses, from the registry or anywhere else for that matter, since the moment (scandalously deferred far too many times already) had come at last for Joyce to give up her bed (and breakfast) to one far more in need, and amble on home which was where, now that she was going to receive topflight chemotherapy injections as an outpatient, she belonged.

He was wishing Belle were here (where'd she gone to this time?) if for no other reason than to be softening the Joyce-blow of the P of A, and to be handling some of the related paperwork which was slowly mounting, though surely he didn't need to be reminded (she was his wife, after all!) paperwork was not Belle's forte. So with tumor at a new instar once again he must consider himself—not Belle, Len, Freddy or some stray around-the-clock aide—solely responsible for all the drudgeries to ensue. Day after day after day after day after day after day. As he imagined with relish his exit walk to the elevator and (curiously) with even more relish the longish wait for its arrival, he found himself agreeing heartily with somebody sometime (who and when was it?) when he or she had spluttered word-daggers to the effect that man was—is—sick by virtue of just being a man, that is of remaining conscious in the face of the annihilating repetition of day after day after day after day after day after day. Repetition of day after day after day is imposed on his mauled consciousness—repetition as the illusion of novelty—novelty as sameness in difference and difference in sameness is thrown to—at—the flea-bitten mutt of his prowling consciousness like a gnarled and bewhiskered soupbone. And the mangy mutt (a.k.a. Bert) always responds yapping and crapping— even if he is physically incapable of yapping (though not yet, alas, of crapping), even if he hasn't the slightest wish (never mind) to yap— for to wake up to the new day is to, by definition, yap at the potential novelty of the new day's dawning over the same sameness of yesterday

albeit freshly maimed to embody the sort of world of difference (if yesterday was *n* then today is *n+1*) that only numerical order can vouchsafe. Merely to wake up and open his eyes constitutes an obligation to
laboriously foment a resurrection of interest in what is never of any interest whatsoever, what is indistinguishable (to the practiced eye) from
all that came before. Yet once the eyes are open (to each new exact
replica of a mystery that has been solved already far too many times
and by no master sleuths) they feel the old obligation to glaze over
with punch-drunk eager-beaverness at the prospect of another clue.
For, sad to say, the numerically different same sameness always manages, tugging coaxingly at the hypersensitive short-hairs of consciousness, to convince them down to the fatty follicle each and every one,
that the sludgelike continuity of sleuthly application must at all costs
be sustained. The puzzle is once again circling the horizon hence the
puzzling-out must recommence, as always in earnest, so as to be fully
achieved in time for—in time for—in time for—But if only he
(man)/I (Bert) could suppress forever this whiff of the maiming different—this laughable but-numerical difference—differentness from
yesterday—that alone provokes me into stalking the old bugbear—if
only he (man) or I (Bert, man but not quite) could elude the push-
and-pull of difference in any shape or form and, lighter of heart, crawl
up instead into the very rectum of sameness expecting nothing but
more of same thereafter and thereafter and thereafter, then all would
be as well as well could ever hope to be. (Elevator summary: the "old"
tension between the dawning day as a new beginning—a unique and
unforeseeable building block in life as a monument—and as an exact
repetition, and simultaneous amnesiac canceling, of its predecessor.)
But if only (he thought, before the elevator, near capacity, swallowed
him up), I could bear (without feeling suffocated and straitjacketed) to
think of my life overall—my life qua transfinite number of its days—

as the construction and cementing of a monumental sameness, *then* all days would necessarily turn out different each from the others. So much novelty—so much meaning, then!—to look forward to. Too bad, then, that I prefer each one of my days to be an upwelling ex nihilo (clearly I prefer the oppression of sameness in the small to the version in the large insofar as the former holds out, with each upwell— though I'd never admit as much—the hope of total transformation) resembling all the others to a T.

Or, as his old buddy Scholem Aleichem would have said (he'd had so many old buddies: where were they all now? and why did they sidestep him like the plague?), he was forever undergoing contraction (*tsimtsum*) to, or rather away from, some fateful pinpoint, only in his case, unlike that of the Ike-Lurianic *Ein-Sof*, such contraction could never be expected to transform—by the very fact of its contraction— the pinpoint into a plenum much less go on to usher in peristaltic configuration after configuration of dross (*kelippoth*)-spewing lights until the last syllable of unrecorded exile—exile as mission for ingathering the divine sparks of humankind's roots shattered among those lights, scattered in 288 different directions—maybe because the mirror of this madness—one Joyce Shekhinah as long-suffering mother, as receptacle of all the nightsoiled tailings of upper worlds (those where Bert professed to engage in his realest doings) too hoity-toity to own up to their state of excretory emergency—was simply over-muddy herself with such punishing dregs (she too was in exile, from her better *Sof*, and was oh so wrongfully being asked to shoulder what was nothing of her own doing: Bert's hectic, willed estrangement from his inmost female waters).

Joyce, to be exact, had other fish to fry. Against every attacker— be it hospital administrator, head nurse or chief oncologist—he was expected to match her animus, target by target. Although the world was a circus of horrors and Joyce one of its stars, staunchly she would go on thinking herself a mere bystander, righteously outraged. So either he must share her point-of-view (POV) shot, thereby getting himself (as said POV went about running down every non-Bert in sight) incinerated only by proxy, or refuse to share it and, becoming by default its sole target, suffer real annihilation.

The attack on her person by non-Berts—whether by disease or, worse, by its treatment personnel—would always metamorphose into attack by none other than Bert who, having failed to prevent it, must (according to Joyce's Second Law—of Hemothymia) be the biggest culprit of all. In fact, Joyce was no less than the line of demarcation between Bert and non-Bert. More to the point she was the sluice forever threatening him with inundation by the non-Berts, all more Bert than Bert himself.

How novel, then, that amid the throes of her being evicted from hospital precincts things were suddenly taking a turn for the better: she'd got herself a drudge and his name was Bert. What better proof that the world, all its Joyce-fire and brimstone notwithstanding, was still ever-ready to accede to her modest requests.

But hadn't Bert been Albert's drudge as well? So Joyce's haggling maneuvers in the face of bedpan death were but a repetition of the old man's. So once again it was but novelty as repetition. So once again he was being thrown a curve ball—an old bone—and, in starkest contravention of the will of his hind leg to kick it to kingdom come, he must learn to love it—her—as he'd never loved the other for here lay his last real-life chance to experience, come away with and instill into his actors and their product the commendable hence marketable sentiments of some average Joe.

Just a case, then, of the very novelty maimed to the same sameness somebody, given half a chance, was always getting up on his soapbox to rail against, but Bert's yapping mutt consciousness simply did not have the wherewithal to rear up on its hind legs and leap for that old bone. The old dog went blind, from testicular twinges. North lobby! Silver zone!

Chapter Eleven

When next he saw the actors (Samuels and GreenHurstWood were both hovering in the background of the studio but he didn't care what either thought, about anything, at this point of time), he told them to remember they were enacting a disease, for which there was no cure, since any measure claiming such a status would merely be appended to the swelling ranks of its symptoms. Johnny-on-the-spot, Gift loudly recoiled from this explanation of what they were doing, and Flowers standing on his cane in the farthest corner was quick to echo back Gift's doings with a gentlemanly smirk. Flowers said: Little Gift wants to will his gestures: he does not want them imposed by anybody, least of all by you, Bert, and he certainly doesn't want them imposed within an overall schema also imposed by you.

Bert tried to make his little responding laugh appear unmarred by resentment, by fear, through bringing to mind what his friends Toulmin Schwartzjopf and Scholem O'Malley had been saying (and in completely unrelated contexts) during so many of their many bachelor-days hiking trips through Bronx Park (though, come to think of it, both were bachelors still). Think of us as mapmakers or surveyors, then, if you like (rather than as disease-mongers), Bert went on, more to Ralph than to anyone for all of a sudden Ralph was bearing an uncanny resemblance to Meriwether Lewis. As mapmakers we have to choose a scale. But just because we choose a particular system does not mean we are being untrue to or distorting the facts. For we can talk about the facts at all only after we have made just so stark but oh so crucial a leap into specificity. (Though now addressing Gift, Bert managed to keep his gaze still focused on Ralph.) There is no alternative to such a leap—except no map at all. And don't imagine that with "no map at all" we leave the facts unsullied by our grubby little hands for in that case there are no facts whatsoever, unsullied or otherwise. But there is a danger here, Flower interposed (as if it were his cane speaking, speaking and pointing)—All hands turned toward the shadow in which he chose to bask.—namely, that you might end up confusing the boundaries (mere ploys) you are obliged to establish in your system so as to be able to entrap a fact or two in its rete—it's your meal ticket—with living and breathing things. But don't forget it's no less of a chimera. I won't forget, Bert said sweetly. But I'm also put in mind of what Scholem Aleichem used to say: Bert, he used to say (during our autumn walks through the rock gardens of Bronx Park: everybody loves Bronx Park, and not just in the autumn), the Torah is unchanging but if it is to have any meaning at all in, and for the denizens of, a particular cosmic cycle—if its letters are to relinquish the bliss of unpunctuatedness and enter into such meaningful combinations as only words can embody then the words so formed must address themselves to (*a*) the immediate matter of the sin prevailing within the cycle in question and (*b*) the cycle-dominant attribute (*Sefirot*) of the Godhead blithely permitting that sin to run rampant.

In seeming retaliation for having been made to dredge up all these painful memories of younger and happier days, he asked Gift to walk around the loft. Gift did not demur, nor did he turn toward Flowers who was busy twirling his cane as if it were a baton. When he did finally turn around he saw that all the other actors—Priscilla, Ralph, Annie, and several new faces here on the recommendation of Mrs. Samuels, a devotee of and former stage manager in summer stock up around the Poconos—were striking the same pose, a pose (from the look of him) he didn't even know he'd struck. So, he said to Bert, I'm supposed to be looking for my future corpse but it's I who's been dismembered— reduced to a single pose that is being multiplied to infinity by your flunkeys. Maybe I'm an artifact or maybe I'm a thought bulging out of your skull, you shit, but for sure there's one thing I'm not: Gift. Gift no longer. I'm an interchangeable part of the Bert mechanism: any-body could play Pudd—they're already doing it—look! they're more me than I am.

And looking around Bert had to admit the other actors bore a striking resemblance to Gift not so much in any single feature (theirs were by and large far more regular though, he had to admit, the re-sults were far less interesting) as in their current poses. Should Bert admit to Gift what had just hit him with a vengeance, namely that whatever the outcome of this absurd project it was clear Gift had been sent as the thing through which he, Bert, could count on being able to do two things at once which were in fact (at least, under certain dis-pensations, that is, *Sefirot*) the very same thing: (*a*) create a product bearing absolutely no trace whatsoever of Bert himself and his preten-sions and, by extension, of his commerce with the less-than-fair Joyce and her soon-to-be-Bedlamized daughter (and thereby redounding in-finitely more than it would have bearing any such traces to the glory of Samuels and Company and, more important, the celebrity, that is, the entertainment value, of Serial Killers everywhere) and (*b*) work out a very private obsession concerning he (still) knew not what: and the more comfortable the obsession became expressing itself in and through Gift, the more it would approach asymptotically a Gift-thing whence all trace of ever-offending Bert would have been, and would continue to be, smelted off and away, into the dross of broken vessels. And what a relief for Bert to be disembarrassed at last of all the foul contingencies that decreed him Bert so as to make way for the Bert-essence—an essence that might, for all he knew, turn out to be utterly Bertless. Something compelled Bert to take Gift aside and say, Two processes are to occur simultaneously and not just simultaneously, but fusedly as follows: while the elements of the Gift sequence are getting further and further from their generating first-term (the hunger to kill so as to satisfy the hunger to be immortal) and becoming each more and more passionate, ferocious and perfectly expert an expression of Bert-rage as Gift-rage as Pudd-rage the further they get from that first term, at the same time and with each additional term a little more of the stuff of idiosyncrasy—Bert-idiosyncrasy (rage-related and otherwise)—will be being pared away, or rather, blasted off, leaving behind what approximates more and more, with each pared blasting, the nudity of a serial characterlessness—not even an artifact for, with the generation of each new member of the sequence, there will be fewer and fewer clues to the identity of the processes by which said artifact has been shaped.

All of this reminds me, said Flowers, no longer twirling his baton, of the timeline of life itself and the little tricks it sees fit to play on us, especially as we age—badly (I speak for myself): we think we are getting mellower and far more tolerant—that with ever-increasing distance from the starting point we can't help but amass the fruits of a more serenely detached perspective when in fact it is the opposing pull of death that is equally if not more (and in some cases entirely) responsible for this breakdown as occasion for smarmy self-congratulation. But more to the point, Bert went on (as if Flowers hadn't spoken though he—and everybody else—knew that he had, and well)—I mean, forgetting for a minute my own project of achieving character-lessness through your depiction of Pudd—the fact that everybody and his brother on the scene has been seeing fit to duplicate your core pose (that of pouncing on your victim to tear his liver out)—which duplication you find so humiliating—so soul-, i.e., scene-stealing—is in fact the key to its—the pose's—and your own preservation, both as Gift and as Pudd and, most important, as Gift-as-Pudd. Imagine what it would be like if it was just you who was posing so: all the energy of the pose and of the character posing would be yielded up to the losing battle against disintegration amid the wind, rain, sleet and hail of the urban circus. As things now stand, your pose is so busy warding off the encroaching contours of the other poseurs/poses and becoming super-fortified thereby it no longer has the time to worry about withstanding erosive forces. In short, your identity—whatever that is—isn't being diluted to nullity among your clones but rather—but rather (most beautiful phrase in the language)—amplified, dilated, reflected to infinity, perpetuated like the seven plagues of Samarkand.

Gift, looking quizzically at all his replicas, said: I am done—to a crisp. As a well-bred Serial Killer, the thing is—*the thing is*: a beautiful phrase, that, the most beautiful in the language—I don't know where—in whom—I am. I am no one in particular, massively imperfect: All the finishing touches are gone. Bert stood his ground, listened, waited, did not visibly fall apart, listened a little more. But he at last spoke out, shouting: You haven't listened to a word I said: you can't be perfect either in yourself or in your replicas because there is nothing to measure your perfection against. Don't you see, with so many strange variants of the same pose—the same murderous moment in time and space—running rampant all over the place, there just can't be anything out there in the real world that can be pointed to as represented by such an item. I mean—such a pose is and isn't representing something out there. And as Gift—after all this!—once more responded by spitting in his face, that is, by turning away with a sneering mumble affirming the implacable line of his jaw, Bert felt he had no choice (if he was to retain the respect of the other actors, especially the newer ones) but to take Flowers aside—keeping all the while every trace of rancor out of his voice—and request that he explain at once to his little protégé that it was precisely now—now that he was ostensibly finished—now that he was positively bereft of finishing touches—that his—sorry: he meant, their—work truly began.

I'm not interested in Gift the perfect specimen, the anatomical norm, destined to win worldwide popular appeal for his bulging biceps and outsize prepuce and already streamlined into a hundred thousand "original" reproductions. What are you interested in, then? Flowers said, looking hard at the cause of all this trouble as if rebuking him, Gift, for having gotten him, Flowers—a man whose far too many far more important commitments entitled him to far greater consideration—to speak his banal (albeit crucial) lines. I'm interested in Gift as a reservoir, a stump-quarry. Yes, it's true (and it's not true) that any of these others could play Pudd as well as Gift plays him now that they've all managed to master each of the Gift-Pudd poses appropriate to a given point in Pudd-Gift space-time. Every one of you, do you hear (hey, you, over there, new mug on the block: look alive!), could play Pudd to perfection and perhaps all of you will end up doing so—maybe our contract will be extended, at least for the national and Caribbean tours, who knows? I certainly don't, not at this juncture. No, what makes Gift unique is not so much the sum total of the boy's poses or any one(s) of them (each hewn in his portable workshop out of whatever archaic torsos happen to be at hand or to catch his jaundiced eye at a particular moment) but rather—but rather (by now you all must know how I feel about that hallowed l'il ol' phraselet)— the refusal of each pose to pass itself off as definitive, not from modesty but as a higher point of honor yoked to the desire to be assured of a future (and the only future for one who lives as Gift must live— badly!—is a future of poses, rather, of posing)—it's this, my friends, that interests me *chez* Gift. He wants to go on posing forever because for Gift to pose is—to live! But he dreads the definitive pose, rife with finishing touches, because that's the one that spells death. Am I not right?

All Gift said—more to Flowers than to Bert—was: You don't know me in the least. But that's precisely it, Gift, Bert replied, edging toward the floor-length windows as his high-school math teachers used to do (though where Bert hailed from the windows were nowhere near being floor-length), for inspiration, while setting out the steps of a proof; and then (to whatever human odds and ends happened to be reflected in the pane): I don't know you in the least and I don't want to know you. I just want to know your odds and ends— your giblets, as the great Auguste Steinberg might have called them— are forever available at a moment's notice for grafting onto others— such grafts as go to make up those combinations that, among ourselves, we style your poses (and soon—mark my words—millions of your fans will be on a similar first-name basis with the little devils). It is, as we know, in the nature of things immunological for very many grafts to be rejected but never yours, or rather—or rather!—yours always manage to incorporate the very act of rejection into the final product—to graft the rejection itself, as it were, unwittingly right onto the conjoint graft-recipient pose of the moment. Through sheer luck you manage—not sometimes like the others, but always—to graft one of your interchangeables onto some unsuspecting (and occasionally unsuspected) part and to come up with a thing that doesn't quite work, that in fact cries out in agonized protest at the intrusion.

Gift has realized what few sculptors—I mean, actors—realize, to wit, that if Priscilla, say, is suddenly made to wear her left arm as her right [after he's raped her and cut off both (common *Newsqueak* magazine Serial Kill fare, this, and with a bit of pietistic outrage of course thrown in by the reporting hack to scumble the rabid voyeur's thrill he's been paid, unhandsomely, to foment)] then this, more vividly than any courtroom testimony or newspaper headline, confronts us with the enormous "threat to society" represented by the Serial Killer's hunger to repeat. With all the right parts (private and otherwise) in all the right places, the character in question becomes a workable contraption able to elicit our pity and terror at every turn. In short, it lets us lick our chops (those below as well as above the waist) with a good conscience. The Priscilla character, on the other hand, in now having to bear—and before millions of spectators—the burden of an arm that is her arm and yet very much the wrong arm, is no longer an "interesting character" [which is the confection (go easy on the strawberry sprinkles, maestro) we paid through the nose to be able to consume] but rather the site—Now, Gift (with Flowers' permission, of course), please stand just like that, and Priscilla (with nobody's permission, of course) get over here and extend your arm so that Gift can weld his elbow to yours: do all that now, please (surprisingly, they both did)—of an instantaneous collision that's already an afterimage, fool's proof that the concept of *what is* can be embodied only by a case demonstrating all that can go wrong with the *what is*, and so the pity we were about to feel and the disgust! (for as a murder victim she is guilty and stupid and perversely—almost foxily—responsible for her dismal fate until proved otherwise by some international tribunal manned by a passel of credentialled big shots and certain never to be convened given the urgency of all their prior commitments) are lost to her forever. Our feelings—and yours—are after bigger game. She—and we—are stunned by her yokage to what is defiantly alien: something is wrong with this pose of hers; we don't know quite what; only we dimly sense there's far more here than can be laid at the doorstep of mere murder victim hood. In short, Entertainment—Serial Kill Entertainment—at its purest.

Once disentangled, Gift said: Why is all this a good thing: wrong pluggings, almost-implausible couplings? Bert replied, Plugging the uncooperative member—yours—into its stump socket—hers— serves to remind us that our will has even less control over our body than over the elements, hence her stunned resistance—the resistance we all muster—and continuously so as to survive but on a microlevel whose imperceptibility is magnified by our ostrichy refusal to perceive it (we don't want to be upset realizing what an effort it is just to get through the minutes, millisecond by millisecond)—has something heroic about it because it retrofits us in the mail of heroes for making the same effort, and non-stop, unbeknownst to ourselves. In short, a single, singular effort of her will to make sense of an uncooperating body is eagerly synonymized by us, the living, with our whole thwarted life history. And all thanks to the hard work of the Serial Killer! Hence, Entertainment—Entertainment as Education at its starkest! (This is a fantasy, Gift sneered: this is what you hope "we'll" do in the dark safety of some suburban dinner-theatre's salad bar.)

She reminds us body is as much our enemy as the most malefic detractor preparing to launch stinkbombs at our profile from the peanut gallery: who knows, for example, when it's going to decide to announce a colon cancer? The fact that Priscilla ends up with Gift's arm rammed into her stump merely foregrounds what is in fact the case for even the most perfect specimens—you know, the ones eating up every available inch of space on the cover of the very trendiest Dedekind-cutting-edge glossies—namely, that nobody—no body!—ever knows what settled hash of parts it is going to end up with millisecond to millisecond. But Gift doesn't want to understand any of this, much less acknowledge the benefit. Your boy (soliciting Flowers, who promptly turned away) doesn't seem to understand that his wasting Priscilla—or, for that matter, her macheteing him, or Ralph here bludgeoning Annie, or Annie daisy-chain-bludgeoning the new girl (Tillie, is it?), or even you, Professor, getting into the act by casually decapitating, say, Gottfriedina—and thereby exposing her to the tradewinds of chance—saves her from perfection. Too perfect she would become non-human. Compliments of me, rather of the fact that our work here masterminds her incompatibility with herself, she is able, through thick and thin, to maintain her stance—her foothold—in the mulch of humanity. For where I come from being human is to be resisting annihilation—worse, maiming—at every moment and at every turn—and with her right arm not quite grafted onto the left side of her trunk, Priscilla (the tenth victim) does just that, sustaining thereby the core of her selfhood, to wit, its incompatibility with every one of its parts and particles. So, by cutting her up and putting her back together again—badly—the Serial Killer alerts us to the precariousness of our own selfhood. He educates—that's my whole point!—as he entertains.

Hold your horses, said Flowers emerging at last from the shadows and advancing on Bert with his cane as if to mow down so much crabgrass. Bert rasped out a What is it (he knew there was panic in his tone and immediately regretted showing signs of it). Do you mind? Flowers murmured, taking advantage of so unusual a display on Bert's part of loss of control to italicize his own superabundance of same, this by brandishing the cane high above his head and then (as invalids will sometimes do) casting it brutally to one side. I feel obliged to warn Gift—and not just Gift but all the actors here assembled—that they will be grossly exploited by having to act out what I choose to call your expendable personal—your prefabs—your building blocks—your muniments (call them what you like)—that is, whatever detritus you end up bringing here straight from the arena of your personal life so-called: a fight with the little woman, say, or the latest abasement at the hands (grotesquely ankylosed) of your aging, overhospitalized paternal granny, isn't that right, Samuels, wherever you are? Boys and gals, he comes to you—and will continue coming—with such detritus— "intimately private"; "intensely—searingly—personal"—expecting, through your manipulations of its rotting core that at the very least you will be able to get him through this, his pain event of the moment and transform it, over and done with, into a shit-pellet—sorry, a postindustrial shard—*before* it demands (no, it already has)—rather, before it achieves—entry into his—your—communal theater. So there'll be no way for you to know right off the bat whether you are in fact working on the commercial itself or merely catabolizing his own private refuse heap so as to keep the burrow of theater activity un-clogged—distracting, as it were, his own private pain-event circus from forced entry into that burrow. There's no way for you to know when—so overwhelmed does he sometimes become, isn't that right, Mr. GreenHurstWood, wherever *you* are? by the goings-on in the world outside—hospital, outhouse, marriage hearse—whatever may be happening among you all means nothing whatsoever to him. The best one can hope for is that, once you have pounced on the personal, private pain event he has assigned (read "dumped upon") you, torn it to shreds and managed to serve it up again as ecologically viable polyethylene, the vacancy will not be menaced (at least for quite some time) by yet another intimate and "achingly personal" Bert-pain-event flaunting the right to rush in where only the truly (inter)personal ought to tread.

But isn't it possible, Bert contended, that Gift and Prissy and Annie and Ralphie are equally culpable when it comes to dumping their very own personal refuse into our arena? Shut up, please, said Flowers, when I have the decency to be doing the thinking for all of us. The problem is he comes here laden with far too many pain events which need, through no fault of his own, to be discharged into our waters. But why should you folks pay, and not the polluter? So I advise you, dearest Gift, to get off the merry-go-round while you still can. Don't worry: there are other productions and, as everybody knows, I have connections in the industry.

Gift appeared to be hesitating: should Bert go towards him and try at once to win him away from his mentor and patron? Should he attempt to explain that the propagation of pain-events by unwished-for relations like Joyce was not always to be considered negatively, that the ability of mindstuff to participate in the brickwork of, say, a thirty-second commercial was not necessarily obliterated by the runnings rampant of pain-events of this kind—in short, that pain-events of any kind could be depended on to fertilize the mindstuff? And/or should he bring up like a bat out of hell what his old pal Charley Peirce (who frequently compared himself to one) used to say every summer without fail during their cigar-smoking marathons at Charley Ives' place—in the wisteria pergola teeming with friendly wasps, to be precise—namely that old Mother Reason would have no being if she didn't at every turn have much too much to work upon, hence that Reason, motherly or not, required the occurrence of *more individual events than ever can occur*—the occurrence, in other words, of chaos-breeding pain? And there was more. Only he had so much difficulty selling himself as a rule. Why even when he suffered the urge to fuck Belle (though such stirrings, owing to his preoccupation with pain-event propagations, were few and far between) he could never summon up enough honeyed ebullience to sell, so to speak, his erection even if it was indubitably there for the taking or the shaking and no further sell, at least as far as Belle was concerned (to judge from the avidity with which she mounted it), required. He simply couldn't bear to allow his old shaft to do the selling for the two of them. Gift recoiled slightly, as if Bert had just touched him—in the same way, come to think of it, Bert himself recoiled whenever Belle touched *him* (unless of course the touch managed to trigger in time such overwhelming cock excitement as could be depended on to smother the usual panicked flight at all cost from tenderness).

In reply to all this Gift said, I'll think it over. Did he mean he'd soon be talking it over with Flowers? Stay, Gift, Bert said, though Gift was not going anywhere, as far as he could make out. Gift looked accusingly at him. Thank you, Gift, Bert added, disregarding the look: Gift was resisting—Gift was pure resistance. I mean, thank you for resisting, for as dear, improvident, ultimately cancered Charley Peirce once said (October 12, 1904: jeepers! I'm much much older than I thought) to our mutual friend Viola Welby on one of her trips in from London (once again it was in the presence of our old pal Charley Ives who'd just staggered in from a visionary junket through Central Park in the Dark and was always managing to be sticking around when it was a question, as it sometimes was, of female fans' vocalizing their adoration of Master Peirce—nothing transformed Charley (I)'s French wife into a jealousy-crazed harpy more than the arrival on the scene of such gal-fans—in the wasp-ravaged wisteria bower as a sort of chaperon): "The experience of effort cannot exist without the experience of resistance" but for all that I've never forgotten, nor must you—whatever happens—that it was Nat Gaza-Strip, several hundred years before (and with a little metempsychosal help, perhaps, solely from that old *tsimtsum*-and-*tikkun*-monger, Ike Luria), who first noted said Resistance—to respectable creation—was worth a damn only when, having flashed forth from deep down inside the worker himself, it then went on—like my pain events—to tilt the whole enterprise in the direction of chaos ultimately reversible.

So, concluded Flowers, from the shadows that were his native element, what you, or rather what Nat of Gaza (wasn't he Sabbatai Sevi's PR man back in the old days?) seems to be saying is that there can be no creation—of commercials, that is, for I seem to remember (Priss giggled: The Professor doesn't remember like us mere mortals—He *seems to* remember, whereupon Annie giggled also.) throughout all his pontification he made a point of restricting himself to the case of the thirty-second puff—No Creation without the creator's thought-some lights (those focused exclusively on making) doing battle-royal with the thought-less ones [focused exclusively, like the old Bronx widow of the limerick, on carrying on with the strenuous business of staying passively immersed in the battened depths of the Creator—the *Ein-Sof*, not be confused with El Sof, his lanky Latino counterpart—the very depths where once upon a time (or as Rabbi Harold Arlen would have cantillated: *ages ago/Last night*), before the -somes took it into their not-so-pretty head to ensure at all cost that the Big Sof got himself smitten by the prospect (and big with its child) of emptying his mystery into a marketable commodity, those -somes a. k. a. *or she-yesh bo mahshavah* were undifferentiatedly at one with the -lesses a. k. a. *or she-ein bo mahshavah*]. And why not, Gift piped up, why should any self-respecting creator—sorry, Creator—worth his (pillar or grain of) salt be reducible solely to his thoughts of the thought-some sort inasmuch as this is to proclaim no less than that the Creator is no more than whatever goes into his creation. Look at me: Hell, I'm a creator but I also chase girls and excel at foredeck badminton and gobble down Chinese cookies, fortune and all.

And right you are, Gift—almost, said Flowers, blowing him what looked (at least to Ralph's ever-watchful eye) like a cross between the kiss adoring and the kiss-off abhorring. For it is precisely—always according to Big Nat of Gaza's Sunset Strip—the just-in-the-nick-of-time intervention of some Ur-principle other than the creative—one of death-drive-style inertia qua passivity—not evil, not destructive, per se but only so serendipitously, as it were, through—zealously, jealously—a currying care for Sof's well-being hingeing (as far as these thought-lesses are concerned) on the nonexistence of anything (especially the marketing of one's mystery) apart from Sof—it is precisely said Ur that makes for tension—Theater—the very heart of creation. Much more interesting, then, than a Creator's will to create becomes his resistance thereto—as long as it's mapped into, and expressible in the currency of, the aforementioned commodity. (We know of course this sleight-of-hand is far beyond Bert.)

Though Bert was able to say politely, I'm glad we all agree, he felt no jubilation at the consensus with his fellows here and now. But at seeing (mind's-) eye to (-) eye with the uncoeval likes of Big Nat and Charley Peirce for once he had known pleasure—something between a flush and a thrill.

Chapter Twelve

Gift still seemed unmoved, though somewhat less tempted by the prospect of flight. Bert decided to exhort him directly and, surprised more than anyone by the fact that he was bouncily back on his feet, said: The media machine is beginning to have a memory—in other words, it's getting ready to lie, and to do everything else besides that a human being who's a credit to his race is expected to do. The interviewer in Schurz Park, where you've just been apprehended—you, Fritz (Langley) (another highly recommended raw recruit who'd been sent over from the Bob Bresson Agency)—turns abruptly away from the too-hovering cameramen and, looking in the general direction of the circulating squirrels, says something to his assistant (you, Annie), a loose-limbed and extremely fair skinned gal in blue jeans and T-shirt, who on top of all this is quite fetching. The assistant then scurries off, somewhat like a squirrel herself, but without a squirrel's heartbreaking capacity to stop, look, listen and munch frantically, all at once and all on the run, and he redirects his attention to Pudd, who (looking straight at Gift), having miraculously disengaged himself from the grip of his captors, is busy holding a knife to his assailant's throat (yes, his assailant, for hasn't Berlio all along been assailing him with the modest request that he, Pudd, obliterate him before myasthenia does?). You see—sorry, you catch a glimpse of—yourself, Pudd, in one of the TV monitors and (in a flippantly ominous newscasterly undertone) things will never be the same. No, what I mean is, strange to say you're intimidated by what you see just as you always made it a point to be intimidated by those photos of film directors you drooled (in their superstar heyday) over in glossy surveys—you know the kind I'm talking about, the ones where they're photographed from a very low angle or in extreme close-up, their godlike status emphasized beyond confutation thereby. And now that you, Pudd—you of the TV monitor—have become one of these idols you don't quite know what to make of—much less do with—yourself. Maybe, said Gift, I'm already having a hell of a time becoming the madman celebrity the image on the screen says I am, or didn't that ever occur to you, smartass? (Whereupon Gift smiled fatuously—flatulently—thereby deleting the expletive at which Bert had not managed not to wince.)

I think, rather, you're intimidated by the new you, Bert replied with as much imperturbability as he could muster. After all, it is a form of capture and capture of whatever kind is never entirely pleasant. But the key—that is, if you intend to keep a head on your shoulders and get around to beating the system of capital punishment at its own game—is to unzip/overpower/analyze the potent mechanism of idol-generation before it can undo you even if in this particular screwed-up case you happen to be the idol in question (which unzipping was always your stratagem when confronted with your rivals—

high-level Mafiosi, cocaine kingpins, politicians with "under- and third world connections"—who repeatedly made you feel you would have to revise your life completely and the hard times along with it if you were ever to amount to anything even vaguely resembling them in their eternal prime). Remember: that it's your very own image being unzipped doesn't make it any less toxic. And what makes it worse is that insofar as anything perpetrated by the media is as if given in, by nature—an insidious nature higher than nature herself— there's seems to be absolutely no reason in the world to be bandying accusations of toxicity about.

The interviewer is now standing beside what appears to be a po-liceman (Gottfriedina, here's nothing less than the chance of a life-time) who's looking very calm and collected (at the same time he feared that to cast Dinka in this role was perforce to allude to her sex-ual preferences, about which up until this moment he'd never pro-fessed to know a thing). Policeman—Dinka—you say to him, Pudd, Take your hands off him, punk, for he is still trying to put Berlio out of his misery. Dinka jibbed ever so slightly then recovered saying, I think *scum* would be a better word. Bert announced: Leave it to Dinka to put me in my place (but once out of his mouth the speech stank of calculated fake abasement): scum it is. You, Pudd, say: I can't take my hands off him. Why? you (Dinka) ask. I won't know until I see it all the way through. The policeman retorts gratuitously (a touch customer, he) something streetwise to the effect that in fact, you're managing right before our very eyes to fail once again: this time in killing Berlio off before he finishes transcribing, from the memory of last night's pre-Pudd dream encounter with it, that symphonic (first) movement (allegro in A minor in 2/4 time) he's at the same time vowed (see his 1858 letter to the hack hag-iographer Eugene de Mirecourt)—refus-ing to treat his art thereby as a Moloch hungry for human victims—

never to force out of the oblivion whence in all good faith it thinks it's struggling heartfully to be born; but of course your public is hardly interested in the sort of failure that cannot even help some poor slob of a masochist-musician to suppress all further effort to achieve passionate expression (that is, expression consecrated to reproducing the inner meaning of its subject, even *when that subject is the opposite of passion*), inward intensity, rhythmic impetus and a quality of unexpectedness so as to be delivered at last (since, unlike his old pal Jackie Meyerbeer, he's not blessed with a remarkable talent for being lucky in a universe where God stands punk-aloof), or at least until the next unholy upswell, of the urge to produce—not opera-comical meat-pies but such large and complex works as by his own estimate (Paris, 17 October 1854) will require two hundred years to taste the benefit of some stretch—*imperceptible* (oh so imperceptible) *in the brief span of one human life*—in human receptivity.

Naturally refusing, Pudd, to take all this sitting down (especially with God standing on the streetcorner), you proclaim something to the effect (here's your chance to extemporize your cute little butt off) that, contrary to whatever he (the cop) may think, not finishing off Berlio here and now has nothing to do with failure—has nothing to do with anything his kind could decipher and put a tangy tabloid name to hence neither he nor the 11 P.M. atrocity-mongers will ever (allegros or no allegros) be able to say of you what all along they've been finding it so easy to say about your far more successful—because far more sayable—rivals, namely that no matter what they get themselves entangled in it ends up existing purely to be failed at insofar as from self-communing serial failure (so sing the -mongers)—be it at holding down a desk-job, or at achieving a "meaningful relationship" chock-full o' quality time and related psychobaubles or, worst of all, at eluding capture—such scum always manage to wring, in defiance of their heartless judges, a biopornographic sob-story wherein Mother—rather, mom: ever since Norman Perkins declared her to be *a boy's best friend* mother no longer exists—is depicted, say, by a whorish hag who though she herself never got past the fourth grade expects her son to become Kurt Gödel II and Father—sorry, stepdad—by some flogging puritan with a frilly-exhibitionist streak. (Forbear oxymoronism's the culprit, then: Herr Serial just ain't *verantwortlich*.) But though your biopornogs will never be able to verify anything—not a single factoid—where the sparks of your own fetid root are concerned, this does not trigger a single—not even the tiniest—fear for the continued well-being of your fame, for such unverifiability constitutes the most straightforward spur to the very sort of progress you wish to abet. In fact, it is precisely (you now include the interviewer in your address) the lack of all verifiability, of all certainty, that permits your work as the product of their snooping thereabouts to go on breathing, to perpetuate itself indefinitely as a semi-malignant tissue of speculations, a bleeding fabric of appellatives, as multifaceted as the Torah. As scribbling snoops, don't they know doubt engenders bulk—guarantees prolificacy—whereas certainty is capable only of coinciding with itself—of shrinking ever further towards, drifting ever deeper into, withering and frugal self-identity.

The T-shirt girl (you, Annie) runs up and announces that eyewitnesses both at the tenement and in the park itself are having the hardest time identifying him, the culprit. At which point you, Pudd, pipe in with: Bystanders have the hardest time taking a good hard look at the culprit emerging. You notice as you speak that plainclothesmen are scattered about: one to each of the bollards marking off the crime scene. The foliage—linden, I, or rather, you think—is vast and blueblack. No one tree trunk can be mapped to a specific blotch for there are no specifics: the trunks, Hardylike—Judelike—are collectively responsible for all their generation's chlorophyll. The cop (you, Dinka) standing next to the microphoned TV host is looking more hardboiled by the minute: but, although his stare bespeaks a disgust of which you thought only you yourself were capable, you can't help believing (and not in the least because you are intimidated) all this is in fact a hunger to please, not so much you—of course not you—but his superiors— he's started writing his report in a little black book. So, his sneer of disgust at the puddle of slime—sorry, scum—you constitute is but a pandering to his (mostly male) constituency's hunger to, by shitting upon it, conquer the world represented for the moment by none other than you—to prove themselves smarter than its most indecipherable intricacies. (But will his superiors down at headquarters be able to figure out that such extravagant disgustedness at your ostensible disgustingness is no more than the extravagant revenge of his impotence on your being in fact completely unremarkable and report-resistant thus utterly useless for purposes of advancement.) Hence (you breathe five fathoms deep, so disquieting is the discovery) the agonizedly reluctant taking stock of a puddle of filth, all the revolted inventorying *malgré lui*, adds up to nothing more than the inventoryer's personal bid, through his very own personal excretion of that puddle, for notice at any cost. Or so you tell yourself.

This thought calms you—as thoughts rarely do—in the face of their ineluctable coming to lead you away. It is getting on towards dusk, duskier and duskier. You continue to be calmed by the thought and a fortiori by a rare sense of your own . . . reality, not just heightened but, so you need to believe, largely—single-handedly—created by this evidently final and immedicable failure (failure: the great reality-conferrer) to have achieved greatness in your own line (oh, the brief bout of notoriety on the 11 o'clock news, even if it should turn out to be something more than a mere glint in a law enforcement officer's pseudoChandleresque eye, isn't fooling you, though you'll be damned if you find yourself acknowledging as much to any of *them*).

You are busy adjusting once again to screams: the screams of Berlio still protesting that you didn't manage to kill him off in time, and the screams of sideliners: 11 o'clock news-intakers-to-be, unsure about whether they are cheering or jeering. You manage to note that an oak leaf is caught in a grating, and that a gull feather is caught in the slight damp of a bollard's crevice, and both are struggling to get free, and even if every oak leaf is absolutely identical to every other and every gull feather to every other, and even if every oak leaf is absolutely identical to every gull feather, the struggle to get free is always different. The cop whispers something to the TV host. The host nods. They are both observing you, Pudd. Berlio starts to crawl away. You pursue. You know they will catch up with you before you can kill him but you go on pursuing, because any act, however ruinous, however resisted (initially), once begun becomes a pathway of discovery, a vestigial organ of hope. Then Berlio (who has made it—who has been allowed to make it—to the corner of East End and Eighty-third Street) stops moving, for good, as it turns out. Aren't you going to try to get away? you cry out (loud enough for media man and policeman to determine your whereabouts). Berlio—you, Ralph—shakes his head, either from the blows received or the shock of so much media attention or from the disease and somehow manages to muster enough strength to murmur (listen carefully, Ralph): I don't want a way out other than death. You, Pudd, feel tainted by the encroached shadow of the media man which (at least at this particular place and time) rears its ugly head like a poster confirming that the world is never necessarily more favorably disposed towards those who deny themselves a way out, or fail to find one. Berlio shakes his head, as if to say the media man has yet to—nor will he ever—understand the Berlios of this world who function according to the first principle that truest mystery, mystery being a good thing, subsists only in complete unknowing of what might happen in the absence of all outs. Darker and darker it gets, with insects abroad—insects that bloodsuck. The kind of oversized woman who even before she opens her mouth—you'll play her too, Dinka, that is, if you don't mind getting all the juicy roles (Dinka's nod expressing her stoical willingness and—more to the point—her awareness—completely without rancor—of being exploitatively suckered into something made to bear—clumsily, inconceivably— the stamp of a windfall)—you know will have the voice of a highly effeminate man cries out that at the very least your balls should be cut off. You turn away from her shrieks right smack into the dogshitty asphalt templum of one pigeon (fluttering its wings because frantically questing a better purchase?) a-humping another. You can't stop turning away because the crowd (taking its cue from Oversize) is about to tear you to pieces (you know how crowds are) but still the hunger is ever so strong—stronger than ever—to go back (to the pigeons) and pay further heed so as to confirm what you're not quite sure you've just seen precisely because it's still so uneradicably vivid, even as afterimage.

Gift piped up with: I go back, folks—Bert—not to wangle a better view on the proceedings—there can be none better than the initial view, that is, if the still-searing vibrancy of its afterimage is any indication—but rather—but rather—but rather—through further thinking watching [and hence contaminating the thing thought-watched with the unreality of my thinking-watching (for except when killing I myself am unreal)] to somehow cancel the status of the event (should there in fact have been and continue to be an event and that event pigeon-humping) as event, to eliminate all trace of it from the landscape, for once the event is proved non-existent there is no possi-

bility of commemorating its existence through a thought whose making only widens my distance from the world as, now, this single event
being thought. Because now more than ever, with my fifteen minutes
falling due, I want to be part—nuzzling deep inside the very crotch—
of that world, right, Wilhelm—Herr Dr. Meister, sir?

Bert said (a little incensed): You shouldn't take it upon yourself,
Pudd, to be consolidating so fast your own particular take on the
world. As a murderer, you should be paying attention instead to the
mullions blazing (night has fallen). You look up, try to forget the bur-
geoning celebrity conferred upon you by your dying—dead—yoke-
mate, the composer Hector Berlio. You watch the day surge and die
and experience pleasure at flushing it away single-handed only there's
a slight hitch—it's you being so flushed, trashed on its treadmill,
while tomorrow this very same day—a day supposedly scuttled for
good—will be reborn unharmed. Once more, Pudd, you should be
paying attention to details in themselves, not forever enshrining them
in thoughts so as to be exacerbating, also forever, your distance from
the world as herniated into—corseted in—those details, now un-
manageable pain events. For then you'll only end up trying (as Gift? as
Pudd? who can say?) to trash them for making the world un-nuz-
zleable when in fact it's the need to confound too-hasty thoughts
about those events with their (now your) invulnerabilizing essence—
and at the very moment you're deep in their throes, no less!—that's
the culprit. How many times in one evening do I have to remind you
(and that goes for every other bum present among us as well) of what
Charley Peirce once told Frankie Harris [whether at that very moment
Lady Vi was listening or (attending to the bumblebee massacre of the
wisteria) not, we'll never know]? What did he tell him? Gift asked
glumly, looking (away) as if he'd have given anything for a sniff of the
bloom, and though Bert would be the first to admit such glumness did

not offer much in the way of an invitation to expatiate, expatiate he
must and (clearing his throat to overpower all the resistance he was
toiling against) expatiate he still could: Peirce *warned* Harris (whose
strutting, freewheeling talk constituted at that stage of his game, *inter
alia*, the trying out of the monster autobiography to come) against so
representing his fuckmanly experiences as to suggest that the moment
of synchronized orgasm had always been inch-by-inch big with analysis, comparison, recognition, and every other cognitive process in
sight. Indeed, he could heartily assure him that the orgasmic Firstness
of instantaneous prick-to-mind consciousness of the sort postcoital
Frankie was so hot to huckster (so Charley affirmed) was pure
myth—the hypothetical by-product of retrospective sleight-of-hand:
nothing was—had ever been—present to the prick of Frankie's mind
in any given bed-instant [no matter what he (drunk on pollen) might
hind-claim here and now] except a spectrum of full-color scrotum
ticklings, which always made it a point to be gone before anybody's
prick—even one as celebrated far and wide (that is, throughout Edwardian London) for being longer and harder than all others as
Frankie's—could think them through to the Second- and Thirdness
of rounded coherence: and to further hammer the point home
Charley, before the night was half over (so country-quiet, they—I
mean, we—could hear samara scythes of every imaginable persuasion
scraping, in their windless somersaults, the underbelly of the hump-
ing turtledoves), went on to regale him (while muttering something
about some consequences of four incapacities or some incapacities of
four consequences) with the very worst of the matter at hand, namely,
that there was no—nor would there ever be any—absolutely first
cognition of the apples of his pudendal eye (whether that apple happened to be tawny-bristling cunt, an erect nipple, a roughcast buttock
squeezed, or a freckly cheek aflush) to which he could retropoint, con-

versationally speaking, with a know-it-all, he-men-only-type guffaw, and that such cognition as did arise would always arise by a continuous and largely unchartable (there lay its genius *loco*) process such as was being traced (and in the presence of a lady! to boot: Peirce later learned but being the least jealous—the least envious—the least success-mongering—of immortals not to his chagrin that Viola and Frank had gone on to enjoy each other's favors that very night and in that very wisteria arbor, under the fatherly swish of the cottonwoods) by Harris's shameless, strutted expatiation here and now. Poor, strutting Harris: like you Pudd, he begins to look as if he might fall completely apart now he's been informed he can never bring back those unique feelings of urethral flooding as they were in and for themselves in the course of this or that Arabian night of maid-initiation, no matter how much of the friction of cognition and analysis he may think he managed to apply to the crumbling, moistening walls of such feelings in their instantaneous heyday and, in any event, at no one instant was there any cognition or analysis or representation or percipience whatsoever, friction-generating or otherwise, to be found in that notorious mind-prick of his, only a shared shudder in conjoint loins which he mistook for a thought. Just as you, Pudd, that is, Gift-as-Pudd, can't bear to think an understanding of life as it unfolded in that Schurz Park clearing with Berlio and the media men and the intractable cop may come only later, in your prison cell, perhaps much later—just before you are electrocuted in fact (it all depends on labor conditions in the workshop of memory)—so Harris could not bear to think that what he'd recounted to Peirce (and to me and perhaps to Lady Vi delightedly distraught as ever in that orchard abuzz with the fevers of springtime) was not exactly—no, not by a long shot—what he'd experienced at any of the ever-recurring historic moments transfigured by the shooting of his wad into the tight little culvert of this, that or

the other semi-willing chambermaid or duchess or suffragette. He
simply refused to get it through his thickish, elegantly balding skull
that the Immediate—the Unanalyzable—the Inexplicable—the Un-
intellectual—ran in a continuous fecal stream through his life and
never more unfordably than at the very point where he flattered himself he was most straddle-legged—that is to say, where (in the lam-
brequined twilight of unspeakable secretions) mind's prick, meeting
up with yet another potential customer, unveiled to said customer's
cunt—and all in an instant—every quirk in the labyrinth of lust. So
when our Frankie spoke of how during a visit to a Moscow cat house,
he'd (magniloquently thrusting as per usual his big, beery cock
straight into and then deep inside his partner's juicy orifice yet always
finding a way to exit just in time so as to massage her pubes yet again
with the tip of his engorgement and thereby postpone as long as possible their little death) made it a point—almost of honor—never to
look his beloved in the face lest he become too excited by her
beauty—by the certainty of having mastered that beauty—and hence
come too soon, or lest his admiration being mistaken for surveillance
induce a rushed effort to simulate final throes or when he—our old
Frankie still—immodestly pointed out how in a Venezuelan ashram
he'd managed around ninety-eight per cent of the time to refrain from
shouting Fuck, or Lick my balls with your asshairs when they're (the
hairs) soaked in my come, not only because the words would overex-
cite him and thus precipitate a premature spurt but also—and more
to the point—because it would trigger the loss, through her feverish
desire to please him, of his partner's undivertible concentration on her
own pleasure (which was what excited him most during the act albeit
what had attracted him initially to such partners was, he must admit,
their maidenly wish to please and to be infinitely pleasing) insofar as
all at once she would become feverish in her attempt to rise to the oc-

casion inaugurated—the same level of daring prescribed—by Fuck and Lick lest she be abandoned for not having been daring enough while her excitement mounted [in point of fact he'd always preferred, in ashrams or anywhere else for that matter, to detect, assess, closely monitor and even more closely subsidize a mounting excitement solely from the lubricity of the cunt concerned which presumably never lied—never felt it had to (and never could) play at shameless- ness (a conventional mimicry compared with its oceanic engorge- ment)—and so to hell with such demonstrations of daring as were all too often but self-consciously concocted to reflect whatever a given night's scheherazade erroneously assumed his own pulsations hun- gered to hear]—so that when our Frankie spoke thus and our Charley (invariably) felt obliged to ram home once again the fact that all this fine-tuning of sensation into perception (First- into Second- and Thirdness) was very much ex post facto—an articulated complex im- measurably different from secretion-feeling whether undergone in Moscow or Venezuela or Chittagong or Ho Chi Minh or Cox's Bazaar—all too predictably Frankie (he of the 1,001 maidenheads) found it—the ramming home—simply unbearable—and maybe that is why he ended up fucking Viola the very same night, in re- vengeful protest, though, come to think of it, it could very well have been a semi-controlled experiment to disprove what Charley clearly thought he'd proved definitively—namely, that the striking in of any new experience was never an instantaneous affair but an event occu- pying considerable Secondness and even more extensive Thirdness workshop time—in short, a process.

Process, process, process, this is what Harris finds so distasteful: his meditations have to spring full blown from Athena's maidenhood or they're valueless—didn't his old clubhouse buddy Charley see this was what made them cheesily unique in the annals of pseudoconfes-

sion? (Charley of course did *not* see mainly because he was too busy seeing something far more important, namely, that the beauty of the
feelings in question, the mind-prick quales, lay in the fact that at the
height of their ticklish engagement/engorgement with the secretions
of the moment they were completely untarred and -feathered by the
machinations of consciousness trying yet again and as ever to elbow its
way into the arena of being and decree just what this particular onto-
logical beastie ought to incarnate, warts and all.) Frankie only became
redder and redder and redder and redder when Charley got started on
extolling the virtues of the feelings (solitary and celibate) out of which
Frank like every man was constructed and (misperceiving a receptive
softening of Frank's formative tissue) then went on to point out that
when he'd talked earlier in the evening about stroking the hindquarters of the Muscovite cat-o'-nine-tails or the Venezuelan ball of fire
surely he didn't expect his interlocutors however comatose to buy the
idea of his having been able to say right smack in the midst of the
stroking, "This (center piece of) ass is present to me," since before he'd
have had the time to create such a reflection from scratch the sensation (of that bristling pudginess) would have been long dead and gone.
And once past he could never hope to bring the quale back as it was in
and for itself except as a corollary of that general theory of himself—
Frank Harris—currently being expounded in a thousand and one
drawing rooms, toilets and railway carriages, and then clearly not in its
idiosyncratic peculiarity but rather as a thing made soddenly present
through every sort of algorithm-crazy extrapolation. And it was precisely the best part of her ass that would be left forever un-present.

But Frank would not listen. I remember how suddenly struck
Charley became by the way the old hunks was now eyeing Lady Vi.
And then the moment of Charley's catching Frank in the act of ogling
Charley's muse passed and Frank was saying in his most blusteringly

clubhouse tone (which was also—at least at times—his most endearing) that, no matter what Charley had elected to blabber in his dotage, he, Frank Q.E.D. Harris, wanted it understood that all he'd recounted and everything he still had to recount (and, mind you, there was plenty left) was/would be recounted just as he'd lived it. I'll never forget, he intoned (just a little too conversationally given the thesis-like doggedness of his intention), the exquisite Dottie Schnitzel-Barf, the buttered toast—the cat's-meow—of Schleswig-Holstein. Poodle ass, I used to call her, because she gave herself (the most intoxicating) airs, quite like some bratty little mutt decked out in Scotch plaids and bangles. Until he educated her—all in a single night, all in an instant—she could not accept the fact that eroticism was based (contrary to what the women's magazines insisted was the case) not on a cosmeticizing away of all decay but rather on an all-too-noisy celebration (rife with brass and crass) of everything gathering decrepitude had to offer in the way of the smelly-belly mediocrity inherent in any *sexual relation between humans* but he managed nonetheless to teach her and teach her good (ramming each and every proposition down her throat and making her beg shamelessly for more) that no sallow trickle in one loving party, no sag of fat or shedding of greyish hair, should go undiagnosed—to wit, unsung—by the other, that is, if that other wished to achieve maximum pleasure and vice versa. The joy of the fuck (as Cleopatra's flunkey spoke of the joy of the worm) consisted (and let nobody tell her different)—this he felt, learned and formulated all in a moment—yes, Charley, *all in a moment*—was simply a matter of responding to a whole new set of secondary sexual characters, to wit, wrinkles and creases and bags and sags (under the eyes and under the knobby scrotum) as well as other equally blatant desecrations of the sacred body beautiful as peddled at every corner kiosk—the carbuncles (if you will) of fate, ranging from benign tumors to overinflamed bursae, and serving, then, as aphrodisiac prostheses not available even in the most advance-guard boutiques. All in a single lesson lasting no more than a split second, he taught her (and for the first time his master bedroom eyes overtly declared, As I will be teaching you soon enough, dearest Violetta) that the common-as-dirt practice of apologizing for this or that hideous flaw was far more hideous than any flaw could ever be, and infinitely less erotic. For eroticism was poker-faced shamelessness and in order for such deadpan to flower lamentation over the less-than-perfect had to be suppressed. For there was something overwhelmingly titillating, after all, not so much in the bags & bursae per se as in the substrate's disgust sliding surely into heroic defiance and even more heroic indifference to the world's echo thereof (i.e., the more massive the decay, the raunchier defiant indifference to it becomes). Or, as one Augie L. S. Rodin (his arch-rival for the affections of that balding grisette George Sand, or Sanders) used to say to his giblets, *More beautiful than a beautiful thing is the ruin of a beautiful thing*. And this, Frank swore—more and more to Vi of course and less and less to Peirce, who was half-asleep anyway (for it was now far less a question of metaphysics than of preparation for the avenging fuck he'd clearly been promising himself in the wake of such unpardonable humiliation by his so-called pal—who looked thank heaven as if any minute he must quit the scene to attend presumably to the newest messages scrawled all over his viscera by the cancer Charley Ives had been talking about earlier, at dinner in town, the town being Milford, PA)— and this, Frank swore, was what he had felt and acted out and understood and refined all in an instant way back when in Baden-Baden.

At which point, Peirce exited at last of course still very much unconvinced and toddled off muttering to himself (or to the bumblebees) something about eternal and inexplicable obduracy—the exasperating self-righteousness—of Don Juans. So, Pudd (Bert modulated out of the key of placid reminiscence), don't be in such a damned fool hurry to tell us what all the details (Schurz-Berlio clearing details, for example) at any single moment mean in and out of time. Whenever you are just remember that particular quip Charley continued to be so very proud of all the way down through his colon cancer's last micrometastases. What particular quip is that? I hear you (Pudd as Gift) asking yourself. Why, the one that stipulates we ought to say we are in thought rather than that thoughts are in us.

Chapter Thirteen

Seeing Pudd was still unconvinced or muddled Bert (preferring the former alternative) went on: You have now heard the experts on the subject of World—it's either funny (Rodgers and Hart); or Barnum-and-Bailey (Arlen); or wonderful (Armstrong); or bright/guilty (Welles); or elsewhere (Coriolanus). Now it's time, Pudd or Gift, to come up with your very own experience of this World.

Gift, beginning to read his script then throwing it aside in favor of his own thoughts (which, if he'd been able to fine-tune them, would have run somewhat as follows): Remember that "story" *Newsqueak* ran on the Jeffrey Dahmer case where the hack responsible set forth in tabloid-luminous detail the hectic-flush desperation prevalent in gay bars just before closing (titillating glimpse of a nightmare world out of the reach of most media fan-club members) when those unfortunate cruisers who haven't yet made a kill—the lowest of the low, then— the Loserliest among the Losers—find themselves willing to hook up with just about anyone or anything in trousers (even a Mayakovskian cloud) and so (so implied the union-organizer of this cautionary tour of a Swiftian Scumbaggia) it was only logical, fitting, ethically sound— whatever you want to call it—that one of the denizens of this sleazy deep, Mr. Dahmer, should turn out to be a Serial Killer with a penchant for Frankensteinian head-in-formaldehyde jekyllisms and that his victim of the night—or, more to the point, another denizen— should end up getting his long-overdue just desserts? In short the unfathomable—in this case, Serial Kill—could be best understood (according to that Newsqueak mini-arbiter of our collective destiny) as depending from the shriveled testes of the merely fathomable—in this case, homosexual lust and longing—with such middlebrow intelligibilizing ultimately finding itself, that is, getting itself lost for good—under the sign of Loserliness in implied combination with Lonerliness, its accessory before and after the fact (along with whatever other junk the two managed this particular time around to pull into The AmericanWorld Picture ca. 2000. In any event, the Newsqueaker proved once again beyond the shadow of a doubt that L & L are the current cure-all of choice for that most unbearable of social diseases, culpritlessness). In fact, they constitute a tabula rasa, these two (on which to project the most lurid fantasies of sexual and/or socio-economic pariahdom, to dread of which Americans are particularly susceptible (thus the obsession with keeping *fit*), a duo available for fast hire by whichever media mogul's minion happens to be trying his hand at so "explaining" (away) some Page-one Atrocity as to preserve those very bigotries that are the demographic handmaidens of big bucks mind control. Hot air, sneer-whistled GHW from the sidelines (so he'd been only pretending to snooze under his bomber jacket), especially the bit about *big bucks mind control*—hell, that pseudoconcept went out with Teddy Roosevelt (and lay off the mainstream weeklies, will you please?). Why not channel all the energy reserved for this cornball editorial page into making your character a real super-duper (but of course always entertaining) byword?

Drawn to Gift's sudden cuddliness by the GHW put-down's fabrication thereof, You hate the media man, Pudd, Bert said, but we can't condemn him out of hand simply because he's not to be ranged along with you, once the world has been partitioned into an infinity of subsets, in that special one housing only those who in some way profit, or think they profit, from the recognition, that is, the acquisition, of dire truths, appalling unpleasantnesses. [I dare (with no less than sublime truth rearing its ugly head) to oxymoronically invoke profitable acquisition since, after all, they're always the very first, these particular subsetters, to smell out the possibility that the blood-and-guts, here-and-now, meat-and-potatoes sensible is somehow *available for a possible supersensible use* (and of course however ultimately supersensible the use there is nothing more self-serving, more -aggrandizing—more pigsty sensible—than the act itself, the act, that is, of using, of putting to good use).] Call it the sublime subset, then, for the just plain folks who dwell therein make it a practice to smell out at the drop of a hat their most fetid defects, or the world's most immedicable inequities, or what they eagerly take to be so—in other words, they are inveterate acquirers of their own—and the world's—detritus though the very first to rant against conspicuous consumption (in any other form). But why berate the media man for being unable, or refusing outright, to get any mileage out of such scarifications as you traffic in so blithely—to cuddle up inside the coffin of the same subset as it were? Let's get something straight: If this commercial is to be a success we've got to make friends with the media and media men. Stop being a rebel, Gift! Think of your pension! But so far, said Gift, looking around (for the absent Flowers), it's only you who's—Never mind me Pudd, said

Bert, raising his voice a bit because he was getting a bit hot around the collar. As they are about to wheel you away, your thoughts about your fate—most of all, about how you may never get the media coverage you deserve—are spun from a great distance and thus end up being about somebody else, a somebody who because you know him (or her) only slightly manages not to trigger the trademark rancor you freely lavish on most others.

In fact, as they push you roughly forward, well past the plaque memorializing Archibald Gracie, you wonder how you ever could have allowed yourself to want a thing so measly, and how you ended up acquiring Berlio's body as the quickest way thereto (you snap up bodies the way other people do seventeenth-century hourglasses, or Adirondack chairs, or bitumen-sprinkled *shabti* dolls fresh from Seti I's tomb). Coverage, being close enough to taste at last, was always, you realize (beside an embryonic high-rise scaffolding of bulbs just off Henderson Place), just the unwitting accessory to a delusion that wanting the unwanted constitutes the royal road to from-scratch rehabilitation. For, as everybody knows, serial killers, or at least a few, misprize their bottom self above any victim and, all things considered, it's precisely this that makes them so much like other people, only more so.

You look at the cop and Ginger (Mlle. T-shirt) and reckon they make a wonderful couple: not even married they're already plotting and scheming hubby's advancement, as Dick and Pat were known to do, for example, and oh so many other yokemates. So why the hell, you ask yourself, is the bond between man and wife considered so sacred when all too often it is but a legalized cabal between two profiteers, a sty of calculation.

In saying goodnight (a first, that is, if one's memory didn't deceive one and it rarely did), Gift was uncharacteristically subdued, even mildly effusive, and Bert couldn't help feeling such a shift must be due

to the conspicuous absence of Herr Flowers (vanished in high dudg-
eon?). Samuels, on the other hand, looked unhappier than Bert'd ever
remembered seeing him (he somehow knew *unhappier than ever* . . . offered infinitely more hope than just plain *unhappy*). Was it all that un-
bargained-for business about Peirce and Harris fighting, amid a positively BronxParkian stench of privet, for the favors of London's too-fair
Lady Vi (which had served presumably only to evoke the boss's own
unpleasantly archetypal struggle with, in his case, overweening underlings)? No matter, whatever Samuels' (and his clients') misgivings
about Bert's compulsive advertence to things extracellular it was too
late to turn back, that is, too late for Bert to turn his back on pals as
immemorially solid as Charley and Frankie could (still) in a pinch be
even if Samuels—or those underlings—might think them irrelevant
to the main design.

When he arrived home, he learned that, definitively, Belle could-
n't be expected to be of any help in his other theater inasmuch as she
herself was now being kept under strict medical surveillance—in a
well-respected rehabilitational facility upstate—at least until the
shock at what she'd perceived to be irrefutable evidence of Joyce's de-
terioration showed signs of wearing off.

When he picked her up at last for the voyage home—since the
management had simply refused to be cajoled or browbeaten (so she
warily implied, but in a manner consonant with her pride) into keeping her on board one second longer—he found that for someone
who'd been so vociferous in her outrage at being ordered to skedaddle
forthwith and been resourcefully making a sideline out of beating her
wobbly breasts in celebration of such heartlessness, she looked surprisingly chipper, crutches—or walker (he couldn't quite make out the
gadget of choice next to the bed as, mildly transfixed, he forced himself to stand there, half in, half out)—and all. But as he watched her

toy coquettishly with her upper denture with one hand as she shielded her brow from the uncurtainable midmorning blaze with the other, he fought very hard against giving way to his first, instinctive reaction, which was to shudder at these curved balls' being thrown at—not to—him long before it had even occurred to him to emerge from the dugout. Only, as he went on watching it so turned out that all he could do was shudder—at the brute fact that once beyond the nosocomial hell the illness, no longer in its element, must completely disappear and who knows what infinitely more demanding impostors would rush in to take its place (for hypochondria even more than that feisty old stepmother, nature, abhors a vaccum). He at least would miss it deeply.

So (the shudder went on to say) with her being once more at large he, Bert, would be sure to have the worst of both worlds: that is to say (a) an end to the cumulative impact of the disease so conspicuous in the hospital setting where her tenure depended, after all, on unremitting upsurge (since once discharged she'd no longer be obliged to keep up the fiction or the non-fiction of a disintegrative process busily at work) and at the same time (b) a being even—infinitely—more (if such were possible and it was! it was!) at its—the disintegration's— beck and call given that she was no longer within the purlieus of protection. So the demands on his time and patience could only get far more frequent and ferocious and would inevitably erupt over a much lower threshold, since now that she was utterly alone—even if there was a passel of servants to wait on her hand and foot—what had rated as merely irksome owing to the proximity of trained staff would all at once flash forth instantaneously lethal given the stark lack of access to such pros on the home front.

Although Bert found in spite of himself (they were seated in opposite corners of what she referred to as the morning room) that he was in some small way seduced by the patient's self-pitying monologue in commemoration of entry into collusion with chemotherapy. Here she was, then, lamenting the taking of the toxins as a revulsion-worthy fait accompli though the minute he began to show, disastrously, all the signs of taking the old girl's surrender to the fait accompli at face value—by singing the praises not only of such toxin-taking per se as bona fide cure but of every foolproof adjunct as well currently available over the counter to camouflage said cure's myriad side effects: miracle contraptions like merkins (pubic toupees) and rectal bibs—Joyce suddenly thought nothing of remarking: But I never said I was going to go through with it, although she did add almost immediately (maybe because she was embarrassed—even she— by the silence succeeding to this skewed acknowledgment that she was no stranger to the black art of talking through both sides of her mouth), So I'll die, I'll die, die, die, die: it's enough (I'm eighty-three)—how much longer can you go on, will you tell me? Clearing her throat: You see what happens when you live *too damn long* [not unaffecting, this very last, so Bert noted: a (for once) truthful admission]— and all this while on the wooden floor in the room adjacent (a pantry?) the shadow of newborn leaves, or maybe old twigs spasmed madly in a patch of sun set aside—in honor of the present occasion, whatever that happened to be—solely for the climax. Of course the palsy, in a farther room, of petioles was not Joyce's affair. She had far more serious business to transact elsewhere, among vital organs dead or dying.

Yet just when he felt Joyce more than ready to throw in the towel, which would be the best thing for everybody, she managed to come up with a question [Here's what I want you to ask Dr. Pratt—when you get a chance: it doesn't have to be today or even tomorrow (how he detested her simulations of flexibility)] that suggested not just a mere will to live, though that would of course have been incendiary enough, but a fibery tenacity contingent on all other wills' shrivelling, to wit, Given that mine is a very very rare case—one of the anesthesiologists just before I went under said (he thought I wasn't listening—why shouldn't I have been? It's my skin!) they could report me—wouldn't there be some entitlement to think that, such a case making mince-meat of statistics (standing them on their head, so to speak), not only is it more than likely that the less powerful dose (no bibs, no toupees) must be as good as—even better than—the most powerful but that it bids fair to cure me completely. So, did you jot that all down, she asked, pointing to the invisible notepad perched atop Bert's right kneecap, and Bert indeed did very much feel he had to jot it all down, to the last syllable of recorded time in fact, so as to be able to present the question in question from every possible angle, and be thereby vouchsafed in return what only unassailably correct rendition might vouchsafe, namely, an end to such errand-boy-type stints, that is to say, an end to all connection with Joyce, errand-boy-type or otherwise.

She was positively leering at him now (in anticipation of the doc-tor's response? delighted that he was forced once again to do her bid-ding?) and because he wanted to rear forward and strangle her it im-mediately—still no loving her so as to be loving Albert retrospectively in tandem hence no making himself fit for commercial-directing ac-cording to company specs—became clear—*clearer than it had ever been*—that the trick where Joyce and her cancer were concerned consisted in separating the Joyce (J)- from the disease (D)-phenomenon in whose show the former was a mere bit player: the desire, then, to rear and strangle was, in the final analysis, but an atavism of the belief—of the infantile need to believe—that the J-phenom was always in complete control of—the veritable mastermind behind (and at all hours of the day or night)—the D-phenomenon—that in point of fact the whole tumor shebang was a ploy, a hypochondriac's near-expert simulated orgasm, to be turned off at will. However, long before he could separate J from D Leonard was before him with a piece of paper dangling between thumb and forefinger (Please call Belle at the sanitarium was the message and even before he was finished reading Joyce (forever on the sniff-out for upstagers) was heckling breathlessly with What is it? What is it? It's only your daughter, he replied a bit prissily, and far more to Leonard than to the mother.

What's the matter with my daughter, Joyce asked. She has her own problems, he said: she's still up at the facility. You know, the one that's about midway between Schaghticoke and Kattskill Bay. Your illness has been too much for her. Joyce's only response was to shrug, partly at Bert's bad taste in bringing up somebody else's predicament, which was axiomatically insignificant in comparison with hers, as well as because she'd heard it all, somewhere, before. He couldn't resist saying (or rather, it was at the very moment he knew he could, and effortlessly, that he greedily succumbed): Sorry I'm boring you, and she couldn't resist retorting, Who said anything about boring me? Look, don't take your frustrations out on me: I'm a very sick woman. To Leonard (and another servant who'd just entered to clear the table): But I forgive him: that's the kind of woman I am. I know he's frustrated with his job and the fact that he's (stage whisper) *not where he wants to be.* For in his business, Gilda—sorry, Gerda—the competition is fierce: he has more rivals than he knows what to do with. Their bigger success—the fact that their names figure on Professor Flowers' Best-dressed list (you can read all about it even in the tabloids)—has always made it hard for him to go on working, poor thing. Bert tried hard not to take the bait but he found himself saying in an undertone he immediately regretted as whiningly detestable: What Joyce never understood is the following: The tabloidability of my rivals' so-called success necessarily convicts it of redundancy: I'm after the fate that hasn't been (that can't be) conceived, much less published. Such triumph then becomes a wearisome rite of passage that I for one—that I alone—have been spared compliments of sufferance by my pretty little proxies—or, in Joyce language, the gut-crunching rivals. And so, those very rivals become my shabti in the kingdom of Osiris. To paraphrase the words of chapter V of the *Book of the Dead*, so popular during the eighteenth dynasty of my salad days, the judgment of celebrity, that is, of all-too-conceivability is made to fall upon them instead of on me, who am spared for bigger and better things, in fact it liberates me for the most fruitful work of all, that which remains supremely uninfiltrated by the shadowy expectations of others.

Joyce, he said severely, at the same time beckoning to the two to have a seat like human beings (he was sure this initiative would gall her), have you never in all your born days heard of the Reflection Principle? Joyce guffawed, only just beginning to secrete the anticipated gall. Of course not, she replied proudly. This was an invitation to elaborate effusive beyond his wildest dreams: Suffice it to say that according to the Reflection Principle (of set theory fame), most characteristic of the true God is the fact that he never begrudges—indeed, actively encourages—the participation of his inferiors in every one of his attributes. For if any one of those attributes or properties—like unexpiring fame—turns out to be possessed only by His Infiniteship then he—the Infinite—the Absolute—*Ein-Sof*—what-have-you—ends up stuck with the mere uniqueness of—i.e., irrevocably diminished by—said attribute: in a word, His Infiniteship becomes grossly conceivable—bounded—a mere flash-in-the-pan—a two-bit sleight-of-hand. So this is where and when Reflection Principle, Inc.—the most prestigious of all acosmist public relations firms—comes to the rescue, making sure that such a fate is never visited upon H. E. *Ein-Sof*. For any time one of your malevolent has-beens or never-wases takes it upon himself to plaster the Sempiternal with some new, vital property uniquely and unmistakably *Sof*ian—call it *X* or Ishmael—Reflection, Inc., immediately gets the ball rolling by announcing a casting call for the purpose of discovering (in the Schwab's Drugstore sense of the term) the absolutely smallest, most inferior entity, possessed of—not by—that very property, the Hollywood-and-Vine upshot being that, instead of impaling *Sof* on the lance of its puny conceivability, the property in question gets foisted off on an ocean of fungibles (all ultimately maimed by the very same shark-eagerness to be designer-labeled as having it). So that whenever I am threatened with an attribute symptomatic of ever-growing celebrity (Joyce looked aghast), *my* public relations firm—one of the best in the business—surely you've all heard of Samuels, GreenHurstWood and Van Ardsley, Ltd.?—sees to it doublequick (it's their press release I've been quoting verbatim) that the enshrinement manages gently to devolve upon some unsuspecting standby at which point I can watch the attribute's gradual disintegration from the coziest of front row seats (all the while thanking my luck stars I wasn't the chump singled out to be annulled by such lionizing). Joyce shrugged again: clearly she wasn't buying whatever it was he was peddling, and what *was* he peddling?—something (to her unbefriending ear) to do, so it would seem, with the surplus value of sooty obscurity (the sootier the better, in fact) as goad to authentic making—and with the special, supplementary afflatus known to issue out of the asshole of the most excruciating neglect and its aftermath of raging self-contempt. But how dare she not be buying?

Once Bert, not knowing what else to do in the time remaining, managed to get Doctor Pratt on the phone in Joyce's second-floor back bedroom (to relay what she'd determined must constitute the only viable interpretation of the data collected on her case thus far), all he replied—and in a tone far less pleasant than before—was: Make sure that for the first treatment session the old girl—I mean, the little lady—comes well-stocked with stool and urine samples. They must be notarized, needless to say, for we could, as I'm sure you already know from last night's eleven o'clock news, Report Her—every step of the way. Do you need a list of notaries public in the metropolitan area, he asked. No, Bert replied, there's a most reliable one in my neighborhood . . . delicatessen.

Chapter Fourteen

Even if the prospect of having to search out a notary public in the wilds of Manhattan made Bert feel crushingly aware of his glaring ineptitude when it came to the little exploits that made life worth living, he was not so incapacitated as to forget his recent resolutions to adopt a posture of unshakable assurance with the members of the actor tribe (it was not fair to make them—worse, the production—suffer for the torments he was being made to undergo with Joyce and her healers); to compel each of them, regardless of age, regardless of experience, to go through certain crucial motions; and (this last more of a vow than a resolution per se) to care less and less what Flowers (who was sure to be present at rehearsals once again—he'd been ill, so Gift said: a nasty bout of swine flu) might pretend to be thinking at every turn. He vowed on his way to rehearsal to get better and better at retaining just so much of a work's core as would be needed to stimulate thoughts propelling the Serial Kill story from crisis to crisis. And the minute he arrived in fact in the pitchdarkness of the New York subway, what did he espy but a platform already emerging—far in advance of entry into what up until that moment (the very fact that up until that moment he'd never been aware of harboring such a prejudice should become a crucial component of the artwork aborning: call it the *acquiring what I already had* component) he'd always taken to be the only conceivable medium conducing to such an emergence, namely, that in which white lights and straphangers ferment amid a forest of mirror-covered stanchions. So here he was discovering, and at his shamefully advanced age! that a subway platform required neither lights nor straphangers (much less glued, one per stanchion, to their favorite tabloid) to subsist after all. (He looked about him at this point, avid of astonished applause.) So, that, in a nutshell, is why subway platforms were born.

But the minute he arrived at the loft, Bert could feel them (not just—least of all—Gift: so much prior rebarbativeness seemed to be waking him up to dewy-eyed allegiance and in some strange way in fact Gift had turned out to be his most effective advocate at least for the moment, or had he?) slipping off, in the direction of their next gig, no doubt. Yes, they were all drifting away to talk about the future—to pine collectively for the first sign of circumstances' being altered enough at last to plausibilize a complete condemnation of their tormentor, to say nothing of the hard work he was forcing them do. But to his surprise he was able and far more quickly than he would have believed possible five minutes before to accept the fact that already they had to be weaning themselves by making plans even if those plans might very well not materialize once the undertaking was over and done with (but over and done with it surely was, in a certain sense, though they were less than a fifth of the way, if that, through the rehearsal process). (But what was it Nona Vincent's husband, James

Henry, Jr., used to say about rehearsals—something about their embodying much more *the death of an experiment* than *the dawn of a success*.) A few were already flaunting other offers, more to him, clearly within earshot, than to each other though he made every effort to listen without appearing to. So, taking the bull of his pain at such a rebuff by the horns Bert decided to speak thus: I don't mind in the least if you strut about a bit, plugging more prestigious projects to come since I know it's not evasion but rather stems from the mistaken belief that you have to savor now what you'll only spew out (from grief or fatigue or boredom or impossibly high standards) once the run is over. And feel free while you're at it to summon forth the terrible thoughts you didn't have the courage to subpoena way back when (before, that is, this pinnacle of your career was visited upon you) simply because they weren't placeable within a detoxifying context like ours. At last, Priss, you can look back—not at the "depths of despair" in some furnished room appointed loneliness whose centerpiece was always the (rotary) phone that refused to ring and accumulate messages the way images in a film by Bob Bresson (at least according to his manager Andy Bazinsky) accumulate a static energy like the leaves of a condenser—rather at your having managed always to generate, despair or no despair, enough credulity with respect to the importance of executing certain tiny tasks perfectly (which perfection is of course crucial to your perpetrations here and now). On the other hand, the wet noodle of retrospect cuts both ways so don't be shocked if the very moments when (amid phone despair) you believed yourself supremely, inexplicably happy are being confuted by a repleteness that, up until a few seconds ago, was infinitely beyond your reach. In short, those jolts of reassessment incessantly generated by our working together constitute, I'm pleased to say, none other than the massive inner strength needed to give the best performance possible, whether as Hector Berlio or Fritz Langley or Glendinning Stanley. By the way, is there a notary in the house? I'm a notary, said Flowers (who was back once more but still addicted to shadow), where's the horse? Bert: Then, would you be willing to exercise your function in respect of some stool and urine samples I just happen to have dragged along in my carpetbag? For a second Flowers looked at Gift as if Gift were now the mentor and he the lowly protégé.

I don't know, Flowers said finally. What do you mean, you don't know? Bert heard himself pressuring. Look, buster, be grateful for my hemming and hawing: a week, perhaps five minutes ago, I'd have turned you and your turds down flat but only because I am too tired to rant and rave against the down-and-outers like you, Bert, do I say, finally, Yes, to your proposal. In short, where are the stool samples you mentioned? let me at 'em! You see, Bert, I too've *changed a lot* since rehearsals began: I'm more humble. But all this humble accepting, Flowers—Yes, Bert, my dear—Is it such fruit of reasoned meditation on past follies as can sweeten only in direct proportion to distance or (as, it seems to me, you yourself in slightly different circumstances once dared to suggest) but a symptom of messy, rheumy imminent death. In other words, how much of Prospero's leniency's sheer exhaustion, eh?

All the actors were moving away from this, the stench of death, too vividly in the air, already stiflingly close. Bert thought at such a juncture it would be appropriate for them to step out onto the fire escape, although the hard snow below turned out not to be as luminous as he'd hoped. In a stage whisper Flowers said, Ever since I met Gift I've been terrified of one verdict and one verdict only (you're a man of the world, Bert, for all your affectations to the contrary: you know what I'm referring to in my best nineteenth-century manner). But now that there're stool specimens *et al* on the horizon to buoy me up and then some I'm beginning to perceive the verdict as workable, more than workable, livable, and well it should be, given the fact that I am an otherwise upstanding citizen with a certifiable vocation to my credit (canonization of my betters) not to mention numerous subvocations (notarizing forensic samples for the artsy-fartsy crowd, among others) of the right sort—you know, the ones that breed portentous affiliations (what nowadays are called *contacts*) faster than you can say Cock robin. There's no reason then why I can't go on living in the shadow of such a verdict for many years to come (that is, if I remember to take my vitamins).

Even if the snow flurries singeing his gristle made it almost impossible for Bert to focus, he forced himself to wave the two plastic bags under the notary's nose. Not recoiling one bit as he proceeded to fish out the stamp in question—searching (in vain, so it would appear) deep inside the right inner pocket of his sport jacket—Flowers insisted that he didn't mind such lowly tasks—not anymore—no, not in the least. At first I thought my canonizing would elicit love, in other words, immortality, but now I know that I freighted my efforts with too much expectation. So how can I help—will you tell me?— liking the little lowly tasks with which losers like you insist on saddling me. After all, as I dutifully point out in the preface to each and every edition of my Canon, the heart and soul of the world of arts and letters—or farts and leisure, same difference nowadays—are the alsorans. Little did I know that I myself would end up as the byword of the subspecies, but never mind that. But the little tasks—such as the notarization of the stool samples you've been so kind as to bring me (does this "matter of some delicacy" involve, perhaps, an ailing blood relation?)—brace me against the unpleasant discovery forever being made as if for the very first time. What discovery, you say? Why, that the star system of the farts world requires more than anything else the exis-

tence—the persistence—of these also-rans—these . . . hopefuls, for
the system's exclusivity is perpetuated to enhance not so much the exultation of the winners as the morbid misery of the losers. As an also-
ran, you—or rather, I—am needed by the media, if by no thing else,
to ply my loser stock in trade so as to generate and help keep salaried
the best way I—or they—know how a whole counter-army of commentators, ambiguous well-wishers and semi-certified panders ministering to (the hormonal imbalances that are the hallmark of) loser
breakdowns, near-suicides, maudlin comebacks in supper clubs. But,
most important, being an also-ran has taught me to curse my fate se-
lectively (a trick few can master precisely because it is a trick and thus
requires grace under pressure): after all, it hasn't been all bad, even if
my mother was an incorrigible slut and, worse, a social climber. (Here
Flowers managed to remove at last what looked like the kind of oversize metal page stamp utilized by the most underpaid editorial assistant in some German-owned medical publishing house, and began
branding the wrinkled skin of the larger of the two bags.) The knack,
my friend (these flakes are so refreshing, aren't they?) is to curse one's
bad without that regretting of the final result—one's self in all its
murk—that only renders life unlivable, worse, unthinkable. The
knack is to curse the bad but not in such a way as to succumb to total
cancellation of the self through hankering after a better version in
some rival. One must learn to hate the bad bad without hating oneself
nor in such a way as to suggest one hasn't the slightest idea how to
make use of bad bad to maximum—that is, media-potable—effect: in
the compilation of a Canon (a modern-day Book of Hours), say.

Take me, for example: I put my rivals (like four and twenty black-
birds) into a list and when finished don't stop there but move on to
other inventions. Being out here with you on the fire escape in the
middle of winter constitutes, by the way, my most stunning inven-

tion—my most adroit change of garment—and the one that may
turn out to be far more enduring than the Best-dresser for which I'm
justly famous. This particular work—to wit, our being out here together with all of smelly Gotham at our smelly feet—in case you
haven't noticed, embodies a leisurely gliding away from what for too
long I too desperately took to be my epicenter. Somewhere down the
line, don't ask me when—maybe as recently as twenty minutes ago
when you first started babbling—I suddenly knew it was only by accepting myself as mere byproduct of all my works past and to come—
that those works, and me in tandem, could begin to breathe, in-out,
in-out, like yogis. So is our standing here on the very margin of the rehearsal process very much the main event no matter what Samuels or
anybody else might say and not just some blowsy peripheral rushed in
to shield the core of the business from prying eyes. His work now complete (for he had been stamping away nearly all through his arioso)
Flowers, as he handed the bags back to Bert and pocketed the stamp
(his insistence on having the fee waived carrying the day over Bert's
feeble protest), said modestly, I think you'll find that these products—
or should I say, by-products—will stand up in any court of law. They
belong to my mother-in-law, Bert felt obliged to admit. A feisty old
broad if ever there was one. Except that her broadship's illnesses—real
and imagined—are eating up more and more of my rehearsing
strength so that more and more I'm coming to feel any work with the
actors is a mere biding borrowed time until the next encounter. With
your mother? You mean my mother-in-law. No, with the head physi-
cian on the case, a Dr. Pratt—had any truck with him by any chance?
I've notarized wastes for/from patients of his, yes, said Flowers, with an
exquisite modesty Bert would never have presumed could be one of
the canonizer's changes of garment. Some products are easier to nota-
rize than others; still others are more worthy of notarization than

196 / MICHAEL BRODSKY

their . . . rivals (Bert felt immediately depreciated). As you can see (sensing his effect?), I can't stop canonizing wherever I go, and no matter how low I stoop: the Joe Haydn of high-density lipoproteins, *The New York Times Book Review* of piss specimens—these are just a few of the judgments I can't help pronouncing on my trek through things human and not-so-human so as to get myself, even if it's only for the brief duration of the utterance, invested with a pathos—a potency— of transfiguration (one flick of the tongue's magic wand and I end up in the seven-league boots of Big Joe Haydn, among others, and ending up that way even if it's only for a split second *makes life worth living*, to use the phrase I loathe most in the world). Here, take them, he concluded, and with these words (though he'd already returned the specimens in question) seeming officially to wash his hands of Joyce, Flowers proceeded to slip back into his old finery.

Returning to the actors, Bert asked Priscilla (a bit blusteringly, he knew at once) to climb atop Gift's shoulders. Priscilla protested (had she gotten the bug from Gift?) that it was not the moment. Her Gioconda smile made it clear there were other—weightier—matters to be attending to. Bert restrained his irritation or his impatience (he wasn't quite sure what it was that needed restraining) and, taking a deep breath, said, Right now I have this indelible image of you atop Gift's shoulders, Priscilla, and I simply can't afford to lose it—to let it go and then try to come back and retrace and retrieve it. For who knows, dearest Priss, through what detours I will be led on my way back to what, I'm, alas! never in any danger of losing. For I'm far too old to be wanting to traverse labyrinths of unwelcome rediscovery. I've gotten to the point—or (as my now-defunct pop used to say) I'm at a stage: pop was always at some stage or other (until shrewish mom decided it was time to hasten his arrival at the stage that is beyond all stages)— where I need to make use of my stock as soon as possible so as to be getting on with the bigger business of becoming an anti-Bert—once, that is, I've managed to divest myself of all the stuff that makes me Bert. Maybe once I'm done smelting I'll find that anti-Bert equals Dr. Flowers or David Park or Cluny Brown or Isaac Luria, who knows? I think, Bert, said Flowers, you dread the pathway back to the thought—to the thought as image or vicey versey—because you fear en route the hindering of hostile elements. That's, after all, why people go to the movies.

Since Bert was beginning to look daggers of obtuseness, Flowers (a bit huffily, so as not to lose face) elaborated: In order to be bombarded by thought-images or image-thoughts directly, that is, passively—thumbsuckingly; after all, it beats having to trek through the slag of inwardness in search of such shards. In the movie theatre they're visited upon you without the inconvenience of detours. But it ain't just the movies that are at fault: there are simply too many media implements nowadays only too ready and willing to perform a fleeting inventory of latent spiritual susceptibilities and to shed a light on this or that byway or recess of the mind as if it were a milkable gland—when and while we all know the sole reason for living is to be struggling with and invariably failing at such inventory but at least to be having it— such inventory—one's very own inventory—*as* one's very own and at one's very own command for the moment the living, feeling mind is baited, and its contents scavenged by some outside stimulus—made to dance to the copyrighted tune of that stimulus [the image of a Hollywood-coded fuck, say, where the eyes, adoring, of the postcoital she are obliged to look up into the eyes, unseeing, of the (thus plausibly virile) postcoital he while absentmindedly dutifully she strokes two or three of his chest hairs, also virile, also unseeing; or a gangland dismemberment in a meat-packing plant at the corner of Twelfth and Gansevoort]—then it—the dancing mind is no longer one's own: it now participates in what is referred to on streetcorners everywhere as mass consciousness. And Bert has assumed the role here, folks, of an outside stimulus—some knee-jerking feature film or video game or prime-time sitcom—with regard not just to you (folks), but to his dear old self: out of the blue he elects to assault anybody and everybody concerned with a particular thought-image simply because at this juncture he thinks he's afraid of losing it forever [what he really fears is never being able to shrug it off—of being wedded to it—and to Bert (as opposed to an infinitely more desirable anti-Bert)—forever] and consequently of having to make his way back to it through the thick and thin of its incorporation, at the right time and in the right place, into the work at hand—in other words, of having to earn it—and he thus prevents you from discovering the contents of your own mind as they relate to this particular mishap of a thought-image—of an image-thought. And that's why he doesn't deserve membership in my canon—sorry, my Canon.

As Annie (Priscilla's best friend) all of a sudden saw fit to ask, So then what do we do now, Professor? the Professor (ever attuned to what made for an electrifying sense of sheer life's being pissed away on stage never to return) was quick (but not too quick) to reply, What do we do now about what? Once he determined that enough brute duration had been visited upon all concerned, without further ado Flowers proceeded to demonstrate his espousal of the common cause by proceeding to answer his own question. We fight for what we believe in. With all your heart and soul: fight. And in fact you will be helping Bert. By defying your master—for Bert thinks he's your master in spite of himself just as I think of myself, with equal erroneousness, as the master of those I relegate to the bolgia of best-dressedness—you force him to confront—or to think he confronts—a new Bert, a Bert molded by circumstances wildly outside his control.

At first he'll balk, or seem to, until he begins to look at himself as all of you must and wonder how he could ever have perceived—or wanted to perceive—himself differently. Owing to your providential champing at the bit he'll be able—when it comes time for him to croak—to breathe a sigh of relief at having contrived somehow to effect a true life-journey since the only true life-journey is the one charted quaquaversal to the course prescribed by our barren dreams of what the journey must turn out to be if it is—if we are—to qualify as a success. Your defiance at every turn—and I don't forget it was Priss who did most, until she was so rudely interrupted, to get that particular ball rolling—of his refusal to hold the fire of his thought-images and image-thoughts for the juncture most appropriate to its discharge will spur him on to bigger and better things. So, sighed Bert, I should be grateful for non-collaboration with that old tantrum, blind ambition. Flowers' temperate hand-waving said, Hold that objection for just one moment while I demonstrate to our contestants how they are to see about sparing you the gratification of your peevish fantasies.

First, face the fact that Bert here will, as rehearsals get under way, be tending more and more to rove all over like a camera, setting you up so as always to be knocking you down. For all his yapping to the contrary, the hope that sustains him as he goes along changing this one's position in response to the challenge set by that one's expression is to come at last upon such a one if such a one there be as is clearly not one of the group—any group—one who stares so far beyond the camera eye and/or is so absorbed by a particularly manic tic or in obsessional fondling of a particular object that never in a million years could he be accused of mugging—one rendered so . . . impacted through consecration to a particular version of frenzy (guarded jealously like a pot o' gold) as to prove completely immiscible in the camera-eye solution. His hope is to stumble on some character who, like an inkblot, will call a halt to the camera's unstoppable legibility. His hope is, for all his labors, to end up having laid down the stakes of a character—you, Priss, for example—so cunningly that when he catches up with it at last, when his roving eye comes to rest upon the challenge of its blind defiance, said character—you, Priss, for example—will be able to explode the entire spectacle to smithereens and leave him, if not the spectator, with something far better. He never stops hoping, our Bert, to end up having constructed a figure infinitely more powerful than he. In other words, our boy never stops tinkering with the mechanism (the willed contortions of this, his very own corps de ballet)—he is busy creating these set-ups: Priscilla on Gift's slender shoulders, for example, with Annie and Ralph slightly to the left of the unflushable toilet cheering them on unflaggingly—so that at least one element will end up being not *of* him though clearly *from* him. And, who knows, he even may really let himself go on occasion and dream about things like gliding straight out of himself and smack into the mold of another—a better—life.

So, Flowers concluded, to answer your question, Bert (however belatedly)—rather, your noisy protest—Yes: you should be infinitely grateful for failure's undeviating attachment to your hindquarters since success, sad to say, would only have confirmed you in your very worst impulses. So now, when death comes—as it must, and to all men—then—then (Flowers turning here to cheering crowds sorely lacking)—then (successful hallucination of the missed millions)— insofar as death rarely coincides with an authentic ripening you'll find it easier far easier than most (for through so much ungracious truck with failure you'll have become a past-master in the underhailed art of making do) to compel the arbitrary moment of your passing to stand in for such a ripening too sorely missed (the final flowering, as it were, of those worst impulses aforementioned). You'll be finding yourself exhilaratingly scot- and fancy-free of any pangs of conscience whatsoever in respect of having neglected to perceive everything prior to, say, your fatal collapse in some subway station (on the L line) as driving you relentlessly towards this very (and no other) moment of truth. So—thanks to failure and assorted hangers-on—the celebrated Death in the Urinal sequence if a urinal happens to be your—or Pudd's—next-to-final resting place of choice becomes a consummation in spite of itself, the very best sort of consummation after all: puniest contingency ends up constituting acme of predestination. It will be your job, Bert, whenever the moment in question supervenes unbidden, to convert it (to Bert's provokingly dumb stare: The moment! the moment, you idiot) into a stillpoint of epic closure. But tending to the unreasonable demands of your mother-in-law has put you—and us in tandem—into a very morbid frame of mind: in short, the end is by no means near though I'll be happy to let you know when I begin to smell its approach.

But why (exhorting the multitudes again) must he forever perceive everything in terms of success and failure? Priscilla's answer was a hurriedly managed descent down one of Gift's shoulders (the right), Annie's, a no-nonsense massaging of the other; and during all this the theater of so much striving, Gift himself, wasting not a single minute, had succeeded at once in getting himself deeply immersed in the wispless night sky, clouds big as galaxies, framed by the window closest to the fire exit.

Despite his disappointment, Bert knew he should be moving on, towards better things. Gently he escorted Gift back; the others sheepishly followed, as Bert had known they would, for Gift after all was still their bellwether: In the paddy wagon, you try to make them understand, Inspector Zohar and his underlings, that a posterity you know nothing about is waiting for you to die. (You begin to wonder whether your personality is indeed being usurped by that of Berlio, for whom an unknown posterity might have meant—might still mean—something.) You see how easy it is to die, and what little impact the dying makes, and how those who fancy themselves defenders of the works' faith, to say nothing of the works themselves (whether those works be serial kills or symphonic allegros: you for one are beginning not to see the slightest difference between the two), are the ones most insistent in respect of the urgency of such a dying, so them there works can get on with the heady business of becoming themselves freed at last of all filiation with their maker (for they can't very well do so living in the mangled shadow as they have been forced to do of that maker).

Cop and T-shirt (in an adjacent vehicle) are continuing to hit it off. Your vehicle stops in what looks like a canyon. Everybody gets out and decides to rough you up a little but before the roughing-up really gets under way they allow you to walk to the canyon's jagged edge (off to the left what looks like the Hudson scintillates: can you be in Van Winkle country already?). There is but a gash (not that far off, come to think of it) where the sunset should be. You try to forget your new-born celebrity. In fact disfigurement (minutes before, they tried to claw you with a twig) is a blessing in disguise insofar as it results in a confinement of your scrutinizing to the smallest possible range: so rudely gored understandably you no longer wish, as formerly, to note the attention of every passerby within a fifty-mile radius for there's no longer a likelihood that such attention will graciously exude the boundless awe merited by your accomplishments: from here on in you must resign yourself to ogling contempt—no doubt about it—every step of the way. You termite forward (a veritable Turing machine), frugally parasitizing your own boundaries as if they were so much sawdusty air in order to be able to turn their remains into parameters of the next exploit, for despite this dread of gawkers' loathing you're conscious of a camera eye lurking round every bend and seeing to it that your moves, even the very tiniest, turn into world-class great-shakes—and hence of now having an obligation—towards your pub-lic!—to be both an observer outside and a being very much trapped within your own little world. Buglike in the most minuscule of cages you're compelled to make a virtue of necessity by nailing down every moment without glamorizing it.

And let me tell you, if my old pal Manny N. S. Farber were still around he'd be Number one on line to praise you unstintingly for these services on behalf of termite art just as way back when (during their salad days at that notorious old fleabag known as The Negative Space Garden Apartments Dormitory and Cafe where any self-re-specting budding termite artist could earn his stripes vocational through one method and one method only: defiance of the landlady and her termagant husband's every threat of eviction) he used to praise *his* old pal Joan (Crawford) for doing the very same thing and, more to the point, for always doing it with the same bravura convic-tion. So, go forward proudly, Pudd, in the knowledge that no less an eminence than Farber has been making it a practice to praise you all over town for this measured eating up of every identifiable boundary of your serial artwork with never one single thought for the world lying beyond its unique moments of ingestion—that is to say, the world landmined with consumer expectations.

But make sure all this praise doesn't go to your head, or rather, your vacuum tubes; in other words, remain a zombie completely de-termined by the finite number both of your internal states (Off/On/Dozing) and of the boundary inputs to (or rather against) which your scene-chewing is programmed to respond—as Joanie Dearest did to the bitter end, that is, if you wish to go on being a ter-mite virtuoso. In short, you must remain a Turing machine for only the Turing machine fulfills the Farberian Ur-condition for a true artist: nibbling away at small sensation (a tape consisting of a linear sequence of squares, each edible square either blank or inscribed with the mark *0* or *1*)/nailing Crawfordlike each moment without glamorizing it (reading the tape, that is, moving one square to the right or left after replacing the *0* or the *1* just read by a *0* or a *1*, the whole operation capped by a change of internal state).

Once you've gotten the hang of Turing termitism you'll always be supremely unable to see the smallest distance ahead, and because you're simultaneously blessed with only a finite number of internal states (instead of the plethora that would end up, if you were, say, the hero of a Victorian novel, breaking your back) there'll be no reflecting back over this or that previous tape-result—no internalizing of external data or of any previous response to the edible tape. You're better off so, travelling light. In short, now you're a killer without a memory— you're capable of dealing with data—with life's input—only immediately—only, as the algebraic topologists would say, in the small. As a burrower you can smell only that milliliter of earth right before snout's blind eye. This is the beauty of the computer-being, you—you as Joan—have become. As you speak your lines, as you act your story, for the overanxious pre-new workweek Sunday night billions, all you can hope to respond to is the immediate input of the moment (the tape square: *0* or *1*) to which you react with your next utterance/gesture (determined as well by your moment's internal state). (The ordered pair $(i\,(1),\,1)$, for example, where the first member of the pair is your own internal state at moment i and the second the input symbol on the tape of life at the very same moment denotes the configuration that determines the next act of your theatrical machine.) So it is only to the unpracticed eye and ear that your plowing ahead one gulp at a time will seem imbecile, worse, inept: to those in the know—those for whom an infinity of internal states, one more subtle and intricate than the next, has long been a much-overrated asset—such plowing must reek of shameless virtuosity. The latter know that as a one-man-band termite artist-cum-Turing machine you, a respected serial killer, better than anyone know that if you have to portray—transmit—seamless duration on stage you might as well call attention at every turn to the sheer impossibility of doing so, and this by blatantly shifting from one discrete state to another (ostensibly propelled by the conviction that such states cannot but turn into time uninterruptedly flowing). If like every self-respecting artist your primary task must be to encode the value of a continuous quantity (pressure on the trigeminal nerve, say) in the digital notation that to the eleven-o'clockers is the only pap worth downing then as the raw nerve in question it is your bounden duty to make a virtue of necessity and wallow in the flaunting of all-or-none signals, impulses that are simply either there or not there "with no further shadings" (to quote my old buddy Johnnie von Neumann), when only seamless flow is in order. So the very worst that can happen is that the cognoscenti will end up applauding your downright refusal to sell out through analog bad behavior to crowd-pleasing continuity-mongering and the eleven o'clockers will curse you for tampering with their bird's-eye view of reality. But their very curses will put your name on their map and they'll end up falling in love with you, their favorite psycho.

Favorite since because you've made a bar(e)ococco aesthetic out of the impossibility of portraying the continuity both of your interior states and of your environment as continuous our spectators can always feel they're in one-to-one correspondence with your discreetly discrete spiritual states and never any more bereft than you of the data needed to envision the next (never forget this-here commercial is, in its own way, a microthriller), for at a given moment you yourself have privileged access to only one such state [registering as, say, pulse rate or cholesterol level or ejaculations per millisecond (vital signs will be broadcast using Met-style supertitles)]. Your commerce, then, with all but the starkest (inner and outer) parameters of the moment, albeit mere vanity's ostrichlike ploy, bespeaks an endearing innocence for the prime-time hordes [in contrast, the performer who, consorting easily thus cunningly with states past, musters their detritus to caulk the present thereby violates his tacit agreement to undergo said present's Firstness and, sans recourse to prefab private stores, construct from scratch its Secondness step by step together with, and as vulnerably—as a-(case)historically—as, those hordes] and for the cognoscenti a one-track, termiteful professionalism (dazzling beyond the wildest dreams of even Manny and Joanie) though why all this hullaballoo since, as pulp fiction's Inspector Marcie Proût of the Balbec(k) Street Irregulars used to like to say about Mlle. Everyman, criminal or otherwise: *A n'importe quel moment que nous la considérions, notre âme totale n'a qu'une valeur presque fictive* (At whatever moment we choose to consider, our total soul has but a near-fictive value): *C'est sans doute l'existence de notre corps . . . qui nous induit à supposer que tous nos biens intérieurs . . . sont perpétuellement en notre possession* (I daresay it's the existence of our body that induces us to assume we're in perpetual possession of our whole inner stock).

So—getting down to cases once again—in an effort, Pudd-Gift, to conceal your deformity at the hands of a brutalizing cop, you are no longer looking up into the eyes of every passing stranger. Everything, Pudd, is simply a matter of knowing how to rise to the challenge of assuming one's own vesture of deformity. And you are slowly rising to that challenge.

You look about this canyon to which their new access of brutality has just consigned you and your camera-eye comes to rest on the media man (how did he manage to get here so fast?) who's handling your case genially chatting off camera with the cops and T-shirt (Fritz—Fritz Langley—look alive). There are so many cops now. And though the media man is loathsome to you and you never so much an outcast as now, still it is gratitude not loathing that is your overriding sentiment: you are grateful to be able to acknowledge your hate, for you still have enough of bad's flair for worse to imagine what it would be like, day after day, year after year, to have to listen to the rantings of somebody like the media man without conceiving you had the right—the duty, even—even if you are his accursed offspring, to loathe him for all you were worth, even if you're not worth much.

Careful, Bert, Flowers taunted from out of nowhere. What do you mean, *careful*? Bert carefully hissed. It seems to me, Flowers intoned, that thoughts about that accursed mom-in-law of yours, who's making it her lifework to hobble your every half-step, are being inaptly stretched to apply to poor old Media Man—Thereby enriching him in the process! (Bert doing his best to make this cry a cry out of nowhere) —and it's not quite a perfect fit, the canonizer concluded, as casually as if he were puffing on a favorite cigarillo. (Truck drivers passing by ogle T-shirt with the double-take codified compliments of usage immemorial whose mimed beef boils down to plain and simple outrage that any cunt should be able to authorize, through this or that provocatory ploy, the long and the short of their anatomy.)

Knowing habitation awaits (habitation being not prison but your story—beginning, middle, near-end—as recordable by the authorities), it has become easier for you to fend off T-shirt, Media Man, and the cops as they try separately and in concert to browbeat and harass you into what is known in the trade as a (pre-prison) Canyon Confession (since they put no trust in the prison authorities' capacity: only they can extract the sort of details that are compatible with their objectives as go-getters who are willing to work hard as long as they are suitably rewarded) for as a story character you've already learned what they'll never learn, namely, that any process, whether that of your fending them off or of their trying to extract at any price the kind of confession they want to hear, has a logic of its own which cannot be rushed and for whose apparent sluggishness you must never excoriate yourself; and that, even if the harassments and the browbeatings and the bullyraggings repeat themselves over and over and over, to the practiced eye (such as yours) there are always slight variations amid all the identical drudgery of welts and howls and it is deep within these (and in your ability to abide by their tempo) that the momentum, that is, the truth of the process, and your own salvation, lie.

So what does it matter if all the T-shirts and Media Men of the world remain committed to kicking you in the teeth and bludgeoning you. Since, as creatures of habit, any concession to forbearance would only crush them (and all hope of perks and promotion) under the weight of its own infinite—Serial—replication.

You peer into the depths of the canyon but just before you're about to jump you happen through the corner of your eye to observe Media Man talking on his phone, a Cellular Phony if ever there was one. (Your first impulse is to berate him for making you a new kind of eavesdropper: the Phony's loudmouth insistence that you invade his privacy is his way of invading yours.) Insofar as it looks like he's talking about something—astounding as that may seem—having nothing to do with peddling you to the billions huddled before their eleven o'-clock P.M. television screen, his immersion in his own chatter alerts you to the fact that not only Pudd exists—not even Pudd in his universally shunnable ignominy—yet this rude awakening neither saddens nor lacerates. You're all too willing to grant—it's a massive load off your freckled shoulders—that the real dramas are always the marginal ones [remember how, while you were uncalmly waiting for Belle to rejoin you after her visit to Joyce at pool-, I mean, bedside, the TV repairman proceeded to call his office from a vacant desk in the emergency room, completely oblivious to the life-and-death struggles going on around him and as calmly as if he were stripping to masturbate, against the memory of a particularly fetching irate client, in the privacy of his own toilet, and how the call managed to advise you ever so tactfully, ever so tonically, of there indeed being a world beyond the one framing your particular version of non-Hollywood (i.e., with all the boring parts left in) crisis (which advice spawned less disappointment than relief)] like Flowers' here notarizing the stool samples on the loft fire escape.

And it is your resignation, at once instantaneous and evolving, to the priority of Media Man's cellular-phone chat that allows you (like the rich indicting the excesses of the super-rich) to expand your repertoire and play easily at playing second fiddle to, *inter alia*, stripped birch boughs emerging out of the canyon's shadow and squirrels galloping gingerly across yours, for all at once you've deduced that the marginals are not going, in their passage into eternity, to brutishly leave you and your earth-shattering crisis behind—precisely because it's up to you to procure them that eternalization at a reasonable price though it's not just a question [no matter what your next-to-last victim, Rainer (or René), may have said just before you whacked his afflatus], of delivering them up thereto through their unending (*unendlich*) change within the invisible heart of your own perishability—you (like all humankind) the most perishable (*Verganglichsten*) good on the market!—much less of telling the angel (*Sag ihm die Dinge*) that comes to judge you straight out of this world how happy they were—the squirrels and the boughs, for example—to be living by perishing within your gaze (*im Blick*). It is on the marginals in their very obviousness (which only seems to call your story integrity into question)—the obviousness of, say, a squirrel shuttling from one acorn husk to another and finding a safe haven in neither—and on that obviousness alone that you'll be able always to depend for an inspired and unforeseeable escape to, that is to say, an unforeseen self-mutation as self-expression in, the other world. Thus do the—*your*—marginals get themselves other-worlded (sorry, eternalized) in tow and in tandem at your own expense and no questions asked. The other world, Ralph prompted. Language, Bert whispered as if he were an innkeeper leading, by candlelight, the only guest not yet asleep to his turret room, in whose kingdom you are not a Serial Killer or not just a Serial. The squirrel's leap may be obvious but the faithfully rescuing description to your judges of that leap, being incontestably the very hardest thing of all to achieve, in any world, will do for you what Abelone's singing did for Malte or Rainer or René—it will set you down anywhere but where it found you and so you'll have come the coveted interior distance that separates the men from the boys.

In a word, once you manage to retreat from the world of your vile acts to that of language, the marginals you (or rather, the aiders and abettors of your media-potability) were so quick to pretend to spurn—from terror lest they steal your (i.e., their) paltry little show—will become the instruments of a self-transformation. In such a world, you are a completely neutral phenomenon at last, one ultimately explainable (after a few false starts) and by those very instruments, now the particles fundamental to your picturability—but a picturability no longer rancid for it is the job of the fundamental particles (marginalia) to take said rancidity upon themselves and decompose it into a potpourri of primary properties needed to pass themselves off as entities of a certain type—spiritualized neutrinos, say—so they in turn, having acquired these hot properties (like Democritean position and Epicurean shape and Newtonian motion and Daltonian mass and Boylesque unresolvability, for starters)—and bearing them like a cross—can go on therefrom to explain you (but a you immeasurably purified, or better yet, neutralized). And just as electrons must be absolutely identical if sharp images of a pay-per-view pornographic turn are to form on our television screen, so will your fundamental particles be absolutely indistinguishable, one from another. (The carcass of your rancidity is now between the particles, never to be recovered. And since they owe their status as entities to that rancidity they will be forever returning the favor by picturing you to your judges in a format radically different from the one establishing you as the FBI's most wanted.) In short, in the marginals' version of particle physics the gross phenomenon of your rancidity is broken down into the only primary properties (now belonging to the marginals themselves) that make your imminent status of Mass Entertainment Figure par excellence comprehensible at last.

Flowers cried out: But the particles are just retroductive constructions. They're "concepts" in the worst sense: they don't exist and what's worse nothing they supposedly scaffold exists. The character Gift is playing's a killer. There's only one way to picture him: as a rancid SOB. Pretending not to hear (although he feared that in the eyes of the actors, albeit maybe for Gift least of all, the face of his integrity had, from so arduous a simulation, permanently gone alternately blotched and pasty) Bert noted, You know now that somehow—even if just minutes before execution—you'll have this other-world opportunity to recuperate all your marginalia and that said recuperation of the recruitees is to constitute an earthshaking process of self-revelation and -discovery having *an inherent logic all its own* within this other world (which idiots only insist on wrongly styling the world of lies but which is in fact the plane for rectification of all the horrible wrongs, and for reparation of all the terrible wounds, inflicted in this, the world of acts where, insofar as acts submit to no shadings, you for one have made such a pitiable showing crime after crime) for there your neutrinos, unpicturable themselves, are this very moment flashing forth nothing less than the incessant picturability of not some PO Most-wanted but rather a madman whose continuous beta-ray spectrum of trespasses, whose rampageous beta disintegrations manifesting flagrant uncon-servation of energy, are, inexplicable otherwise, redeemed and exalted at last (and without the least little recourse to such farcical Holy Psy-cho hypotheses as've been made fashionable by Jean-Jacques Laing and R. D. Rousseau, among others). (And it doesn't matter in the least that your neutrinos leave no slot or spoor in the Wilson chamber of the foggier emotions, nor that for the time being you can only hallucinate them as sporting, in flashiest Fermian rake style, a velocity c, a mass of zero, a neutral charge and a magnetic moment also equal to zero.)

Only such neutrinos pullulating in the world of language— where any story character worth his pillar of salt belongs indisputably as well—allow you to heap scorn on the succession of rancid selves obliged to perpetrate unspeakable acts, as if—albeit, alas, only as if— you (for one) are well out of, well beyond, the mulch of those selves [and so what if some crusty old Storm Trooper—Marty Heidigger, say (prime culprit here as elsewhere)—then takes it as his bounden duty to be the very first to excoriate such excursions into the world of acts as are required to procure the marginalia earmarkable for neutrino-dom in the other world (because motored in his jaundiced view by a single aim: to return filthy-rich with the booty of consciousness whence to rustle up a hearty stew of invective against the squirrel self now transmuted into any number of one's fellow men) simply because Farty Marty refuses and will go on refusing to get through his thick skull the fact that only by depicting a canyon squirrel at its most obvious can you, ur-culprit in quest of rehabilitation, hope to allegorize (i.e., pillory to your heart's content) the so-called forces that drove you to Serial Kill in the first place and are continuing to tear you apart and (possibly—who knows?) through this cautionary tale spare billions a similar fate of foisting off on such forces the responsibility for their hemothymia thereby giving it free rein till the crack of doom?].

And all this, Flowers sighed as if puffing on an authentic hookah, through some lame description of a squirrel's tail which then obediently materializes into (*a*) a scathing indictment of postindustrial capitalism and its whipsaw egging on of the individual to break the bonds of his (phantom) fungibility and affirm an (infinitely more phantom) uniqueness beyond price (even if it means undertaking a killing spree of unprecedented dimensions) as well as (*b*) an indictment of the indictment particularly at those points where *a*, in the name of pseudointellectual high-fashion, comes perilously close to depriving murderers of that tool most crucial to their rehabilitation: a good old-fashioned sense of personal responsibility. Although he was already looking around for some vote-of-confidence echoing of the guffaw that had experienced birth pangs somewhere in the middle of this speechlet, it was clear there would be no bringing even the guffaw itself to completion owing to an atypical compassion for Bert—the canonizer couldn't remember his having ever looked quite so pitiful.

So never mind if your detractors fail—refuse—to see that you've no choice but to stage a one-man flying circus-cum-battle-royal through conscription of the very marginals whose flowering escaped your immediate notice way back when on the road to ruin and which, now unutterably fresh, you thus manage (given the requisite knack and savvy) to refund to yourself at the moment of greatest need—for on-the-spot transmutation into the neutrinos—the building blocks—of your rehabilitation and (thanks to what the neutrinos

214 / MICHAEL BRODSKY

have been busy making you out to be) as far more than a mere killer ready for the amenities of death row. So never forget you're Far More than a Killer and that you can be of use to others only under this quasizodiacal sign. Starting now, then (on the threshold of your prison cell), you've decided (for your own purposes, needless to say all altruistic) to take the laws of the media and of all the media's men into your own hands and thus determine for yourself the dimension of events (and not just those in which you played the role of vicious perpetrator). You refuse to have your story interrupted by a toothpaste commercial, say, and a trailer for some film about bisexual dinosaurs terrifying Middle America even if in respect of this planned flow of incoherencies that is prime-time television there is in fact no such thing as an interruption per se: let's face it, man, your story is by its very nature a TV story and a TV story is untransmissible through the media and unreceivable by those who are parasitized by it nightly unless that story's ragged sleeve of care is being incessantly pecked at by such daws as commercials and trailers and trailers for trailers. Indeed, expect even in the course of your very own story as you may already be tending to call it to be interrupted (or you may as well write yourself off as a total failure—your celebrity career no more than an aimless uncelebratable careering) by trailers for the story, for what does all this frenzied miscellaneity of audiovisual attack embody but a herculean goodwill effort by sponsors and producers to mimic the world itself.

Chapter Fifteen

As they escort you into the station house (it's on the West Side, not too far, it seems, from the George Washington Bridge) you can't help but notice all the bystanders noisily pointing fingers your way. [Night is mounting over the Hudson below: this moment—traffic moderate at the water's edge—will, suffused with its Peircean quale, never come again, so you have little choice but to bid an especially somber farewell to the real star of its show—these intricately scalloped (every edge a Pike's Peak) clouds, the overriding aim of any one being to countersink its dolphin lips into some other's ticklish rump.] You let them know you recognize them back and then some—but that their play of scrupulous certainty is fooling nobody. When you leered at them in the narrow bulb-riddled hallway and out on the landing, they were unwilling to return the challenge by undertaking the good hard look that separates a true expert witness from mere apers, so now to hide that chicken-livery here they are vastly overdoing recollection—

packing far too much vehemence into their moment of culprit identification (as if they could ever in fact be depended on to distinguish you from a horse's ass).

Inside, after the routine lineup, they speak with reverence of the deceased. The ideal neighbor, as it turns out. A neighbor who was also a beloved friend. Before they assign you to a cell Media Man, ever the muckraking crusader, notes that only the very poor, the very old and/or the very (artistically) underappreciated appeared to be living in such a building. And you, Pudd, are in ecstasy absolute to be able to agree with him (though has he ever solicited your agreement?) on such neutral terrain. It's a pleasure (you weren't sure you were still capable of any) to be able to nod graciously—to concur—without suffering immediate self-indictment as self's betrayer.

Arrived at the Tsimtsum Correctional Center you're not quite prepared for the jeering—the attempts, even, at stone-throwing—of Tsimtsum Township residents as they watch you get marched past perimeter fence after perimeter fence topped with razor wire into a fastness where no window ever opens. Later you wonder if there weren't a few inmates with limited excursion rights sprinkled among them. In the superintendent's [Bert: Flowers, my boy, I've been considering you for this role—seriously: Flowers (that old ham), not surprisingly, blushed] office you are obliged to tell your story once again—this time, to the prison assistant investigator (that's you, Priscilla—no ifs, ands or buts about it). He shows surprise, even hurt (hell, prison personnel are human), whenever you denounce some minute deviation of his paraphrase from the account given (the idiot dares to refer to Berlio's B-flat minor allegretto: imagine!) but after (once he gets the hang of it) the playback manages to become nothing less than the purest echo of that account you are even more incensed for his precision, by robbing you of your status as corrector, has thrown you back on the bruteness of the facts themselves. Though deep down (though you'd never admit it to a stranger, much less to yourself) you're more than satisfied with the way things have worked out since through capture you've been spared any further pursuit of your *dream* so-called. Fuck your dream. That's right: you go ahead and fuck your dream—of becoming the world's most inventive Serial Killer—and end up mightily pleased at the monstrousness of the issue—pleased at the feat not, mind you, of lavishing some expletive undeleted on the number one platitude of mass culture: Little man on the street, stand by your wet dream (at a time when the dream never counted for less, or rather, when the dream itself, whatever its particularities, is in every case never more impregnated with the spirit of the very market pretending to cherish its airy otherness) but rather of marking through said lavishing the distance you've had to cover to be able to at last realize this frontal attack on the zeitgeist.

The horror of capture (as with all other Pudd horrors you immediately feel proprietary: after all, its novelty enhances), then, is turning out to be the road to discovery, specifically that being (to the extent that it's real being) is still potent enough to vouchsafe, by denying you the fate-shape (World's Greatest, Most Famous and Most Uncapturable Serial) sketched by the long tantrum-symptom that is your life, a not-quite-posthumous go at the only -shape worth having— that uncontaminated by demands too desperate to be truly vital. And suddenly everything—not just the swallowing of your shadow (flung across the superintendent's rolltop) by that of the crow's-nest above central control (painted a cheery East River tugboat blue or is it tennis-ball green?) and the fifteen heavy steel sliding doors you're about to encounter en route to cell block *i* but everything, everything!—is applauding this, the last chance to make good unstraitjacketed by your own ultimatums.

Bert thought he'd just held forth most eloquently especially when it came to the thorny question of fucked dreams yet here was Samuels furiously eroding his knuckles despite the efforts of—of all people—GHW to divide him from so pitiful a quarry. What was it this time? The apparently gratuitous mention of Turing? of Manny F? of Joan Crawford in (post M-Piercean) flamingoroadlike flower? of Marcie—or was it Malte von—Proût? Or just the out-of-the-blue collocation of these unworthies as unseemly reminder that Bert simply couldn't keep his mind on the game?

When he arrived at Joyce's house for his midweek check-in the maid informed him it was only minutes before that, in the throes of excruciating abdominal cramps, she'd needed to be rushed—half-in, half-out of her polka-dot peignoir, and cuddled by Leonard, Belle and a representative cross-section of attending physicians on indefinite retainer who (according to Leonard, himself at death's door) knew her case best—to the emergency room at Metropolitan Memorial (was this the correct name of the institution?). Though it left, as usual, much to be desired in the way of amenities, Joyce, was not, also as usual, allowing the arrangements, a trifle stark though they might be (two main drags lined with occupied gurneys facing a mercilessly overlit quadrangle of metal desks heaped high with color-coded charts binned and unbinned, computers, and junk-food debris and junk utensils), to snarl her repudiation of Belle's reminder of all she still had to live for—Belle, just released herself from the semi-private nursing facility upstate where upkeep and assessment had cost him an arm and a leg and looking heartbreakingly fragile.

As for Leonard, standing over in a windowless corner as he was now doing, Bert was embarrassed to admit that up until this very minute he hadn't noticed the peaked and hapless consort supported himself on crutches and in fact one of his lower legs had all the earmarks of a prosthesis so that immediately his own rangy stride was retrofitted to a horn-tooting complacency. Since each of his accessories—arms, legs, buttocks, penis—was being recruited (but on whose say-so) to nothing less, then, than the heartless flaunting of a surplus good fortune, where others had none at all, Bert suddenly had no choice, while continuing to get snarled in banality traffic with the soon-to-be-bereaved, but to inventory every single accessory's every movement possibly witnessed by Leonard if, that is, he wished to be able to rest easy that all this flailing was no flaunting but a merest persistence in his own being. Yet how prove himself—not just to Leonard but to all the wanderers left unattended hereabouts—guilty of parading no more thew and sinew than were needed for barest posture. Yet how determine (like old Auguste at his Steinbergian giblets) how much body, and how many members thereof, were really needed to complete any given trajectory; how much core to achieve, say, gesture's fullest evolution on the way to the crapper. How satisfy Leonard (so as to be able to hold up his head to the cripple at last and ever after) that he, Bert, made it a point of honor never to incarnate, as equipment for any day's deal with contingency, an iota more than the barest minimum of purpose.

Oh I know, Leonard said suddenly, as if by so declaiming he was throwing his crutches away forever, you feel sad over my fate, but not my wife's—you hate her guts and rightly—but unbeknownst to you you are that also—sad over the lady's fate, I mean. In fact, you are overridingly sad because you don't in the least know where you and, more to the point, your work—I don't forget your work even if Joyce does: did I ever tell you that in my wild and woolly youth I was involved in some summer stock productions?—stand in terms of the disease, which is no longer—was it ever?—just Joyce's disease (don't make my mistake of letting her steal the show) but I'm pleased to see

that despite the sadness you're not making a pest of yourself with regard to the gruesome details—assuming there's a medico you can
har-ass for same at any hour of the day or night—in order to feel it's
running its course and that you (and your grief, that is, your work)
run parallel to such a running. With time you'll be learning your commercial can run its course without any propulsion from Joyce. Until
then please continue (until further notice) along present, if not necessarily altogether pleasant lines, and maybe all at once you'll come to
feel in your guts that as a reparative tack on the part of the gods (who,
for all we know, are never tone-deaf to the right gurgle of ingratiation)
for so continuing or, better yet (and infinitely more mysteriously) for
no reason whatsoever, as long as you go on abstaining from gurgling
impatience things can have no choice but to turn out well. The only
problem, Bert my boy (suddenly it was as if he'd gone from long shot
to extreme close-up without missing a beat), is that within seconds of
your thus playing dead—in the hope that the things of the world,
animal, vegetable and mineral, take the cue—every thing so inter-
pellated: clouds, turds, micro-infarcts, interracial beauty pageants in
nursing homes, in short, all your intergalactic circuit rivals for the
same scrawny patch of shadow, must surely decide to take advantage
of this timely collapse, sham or otherwise, to outpace you on that circuit for ever and ever. In short, if only like some *Arbeit macht frei*-style
goosestepper (without the messy cattle-car experience) you could
have learned by rote the overarching brute fact of life, to the effect
that everything as you know it and, more to the point, as you don't
know it is in fierce and grievous competition with everything else,
even—especially—for the things they—the competitors—crave
least, and as much as a single second's secession from the jousting
swarm converts one into the rheumiest anachronism. So don't you be
expecting any of the jousters, including Her Majesty, to take time out

to utter sweet nothings in your ear about Joyce's time having come.

I don't expect a fucking thing, was what he found the strength to say to Len, crutches or no crutches. When her (expletive deleted) death, which I admit at this point I desire more than anything on earth, finally takes place it (bis) will, as punishment for my overweening impatience therefor, take place missed and any savoring of this release too long awaited to have been realizable will be lost in the shuffle of tossing preparation for (*idem*) calamities far more grievous than her transfinite longevity ever could have been. More surprising than Leonard's momentary intimidation, however, was his kindness (its gist paraphrasable thus): Joyce is simply infecting you, that's all there is to it, with her fear of savoring the moment, so don't let her. You won't be cheated of her death: you've earned the right to it. Oh yes, I know, at the onset of every new setback (and what would dear Joycie's organic architecture be without its setbacks?) she immediately gets busy nostalgizing the one that came just before to the point where you, as bystanding bedpan Charlie, always end up excoriating yourself heartily for not having, way back in the mists of time, exulted enough (when offered the only chance you'll get ever again to so exult—that is, if Joyce has her way and she always does) at what her retrospection suddenly, baldly illuminates as rare good fortune now that authentic bedpan disaster is (at least according to the eternal patient) once more upon you, failing to perceive that the current disaster is also sure, from the (disad)vantage of the next, to have its day as an irrecoverable arcadia. But unlike these setbacks existing purely to be superseded, the savoring of her death will not give way to disfiguration.

Whispering, Don't listen (how can you let him say such horrible things about mother?), and (much more kindly, lest she lose forever her only real friend in this world of unbefriending parents), I'm sorry about Joyce: we've just got to take it a day at a time: I'll try to be more

222 / MICHAEL BRODSKY

helpful and not fall apart, Belle almost dragged him down the corridor into the visitors' waiting room where, following the markedly under-played entrance of another woman, obviously an aspiring actress, she proceeded to grow noticeably, fidgetingly—dare he say, theatrically—uncomfortable. I'm afraid she'll take you away from me: especially after all you've had to endure from Joyce. He could express his exhilaration at this sure sign of being crazily cherished only through a bark of out-rage at the fear provoking it. The woman, who was wearing, most be-comingly, a plum-colored beret at a mournful angle and pumps with ankle-straps, walked across the room to the cigarette machine (a flush-ing toilet was audible). As the coins rattled through Bert and Belle, both, caught her reflection in the contraption itself as well as (profiled) in the depths of the pane separating all concerned from the mottled night sky. For a while, as she walked away from us (after the grand en-trance routine), I was feeling more and more able to discard her as if she'd never existed. But the minute she got to the cigarettes she became a new threat because she's a new woman, or haven't you noticed? and I'll have to be combating her all over again in order to hold on to you. A pain-inducing being, said Bert (thinking more of Gift, because of the insult-to-injury represented by his youthful beauty, than of Flowers), can never be wholly discarded. I've learned that from working with this young man—Gift I think he calls himself—among others—think I may have mentioned him, no? No, you never did, she obediently an-swered though her mind was clearly elsewhere, albeit not necessarily on the cigarette lady even if she wasn't forgetting to lower her head under the sad weight of its deference as the creature, puff-puffing on a long stick, floated by. Bert forgot his impatience for Joyce to die and al-lowed himself to be moved once again by what in Belle affected—af-flicted—him as kindness, *that is*, her credulity before others' self-advertisement. Immediately, she looked at him sideways in spite of herself.

The sidelong look was too much for his nerves.

He answered: On some level, you're kind, you're good, but on another I know that such kindness is sheer credulity even if I also know this isn't so in the least though why must I abstain from saying what I'm drawn to say simply because I know it isn't true. At any rate, Belle, whatever your kindness happens to be I mustn't fall into the trap of making it the supreme category in whose shadow everything else shrivels. I've got to stop thinking of you as some kind of unsung genius of goodness for in that way I only intensify my own estrangement from others (especially the actors and just when I need them most). Seeing the look of incomprehension (or was it the fear born of comprehension?) he concluded, So if I start seeming a little distant—don't panic: I'm only struggling for the first time in our married life—now that I'm in over my head as regards the enterprise on which that life's future depends—to undergo you, sweet Belle, to undergo all that is Belle, *that is*, your gentleness—for you are, always will be your gentleness and nothing but (or is such an equation proof of my perversity, but perpetrated against whom or against what—my love? my hate? my love as hate? you, Belle in herself? you, Belle as surrogate mother of us all?)—as it— the gentleness—the gentleness that is Belle and nothing but—must (if we both—and the enterprise—are to survive) be undergone, that is to say, cum mere fact with no more density than any other.

In short I mustn't make your kindness, like Joyce's death, the focal point of all my efforts. I've constantly got to remind—convince— myself there are perpetrators of kindness, though few and far between, outside the Belle-domain just as there've got to be, outside the Joyce domain—much as I hate to admit it—practitioners of the same sort of venom-spewing.

In short, I can't help hating your kindness for it is indiscriminate kindness of the worst kind, found(er)ed on the misconception that if only you can solve the current round of problems there'll no longer be anything to stand in the way of Joyce's finally bestowing her favor upon you. But any idiot knows of course Joyce would be nothing without her problems: it's how she lures you to your regular, signature ingenious (her ingenuity *pitted*, like a teenager's chin, against yours) misreading of the accursed mother/daughter dyad, and dutifully you take the bait every time, and so the problems will never end. He was quick to add—not, however, that there were any signs of grief or rage—But don't get me wrong, I'm grateful for the opportunity your kindness and your kindness alone provides for knowing Joyce for if I am to know Joyce then I must know her outside her natural habitat—for the essence of any thing can become visible only outside its natural habitat and what habitat is more unlike unto Joyce's own than that encompassed by your kindness.

When he awoke (analysis is exhausting) Belle was leaning asleep against his shoulder (the tendinitis-afflicted one). An orderly in off-blue stood over him. He closed his eyes in the hope of eventually reopening them to, as in his dream, a perfectly recurved streetlamp pulsing into half-life amid too few boughs in bud against an iceblink sky. The orderly announced (Bert now remembered him, cordially graceful, from one of the side aisles off the ER's Grand Concourse) he'd be only too happy to comply with the patient's wish to be moved a bit closer to the nurse's station—that is, with the permission of and a little help from her (titter) gentleman friend. The gentleman friend tried to restrain his rage as best he could—his iceblink dream had *given him to understand* that Joyce was just about to reward him for centuries of loyal service by doing the decent thing at last: dying within the precincts of this institution which, who knows? might someday bear

her name but here she was instead getting ready to convene (if the orderly was to be believed), and with full administrative empowerment
to boot, yet another of those interims of which his life constituted little more than the missed beat—and the best way he could, or so he
thought at this particular juncture, was to intermingle with their
present variant as few of his own homoeomeria as possible For he
feared—as, let's face it, he did in respect of *all* events (even Belle's laying her sleepless head on his cold shoulder) not just all the Joyce-epi-
centered ones—that the greater the number of particles seeping towards participation the larger the probability of its—the
event's—irreversible and infinite serialization. Furthermore although
it was already late in the game he still couldn't bring himself to believe
(ER trappings and massive doses of chemotherapy notwithstanding)
in the direness of the malfunction he was forever being asked, and not
just by orderlies, to service: either the tumor's proliferation was a hallucination or if not then its use as a ploy for putting him through the
wringer far outweighed any inconvenience to the patient herself
(oddly enough, or not so oddly, patient's very own accesses of mini-
mization—at times, albeit few and far between, she needed to make
light of her condition so that the around-the-clock attention she demanded could be devalued in tandem—had gone a long, or at least a
part of the way towards fostering such a paralogia). Back from the
main drag (the orderly, defiantly affable to the last, had, over Joyce's
insistence that he possessed no sense of direction, done most of the
pushing and all the steering) Bert announced, with a sigh of deep disgust (if only he could get Ralph, aghast at the law's delay, to emit a one
as deep), that Belle should be happy to learn her mom remained (the
nurses and their gentleman callers, as she called them, were a noisy lot
and now she was much too close to the goings-on) as dissatisfied as
ever.

To distract him? Belle said: Unlike you, I just can't believe in my suffering at the hands of Joyce. I can't begin to believe it gives me any authority, that is, a unique perspective. I am a nothing, Belle insisted. He did not like to hear that Belle reduced to a nothing after so much suffering at the hands of her natural mother, for mightn't this mean his work with the actors was a nothing too, and a nothing forcibly contingent for its recurrence on extraction from the very context (the Joyce context, concrete and undislodgeable) forbidding its every installment. So, he mutely panted, his work among them was nothing outside the threat directed toward and against it by Joyce: the *Ewige* patient. With Joyce gone (should such a miracle ever supervene), no more commercial. Beside himself Bert (and at this point he didn't care who the hell heard him) cried, You must learn to be fertilized, Belle, by the very thing(s) your first instinct tells you exist(s) solely to disqualify you for being. It's like me and Flowers. Belle looked away but he persisted. There are props to be had, Belle, mark my words. Belle replied, I would like to believe in what you're saying—God knows I'm not well. And the only suture for the wound seems to be further laceration. But now, ma Belle, you're on the road to rehabilitation—if only we could have known then what we know now, you might never have had to be packed off upstate for you've learned, or rather, you're learning, how to stagger your laceration.

Why are you at war with this guy Flowers? Belle asked, looking at her watch. Partly because he did not want to answer (although he knew that, rather than have Belle go on making nervous conversation, it was to his immediate advantage, or at least not to his detriment, to do so), Bert said: Stop worrying. By way of afterthought, or what he hoped sounded like one, he now showed no objection to noting (the tone was dreamy, once-over-lightly protreptic), Often when two beings—like Flowers and me—enter the same domain, be it lime-pit baseball or hematology/oncology, the rift already subsisting (hell, they're fellow beings, after all) quickly becomes wider and deeper. In short, instead of such strivers' targeting the coarse world outside said domain as their truest enemy, each prefers (from hatred of self? of the striving in question? of that striving as extension of the hated self?) to make even the faintest whiff of homologous striving in any other reasonable and just cause of homicidal stirrings. In shorter, rivalry makes mincemeat of brotherhood. Why that is, I'll never know, Bert added sweetly—so sweetly that he was seriously in danger of falling in love with himself, or rather, with the blue blood capable of *Why that is, I'll never know*, for rarely did a turn of phrase manage so economically to turn him into a being who was all at once (*a*) too innocent to know the reason for a state of affairs he'd nonetheless been clever enough to depict unflinching and (*b*) humble enough to admit he didn't know the reason for said state of affairs and at the same time free of all rancor towards such beings as would be deserving of excoriation within the context of the reasons he knew only too well, albeit without wishing to know, or to let it be known, that he knew.

Now they were silent. The sun was rising: undulating patches on gingko and linden trunks. He suddenly felt it his bounden duty to amble over to the nurses' station and (to use a phrase she particularly detested) look in on the patient. He glared down at Joyce, lulled perhaps to indifference, hence rancorlessness, by the jolts of her own ordeal. She didn't appear to see him though she wasn't asleep. He went on glaring and glaring and glaring. When, finally, two orderlies arrived to wheel her around and out (she thereby turned her back on his heartlessness forever) he waved weakly at the spotted folds of the sheet covering her frame—shrunken *almost beyond recognizability*, he realized for the very first time or, to survive the shame of the moment, was he just mouthing a self-glorifying phrase he'd heard or read somewhere. Tests, tests and more tests, my friend, announced a nurse, also left behind, over a counter overloaded with smelly discarded dinner trays, but more to her monitor's blank screen than to him: First radiology (silver zone) and gastroenterology (topaz and gold) then maybe urology (emerald); your mom, poor thing, ain't—let's face it—responding too well to the hard-line poison.

But once she was comfy-and-cozily propped up among her very own pillows in the in-patient chemotherapy subunit (given the direness of her home reaction they needed to keep her under observation), Joyce (rapidly becoming her old self), was able, between sips of visibly steaming tea, to hold forth foretellingly on the side effects that must supervene once they stepped up the miracle dosage (which they'd be sure to do now she was their captive), and quite convincingly Bert might have added if anybody had been interested enough to ask.

But when Belle extended her hand in commiseration Joyce quickly withdrew her own beneath the sheet—more than anything she hated to need to be touched. Bert's only protection against being compelled (because of the excruciating pathos of that exquisite offer baldly rebuffed) to fuse once again with Belle, the unloved child, was to note that in starkest contradistinction to Joyce, who could love nobody but herself, Belle was able to love everyone and was in point of fact always inventing new targets for this upsurge that constantly did her in (though she didn't care since her desire was stronger than her pride) so that inevitably, on the emergence upon the scene of such a target, all its predecessors, now perceiving themselves, as contracted sole object of her affections (for that was the message Belle's loving invariably conveyed), simply too, too rudely and rankly abandoned for words—all these suddenly cashiered Belle-loveds, had, in their jealous hurt, no recourse but to excoriate not the new recruit nor each other but rather, as incontestable exclusive culprit, Belle herself, and all because unbeknownst to her, poor Belle's loving kindness, her sheer goodness (and there *was* such a thing in this world, of that Bert was convinced) had the disastrous effect of inducing over and over and over again and, worse, fostering for all time in any given love-target, however peripheral, the illusion that she lived and loved for the loving of that target and that target alone and would quite frankly therefore never be caught dead needing any other(s), yet here she was (by the very nature of that lovingness constitutive of her gentle being) eagerly seeking newer receptacles for her inexhaustible upwelling, so how could the upshot not have been the one now universally obtaining whereby every one of her targets ended up feeling so cast overboard (rather than brightly and beautifully assimilated to a wider and wider family of loveds from whose pool of shared resources he or she could expect only profit in every way superior to the benefits conducing from an exclusive lien on her affections). Rejecting such resources as worse than none at all, each strove to become more rebarbative in his or her need than all the others combined hence, in the long run, were Belle and Joyce, though vastly different, in fact even barely distinguishable as sisters under the mink? that is to say, Joyce had a long line of loathers inasmuch as she was incapable of breeding loving among her fellows and so did Belle—have her equally long (perhaps even longer) line of loathers—insofar as she was forever fomenting the delusion that her infinite capacity for loving was the exclusive property of its newest target-receptacle, of which too-seductive prospect he or she—target of the moment—was certain to be disabused the minute a successor swam into her ken.

But so preoccupied had Bert become with the one-to-one mappability of the infinite series of Belle's loather-fans right smack into that of Joyce's and vice versa, in particular with the fact that like any true transfinite worth its salt each series remained unaltered by the addi-

230 / MICHAEL BRODSKY

tion of one or more of its members, and that in many ways [to paraphrase another of his old pals—where were they now? and why didn't
he try, as Belle was always urging, to resume contact (must be that her
breakdowns (so Belle) caused him a flogging embarrassment: how
wrong the poor dear was!)—to wit, the geologist Bad-time "Charley"
Lyell] no sooner might the calendar of ex-fans appear to be completed
than Joyce or Belle or their respective major-domos were called upon
to intercalate, some new, vast constituency thereby smashing to bits
somebody somewhere's unspoken hope that this to-the-crack-of-
doom agglomeration would, through a convulsion worthy of Cuvier,
come at last to a discontinuous end and a golden age redolent neither
of fan nor of loather be ushered in—so preoccupied had Bert become,
here in the facility's super-elite Cantor-Dedekind wing (or was it a
pavillion?), that there was a lag of at least several minutes before he realized Joyce was in fact extending in his general direction an amber-
tinted vial with an off-white cap. Struggling to remove the cap with his
decidedly unpianistic-looking fingers he coldly grimaced but how explain (especially now that she was grimacing in retaliation) that, for
once, the grimace had been prompted not by her lying there but
rather by a schoolmarmish desire to suppress the impish conjunction
of a yawn and a belch. What's wrong, she (now appallingly wide
awake) made haste to inquire, as if it—Grimace & Co.—might be a
first and most unwelcome sign of some competing ailment which
would go on not only to rob hers of the spotlight its gravity deserved
but also to render him far less available, as amphitheatrical stage designer, for periodic adjustments thereof. He shook his head he hoped
definitively (perhaps the bottle cap could be used as a prop back on the
art front) for he knew only too well that this preliminary prying constituted far less some compassion-clogged request for information
than a command that whatever it was she'd already astutely labelled as

a most inconvenient prefiguration of disorder at once declare itself null and void. Yet handing over the tiny pills (shocking-pinkish they were) he'd managed to extract (once the cap was—given his legendary lack of manual dexterity, miraculously—unscrewed), neither of them quite sure just why she'd relinquished the bottle in the first place and even less so why (even more illogically) he'd insisted against all odds on prying it open, he suddenly was supremely happy—she hadn't balked at his proffering the pills hence it could be assumed she'd at least tolerate pill-to-hand if not hand-to-hand contact. No better way to exploit the euphoria, as much on Belle's behalf as his own, than by hailing a taxi and heading straight for the rehearsal studio.

Chapter Sixteen

Before he entered he could hear them (was that knuckle-devouring Samuels referring to him as a namedropping fraud?): clearly they believed themselves unheard or perhaps at this stage of the game they couldn't care less if they were. Why did they choose to stay stupidly on? Who was Bert (there were droves of better, not to mention more bankable, TV directors) to be ordering them about, or rather, refusing to do so, at least with the brutal brio they had every right to expect? You stay he heard Gift say (over Flowers' guffaw), because you ain't got nowhere else to go. So Gift was reverting to the old crust, continuing (Bert was, thankfully, in deep shadow) thus: Bitches, she does, about having to climb on top of my shoulders but in fact she's eating it up—considering the alternatives. I don't, Priscilla said. Bitch, Gift hissed before the words were half out of her mouth, you rant and rave every chance you get—I mean, about just not getting *it*: as you've made us understand, you're the kind o' gal who on any day of the week at any hour of the day or night—and Sundays that goes double—'s sure to be standing on somebody's shoulders, sometimes twice or even thrice daily, so why is he fixing on that of all things and, worse, making you draw it out—underline it, so to speak? Why, in short, is the sonofabitch making you regurgitate your most intimate preferences, rather, your most automatic ones: they reveal nothing about the real you—what you insist (until you, not to mention everybody else, are blue in the face) has just got to be the real you [or, so runs the (unspoken) rest of the proposition, why bother go on living]—the Priscilla nobody knows.

As Priscilla (Bert could see through the door of shadow, ajar) was now turning away with a hurt, an almost nauseated, look on her face though not, it would appear, for Gift, more for herself, for all those intimate and automatic preferences that consistently sabotaged the real Priscilla's maiden voyage towards universal acclaim, Bert (believing it was the only gentlemanly thing to do), stepped forward to acknowledge yes on the one hand he was not particularly interested in Prissie the individual but that on the other there were no bounds to how far she might, merely through the most intimate micromovements constituting a sort of body script, manage to lead them all (turning to the group at large while studiously avoiding Flowers, who as it turned out wasn't listening: his eye was on the sleeping world without). Here Priscilla turned to Gift and made as if to mount him, but he pushed her away, not rebuffingly—with gentleness in fact. You're too late, said Flowers, resentful out of the blue of any further demands that might be made on his busy protégé. No, Gift replied portentously, studiously avoiding his mentor's gaze: in fact she's too early, but her time will come again, and again, and again. (Though Bert had to admit Gift seemed to be wholly on his side at last, nevertheless he couldn't help feeling each time the younger man elected to crank up his fever of advocacy yet another notch that somebody somewhere was merely taking bites out of his soul.)

Priscilla bowed her head, the entire company following suit, as at news of a fellow-trouper's death (Gift's stance, on the other hand, suggested the taking of a long overdue curtain call, eggplant-throwing claques be damned). Bert, rightly judging that at this juncture his only recourse was a winning smile—too sweet even for his own taste but he was impelled to emanate something utterly antipodal to dissension in the ranks—said, I refuse to take all this as negativity per se. For what is her life, what is anybody's, but a procession of nostalgias for what, until a minute ago, we thought we were—really were? (Flowers suddenly looking as if camaraderie's most plangent note had just been struck, Bert was tempted to simper, A little mood indigo, maestrino.) In other words, our Priss is no diabolical wet blanket: she's simply confiding her sorrowful frustrations—the stock in trade as we all know of every underemployed actress's salad days so (clapping his hands, square-dance caller style) to the big bow window—quickish, like bunnies! See that yellow streetlight down there—quick, quick, quick, because in a second it's going to change color (it's starting!)—against the horizon's lopsided glow. There it goes: so now what's left us but an afterbreath of infinite loss as we strive nevertheless to get on with the business of New Yorkerly five-way-street-survival, for (let's face it) red will never—no matter how hard it tries—come up to the standard of yellow, instantaneously (if in most cases unperceivingly) enshrined in our hearts. So we, the unlucky few, like billions of others, will spend the rest of the day, that is to say, the rest of our days, in the deepest mourning for loss of yellow yet without the ghost of an inkling that we mourn.

Bert noted that Ralph looked daggers but was at least for the moment speaking none and that Gift was shaking his head at something Flowers had just uttered in a stage-whisper. Priscilla: He's trying to tell you it ain't nostalgia, it ain't nostalgia [turning towards Ralph, who looked with sudden shyness away (from budding infatuation? Bert wondered, shyly, himself, but could infatuation *be* budding, like a writer or a love affair?)]—it's just that suddenly, from this pinnacle of fellowship, I feel in duty bound to look back at the particular solitudes that have constituted my life thus far and be properly astonished at the brute fact of having managed, despite all odds, to live through them, to make them work on behalf of my own work. Yes, cried Flowers, stamping his walking stick on the wooden floor so that the very panes trembled in the glittering New York City night: exactly: to be sure: quite so. You wonder how you ever managed to see them through (but not through them) to their conclusion, how you ever succeeded (for succeed you did, little girl!) in transforming each solitude (there was a sudden menace of alarm in his tone which seemed to render him more virile, at least in Priscilla's eyes, for she flushed and began picking at the pinkish nap of her mohair top) into its very own theatrical form. In a barely audible whisper evoking the eternal combat between flirtatiousness and dread, Priscilla said: Stop—I can't think straight— you're killing me—I'm already infected with the chill of those soli- tudes.

Sensing things were getting far too steamed up Bert said: It's time we began. I have nothing to say, nothing to contribute, said Ralph, the actor (he suddenly realized) he loved best among all the others. It's precisely when you have nothing to say that you have most to say, Bert replied, for it is then you enjoy a rare—a miraculous—respite from the inexhaustible upsurge of pain. At any rate, into your prison cell, Ralph—I mean, Gift (places, everyone!)—enters a non-denomina- tional man of the cloth, come to have a (non-denominational) look at the soon-to-be-fried. Adding (without taking his eyes off Gift), Until we find the person who's just right for the part in question, would you mind very much, Herr Flowers, standing in? Bert proceeded (though not before succumbing to the rare luxury of a brief amazement at his ability, downright suave under the circumstances, to have taken the Canon-fodderizer's blank look for the heartiest of affirmatives) to put this newfound very reverend through his paces. Remember, so you tell Pudd, adaptation to one's fate is never once and for all but a day-by-day—a minute-to-minute—affair. Just because you can adapt in/under a rainstorm doesn't mean that tomorrow, in the immediate vicinity of a particular postpluvial cloud you will be equally well forti-fied. You, Pudd/Gift, then feel compelled to ask him if by cloud he's re-ferring (you sense he's getting a bit tight around the collar and that was your goal) to the camel-weasel-whale "that great baby" Polonius professed, hoping thereby to retain his franchise in Asslickers Anony-mous, to have caught on the wing one autumn afternoon. Now you begin to grow impatient, looking not at all like a man who every day is newly, differently ordained, and so he is not taken completely by sur-prise when you come forth barkingly with: So, do you choose freely to convert or, better yet, Are you converted? Though obviously you are, Reverend Father—taken completely by surprise, I mean—when Pudd comes back equally tellingly with, I most certainly do not/am not and never will/never will be. Convert/converted, he adds unneces-sarily. But you, Reverend, can't hear because (as you go on to explain) you need just one more patsy to round out your baker's dozen for the month of May and thereby fulfil the quota that will cap you a much-merited promotion. Mine is a faith of practical objectives, you mur-mur, not at all grandiosely, though the temptation of grandiosity being too great to withstand you then add: In such a mobile: indeed, unlocalizable society as is encompassed by the prison, the purpose of any faith worth its salt lies not in the preservation of an historical con-tinuity, much less in the accretion of particular views or practices;

rather it is epicentered around the experience I like my bachelor fathers before me—Charles Grandison Finney, Dwight L. Moody and Billy Sunday, to name but a few of those who helped sire my sunburst—choose to call The Great Conversion—specifically the minister's ability to induce the experience that wins souls in measurable numbers (Proverbs XI, 30: "He that winneth souls is wise") which accumulations become thereby the point on the classificatory grid in relation to which all institutional scum can be straitjacketed. And to make sure the results are fully coded down to the last detail I always make sure to bring to the after-sermon inquiry sessions (held in the diagonally opposite corner of the cell approximately thirty minutes after the moment of definitive conversion) the same sort of decision cards—sorry, "decision cards"—used by Brother Moody himself, or rather by his teams of follow-up assistants, when they went about systematically recording the vital statistics (here limited to a "10-best" list: name, address, age, sexual preference(s), marital status, favorite sport(s) and/or card game, favorite auto make, favorite Fortune-500 company, favorite basketball team, favorite talk-show host and/or sitcom, favorite computer brand) of every last soul saved.

You, Gift, can't resist pointing out that whatever the Very Reverend has to offer in the way of end-of-the-line salvation seems to have long been whittled away to near-nothingness by all this flailing to measure inherent unmeasurability for how measure conversion, and why this need to measure at all, unless it's a question of results' having to be delivered up to some insatiable beast. Smelling your advantage, Pudd (Flowers is unnaturally silent at this point), you add, but not too exultantly, doubtless it was at the very moment when he perceived he'd lost all sense of what a conversion might be or that he never had any and couldn't hope even to begin to define so mazy an event that in revenge for the eternal collapse of his ambitions he fixed on the idea of measuring conversions come hell or high water, whatever they might or might not turn out to be, stumbling serendipitously on one of the basic laws of animal life, namely that the only way to cancel the stigma of a wrong-naming or an inability-ever-to-name is to quantize the thing unnamable to the point where, accumulations being so tall and the memory of the public so short, the scandal of its undefinability and even (as in this case) non-existence may safely be expected to have been blithely bypassed amid all the applause for the loom of large numbers. Consequently you're more aware than ever that it's definitely to his advantage to believe or to think he believes or at any rate to have you believe or think you believe conversion takes place not once and for all but anew at every moment (thereby multiplying his opportunities for intervention at least a trillionfold) and even if an instance seems the exact replication of every other it is in fact always a unique point on the curve of the world since [this is now your (instantaneous) discovery, Pudd] any instance is always being deformed through the pull of death, which pull is increasingly potent and thus capable of inducing greater deviations from all instances that came before, only confronted with so inexorable a pull one naturally can't help wondering if there really is such a thing as mellowing into forgiveness or whether it isn't in fact the outcome of vengefulness's having gotten simply too tired to campaign against every single fucking bastard in sight.

So what do you suggest, ask preacher and warden (he's just come in: Fritz Langley, here's your chance to rechew the scenery) simultaneously, that we lay off completely? convert each other—rather than the inmates? Though you are at first buoyed up by the retort you can actually taste (it's a bit salty but not excessively so) on the tip of your tongue yet even before they're done, and even if you are only too well aware the problem is exactly the sort that ends up eventually con-

239 / CHAPTER SIXTEEN

fronting every man, and not just the one on death row, and despite the
fact that you thus have a duty, before the switch is pulled and the mixture of sodium pentothal, pancuronium bromide and potassium chloride coaxed into your vein, to help set the future terms of such con-
frontation, far more pressing becomes the overpowering hunger to get
away—from the problem, that is, whether confronted or not—
which hunger is the harder to suppress the more you manage to convince yourself that once you've gotten away from preacher and warden in the dawn's early soot you'll be free—free at last to discover it
was only here, in this place, and at this particular point in time determined by an infinity of coordinates (preacher, warden, soot et al) none
of which are, thankfully, replicable, that there could ever have been
such a problem in the first place. With every passing moment, then,
this problem is proving to be more and more an artifact of the moment, or so you maintain to the cockroaches under the sink.

So there's a kind of rough justice in the fact that if you couldn't
manage a change of scene a change of scene has nonetheless come to
you for at this very moment who should enter (picking his nose: his
fingers are especially busy in the nostril less hirsute and, biggest surprise, not unRachmaninoffian in their sinewy slenderness) but the executioner himself [to be played by none other than our dear Gottfriedina whom, as you might remember, I took it upon myself to
singlehandedly rescue from a career far more lucrative in the state-of-
the-art dungeons of hematology/oncology (come forward, Dinka my
love—we'll stand for none of your milkmaid shyness)].

Once Gift was out of the crapper Bert had every intention of explaining how in the postmortem quiet of the execution chamber Pudd
would have been fingerprinted—Gottfriedina's job, that—so it could
be verified that it was indeed Pudd and no other done in for the good
of the commonalty and so the coroner could then come in and, in all

good conscience, take away the already rotting body. The fingerprints went along with the execution warrant and both went the way—to the central office to be duly filed—of all bureaucratic horseflesh. And he'd make sure Gift-Pudd as the star of the show (a plug for serial kill type entertainments, remember) never forgot there were always, amid all the grisly clockwork, at least two chronologies at work in Deathville [the one started by the operations officer on the day of the execution and the chronology of the deathwatch officer in the holding cell which as everybody should know was an open room cut straight down the middle by a wire mesh where on one side (with typewriter and telephone) sat Boswell documenting everything that happened in—no avant-garde antics, please—strict chronological order including every telephone call for the to-be-executed had unlimited telephone access (and perhaps one day the Pudds of the world would be able to look forward to playing the Cellular Phoney—as if they were out strolling on the very sidewalks of New York—during their last minutes on this fucking earth) as well as unlimited opportunity to fuck] just as there were also always two at work in the vicinity of Joyce's gurney, namely, the time-scheme of her desiccation and atrophy, and that of his hunger to get away counterpointed with hers to have him overstay, though she could barely stand the sight of him.

   Yes, there was so much Bert still had to reveal about what went on (if only Gift could begin to see his way clear to giving a final wipe to his ass) in the little lifetime just before execution—not just the fact that Boswell kept a log of all visitors so that if, say, the Dowager Duchess Dottie O'Dowd decided to deign to drop in then she perforce became a permanent part of the corpse's entourage down at the central office, but more to the point how at 8:30 Pudd's gurney was prepared to receive him, and blinds dutifully drawn; and how at 10 PM the execution team (ET), wearing highest-priority security badges of course, arrived to load an evening's hemlock into the LIT (lethal injection machine); and how at 11 PM the chaplain (he who measured professional success by number of recorded conversions per square millimeter) reported to holding cell for farewell chat (HCFFC); and how at approximately 11:36 PM the ambulance and hearse pulled up at the sally port amid a deafening absence of fanfare; and how through all this tomfoolery the doc went on testing and retesting the EKG gizmo and the saline solutions and the IV lines; and how at the last minute the governor's designated rep was scrupulously contacted in case of a (highly unlikely) stay—only the longer his mind's eye went on elaborating such microtraumata the clearer it became such detritus configured one unmistakable event: the slow death agony of Joyce until not so suddenly but no less astoundingly for all that he was overcome by a sensation altogether new: infinite pain for her infinite pain (it was against his principles to sentimentalize but this was second sight, not sentimentality— not even sentiment). Through the unwitting superimposition upon the Joyce-calvary (and it was a calvary, most of course for her but for him too) of (of all things) the Pudd/Gift's execution (still very much to come) with its own onco/hemo-twinned bric-a-brac of soiled gurneys and infecting IVs and EKG wagons and fumbling medicos, he (or some demiurgic biggish brother) was managing to purge the former of its inflection of raging rancors: his and hers (hadn't she in fact murmured Thank you, weakly thus rendingly as he was leaving the last time?), hence it was no longer possible to keep track for Gift's sake of what still had to be depicted (the fact, for example, that in the press area, once the ordeal was over and Joyce or rather Pudd was gone for good, a nominated media witness needed to be available for questioning by the mediamites who hadn't been as fortunate as he though of course it was to the chosen one's advantage to cheat a bit on the gruesome details and render them exclusive thereby to his rag).

242 / MICHAEL BRODSKY

But with Joyce the condemned man tugging for the first time in ages at his heartstrings there was simply no thinking of the execution chamber. [Not even if here was Gift emerging from the toilet at last and looking in the half light (his breasts pendulous and surprisingly hairy) more Pudd-like than ever and not just any old Pudd but a Pudd finally ready for his farewell gurney (albeit this undressed vulnerability's suddenly granting him a queasy upper hand over the heart of the heart of the wound that was Gift-cum-Pudd-cum Gift merely sent Bert flailing back over past encounters towards proof that insensitivity *then* prohibited—as director, as executioner—his calling the shots *now*.]

Indeed, the space before him was already expanding, willy-nilly, to the dimensions of the emergency room at Mount University Metropolitan General: in fact (or fiction that was infinitely more corrosive than fact) he remembered precisely how, as she lay there—just one among the big communal bloodbath's far too many untreatables (having been rushed through the sooty winter's night) overexposed (on a gurney already soaked through and through) to the scrutiny of all and sundry—one of the orderlies had proceeded, with a poise positively breathtaking, to draw a curtain around what had seemed only moments before to be the most wide open of public spaces—one boundless beyond any hope of even the most nominal partitioning, much less the sort of unbreachable quarantine capable of shutting out everybody including him. How theatrical the moment had been, transforming all that came before: thanks to the orderly's exquisite sleight of hand E.R., formerly a chaos of Times Square anatomy lessons, was currently—had never been anything but—one life-experiment that, unlike so many of Bert's own, hadn't failed (maybe because the orderly didn't try too hard).

Thus there always came a moment—what with the doings of the

recruited private aides and/or the non-doings of the goldbricks there-amongst and the assistant dietician's attention to the spiritual needs of the soon-to-be-deceased and the visiting chaplain's snubbing of the itinerant social worker and the harp and organ movers waiting impatiently in the wings and the TV going full blast without sound and what with the painkillers administered rectally and the anxiolytics administered vaginally and the anti-nauseas administered intravenously, and the aides trying to impress the fancy visitors with their expertise and the visitors trying to impress the aides with their gentrified devotion and the eagerness with which both species angled for the biggest fish of all, namely, plausible deathbed chitchat: in a word, what with *a* and *b* and *c* and *d* and all of the above and then some and everybody and his brother babbling and by so babbling trying to keep their filthy hold on life—when the patient (remember him?) completely disappeared or more to the point when, in all the fracas (or so the curtains said, and who knew better than they?), the patient's moans, groans, incontinence and scraping with still-youthful fingertip on bedpan edge or inundated plastic sheet inevitably became of only incidental interest and in the overwhelming majority of cases not even that and never more so than when some hefty kissin' cousin fifteen times removed felt blood- (and-guts-) empowered to sally forth and address the death spasms (as if they were a not-yet-quite-adorable toddler just learning to hold its peace not to mention its byproducts) in a very loud voice of course inasmuch as whoever made it a practice to moan, groan and overflow must surely be hard of hearing.

But all he could think of to say was: I wanted, now that my mother-in-law is dying (no chemotherapy—however foolhardy—will save her and not so deep down she knows it as you, Pudd, must be knowing it every minute of your waking life inside the holding cell), to bring her to you for I never believed as strongly as I do at this very minute that the rigors of the ER and beyond as undergone by poor Joyce (and poor me right along with her) must constitute the key to your collective embodiment of Pudd's death-defying act of institutionalized dying (indeed, the chemicals involved are pretty much the same, even if the proportions dispensed may vary). In other words, you can bet your bottom dollar (sensing a momentary waning of interest, or compassion for his poor mom-in-law) it's only through Joyce that you'll reach Pudd and through Pudd the several hundred billion pornography-of-death addicts whose susceptibility is worth billions, at least to the media. For what is the difference, I ask you, between me hating my hatred of Joyce even among her death agonies and some anonymous member of the press gawk-annotating Pudd's final and unejaculating spasm?

Yet before I do anything so rash as to drag Joyce in here for your edification, I want to make it clear that death is not just horrific for like any nightmare worth its salt it's never without moments of high farce thanks to the industry's ever-readiness to step in at a moment's notice and ensure that the full strength of its workforce is put right smack behind the case at hand with, naturally, a view to partitioning his or her life-and-death agony into a maximum number of sequential crises all in clamoring need of some highly specific thus understandably costly sort of professional per-hour intervention. For what process of decomposition is complete without the funeral-home flunkeys, cantillating chaplains, bereavement counsellors, accountants able at a moment's notice to funnel more than ninety-five per cent of all available inherited assets into banana republic dummy conglomerates (provided the necessary letters testamentary are in order) and fly-by-night hotline therapists. And in the midst of the death industry's doing its stuff there are of course the fringe-benefit bumps and grinds of the corpse (-to-be) herself which must, however (if they are to corner the market on magisterial pathos), be viewed (as paraposthumous Pudd welded to his gurney also must) in a certain (preferably fading) light (albeit not necessarily that of a neglected old master on the order of, say, blasted birch-obsessed van Ruysdael).

I might as well tell you (what, after all, have I got to lose): her condition is growing more critical by the split second; in fact I'm a monster to be leaving her alone for so long. No, what I really want to say is that when the death house's interfaith chaplain (just as post-ER Joyce was getting all comfy-cozy on her in-patient chemo unit bolster), thrashing daintily past the IV stands (they travel in droves) to introduce herself, asked if she could intone a little prayer for the sabbath Joyce, *of all people* [as my older daughter would say, but never about her (oddly) beloved grandmother], and of all things (even if up until that very moment she'd made it a point of honor to be obstreperously intolerant of any ministrations the least bit redolent of last rites), graciously agreed though, granted, it was no Everlasting Yea. She listened patiently to the plainsong that the lady of God gently (and beautifully) coaxed into the portals of her ear and when the performance was done, to the chaplain's whispered codetta of Best wishes for a benign day of rest she responded with a simple Thank you, appending a— even more miraculous!—clearly heartfelt, hence almost heartbreaking, You too. But into the depiction of such sudden sweetness is there any wonder at my wishing to insert just a dollop, as the cookbooks say, of her old rancor, for I fear that with the ebbing of its lifeblood ebbs my own. In a word, friends, the overwhelming restraint of Thank you/You too sears unbecomingly even now—at least that's its effect on *my* deadhead vitals, especially during this, the time of day Joyce has for generations been making it her business to deprecate above all others—in a word, dusk—for, in case you haven't noticed (what with there forever being some pane-stunned plane bough or other struggling in vain to slough the shadowy second skin cast along its leprous arc by the leafier fellow upstairs—before all turns to Shadow), in this-here rehearsal studio it's always dusk.

Convinced she was reading my very thoughts as I played (badly) door guard, the chaplain assured me (once floor nurse and aide on duty had joined forces to empty the patient's bedpan and capsize the patient in tandem) this nightmare, too, must end but directly she spoke, insofar as such assurance was not in the Joyce-tradition, a flood of counterarguments came to the rescue. Were the moments with Joyce (following the centuries with Albert—you don't know Albert: Herr Flowers, come, do me a favor and *be* Albert, won't you, just for a little while?—only kidding, of course!) indeed the stuff of nightmare (after all, my duties had by now—like the sex scenes in a Hollywood blockbuster—been pretty much codified)? Or granted her dying qua muddled rectification of Al's was every inch a nightmare and then some, did this have to mean I wanted it to end insofar as the ending of the Joyce nightmare which was at least a nightmare shared with others must only reestablish the centrality of my—our—own, sharable with (our many glorious collaborative moments notwithstanding) nobody else?

What all this is leading up to is the fact that out in the world (with three livid knuckles he wiped away a tear) death just doesn't take place and never will (not even in Joyce's holding cell which, except in a few particulars, resembles Pudd's to a tee)—merely gets passed on for safekeeping and your job as artists is to play it out so when all is said and done the prime-time billions may affirm that you, Priss, and Ralph and Gift and Fritz and Annie and Gottfriedina O. Jones—that you at least and you alone truly did die (for it's only on stage that death waxes final), whether or not the script has condemned your characters to go on living and breathing. Trouble is, with all the expertise now at your fingertips I know you'll soon be leaving me far, far behind.

Priscilla, getting down on hands and knees, murmured: Don't abandon us now, Bert, when clearly we need you more than ever— more, probably, than we ever dreamed we might. We favor him, said Ralph, the way we might favor a sprained ankle or a subluxated scapula, eh, chief? But you've no desire to cast aside what you're finally beginning to recognize I'm capable of teaching, to wit, that all the volcanic doings in off-stage space are always several steps ahead of any stabs taken at their annihilation in thought. In short, thanks to me you're further along than you've any right to be—Oh Bert, I'm so glad, said Gift, coming at him this time from the direction of the fire escape.—but let's quit the gabbing, as my old pal Jimmy Cagney used to say, and assume our regular places at the barricades. You, Priss, last I heard, were atop Gift's shoulders. And Ralph, you were cavorting in a corner (any of the four will do)—as is your wont (at least since you've been among us)—my favorite in fact, for there's a sweetness about him that defies comparison. I was your favorite, insisted Gift. For it's Ralph who's always gotten us through when, for example, the lights didn't dim or the toilet flush. Clearly he's not to be ruffled, is our Ralph. Bert turned to the company at large and said: Ralph, my friends, is what very actor should be and all too rarely is: a maker of crises whose building-blocks are of the humblest—merest big-brother hand-me-downs of that great god street-life. In a word, I will always reverence Ralph and his doings whatever should become of me and my own (well do I know it won't be long—again I've heard you all whispering about the auditions you've been squeezing in between rehearsals though, believe me, I don't begrudge you your hustling or even the frantic need to flaunt its windfall—before we go our separate ways) for I've just been made to realize (thank you, Gift) that at climactic moments—when, for example, Priss was about to mount

Gift's shoulders (so he could fling her into the nearest Central Park ditch) and always found a reason not to—only Ralph managed to take full advantage of such contingencies but what do you say we let bygones be bygones and try to get on with the last rehearsal?—Yes, the Last Rehearsal, before the dark of, first, the cast party (can Joyce come at least to that?) then the premiere at Madison Square Garden, or is it Weill Recital Hall or Shea Stay, at which time assorted moguls will decide whether they want my—our—work to go prime-time or just play itself out live (to packed houses, of course): Ralph, would it be too much to ask you (the only man, obviously, for the job) to lead them in a warm-up.

Ralph, bowing, took the trembling hand of Priscilla, she resisting from a mixture of shyness and, yes, resentment, for who was he, after all, to be receiving so much press? And while all this is going on I want the rest of you to be observing Ralph from different perspectives and to report enthusiastically on what you're privileged to see. It is the sense, Bert continued, choosing to ignore Priss's sullenness, that any event, however paltry, however mediocre in itself (the more so, in fact, the better), can be viewed from an infinity of standpoints that is the key to success in our field. Such a sense must turn out to be invaluable to all of you, even those who end up in showcase vanity productions on the Gulf Coast. Gift turned to Flowers who, taking the look, big with unspoken panic, as his cue to smile knowingly, tried to catch the panicker's eye before his own (full of the cocksure promise that Gift for one need never worry about going slowly, or even rapidly, so far downhill as to end up showcasing his decline on the Gulf Coast, wherever that happened to be—not as long as Flowers had any say in the matter, that is, and he did have a say—plenty or at any rate enough, through one simple phone call to the right Canonized, to reverse the irreversible course of things) clouded calamitously back over, this time perhaps forever. There would always be a place in the theater for the Gifts of the world, if not necessarily for Gift himself, to say nothing of a place in Flowers's heart, itself a theater of incomparably vast dimension and, more to the point, perpetual audition where men and women *in good standing*, this last being sternly insisted upon in the application [available pending SASE from the Old Soldiers Never Die (Gen. Doug MacArthur) Foundation], were encouraged to come forward and face ranking and serialization for without such an assurance of winners and losers (and also runners-up to season an otherwise sodden stew) life as we know it would die out.

Gift, Bert saw, was at home in Flowers' message although Bert himself could no longer focus on Priscilla's quest for a still point on or off Gift's shoulders no matter how perfectly each ravishing posture simulated emotions she would never (so averred the posture) in a million years have dreamt she was capable of depicting, especially in front of an audience. Still erect on his shoulders which faced the bay windows facing Madison Square in all its equinoctial glory (GreenHurstWood's mother-in-law had very generously offered them the use of one of her many vacant pre-war duplexes for a small honorarium), Priscilla explained that being so poised (something urgently soblike in her tone demanded that Bert resume paying attention) vouchsafed her a particular detachment when looking at the world that was otherwise impossible at her advanced age.

As I bridge Gift's poles without toppling I am transformed into the very opposite of what, willy-nilly, I always tended to be: all of a sudden I'm forever changing and always the same. My work here, on the other hand, said Ralph while gently lifting her off Gift's wilting frame, has made me realize I've reached a point where every moment in my life is identical to every other, the disparity between any two, no matter what their contexts, being smaller than whatever quantity you might

250 / MICHAEL BRODSKY

care to adduce, and . . . and . . . and . . . Edging toward the toilet Ralph
looked around (it was almost morning: there was a breath of spring in
the air though it had snowed the night before, then rained, then
snowed again) with incomprehension, even outrage. This was clearly a
key moment since for the life of him Bert didn't know whether what
he knew had to be said (though what made him so sure) would play
itself out as Ralph's—i.e., Berlio's—predicament or somebody else's.
It would be nice—a nice surprise in a world celebrated for its unpleasant ones—if what there was still to be said could, rather than
constitute out of the blue a new beat, be given to Ralph a.k.a. Berlio.
But that's precisely why we're here: to help you go on, said Gift, massaging his left scapula as if it were a jilted sweetheart. Emerging from
the toilet with a certain matronly flurry suggesting his thoughts were
still on what hadn't managed to occur within, Flowers immediately
observed that (his flourish signified that Ralph for all he cared was
more than welcome to try his luck where better men had failed) it was
Bert who must be blamed if all moments smelled the same.

Before Bert had time to shrug away all this abuse—he sorely
missed the comfort of Belle's always welcoming, if frequently spurned,
arms—Ralph re-entered and, a bit shy, demanded to know why he'd
said it would be a thing most capital if the others were to view him
from different perspectives.

Chapter Seventeen

You are the executioner—you're Berlio but you're also the executioner—you pull the switch—so stand still (like the captain of a small fighter plane in use temporarily as a yacht) and as dourly as you know how let *the others* have their fill of watching you while they take their seats. You don't notice—you're too busy grimly making sure there are no air bubbles in the IV line to be inserted in Pudd's arm or, more probably, given that he seems to have the tanned hide of an old doper, in his groin though, strictly speaking, that is done before there are any witnesses—about forty-five minutes before the execution, to be exact. Rather, you don't notice because you're too scowlingly busy depressing the lethal button (sliding your thumb off so it recoils with a firecracker report) ensuring the flow of the drugs through the line though, again strictly speaking, there are three or four button-depressors and none know whose touch is the overdetermining one and for that matter whether it's the sodium pentothal or the pancuronium bromide or the potassium chloride delivering the coup de grâce, and all this so that somewhat later when, in another world entirely, that is, a wee bit further backstage, you're observed after signing a notarized return warrant of execution, by the witnesses being respectfully escorted from the bleachers, to be completely transformed, that is, chatting casually, almost lightheartedly, even effervescently [presumably with the doctor—that's you, Flowers—who—after getting ready to pronounce death from the EKG machine hooked up to the gurney, although our particular Kildare might have volunteered, as his kind are wont to do, for far more than just gawking at the impulses flat-lining out (for a major role, say, in elevating the groin vein)—then goes on to add just the right touch of professional illegibility to the death certificate but, then again, maybe with the gal whose job it is to lower the death chamber jalousies after the show or with the local coroner who's come for the body looking himself like death warmed over or with the kid fresh out of community college doing the fingerprinting which, with the return warrant, will prove the corpse is just whom he claims to be and nobody else or with, worst coming to worst, the deathwatch officer who, in his bid for literary immortality, was there all along Pepysizing every single stopwatch-timed micro-event and now needs to replay his grim scrupulosity]—all this, I say, so that somewhat later on said witnesses—and they call themselves men of the press!—can wallow in wonder at their lack of foresight (though who in fact could have imagined a constipated dourness of this magnitude, and in extreme close-up yet, giving way in record time to such supple long-shot conviviality) for it is precisely to have, in tandem, their own lack of foresight mercilessly exposed at every turn that our clients—consumers—spectators—customers are paying top dollar: repeated learning from their mistakes handsels a future flawless clairvoyance. But what is the value of all these . . . shifting exposures? bleated Flowers (like most ivory-tower academics he was the windiest proponent of life in the raw). This (turning to the bewildered troupe) is what you must ask him before it's too late and your careers nipped in the bud.

What's the value of all this, the old fart asks (Bert heard himself howling and didn't like the sound). For starters, how about as proof that life's every avenue is wide open to all the others (not even the smelliest pig-alley is airtight) and just as the body offers, through its infinity of orifices, an infinity of routes to self-loathing (eating, for example,ës an advertisement of private function far grosser than masturbation, and not, as is too commonly thought, good fellowship's right-hand man) thus there is nothing to confute any A's turning out to be Y as well as X, especially in those cases where X is not $\sim Y$. You must remember, my dear Flowers, that most of our watchers have never really managed to swallow the fact that, for instance, a former mediocre actor could become President (though their attorney would say it's the mediocrity itself got in the way, the masses being at heart ferociously elitist) or that Garbo's reclusiveness did indeed regularly prolapse into little walking jaunts with friends—in short, their cult of absolutely airtight categories must be smashed and its hierodules made to re-realize that, *inter alia*, Serial Killers can be charming entertainment figures hence the age of the Serial ain't dead yet. Taking a deepish breath meant to mean there are no absolutes—not even Sir Anthony Absolute is an absolute—Bert said, You must, Ralph, allow yourself to be viewed from an infinity of (unsuspected) angles because that is what our predicament (ours, mine, everybody's: those of us, that is, minded enough to be capable of predicament)—I mean our life—is all about.

If only I could manage to persuade Flowers to get (Bert was about to say *his blubbery ass*) out of the way everybody and not just Ralph would see I'm trying to make you advance-guarders in the deoxymoronification of the world—we can seep right out of our airtightness and occupy another dimension (and not only, or rather, least of all its antipode for antipodes have a way of turning out to be spittin' images) as Ralph the Executioner just did going from dour to dazzling not to mention Joyce (who'd ever have imagined transactions with bedpan Charlies and cantillating chaplains *et al* would transform that old serial killer cum cancer victim—and I'm not ashamed to go all mawkish when I think of her—into a creature of goodness for she's definitely well on her way to becoming one and everything else she never was (though postponed to her gurney spasms so she won't have to regret the repercussions of its extravagance) and it would be wrong, so very very wrong, to proclaim her shift a mere artifact of grand-scale incapacitation, as if she hadn't premeditated every station of her dying as purest expression of the will to make amends appropriate only within the frame of that dying.

So let's go back, said Priscilla. This very minute. Back to what? Bert and Flowers gaped in unintentional unison. To the beginnings, she said. I mean, of his death. Didn't you say (lying down on the cold wooden floor warped by moonbeams) the institution entitles his last moments to anything he wants. She extended her arms in welcome. Look, he wants me. Turning to Flowers only once, at most twice, Gift advanced towards Priscilla, bent over her, then moved away. Don't look at her face, Flowers cried, as Gift proceeded to put his hand across the center of her body. Why, he asked, while trying to get busy kneading her pubis. Because you'll get much too excited, you little prick, and flub your lines, that's why. But I don't have any lines: at last I'm emancipated from the bondage of lines. Exactly right, replied Priscilla, your patron (and here she was heartily supported by Dinka who, suddenly emerging from behind the bar, began gently stroking her forehead as if she had a raging fever) couldn't care less about lines, flubbed or otherwise, but he is concerned—and it's all to his credit as a theatergoer—that your surveillance might trigger (so eager to please as he suspects me to be—he's overidentified with poor Priscilla as the too-complaisant passive partner though what is active and what is passive when it's a question of cock and cunt, or a cock and a cock, or two cunts) some bald exaggeration of the throes of ecstasy. And don't throw in any of the usual obscenities, Flowers added, pretending to thumb disgustedly through (what was later revealed to be) the advance proofs of the Spanish-language edition of the present year's Best-dressed though clearly flushing with self-importance at Priscilla's compliment and as regards this business of *overidentification* maybe— who knows?—even at her unwelcome penetration. Since uttering four-letter words, said Priscilla, deriving added deductive strength from Dinka's proudly maternal gaze, will result not in the explosion of my own defiance but simply in an overanxious effort, lest I be abandoned owing to insufficient gaminess and never again called back for further service as death-row plaything, to rise obediently to the occasion of yours, warmed over as it may be. Exactly, said Flowers, and once you see she's not excited, merely anxious, you'll get (because anxiety is contagious) anxious too and angry at the anxiousness because, hell, it's your last night on this hell of an earth and you're supposed to be excited, not angry, not anxious, so anxiously angry how can you expect to play to the hilt the role you were born to play (serial killer on death row who does not repent but rather experiences gratitude for the opportunity to personify evil bracket- and exterminable at last for, let's face it, of evil is there anything more constitutive than to have tortured without mercy defenceless widowers and orphans, say, and then be able without missing a beat to stand forth positively shameless in one's peevish preoccupation—peevishness worthy of some vinyl-vested Serbian ethnic cleanser who undergoing, glass-boxed, token international-criminal-court interrogation at The Hague about having, among other things, forced one interned Muslim in his charge to chew up the testicles of another, can focus only on the little something-left-to-be-desired in the consistency of his breakfast eggs—with the fulfillment status of one's orifice needs) hence justify my ultimately presenting you to the canonized as the best possible—the only conceivable—interpreter of their most challenging future works for stage and screen. In a word, Pudd, you've got to prove you're equal to the grossest implications of my thinking about the thinking done by the families mourning the victims of evildoers (hence a fortiori of the doers' partisans for whom such families' thinking-cum-raging grief is a contemptible joke without a punchline for there will always be sons of bitches perverse enough to backstop/-slap mass murderers and their epigoni given that mankind's strongest urge is to flout the incontestable), specifically about how the infinitely patient torturer of their son or daughter may at this very moment be spreading his butt for an unimpeded shit or his thighs for a leisurely greasy fuck or his jowls for some fashionable bistro blowout, for so thinking about their thinking inevitably I wonder how they can go on living except from second to second inasmuch as to live as their likes now must enjoins the highest tolerance for the unthinkability of such phenomena and a tolerance far higher for the death and grief industries' ever-ready reproof of all this wallowing. Clearly then, Gift, I mean Pudd, you must prove no matter how heinous your crimes the main concern is still and always you yourself, to wit, the satisfaction of that self's animal urges (which is not to denigrate physiology entirely, for we all know how much better qualified we are in mind or heart to square the circle, say, or feed the homeless after a good lunch and its even better expulsion), but if you allow yourself to contract her anxiety you can kiss any credible embodiment of the peevish complacency of pure evil—evil without tears—goodbye (though there is a school of thought arguing that the closer the killer gets to total absence of remorse for his crimes the less he can be held responsible since clearly he's a moral moron).

Just out of curiosity, Bert said, is this the primal moment you were yearning for? Looking as sullen as Joyce in her worst moments— when the illness that was to be her deliverance from the dread of death refused to rear its head—Priscilla said, All I know is that I lie here, being slowly and patiently excited by Pudd, while Flowers (the prison chaplain who still hopes to chalk my trick up as one more feather in his conversionary cap), trying hard to fight off the sniffles of scopophilia, half-turns away and Dinka stands (but not idly) by with a damp rag for as one of the deathwatch team she knows only too well (we've worked together many times but it's never been so difficult: if I don't watch out I'm gonna fall madly in love) how much I loathe the smell of semen, especially when it's hot off a death-row press. So in an-swer to your question, Bert, Yes, this is, or rather that was, the moment after all hence the commercial envisaged by Samuels and GreenHurst-Wood and their team of investor specialists is now officially unleashed upon the world—without our consent, it is true.

Bert could only shake his head sadly (the originary moment in liv-ing color wasn't giving him as much pleasure as Priscilla had led him to believe it would): As my old pal Joe Schumpeter said to Green-HurstWood the day the latter had the audacity to suggest that the reins of this enterprise should be handed over to him and him alone and *tout de suite* since unlike his pimply colleague he'd been around when such commercials were in their infancy and so much more gen-erous in the divulgement of their lineaments: It is a mistake to believe that the primitive form of an institution (in our case, sexual arousal) reveals its nature *more purely and with fewer complications* than later versions. In fact, the more you develop your characters and the interrelation-ships among them the more each and every role—sexual and otherwise—will stand out more sharply which is not the case under prim-itive conditions when any given function is mixed up with a host of others. Though Priscilla in her originary moment seemed utterly ab-sorbed in her role, she was in fact preoccupied with a million and one other tasks (like getting herself utterly paralyzed with anxiety about whether or not she'd be able to rise to the occasion of Pudd's lust by matching it four-letter word for four-letter word) which will, hope-fully, in the course of (what may seem like the long years of) our working together devolve upon others—not just on other persons but other things—chairs, tables, saplings sagging beneath the weight of puffball cloud torsos, even (if worse comes to worst) airconditioner-stub shadows like the ones that each and every sunrise slue and skew the hotel front directly opposite into (or haven't you noticed?) the very snapshot of its own collapse—therefore it is hardly here and now that we can begin to understand the loverly function exercised by Prissie the death-row hooker for in these early rehearsal days she has too many other things to do, like deciding how and when to simulate gaminess in order (even if it's the state that's paying) not to be thought a killjoy by her client which deciding has, contrary to popular belief, absolutely nothing to do with the loverly element per se, so you men and women of the future don't be looking to such incunabula for the last word on How to engineer a good hard pre-execution fuck. It is only when things get far more complex, or at least more complicated, that Priscilla will be able to give way completely to her loverly function as will Gift to his shamanistic one for by then there's bound to be somebody else in the cast (dankly sprung from so much complexity) ready to shoulder, *inter alia*, the burden of anxiety about not being un-inhibited enough for Gift's—I mean, Pudd's—taste and, come to think of it, it may not have been pudency that kept Priscilla from cry-ing Shit to Pudd's Balls or Cock to his Cunt way back when but rather—but rather—but rather—fatigued preoccupation with all the other tasks she knew had, albeit infinitely less incendiary, somehow still to be gotten through.

There was a long silence then each chose to stand at the furthest imaginable distance from his starting point as in the center of a new world abounding in even newer odors, not always agreeable. They joined hands and intoned but drew back soon enough as they discovered, or so it seemed to Bert, they hated above all else to touch and be touched. Sensing he could have a full-scale revolt on his hands Bert saw no recourse but to make nice by promising his flock (if only they managed to get through this, whatever this turned out to be) the most marvellous dress-rehearsal celebration the commercial world had ever seen. You've already promised us one, said Ralph. In any case, Ralph my boy, I want to emphasize the importance of commemorating our fumbling. A week from tomorrow night, Bert announced, in a restaurant-café not far from here [take the *L* to Smithson, switch to the *F*, corner Rivington (two stops), and walk about fourteen blocks to Jack T. Ripper's] we'll be holding a little cast party since—and inasmuch as you've been trying to teach me for longer than I care to remember how you've got to be moving on (even if the rehearsal process hasn't even officially begun) to bigger and better things—since clearly you are the cast.

Is there anything particular I should be bringing, Priscilla asked? Does your wife like toilet water? eau de cologne? All kidding aside, Flowers grumbled, how are we to be showing our thanks for all you've done and, more important, have yet to do. Sounds more like vindictiveness, if you ask me, murmured Gift. Bring the proofs of the latest edition of your latest Best-dressed, Professor, said Bert, a bit surprised that Flowers regarded himself as a member of the cast and even more surprised that nobody was challenging such presumption, least of all

Bert himself. Once we're all good and drunk—including my mother-in-law—you can serenade us in a nice clear voice. The Professor sighed as if to say, These director types are more than just impossible: they're—Bert beamed, relishing (he could read the sigh) the off-chance and (he had to admit) something more than the off-chance that he was indeed impossible: after so many years of toeing everybody else's line here he was proving, at least for the moment, supremely un-budging. Places, he intoned.

All of them moved to the window, Flowers (his view of the pane obstructed by their bulky reflections therein) stepping delicately aside.

Let's go through the scene where he slowly or not so slowly meta-morphoses, before the eyes of his last victim come to bid a fond farewell, into the equivalent of what Joyce, that is, all our dying loved and hated ones, has recently become for me. [Although Bert ostenta-tiously chose to ignore him Flowers, somewhere in the shadows, went on guffawing all the same (symptom of a diminishing influence not just on the commercial but on the entire world of letters?): This skew-ing the final moments of a piece of hackwork in the direction of Joyce and other real-life bugbears will do the piece in as surely as the bug-bears—but with far more panache—did you in.] The silence of the cell—that is, Pudd's silence—is complete and you, Ralph, the victim in question (how spick-and-span), cannot help being even more pity-ing than you intended to be but it's all right since didn't we say the Prospero-like silence of the dying—however much it may constitute the merely contingent spasm of some involuntary decomposition be-yond their control (the gut tumor's having attained, say, the lungs at last) and however heinous in the course of their nine-plus lives may have been the bludgeoning articulation of their contempt (which se-rial killer cut out and burned his mother's vocal cords to ensure that no such posthumous articulations would foul a single throw at the dartboard of her severed head—was it Pudd?)—bids fair, when it comes time for delivering the final judgment on their character, to be weighted in perhaps too favorably as a vital statistic hence there's absolutely no shame in your suddenly finding yourself slobbering or half-slobbering in response thereto. And along the same lines— though come to think of it they're not (the same lines, I mean)—neither you, Priss (as house pussy who alights on the condemned, after being kept too long on ice—or fire—in preparation for just such an eventuality, to prosecute the terminal fuck whose success will enable you to beef up at last your bid for institutional tenure), nor you, Dinka [as the house evangel who—ceaselessly trolling the cell blocks for souls as he himself trolled the megamalls for cadavers—materializes in one last attempt to chalk him up as a conquest and the greatest one of all, thereby ensuring that the CV affixed to your application for the Leavenworth or Dartmoor chaplaincy truly outshines all congeners (nobody's taking a cheap shot at you, my boy: I better than anybody know what it means to have to publish or perish)], should excoriate yourself for, once within, climbing the walls of his cage and retch-recoiling from all the piss and puke.

But you first, Ralph. A.k.a. Hector Berlio, you've come, under institutional auspices, to make last-minute peace with your assaulter— not that it's easy to confront him; for one thing, the wounds he inflicted—or rather, that you allowed him to inflict—are still (and in all weathers) smarting. You see no alternative, as Pudd picks at his last meal (a veritable feast), but to post yourself at the window and though being steeped in its fog starts at once to be a real pleasure, you're uncomfortably aware—far more than you care to admit—of the chaplain's disregard (he's just come in and put his arm around you)—lean? hungry? resentful of your obtrusion on what might still turn out to be the very cream of his conversions? Nevertheless you make a point of telling yourself that he's a chaplain after all and can be beset with only the very best of intentions where you, not to mention the rest of the race, are concerned, and then again (in case you've forgotten) there's the pleasure of that fog—nothing to sneeze at under any circumstances, and almost Dutch-avuncular in its obliteration of all but the landscape's most essential features (though who's to say it's always the most essential that survive) but even the most essential can't quite quash a disquieting nostalgia for the old totalizing hodgepodge where every form is—was—flagrantly just as good as every other.

The aftertaste soothing less than promised, you turn your attention to Pudd who's pushed his plate away and is weeping copiously. You tell him you're well on your way to forgiving him and that he at least—unlike the myriad who are slated to suffer through the slowest of slow tumor-metastases which will put them at the mercy for decades of overpaid, foul-tempered health professionals and their underpaid, foul-tempered sidekicks—can look forward to a painless death. He sneers, then—a sneer not being incendiary enough— belches Who cares about forgiveness, in your face. I just can't seem to forget my rivals, that's all, even now. The chaplain (as if sniffing readiness to lay aside at last the burden of self-inflicted spiritual torment) intones: Dread of death hasn't diminished his envy of others, a common enough affliction among—Can you blame me—it's *their* hyper- and hyposexuality and asymmetrical ears and webbed feet and epicanthi and dyslexia and speckled tongues and crack-of-dawn bedwetting getting all the publicity, the author experts making the rounds of the talk shows (or don't you ever listen in?) dissecting only *their* aura and wooing and trolling and totem phases while I, just because on the surface I appear to be a fine figure of a man—and my mother wasn't an alcoholic whore and my father wasn't arm-, liver- and kidneyless— am stamped unsuitable for star-processing. [He seems, interrupted

Flowers, to be a bit like you, Bert, in your endless teeth-grinding over the fact that I will never include your productions in my canon. Touché, maestro, Bert replied, but not to his interlocutor whom he could no longer bear to look at, rather at the fog so similar (or so he desperately needed to think) to that just outside the holding cell.] By the way, this outburst is your cue as chaplain, Dinka, to say something along the lines of, Pudd, my dear boy, you must scuttle the delusion that a life unscaffolded by the euphorias you ascribe to your rivals is a life unlivable. You have much to be thankful for, my son, and if you will only sign this decision card attesting to the warden and his cronies your last-minute willingness to be saved we can all go about our business with a lighter heart (Pudd slaps it out of your hand).

Pudd lying down on his bed as if it's the springs of the gurney he's testing refuses (superfluously, since his gesture's said it all) with an almost imperceptible headshake: He won't be the agent of this goddamn man of God's preferment. Stretching towards what looks like a steel night-table—which does not quite abut on the wire mesh separating him from the deathwatch officer (Fritz Langley—look alive, Fritz) nodding off at his typewriter while the telephone's rings go unanswered—he lifts a toothbrush back over his head, its slack bristles dewy, and extends it towards Berlio (nothing more exhilarating than the hard-won discard of some object—be it ballpoint pen, pot of elderberry jam or jockstrap—worn legitimately down to the bone) then raises his arms interrogatively in sign of being permanently stumped by the absurdity, maybe even the stupidity, of it all only to drop them like crutches (think you can manage the sequence, Gift?) immediately after in order to be able to get on with the far more important business of scraping the plastic counterpane with the nails—more like hangnails—of both middle fingers. (Just like Joyce, eh, Bert, remarked Flowers, during several of her last moments.) Don't get me wrong, Pudd continues, sometimes I want desperately to be nothing more than a statistic: after all, how similar, when you get right down to it is everything to everything else and even if vastly different, how easily, once we finally get it embodied, or rather disincarnated, in a particular train of thought to move past that jumping-off place into the most undreamed-of diametrical constructions, the moral of the tall story being that it never matters where, when or how our thought-packet odyssey begins: we always can manage to end up where we've deluded ourselves into believing we least want to be; and anyway, do you really think I would permit my knight-aberrancies to be paraded before those studio audiences (who look like they came out of a crackerjack box) just for the sake of hearing myself talked about? No, sir [rising slightly: Tell me this, chaplain (flicker of CV-related hope on the latter's face), Have ambulance and hearse arrived at the sally port?; chaplain (flicker gone, dewlaps completely deflated): Haven't got the faintest idea], the sole purpose of merciless analysis of such aberrancies whether by me or some proxy self-styled expert— one that avoids, of course, all extenuations and looks every painful contradiction full in the face—is not to rummage in the bowel of ap- petites that are all, drearily, always the same but rather to perforate the very membrane of thought so as to disrupt its normal processes of self-replication and reprogram the code determining the shapes of products' linkage, and foment thereby a glorious revolution *beyond*— after so much bedwetter's-laundering-in-public-type overinvestment *in*—content (smut-and-dreck depiction) though, needless to say, rev- olution, glorious or otherwise, doesn't always erupt.

What are you supposed to be depicting, lying there? asks the chap- lain who's lost all patience with this poseur (the SOB may very well succeed in snarling any further career progress). My death, Pudd replies, or rather, the cash-value, so to speak, of its nearness. You ain't in execution mode yet: this is just the holding cell—so hold your horses. Or rather (you, Gift, as Pudd can't resist), my four horsemen of the apocalypse. I don't need the sodium pentothal and the EKG and the IV line about to be set by some clown and the about-to-be-raised blinds to hit me right between the eyes with the fact I've had a life but it's just about over and, more to the point, that having undergone it I'm entitled and then some to my very own take on what it's turned out to be and on what counts in it and what doesn't and on what's sham in it and what isn't (*it* of course now being not just my life but Life itself), in other words, I no longer need the talk-show gurus (you on the other hand, thanks to me, are about to become the most illustrious of the current slew) to guide me towards perdition: I can find my way on my very own thank you very much.

Then you're doing okay, says chaplain Dinka (Bert: Get a little closer to the mesh, dollface), forever looking on the brightish side. Yeah, sure, I'm doing okay, Pudd counters with a savage derisiveness yet just as suddenly his features are achieving a radiance the chaplain (though he professes to be forever on the lookout for mortal beauty, even amid the flotsam of his own sex) could never have predicted and you, Pudd, being inexplicably moved by his confusion, feel obliged (no use telling yourself he's far better off in a thousand different ways than you'll ever be—a fatcat, what—and, what's more, inherently—by self-definition—unworthy of your pity) to reorient him by admitting *Yeah, sure, I'm doing okay* was uttered in imitation of and extemporaneous homage to none other than your old mom-in-law, I mean, your old mom, Joyce T. Pudd, for on the day you arrived (late) to take her home from the clinic after a five-week stay for shigellosis (accompanied by a part-time Medicare aide who after just ten minutes with the patient already looked seasick-wobbly) which was also the day chosen (dreading as you did that she might very well take it into that anarchic old poll

of hers to provoke said aide to quit and visit upon you thereby sole responsibility for her upkeep, an honor of which you felt insufficiently
worthy especially now what with so many swansonglike serial kills to
architect still but, qua full-time civil servant, so little spare time) to
bludgeon her to death, excise her vocal cords and flush them down
the toilet, and make (in the tub-in-kitchen-type kitchen) a dartboard
of her trunkless head—on that day of all days and with so many
things in the works already you nonetheless managed to interpolate
(being superefficient) a thought to the effect that, having squandered
various and sundry lifetimes including her own elaborating nasty tri-
als (not unlike the one you, aideless, were surely about to undergo) for
coffles of husband-slaves and lover-pimps as well as miscellaneous
tumbrelsful of fractional siblings, she was without a doubt (all viriles-
cent moans and groans notwithstanding) doing triple-A-okay to
which she then replied, *Yeah, sure, I'm doing okay, Yeah, sure, I'm doing okay,*
Yeah, sure, I'm doing okay, but this time, and only this time, her reply was
a reply startlingly—nay, rendingly—quizzically—resigned, and sat-
urated with a lambent irony that echoed back, in order that a goat-
song sadness might magically transfigure, every single tone (and every
half- and quarter- too) along the diapason of your own (hey, let's face
it, man, you know and I know the inoperable tumor was in its last
stages and had already sent its most belligerent envoys to every vital
organ on her map so how A-okay could the old girl really have been,
unless you believed, as I sometimes am still guilty of believing, that is,
where my not-quite-on-the-verge-of-being-beloved Joyce is concerned, that the tumor was but another one of her ploys hence re-
sorbable at a moment's notice) and, what's more, it was denuded—
this reply was—of any of her hallmark signs of having begun to
hoard-chew the cud of an unforgiving, unforgetting, to-be-com-
pounded-hourly rancor and so I ask you, Pudd—or rather, you, Pudd

(get ready for action, Gifty), ask him, the chaplain (with one wall-eye glued to the execution officer it's obvious he's terrified of what that worthy might decide to type out regarding your last encounter)—if it's any wonder that such a reply—a reply to end all replies—should induce far more than a merest millisecond of token remorse, should in fact compel you to utter the very same words in the very same tone and with the very same economy the minute some provocation even marginally reminiscent of your unfilial own manages to rear its ugly head.

To prove he's been listening intently, the chaplain, without conviction, mutters, Don't, Pudd, be always waiting to commit the next *wrong*—the next unfilial—act and don't underestimate your strong sense of grief, not just for the dear departed Joyce T. but for a whole slew of victims to which Pudd brightly replies—almost too brightly, for after all he should respectfully be making ready to meet his maker—There ain't much time left for many more wrong acts, let alone underestimated grief, is there, reverend? but the reverend chaplain hasn't heard: he's pacing nervously (Dinka: paces, please!), afraid that several counts against him of obtuseness will be entered into the official record compliments of the flunkey behind the mesh whose unflagging zeal may be just pretending to doze. In fact he's experiencing an uncomfortable urge to hit his charge—Pudd: the about-to-be-sacrificed—but gritting his teeth and scrawny buttocks he can much to his surprise still invoke the holy spectre of what the human resources pod-folk refer to as *career development* (not to mention his pension and dental plan as well as the other laughables that are excruciatingly irrelevant in the large yet so damn important in the small for life after all is lived only in the small even throughout those drunken protestations of inextinguishable fidelity to such large claims of the ideal as seem to do the small to death) and thus begin to take several broad

strides forward in the spiritual plane even if turning round to recon-
front his client what should he discover but that suddenly it's a battle-
royal in the Old West yet again, this time over the burning question
who'll be the first one compelled (as in some law office, meatpacking
plant, nurses' station or teachers' lunchroom) by so miasmic a silence
as was now their microclimate to lay the phatic pellet required to dispel it.

As you are being led away for your final ablutions (Berlio—maybe
now he'll be able to finish that A minor allegro!—will wait until you
return: there's still so much to squeeze into the minutes remaining),
the chaplain feels obliged, over the murmurs of the deathwatch officer (you'll be doubling, Priss, as chaperone & towel boy), to urge
against underestimating the extent of your grief, my son. Why, you
wonder: does he really believe, and at this late date, that with the slap-
dashest of moral rubdowns he can still get you to cotton to the
prospect of a formal (i.e., a feather-in-*his* cap-type) conversion?

In the shower room, the attendant (dearest Priss, we haven't forgotten), while nonchalantly slapping a towel against his collops, tells
you he's just had it and from none other than the warden's top screw
that everybody's favorite man of the cloth won't be visiting you again
between now and sign-off (he was seen backing his Volvo out of the
parking lot not five minutes ago). Before you can ask why (not that
you had any intention of abasing yourself thus) he explains it's because
as far as the chaplain's concerned in deliberately rejecting an incomparable experience which would at the same time have been singularly
advantageous to both convert and converter [though not—as is all
too commonly (and ignobly) thought, more so to one than to the
other] you've proved yourself the worst sort of loser. However much
sorely tempted to suggest it's rather because you've dared to challenge
the very concept of conversion, you force yourself to go on merely lis-

tening, better yet, striving to italicize that listening's complete absence of rancor, for who knows what hidden cameras may at this very moment be preparing a semi-perishable document of your last moments for the edification of every similarly fated eight ball slated to come after. All the same as you begin to strip you can't help noting if only for the benefit of your attendant friend (who looks as if he'd like nothing better at this moment than to strip down to his short hairs right along with you) that men of the cloth bear an uncanny resemblance to airwave headshrinkers: they begin to favor the patient (or, as he's more commonly called nowadays, the client) only when what they perceive to be his affliction allows them to blazon forth in all the prepackaged glory of its expertise their particular specialty of the house—the rehabilitation house of cards, that is—but if his misfortune has the even greater misfortune of not falling within their puny purview—c'mon, Gift, what are you waiting for: strip!—then they proceed at once to dismiss him as incurable. You are aware the attendant is looking at your body with a revulsion unmitigated even by morbid curiosity and though you heartily regret not having made the most of the gym in cell block *i* all these dreary months of waiting for the end no amount of revulsion, however much you yourself may support it, is going to prevent you from concluding thus (so that everything remains crystal clear for your epigoni among whom you suddenly number him): In short, the client realizes his affliction can't get any more unforgivable not because he as the afflicted happens, say, to have served up his shredded next-door neighbor *alla parmigiana* to some giant crawlspace rat but rather and far more direly because it doesn't fit the specifications of what they—the giant crawlspace rats of mind-ministering—have been trained to identify as treatable.

The attendant begins to yawn (good, Priss): he went to bed much too late following the Tuesday night gin rummy game in the screws' quarters. In addition, there was that little matter of the hard-core videos marathon to take everybody's mind off *the other execution* but surely Pudd already knows all about it and the fact that he and his (defunct) predecessor of the night before are slated to constitute the first same-week—same-month—same-quarter double-header in the prison's history. You assure him you're not in the least offended (blushing and cringing notwithstanding).

He escorts you back to your cage and something in his lope [a cross between Mitchum's (unfazed) and Fonda's (pondering)] tells you that it's time to get ready. From the only window in the skywalk connecting cell block *e* with cell block *i* you can just about make out an airplane's tail which at first you mistake for a crescent moon, worse, a crescent cloud, worst, a mustard-colored tug trimmed with blue, only you don't understand why it, whatever *it* was, shouldn't have stayed framed until you gave the signal for dismissal. Once back in the holding cell the attendant, adopting both the tone and manner of the chaplain (while pointedly disregarding Berlio who's waited faithfully—could be he's finally started sketching his soon-to-be-legendary A minor allegro in two-four time), takes up where your skywalk exasperation left off by saying (he makes sure, however, to keep the towel he provided you with at a distance: you've thrown it across a chair and it looks blood- and pus-drenched), Don't despair over not having managed the whole of that body, whether crescent, cab or plane, up there in the big sky. Take everything that comes your way dismembered—especially now, en route to the gallows—as a blessing. But, you pout (and you're even more hideous than usual doing so), the tug—I mean the cloud—I mean, the plane—is only a shard, a part-tug, right down to its mustard-colored vents. I have a right (you stamp your foot like Rumpelstiltskin) to see things whole for once, before I die. There is no such thing as a partial object, the attendant replies, and Berlio (for your own good or because it strikes a familiar chord, having little or nothing to do with you but everything to do with his art) semi-concurs with something to the effect that, rather, in your privileged threshold state any thing lucky enough to cross your gaze should be permitted to fuse with the desperation or the rage or the calm or whatever the gazes of the near-dead are supposed to portray so as to be transformed into its own one-man band of wholeness.

Why, at this stage of the game, still insist on laboring under all the misconceptions of what such things must look like if they're to enter into their own majority—they have no look worth a damn until we transform them, anyway. The tug's rear-end, the plane's tail or, for that matter, a horse's head stalled at the curb and, from your momentary worst seat in the house behind a protruding Mack, rid at last of all attachments including driver, driver's whip and load of fat-assed passengers rabid for a lark and from out of town to boot—these are not parts but wholes-to-come and as such demand savoring in all their novelty constituting as it does an altogether bracing attack on the sort of prefab wholeness that not only no longer applies but actively suffocates. (Take it from somebody not quite back from the dead.) The way matters stand, notes the attendant (who, in taking up Berlio's slack, cautiously lifts the towel and secretes it somewhere in the vicinity of his inner vest), only the plane's tail end, say, or the tip of that damn beast's inspanned skull steaming just above the puddly asphalt's yellow about to go red then green has something in common with—I won't call it your plight (too self-serving)—your status, then, and hence an impossible thing or two to teach [for you've still got a(n impossible) thing or two to learn] about bearing that status with manly dignity for never forget at this point (and perhaps at every point) of the careering you've dared to call your career you yourself are little more than the butt-end—the stump—of your own incarnation, its only

real core and substance being, I might add (but I won't out of respect
for the almost-dead), already buried with and among your victims (especially mom—she of the brown Betty and creamy hot cocoa with
marshmallows), but most of all be grateful that the aforementioned
impossible thing or two these deadhead snippets (compliments of the
institution's central casting department)—whether of planes or
clouds or horse heads or horsehair sofas—have to teach about dignity,
manly or mannish, *is* impossible for to end up being at home and at
peace would be to stand traitor to your own unassailable conviction
that unrightable amputation leaves no time (or place) for home and
for peace But in *seeming to crave* such blessedly unattainable dignity,
you're, like all the psychodespots for whom humanity conceives an infatuation, having your cake and eating it too: clearly you're not a traitor to amputation since—precisely through incessant warring of your
conviction that everything's nothing but a procession of rutted torsos
left to mummify beneath the sun with some equally incessant Lurianic
craving to revitalize and restore those torsos to hale-and-hearty mint
condition as museum-public as a frog—hell! you yourself are the very
embodiment thereof.

Small wonder, then, Pudd, what with all this polemic being forced
down your throat, you find yourself admitting [it's also—doubtless
primarily—a roundabout way of revisiting the scenes of your
youth—of proving (most of all to yourself) somewhere down the
road you've had one] that in fact an old buddy of yours from, of all
places (since you've no recollection of ever having set foot therein except maybe for a long weekend of corporate flunkey-related drudgery
ages and ages ago—in any case, long after the buddy in question was
no more), Chicago's South Side—come to think of it, the oldest
buddy of all (Leo Strauss by name, late of denazified Heidelberg)—had
had you pegged right from the start along quite the same lines for, in

some arcane XXX-rated video (one of many) leeringly entitled *Natural Right and the Distinction between Facts and Values*, he pointed out—or rather directed Shanghai Lily, the opuscule's ill-fated but fun-loving heroine and your favorite alter ego, to point out but to her pimp/stepfather (though every member of the South Side's raincoat and brown-paper-bag brigade knew it was you she was fingering), and virtually only seconds before with a thrust of his prick he silenced her forever—that you—or rather, he—was just the sort of gangland butcher who, knowing instinctively that for its driving force the world of amputations demanded an amputated individual, could never settle—and much to your grotesque credit, you've never done so—for the paunchy elaboration of a Serial Kill ethics-cum-amputator apologia insofar as, ethically soothing and apologetically suturing, it'd only disqualify him as such. If seriatum amputation was to be your—or rather, his—raison d'être then (thus Leo's Lil) as artisan of the truest raison d'être ever to draw blood said butcher had to be amputated himself, i.e., forever hankering after an impossible reconstitution and rehabilitation (R & R) of his victims well before they became his—or anybody's—victims. So if—so sententious Leo went on to say or rather so proxy-mad Leo had *his* alter ego, namely Cyberpenile Pete, Shanghai's lanky lover, go on to say, in the very same video, this time about one Poppy Knish, Waltz King of the Underworld and a but thinly disguised version of Leo's oldest buddy, Maxie C. C. Weber (C for Charismatik)—he, Poppy, was to go on living his truth among gashed amputations current and prospective and remain vindicated in the certainty that there was and would always be nothing but amputations then he simply had to start with himself and stay permanently haunted and taunted—i.e., amputated—by a Petipa-style vision scene of a world unattainable rid once and for all of such abominations and, more to the point, of the craving to visit them on the heartbreakingly unsuspecting, the salvo of course being that any on-the-sly exaltation of the aforementioned certainty into a tension-free work ethic was out of the question since the success of the enterprise must only prove that (*a*) the envisioned world—stumpless and un-gashed—was indeed attainable (inasmuch as it had just been attained, deep within the newly tensionless thus stump- and gashless soul of one P. Knish, hot new ethics-cum-apologia maker) hence (*b*) the condition crucial for the prosecution of his holy calling (amputation), namely that the sole medium (amputatedness) hospitable thereto be a *universal* one, was, through the intervention of so elegant a counterexample, now and forever unfulfillable.

So, concludes the attendant, always eager to graft the strong arm of an employer-related puff onto the stump of an utterance, Be bloody grateful for institutional coigns that manage to serve up only the amputation of things (e.g., fighter planes) as they are: after all, you're an amputee and it's never too late to start getting used to living life among your own kind. However, being used to salesmen you, Pudd, can quickly rejoin, But I've just been explaining how, via Euclid's elements, my old pal Leo was able to prove that by not acknowledging the loss of the whole and not pining after it we—I—lose something far more valuable than manly dignity [whose cultivation is contraindicated, anyway, for those who wish to live out their (homicidal) truth to the bitter end]. Too great eagerness, Pudd goes on (as if the attendant was no longer to be seen or heard for love or money), to achieve a status, any status, even if it must be the status of amputee, and to take one's place in the world at last thereby, causes the sidestepping of that whole slew of sweaty exertions required to deduce wholes from parts—not, however, to resurrect the wholes in question but rather so that the parts may suddenly find themselves glorified from having to perform *the work of the unresurrectable* (a.k.a. poetry). Consequently, if through some mishap one is onused with dismemberments, as I have just been, and on my way back from the shower, no less, and on my way to the gurney, no less—then isn't it true (attendant stopples his ears and drops the towel in the process though maybe he'd have dropped it anyway) that only by striving to be more than the part I'm condemned to remain no matter how hard I strive, in or out of the death chamber which stinks a little of my stomach's posthumous contents, do I begin to become whole? So, Pudd chuckles in spite of himself (do you know how to chuckle, Gift—it's harder than whistling!), it's you who don't understand, Mr. Attendant-in-Waiting, but at least you have the courage (unlike most of your co-workers and all of your superiors) to come forward with the ugliest secret (far more damning than, say, a lingering preoccupation with the repercussions of a successful or, better yet, an only semi-successful shit, or the smuggish well-being triggered by anticipation of all the greenbacks to be embezzled from a nurturing employer or, better yet, shovelled one's way hot upon the death of a not-so- or, better yet, dearly beloved) anybody at this point in time can divulge, namely lack of understanding, for with technology so rationalized and with its every conceivable tool at our fingertips, there just isn't any excuse for such a lack, certainly not slowness—why, slowness is a thing of the past thanks to the aforementioned muniments—which leaves as the culprit sheer perverseness.

With a look that you, Pudd, interpret as meaning, Go easy on your executioners; they know not what they do, Berlio begins to gather his composing utensils (notebook, calligrapher's ink, etc.) together in sign that he'd like to leave but wouldn't dream of doing so without his host's blessing. Pudd sees but something perverse—something . . . murderous—makes him go on pretending not to. He wants what the man he's maimed, perhaps permanently (and who still suffers from nausea, vertigo, hematuria), cannot give—what no man can give. Berlio is looking more and more afraid to tamper with the silence but finally he goes ahead and breaks it with a remark, aimed more off the attendant (who also looks as if he'd like to flee but doesn't quite know why, or how) than directly at Pudd: I'm proud of you. Most people— I, for example, until you had the decency to try to do me in (or, using your term, to *partialize* me)—make no effort to see themselves in the only correct way, namely, as a fertile ground for exposure of delusion and wet dream, the traits on which they mistakenly believe their very uniqueness rests being a (secondhand) furniture largely expendable except as (firsthand) fodder for such a project the details of which I must confess to not having quite worked out, but much more of that anon (in my A minor allegro, to be exact).—After I'm dead, you mean, Pudd says, with, surprising (most of all to himself) full-fledged belly-laugh éclat—Few, unlike you, Pudd, have the capacity to rejoice in flaws, contradiction, inconsistencies, blundering double- and crosstalk, and assorted hot air balloons, reacting thereto not as the sacred occasion for pride, but rather as they might to some Petri dish chock full of the putrefactions through whose treated analysis self-understanding may emerge at last. How do you know he's done all this, asks Priss the attendant (a bit jealous?) to which Berlio equably replies: As I sat here waiting for Mr. Pudd to return from the showers, feeling (taking a few stabs at writing my allegro) I too was on my deathbed (something about the way light refuses to percolate through his last cage's rustproof bars) and hence having no choice but to literally jump out of my skin and titrate all I needed to think I was against all I in fact knew myself to be, suddenly it became clear what all along he must have been doing to get so self-savvy [by the way, like him I never—well, almost never—make the fatal mistake of confusing contempt for the uncovered symptoms as conveniently imputed to this or that unsuspecting other with proof of their non-existence within therefore when, out for a moonless stroll, I happen to come across a man (A) feeling, in the presence of his lady friend, compelled to write off some passing stranger (B) as a *fag pure and simple* I am at once alerted to the fact that heterosexuality A is under siege even if the lady in question now feels justified in breathing a sigh of relief (at its complete absence of tentativeness)].

The attendant has moved close to the door but with another remark, more brutal this time (behind the screen the typing's louder than ever)—to the effect that Pudd and his moll (meaning the artistically oriented Hector Berlio) are the ones who don't and (what a pity) never will understand—it's clear he intends to go out (like a terminal cancer victim) Parthian-shooting his weary way to freedom. In the wake of so much effort to explain it's hard, Pudd, to listen to his denunciations (as long ago you listened to his yawns) without jumping anew to the conclusion that *there's no point in going on*, especially regrettable now insofar as going on would appear to encompass nothing less than participation in the completion (and, right here in the can, maybe even the premiere) of the Berlio allegro, but to your not entirely delighted surprise you listen without the usual panicky foregone conclusion. You listen for once as if the fate being outlined is to be visited upon (or rather—or rather—or rather—as if its blatant untruth must be shouldered by) somebody else, probably Berlio, maybe because all you can think about at present is what you think you're hearing in the courtyard below: an arched leaf's expert mimicry, in somersaulting over the grassless turf, of a large-sized pebble rolling down an incline of its fellows, and what you think you're—but can't possibly be—seeing, to wit, honey locust fronds not quite eclipsing a newt-head's unaccountable (it's broadest daylight) kilowattage.

Before he skedaddles you manage to stand your ground and tell him he's lying through his teeth: it's clear even—especially—to a condemned man that he doesn't believe one word of what he's been saying about objects, partial or otherwise, and the other keepers are just as devious. That your combativeness has increased Berlio's nervousness is signalled by a low cough (though maybe this too is but an aftereffect of the maiming and has nothing to do with present circumstances). So what, says the attendant (already swaying himself silly in the hammock of a phlegmy guffaw stitched together with, doubtless, all the exhilaration borne of certainty that he for one may depart any time he likes whereas you . . . you . . .), if we ignore the discrepancy between what we say and what we know—sometimes the lure of the word must take precedence over anything we might think we believed, that is, felt obliged to believe. If we restricted ourselves to saying, even out of respect for the near-departed, only what we believed we believed, what deprivation. Fact is, certain words in certain never-to-be-repeated combinations, whether we believe what they have to say or not, are things—sometimes, with (as you see me now) inmate's piss-, spit-, blood- and semen-stained towel between my legs, I get to thinking about how maybe they're the only things but that could just be the body fluids talking—and it's blubbering fear of those things' oozing away before being summoned forth as witnesses to the blessed event of our rehabilitation or resurrection or whatever it's called when the self-hate stops for good (that's right, self-hate—you heard correctly the first time: we attendants also have our demons so stop trying to steal the show) makes us go on uttering every chance we get especially when the chance, fat or otherwise, is completely unwarranted by *context*, that ur-hobgoblin of little minds. I ask you why, then, Perlio, or is it Merlio, we should deprive ourselves when we've only one life. Berlio nudges him as if to suggest it might be just a wee bit indiscreet to bring up the matter of life with you, Pudd, about to end yours but the stage-whisper makes you wonder whether, allegro notwithstanding, his forgiveness isn't one more self-aggrandizement in a life consecrated to nothing but.

Pudd, you can't help feeling Berlio speaks without conviction: the sweet talk's an exit line masking impatience to be gone [after all, he's got what he came for, whatever that happens to be: inspiration via institutional exotica (the rarest kind)? delectation over his maimer's long drawn out hence all-the-more-excruciated comeuppance?]. In fact the air (as if his very lips were kid-gloved) starts to simmer with We simply must get together or some such pap only now, appearing (aghast) to remember where he is and why, the words stop themselves just in time though somehow you'd be more than willing to bet stopping's part— the beauty part—of a whole routine. Small wonder, then, that incensed by your ex-victim's self-interest—a self-interest you didn't want to see under the crust of so much musicality—your only recourse (before you reward yourself for the last time on this earth with a final planned piss) is to rectify the failed murder [spurring your renewed sense of mission is what up until now was perceived to be—almost bypassed as—a detail too irrelevant for revulsion, namely that pimple in the hollow of his cheek rhyming not wisely but too well with the spider naevus exactly at the spot on his chin where any other self-respecting titan would have managed a cleft: somehow a fact so atomic takes (the pimple-naevus axis at all cost needs to be smashed) the bevelled edge off whatever overwhelming sense of arbitrariness—gratuitousness—superfluousness remains after having infected your first try], that is, if you can lure the bastard back over the threshold. You advance: he fidgets! not realizing fidgeting's incompatible with his professed motive in visiting which was to concentrate hard on forgiving, forgetting and holding your hand en route to the gurney. As you make like Byron's Assyrian he turns away but clearly doesn't deem such fluttering inattention to have been at all incompatible with, look! this sudden eruption of a gaze (Ralph: gaze!) ravenous in its solicitude. Like most people—and for all the unfinished symphonic allegro-mongering, your victim *is* like most people—he's as forgetful as they come when they come, that is, when it comes, to draining the boils of his own inconsistency though on the operating table of being he'd doubtless lance anybody else's (and sans anesthetic) without blinking an eye. You, on the other hand (unlike most people), spend your time forever weighing the possibility of indulgence in any act against the inevitable scandal of having to someday perpetrate one or more of its myriad inverses, with all of which it's of course ethic- hence aesthetically incompatible, so is it any wonder you've ended up abstaining from everything except murder, the sole act without an inverse; indeed, there's been absolutely no hesitation about twisting the knife or pulling the trigger or tightening the extension cord. Berlio, however, clearly is not one to ignominize self-contradiction: he can make a mad dash for the exit and a minute later simulate (though more than ready to swear on nothing less than the life of his allegro that he means it) sincerest regret at having to abandon you to your bitter end (in fact he's already done so) so to hell with him (in any event there's that ultimate piss to prepare for mentally) only you just can't seem to forget, now that rhyming pimple with naevus suggests you may be able to achieve his murder at last and achieve it as a necessary act no less, how much he must matter as a rival for what would life be without rivals and not just in the serial kill domain. A rival's, you're suddenly aware as you look at Berlio—your arch-rival, in fact (Gift, give him a look—a real look; and you, Ralph, made like your being looked at)—somebody authorized to inform you (in other words hell-bent on doing so) that your persistent failure, a.k.a. your being, consists in having never, from sheer perversity and *so you've only yourself to blame*, executed plans the rewardable way.

281 / CHAPTER SEVENTEEN

Yet Berlio, very much over the threshold, 's already managing (scotfree) to get on about his business of achieving wealth and fame at your expense, over your dead body to be exact, for isn't it said body's mania that is responsible for whatever's noteworthy in his production values—this rival, this allegro grinder, this Berlio, is now irretrievably post-threshold (what's more the attendant, knowing from vast experience how eruptive death-rowers tend to become in their last moments, is on the qui vive) thus clearly well on his way to safety among the cheery shadows of the corridors' main artery while you . . . you must prepare to meet the eternal gurney-maker. Still, you immediately decide to wish him the heartiest godspeed.

To your surprise the chaplain (Dinka!) is back and though Berlio is gone (being allowed to lick his chops over your doom has obviously been good for the business of laying out the allegro's final movement, a theme and variations), the attendant remains. Even more surprising, the former's singing your praises to beat the band, assuring you you've always managed to pick the right victim and so on and so forth although the praise quickly begins to sound spewed like bile. Attempting to drive them into a corner (if you can't kill Berlio why, they'll just have to do) as if to advance were to meet their dares head-on, you're reminded of all the other humiliating encounters that have had their fifteen minutes of non-fame in this cell—by the way, is the chaplain (whose failures are more yours than his own) still going to try to work his conversionary spell and finally get you chalked up to his credit side?—yet in spite of, or rather—or rather—or rather—because of those encounters there's almost too much matter here for exhilaration (that old time-Peircean *occurrence of more individual events than ever can occur*) if not quite gratitude; for one thing they'll never come again at least during your current life cycle [Ma Gurney, here, stands (stalwartly) in for the fatalities of old age—the very fatalities that caused, in other words, permitted, Mama Pudd to at last begin losing all interest in *her* encounters]: That there'll be absolutely no revisitings during these, your last moments' formative years, of encounters recent or remote (they just ain't localizable as a site for this or that recycled wrinkle of self-emendation) means no more tortured thinking about the far too many better substitutes that might have caulked their slot [but so what and who cares—you certainly don't—if it's thanks to these very placeholders in all the perfection of their imperfect courage to be placeholders that you're being allowed, in a madly accelerated rest of your life, to toy with such regrets here and now and for all the world as brandishingly as an express bus charging the Grand Concourse (Yankee Stadium presides instantaneously over its steepest ghats) in duskiest dead of winter].

With attendant and chaplain looming huddled hence far too massive to overtake, you flee to the window towards the sound of leaves (they either bray like gulls or squawk like pigs) and when you turn around it's the warden himself, unepauleted and unshakoed, standing before you. He says (Flowers, get busy—no way out: admit it, your ham's been coveting the role from the word go)—a bit too stingingly, however, for your taste, at least for your taste of the moment (after all, you're about to die)—Look how much at ease you seem to be here in your very own little cubicle; 's that your assistant over there (pointing to the deathwatch officer nodding off but not quite)? hahaha: who would ever have thought you'd turn at last into that bugbear of all Serials: an exemplary prisoner. (You know that, without seeing without even hearing, the other two are guffawing.) In fact I could never, you murmur, aware how self-defense immediately serves to put you ever more weakly on the defensive, be less at home than I am now [though the deathwatch officer's nod (nod, Fritz) is of course to be commended for working extra hard even at this late date to simulate soggiest welcome]. It's just that fully aware of how little time remains (more than suggested by, for example, your sudden presence here) I'm trying to savor this, the very last look from my window. Your kind after all can go on for ever and ever savoring such perspectives but I . . . I . . . Don't you see (out of the blue), the warden starts fuming (no sweat, Flowers: fuming's one of your specialties), nobody wants to suffer through your last-minute visions (mock-reproachful glance at the still-guffawing duo)—all a not-so-veiled plea for the stay that will never come. In short I've no choice but to demand that your scaffold arioso (who do you think you are anyway, Gaetano's Fulla Bolena?) be cut and cut severely since it now must be obvious that a fate like yours is plausible—is *real*—only when another is scat-singing its blazes, that is to say, only when some beefy ex-star athlete's smile (as big as the Ritz) gets busy naturalizing it over the ll PM news.

You turn away from the warden as if he's a blind window giving on a blind alley to lie down on your cot as if it's the fateful gurney, wishing the warden would have the decency to dim the lights (after all, the filming of your promised end is about to begin).

As if reading your thought the chaplain (though looking at the towel boy) says, The work's failure is because you refused to immerse yourself in construction. You, Pudd, ask, What work do you mean, father (*father*'s a classic Warners Brothers touch)—work of murder? On the last phrase he manages (how?) to give the impression of turning, though in fact he's been looking at him for well over five minutes, expressly to the attendant to procure a sharer in, or better yet an (awestruck) witness of, sadly pitying laughter. The attendant does laugh but too late to convey unison. You regret, as always, not having followed your first instinct which was to remain silent but being, also as always, a fast learner—a professional apprentice as it were—you manage to pre-empt the silence now supervening and make it, through an elixir all its—all your—own, convey the next question (maybe just a variant of the one before), namely, What's construction got to do with it. A wiliness of construction, the chaplain impatiently corrects, but such wiliness is not for one who has—or thinks he has—far too much to express and far too little time to express it. That one's elements are far too incendiary to be presented outright hence each must become its own camouflage and with so much camouflage already at work in the world of the work it's evident there's indeed far too little time for the artifice that should govern the work as a whole (with such a one in charge, the work as a whole is left, alas, to its own bared devices). In short, your sort of cunning is active only just so long as it can collude with things overwhelming out in the world—things that must be forever infiltrating the work or else the work—I'm talking about *the work of presenting yourself as an exemplary prisoner*—will be found flagrantly . . . lacking. Instead of acquiring just a few simple, relevant elements and arranging them in such a manner as to simulate exemplariness—specifically, conversion to the prison faith just in the nick of time—you refuse to set any limit to your acquisitions and, what's worse, each, no matter how alien to the situation at hand, manages to get yoked only the situation itself—to wit, conversion—has disappeared in the process or rather been replaced by the far more authentic, albeit much less interesting, avowal of non-conversion.

You never succeeded, then, during all the time I tried to convert you in exercising sufficient foxiness to fool me—your reader, so to speak—into believing I'd done so (your triumphant simulation, don't you see, would have redounded to *my* credit and, constituting the most dazzling entry on my CV, would surely have landed me that coveted post at Leavenworth). Therefore I won't be able to *report* your conversion scene the way some hematologist-oncologist, say, with an afflictee

(truculent but feisty) boasting not one but two rare tumors and—
beat this!—each deemed hitherto absolutely impossible of cohabita-
tion with the other in a single corpus, might get to expound upon
such a prodigy in the appropriate peers-only-type rag.

The chaplain and the attendant laugh. Why, you wonder, do such
types come, like undescended testicles, in pairs? For a moment, forgetting you're not free to come and go, you think of storming out and letting this act constitute, according to the chaplainly specifications of
deceiving through magicianly manipulation of the smallest fixed
number of elements, the masterpiece of simulated conversion that
you, forever in quest of an impossible maximum, were unable to create. Instead you elect to remain saying, Conversion, simulated or otherwise, means nothing, nothing at all. But—the chaplain stammers
(not very convincingly: he's far better at eloquence unbridled). But
how can you piss on the notion of conversion says the warden, inter-
vening at last. Don't you understand, you cry out (more to the gurney
than to anything human), I've been submitting to conversion in order
to be able to suddenly turn around and shower the process with contempt (not that I necessarily contemn conversion more than any
other loathed sign of growth and development): why, after all, should
I be confined in its straitjacket qua little scumbag. So in spite of me
things are proceeding according to plan.

And what might that be, asks the warden, forever on the alert for
looming breaches of prison protocol in this, an election year. Ignoring
him you reply (to—because he's half-asleep!—Mr. Deathwatch) that
your aim is and always has been to provoke the spectators of any one
of your enormities: media, police, church groups, plain old armchair
maniacs (you point, here and now, to the chaplain but the remark's
clearly directed, as well it should be, at our studio audience) to encompass its next move—an open writing, so to speak, whereby, in

comparing their version with your own, they're forced to admit the superiority, that is to say, the economical inevitability of the latter construction albeit not because of a withholding of some vital bit(s) of information for priding yourself on playing fair you make it a point to traverse the same terrain as everybody else. Sensing the revelation has secured its audience by the balls, you don't just add—you *hasten* to add—that your every move as a serial killer was broadcast with the express intention of generously provoking the countermove of some interested party and not necessarily one with aspirations in the same direction but in any event never in order to get him just in the nick of time to shoulder your culpritude: you exposed your directorial decisions to view and review at every turn so the masterstrokes they constituted could be perceived, either immediately or eventually—it didn't matter: you had no intention of rushing your victims' spasms—to have arisen from a mere common-sense manipulation of whatever was at hand (bits and pieces of time and space, chance and necessity—orts, in other words, within everybody's reach): as long as you remained at large you wanted it to be known your story—your next move—could be everybody's (was it your fault you were always the first to make the only move worth making, specifically the one that got made before anybody else could make it?). The sine qua non of success, then, though God knows you've had little enough of it in your time (but cheer up! as my old boon comp. Freddy, or was it Friedy? used to say after just one shot of Johnny Walker: Some slobs are born to be born posthumously), is, from your point of view, to be able to outsmart all emulators without recourse to any perceptible gimmicks but if worse comes to worse and a few have to be dolloped into the perpetrative stew, to know in a pinch how to keep any sidelining old farts (present company excluded) believing you still subsist, like them, at a level of minimal datum-secretion, and that never in a million years would you dream of intussuscepting even a single additional worth a shit up the ass of what's clearly a shared stratagem. (So you are capable of simulation when it suits you, snigger the attendant and Mr. Deathwatch, almost in unison.)

Thank you, says the chaplain, beaming [you're momentarily amused by a thought almost too impish for plausibility, namely, that Pudd killed to be obliged to dredge up hence redeem the pettiest details of his supposed whereabouts at the time (*Ate a hard-boiled egg on a bench right across from the American Museum of Natural History, went and bought an hourglass in its gift shop as a reminder that my luck was running out then took a muddy walk by the lake, turning away in disgust from all the contented-looking couples in canoes—and there were plenty, let me tell you*), since such details are worthless, i.e., retroactively unmasterable, until Secondarily embedded in a crime story]: It's clear the closeness of death makes you more real than you've ever managed to be. True enough! you reply—indeed, you're being slowly disembowelled of the onus of unreality you've carried around like a dead weight since birth. At last I've come to accept that my body's my soul or rather that soul is body's all-too-sloughable second skin even if accepting body means accepting it as my worst enemy for it's the body that runs the freak- cum peepshow of determining our final cause, in other words, our essence, that is to say, the specific lethality visited upon each of us so that at last we may be made meaningful to others through our unspeakable agonies in becoming one with what we are—a testicular tumor for example—and may start acting like the (testicular) creature said fate's decreed us to be—even if it happens to be the very creature from whose cursing on the street-corners of every big city we've always managed up until now—thanks to a Schrödinger's cat like indeterminacy—to successfully shrink thereby proving we're about as unlike as any two creatures could be.

But all he does is smirk, this chaplain of yours: For once you felt free enough to bare your soul before him and his only response is a smirk, and an ugly one, at that. Turning to the warden as if to finally dissociate himself publicly from your remarks he sneers even more bitterly: Always giving names to things that don't exist (yourself) so as to be able to talk about things that do (the fact that we're minutes away from take-off). The towel boy notes, as if he's the night watchman croaking the hour: The chaplain's impatient for you to die so he can begin at last both to know and to falsify you (it's his way with terminal patients: come to think of it, it's every survivor's way with the dead).

Initially you were undone by the sneers but faster than you would ever have imagined the sneers are no longer appalling: they now qualify as fairly friendly fire's induction into the minefield of bleachers humanity waiting to see just how slowly somebody can give up the ghost. The deathwatch officer, yawning as he lifts his head skywards or vice versa, rises from his desk (he's one of those for whom even a yawn may, should the need arise, be adduced as further proof of stamina unabated). You're more entranced, however, by the towel boy's towel, now loosely tucked under his right arm, and though you've noticed it before (in fact, there hasn't been a minute when you weren't busy— far too busy, in fact—noticing it) for the first time his carriage truly registers, resonating as it suddenly does through sharp contrast with (critiquing, as it were) what used to be your own—your own at the precise moment when, departing the scene of a crime and anticipating a long (extensively televised) siege, you succumbed to carting off valisesful of perishables (only the media choosing time and again to overlook you, all that was to be derived from your foresight was a subluxation or two). In a word, all that's left to you—*your* A minor allegro, as it were—is this hallucination of the towel boy living sparely and sparsely for the moment with just a towel under his arm to prove it hence in starkest contrast to you who was always busy plundering and hoarding as preparation for a besiegement that never materialized though clearly you would have given all your road kill to be able to sport an identity as coherent as his—JohnMarcherlike, you see it now when it's too late (which is precisely why you can see it at all) yet in fact there may still be time to look forward to (if not quite forge from the inside out: there ain't no inside inside) just such an identity.

As warden and towel boy step aside, presumably to allow ample room in which to dress for death, all you, Pudd, can do is look chaplainwards. Your love for the towel boy—or is it, niched so neatly, the towel you crave?—renders the other more heinous than ever and if his mad-bull gaze is any indication the compliment's being returned in spades for by now he must know that at last, and in spite of him, you've managed to get yourself very much converted since what after all does this towel or towel-boy attachment reflect but conversion (so what if he elects to diagnose it as conversion hysteria) though his having, by acclamation, now replaced Berlio as the one you'd most like to kill may simply mean you'd like to kill instead the thought that, with literally milliseconds separating you from the gurney of gurneys, all you're able to consider is the shame of letting him down—you, who might have been the occasion of his greatest professional—or (what precisely are the old hunks' credentials?) paraprofessional—triumph.

No time—the chaplain's on your right and the warden's on your left and the towel boy's leaning on the chaplain which for some reason you can't quite explain is very much as it should be. They set you down on the gurney's gray horse blanket folded lengthwise and the warden (who, as it so happens—or, more precisely, as it turns out—frequently doubles as EKG monitoring quack) proceeds to perform (getting all vital signs: blood pressure, temperature, pulse, respiratory rate—the works!) what's known as a pre-kill physical. After all, if you weren't definitively alive at 11:55 PM it'll be pretty damn difficult to es-

tablish that you were IV'd to death at 12:03 AM. You turn away sor-
rowfully—you don't have enough strength left to feel rage or even
disgust—from the stain that's impossible not to observe at the level of
your feet, now bare. Mr. Deathwatch and towel boy start to strap you
down—legs, shrunken abdomen, chest (were you hairy or hairless?
for the life of you, you can't remember)—employing, among other
things, leather straps with tarnished blue buckles but you still have
enough mobility to look for—at—the warden and once his gaze is
appropriated you move it ever so gently in the general direction of the
two tiers of bleachers with their red plastic chairs which constitute the
witness stand (none yet), as if to say How can you allow *them* to observe
me subjected—and most unnecessarily—to so crude a ploy of maximum restraint? In deference to all the trouble taken to get his gaze
precisely trained he goes slow in refocusing on you and, indeed, the
very slowness affirms that having thoroughly studied the problem he's
now in a position to deal with it to your complete satisfaction. He
whispers: They won't see the buckles—how can they when, look,
you're white-sheeted from toes to chin.

Lowering your head, you're surprised to see Berlio [he's upside
down, as you must be so you tell yourself, and seated very much apart
from what look like the state witnesses as well as from members of the
press (the place is quickly filling up)]; looks like he's writing—by God,
it's that old A minor allegro again—drawing inspiration, hand over
fist, from your capsizing. The warden, unfumblingly placing the IV in
your arm, announces there'll be no stay after all (you did decapitate
your mother, he reminds you, but not sternly: his vast experience of
such things tells him it was a case of chance-medley, pure and simple)
then asks if there's anything you might still wish to say. To the press?
you can't help wisecracking (secretly you're thrilled he didn't end up
having to do a cutdown in your bull neck or, worse, your bubaed

groin—worst, through a hemorrhoid). The execution officer (Annie, get your gun), though clearly hating himself for being overkind, murmurs: It still might arrive . . . You want to reach out and slap him down but remember, with relief, that you're strapped down. Instead you *content yourself with saying*, Even if the letter—the call—the billet-doux from the governor were to arrive, it would no longer satisfy, its beautiful justness already blighted by the many tantrums succumbed to in the face of its continued deferment (in short, my young friend, nothing is valuable unless beyond conceptualization's adulterating power: only if we don't even know we want it can we expect to deserve it). So I've got to admit that in my case things have turned out for the best with this rupture of every expectation of a fair shake (and at the same time I'm aware many must ask, and rightly, rightly, why I of all people should merit, etc., etc.). One day—today—I wake up (only to realize that soon—in a minute—I am to be put back to sleep—for good) and discover the tantrum-ridden desire for a stay has done gone wrong and my last (almost-) victim (who has the gall to be occupying a front-row seat) is ever-ready at a moment's notice to translate spasms into hemidemisemiquavers. Yet at the same time I'm sad somehow (I don't want to be this old grotesque about to be inked to death) but the sadness will pass. Was that GHW—indeed it was!—and, through his gnawed knuckles, Samuels in unison muttering Balls! Balls! Balls! (Maybe he *had* gone a bit far what with mixing Billy Sunday and—of all people—Leo Strauss, not to mention Warner Brothers' G. Donizetti and Yankee Stadium's Lord Byron but such a hodgepodge provided the very illumination Gift & Co. could not—he was convinced—have done without.)

It is here that the chaplain intervenes. What an ingrate, he cries, accenting every syllable to remind the warden (who's known to be partially, or facultatively, deaf) that as regards a client as ornery as you he just can't be held responsible for his failure. Here you are about to live the event (you're tabloid-famous, for crying out loud!) you always coveted (at least in the plane of language, wherever that is)—the kind of event that, visited by the old masters on their corpulent models, was singlehandedly responsible for making them masters—only upon discovering (poor thing!) the enormous disjunction between event as lived in language and that of sagging flesh and aching bone what do you do but fart despair's old sweet whine.

You make a desperate effort to dismount because none among the inescapably fixed number of elements—buckles, IV, semen stain, etc.—constituting this too self-contained gurney event are usable in concocting the properly killing retort but even if they are and even if you know for a fact that only from within such a group—as would have done Evariste proud—can truly new and undreamed of elements *like* a properly killing retort (or redemption for a lifetime's atrocities) manage to emerge, you don't feel quite up to working on it. What you must do is get back in the world because in your eyes the world remains the only legitimate source of armaments against the world: you can't construct a retort, much less a memorable—a magnum opus-style death, from so paltry a passel of orts (among which you lucidly number yourself) as are being deployed for somebody's delectation here in the killing room. But since the chemicals appear to be already entering your veins (a bit flushed in the armpits and between your buttocks, you are: a sure sign) it's getting harder and harder to even consider dismounting so you cry out to the warden who's making his escape EKGwards (if he disappears, you think, Mr. Deathwatch might very well do in a pinch) that though nothing would please you as much as getting at last into the spirit of a straightforward and easy-to-follow storybook kind o' dying there's suddenly just too much to think, detourishly, about along its Appian way.

Chapter Eighteen

As the troupe (dawn was breaking) went solemnly for their duffel coats and bowler hats (even Flowers' customarily ironical tata *sounded visibly shaken* by Pudd's death by injection), Bert (adding unnecessarily, That's it, folks—that's our commercial in a nutshell) urged them to remember the bash, not that he had any idea it was to be there Gift, of all people, would graciously administer, before he managed to get halfway through the revolving door, the first of what were to be many shocks (since Joyce was in post-critical condition, Bert felt supremely safe in having brought her along) by informing him rumor had it based on *their* (comrades-in-arms at last!) current work he might very well make it in- (or was it on-?) to Flowers' Best-dressed some time before the millennium, albeit (Gift couldn't help adding) in a strictly provisional capacity. Bert gave vent to a shrug, not quite sure what it meant yet heartily wishing it could be understood to mean even if the millennium didn't pan out that you could be sure he'd be doing his damnedest here and now to convert obstacle into opportunity by making whatever puny ray of hope still flitted about the chafing dishes pretext for revelry.

The minute champagne was duly ordered (Flowers, though hardly a member of the Bert-claque, insisted on paying for the first six bottles), Belle, the gala's cheerleader de facto and de luxe, heartily applauded but declared it was Bert's responsibility to pick up the tab for every item consumed. He saw clearly up to now he hadn't been quite believing in the ordering or anything else connected with this blessed event, not to mention the event itself, until Belle herself saw fit to second the canonizer's motion—or rather it was only with the old snaky-bovine disintegration of Joyce's features—she was propped up on cushions far more denatured than Pudd's gurney quilt—in reaction against such conviviality that he was being made to understand how things stood. Something in her blooded gaze allowed him to grasp at last that the goings-on constituted not a celebration of Bert's achievement (for feeble it was and feeble it would remain no matter how many of Samuels' clients and flunkeys ended up sponsoring its afterbirth) but rather—but rather—but rather (for she was the true star of this and every other show he might care to name, not to mention the true epicenter of any hurricano)—a stab (alas, equally feeble) at rectifying [as her own dying was a rectifying (still) of Albert's] all previous shows of disrespect and as such it of course failed even more dismally than the commercial itself. Surely it was all meant as placation, however oblique, however inadequate, of Joyce and Joyce alone—and long overdue for she was the only one who knew what it was to suffer (and not just as a side effect of shotgun chemotherapy) hence being so deeply attuned—to the torment engendered, for example, by Bert's own sense of his mediocrity—understandably she couldn't very well expect to enjoy herself, that is to say, be expected to sanction the enjoyment of others, which was nothing more, anyway, than the blue ribbon earned by an abscess. (Flowers flitted by and evidently empowered by the Champagne for Everybody coup snickered, Be nice to Si-gnora Meyerbeer, Rossini, she's obviously gotten off the old deathbed to pay you homage.)

The actors were, Bert had to admit, being far unrulier than they'd ever been which would account for her disgusted look's disgustedly inquiring: Can't you, with dying me here, manage to control your tribe? Where was the sweet and docile Joyce of recent times, he wanted to wonder, only he'd lost all sense of wonder and even if he hadn't there was no time to devote to her/it.

Only Fred, obviously himself near death and maybe much nearer than Joyce herself (or was this Leonard?)—in any case only Fred/Leonard was making a noble effort to overcome his indifference where Bert and Bert's strivings were concerned—to celebrate whether or not there was anything to celebrate (*was* there in fact anything to celebrate?) and thereby (from time to time he touched his right buttock with the pale, mottled back of a palm, coquettishly, as if it was somebody else's: a lady's—in distress) elude all mortal symptoms. Indeed, it wouldn't be too much of an exaggeration to say Fred's struggle—in psychotherapese, his task—was (Bert's long, languid glance tried conveying as much Bellewards) to transform himself into the very life of the party so as to, *pari passu*, effect lateral transmogrification (even if only for five minutes) into one no longer at death's door—and if the only available means was exultancy over his favorite stepson-in-law's belated theatrical success then, shit, he was *as more-than-willing as the next guy* and then some to make whatever efforts were required.

Was Bert imagining it or was Fred/Leonard currently exclaiming to Prissie and Ralph (who were holding hands, a bit too tentatively for

Priscilla's taste Bert could see, especially since it must be clear as day to everybody Gift had no further interest in her): Will you get a look at Bert—your director, I mean—sitting around with his hands prissily folded against the rave reviews which he knows damn well are sure to come soon but not soon enough for his taste. And Bert had to admit it was a pleasure to discover, smoothing down the monogrammed napkin on which they lay, that the objects in question were interlocked just as F/L'd managed to (skewedly) assure him they'd be and with a highly uncharacteristic placidity to boot though he didn't feel, what with Joyce having an access of direst pitiableness and Priss succumbing to inadmissible pining (he suspected Gift might end up being the great love of her life), quite up to admitting as much to the hands themselves. Priscilla looked like she positively loathed all this talk about hands perhaps because it was uncomfortably redolent of (during that too-brief peak—literally and figuratively—atop Gift's shoulders, hers no more) the caressive play of her own (where was Gift now that she still needed him, albeit differently and in a way that had nothing to do with the commercial which if it did turn out to be a success would redound to the glory of Bert alone so what concern was it of hers, in other words, Was she turning into an old maid overnight? her stare, momentarily as wild as Joyce's, dared to ask).

Edging away from Joyce's dying with a tenacity that outpaced all her efforts to avoid the (even Bert had to admit) far more blatant odors of his own decomposition, Fred/Leonard, leaned hugger-mugger over Priscilla (there was a teardrop in each eye) and began to whisper, but loud enough for everybody to hear, what sounded initially like the sheerest mumbo-jumbo but the more he did hear, the more convinced—with an eye of course to the enrichment of some future production, should there happen to be one—Bert himself became that said mumbo-jumbo might very well be constrained to cohere [after all, hadn't he moonlighted extensively (Kew Gardens, Fresh Meadows, Flatbush) as a small claims court reporter (the first time Belle turned up pregnant, wasn't it?)] along the semi-eloquent lines of, say, Yet the more I thrash against her (she was my wife once, and I loved her madly) the more I feel enmeshed in the warehousing of it—her behavior, I mean—or should I say her behaviors? jam-packed as they are or rather have come to be (for you didn't know Joyce in the bloom of her youth) with ill-will and other confections—warehousing it as template for my own contortions which are sure to erupt someday but let's not talk about that now (Bert suddenly pitied Fred, for Fred it definitely was—Leonard must have died, being no match for the demands of Joyce's illness)—but isn't this what actors do—the good ones, I mean? Priss just stared coldly, as if Fred were Gift or a scrawled message from Gift. I don't understand, she finally said, but Fred stuck to his guns: Surely, my dear, there are people in every actor's life he vows to be as unlike as possible yet whose tics he incorporates in spite of himself so that the minute he walks out on stage—poof! who does he turn out to be but those very people—and all at once, too. Priss shrugged, her mind still on Gift now, Bert noted with inexplicable sadness, drinking champagne out of his own shoe or (for the benefit of any tabloid reps who happened to be in the vicinity?) pretending to be. She is teaching me, the old bitch, how to die and, dying, to cause others to die not a little in the process. Neither did this summation make an impression on Priscilla. As if responding to the outcry at the heart of her shrug, Dinka was now at Priscilla's side. Hey, Fred murmured, in a tone whose contempt he couldn't quite mask by trying to sound much drunker than he was, weren't you Joycie's nurse up at Mount Metropolitan University General right before she had her jejunum resected? As she bit hungrily into two canapes at once Dinka managed with dignity to speak volumes by nodding yes.

Yet at the same time I'm nothing like Joycie, at least not yet. In short, dearest Priss—I can call you Priss, yes? no?—I want no part of humanness if Joyce hails therefrom. Priss, evidently intrigued and maybe even aroused by the quiver of Fred's nostril stamens, now sounded much less rebarbative, going so far as to point out—and not in the least unkindly—that Fred's sentimental education might have to remain unachieved until he took to embracing the very humanness Joyce embodied. If it repels you it must be in and of you, she said with an emphasis that couldn't help, Bert suspected, having her own Gift very much in mind.

Belle, busy overcompensating for everybody's dire neglect of Joyce, was once again desperately trying to save her from herself, selves, any disconcerting memory of those selves—by dutifully asking, *inter alia*, if she liked the champagne and were the baked oysters up to snuff and did she need a glass of tomato juice for her pain—no, her pancreas—medication? And Joyce dutifully on cue and in her nastiest tone (as if a truly loving daughter must settle, rightly, for nothing less) sneered: Oh that's not important, nothing importing as far as she was concerned but the next turn for the worst. Bert thought, enjoying its metamathematical simplicity: Joyce's repudiation of Belle equals Flowers' repudiation of Bert in favor of Bert's rivals and, indeed, during the moment it took to descend upon mother and daughter in order to truncheon the former (the plight of the latter, though, might stand a far better chance of rehabilitation if she was arraigned as the sole architect of her misfortunes) he felt completely out of reach of those rivals not to mention beings like Flowers who, by invidiously comparing him with this one or that and then by way of encore pitting him against them all, were much worse than rivals. For this one rare moment, as his look spoke daggers and Joyce's answering one unwillingly confessed relief that, all probabilities notwithstanding, her jugular hadn't in fact been severed, he'd managed to slip out of himself to become himself, hence incommensurable with all others except that self, to smelt himself down to the smallest subset of himself—a set so small as to be invisible, i.e., invincible, to the eye of invidious comparison—and serendipitously to take pride in his mean feats as a director of TV commercials even if nobody else did nor ever would. For this one rare moment, in bristling on behalf of Belle's unsung solicitude, he was himself alone and not a failed version of his rivals as Flowers always seemed to be trying to make him out to be for he'd just achieved something that gave him (no matter that strictly speaking it wasn't an act at all—merely a react . . . against a mother-daughter act: for the purpose of the present self-promotional campaign it must pass for an act) the sense of no longer living in their shadow. His act was his and his alone though admittedly there was a sense in which the act or the non-act—in any case, the righteous outrage on Belle's behalf—in deploying the vexatious strength he found it so hard to muster on his own could be said, now that the glowering over Joyce's near-corpse had done its work, to have robbed him, as his rivals or rather their Flowers-masterminded enshrinement had robbed him, of himself, though for the time being he didn't mind in the least being so robbed.

Become the shadow of the valley of death that Joyce was trying in vain to escape at all cost he felt strong as he advanced Bellewards to claim the reward of his knight-errantry. If only this wife of his could secure what through no fault of his own had made him momentarily strong beyond the threat of rivals.

Or, if Belle could only see her way clear to securing an obsession—even if with, for lack of anything better, that very threat of rivals—which enjoying far higher priority than would hence exercise complete control over all shocks emanating from Joyce's epicenter. It was what he had and what made him strong from moment to moment except for the moment, but a moment ago, when he'd been be-yond such threats: he couldn't be humiliated there, in the domain of obsession with rivals rampant, because this was where his humiliations could be depended on to overwhelm and thereby inoculate him against all further humiliation. If upon re-entering his domain he had momentary fears of being—by humiliating thoughts along the lines, say, of *Why oh why was he excluded from the canon and Tom Q. Pudd begged to accept membership in perpetuity?*—engulfed beyond all possibility of exit then he had only to think for a second beyond those thoughts and realize everything here was soothingly symptomatic, of the same old raging despair, so in fact there was nothing to fear—it was all just a matter of gritting his teeth until the wave of humiliations subsided foamless and if he was good at anything it was gritting his teeth—so good in fact that very early on he'd gotten into the habit of seeking—in other words, creating—just the situations, the most recent of which being the harpooning of Joyce (yet another dialogue by proxy with his hated rivals and their master), to necessitate re-relegation to the domain where that too-dependable source of instant gratification, and not cot-ton, was king. In short, in his obsession he had what few people had and a place all his own in which to cultivate it: if only Belle could pro-cure something similar since Joyce's obsession was slowly eating her up precisely because she had nothing to oppose. But was this really just what the doctor would have ordered—wasn't *his* obsession in fact merely the dutiful elaboration of an inescapable, twinned, strangu-lated linkage with the one he claimed to detest, a too-obvious (for all the surface discrepancies undeceiving to the practiced eye, and no doubt even to the most unpracticed) homolog of Fred's warehousing Joyce's ill-will as template for his own future contortions? Wasn't Bert, like Fred, like anybody else who'd (as the eulogists say) ever had the honor to know her, just acting Joyce insofar as everybody was an actor? Good, bad or indifferent and willy-nilly weren't they all actors—not one eyelash-flicker being genuine in the sense that it could be called selfsprung and -concocted?

Bert knew clearly no point, then, as he went on skedaddling more than sauntering and less towards Belle than away from Joyce in continuing to ask if his obsession (with Flowers-designated rivals) was an escape from or a fusion with the latter (of course first choice was but a coy masking of—in fact a skewed emphasis on—second as the one and only) or, for that matter, in wishing a homolog on poor Belle. So maybe, when all was said and done, it would be seen (though not necessarily by Bert) that the Flowers obsession had been manufactured for the sole purpose of achieving the only kind of self-sufficiency conceivable in a Joyce world (for in Bert's limited experience the world was quintessentially a Joyce world, that is to say, a world where the only thing better than non-being was being obsessed) and if this was the case—and each passing minute suggested more and more decisively that indeed it was—then surely she had been, both on and off the podium of mean-spiritedness, the most excellent of teachers where obsession was concerned since who better equipped than Joyce to instill in any willing pupil—and even more in those ferociously unwilling—a sense of inexhaustible value of disciplined commitment thereto? Despite debilitating disease(s) and well on into the valley of their shadow of death, she'd somehow managed to teach him to love if not her very own *cause célèbre*—to wit, herself (and probably she wouldn't have borne such love—no, not for one millisecond)—then something far more crucial—that is to say, far more corrosively self-constitutive—namely the mechanism of all such (lost) causes far and wide.

So it was not disinterested defense of Belle that had made him momentarily strong but reactivation of obsession via—as antidote to terrified—terrorization of the undisputed master of obsession (in his efforts to escape Joyce at all cost he'd gotten about as far from the parent trunk as any feeble offshoot forced to double back on itself can be expected to get). [Not that Joyce-bashing *really* made him strong, even momentarily; it was just that by stooping to defy a pitiful old lady, instead of the pundit-punk he should have been defying, he knew he could sink no lower on the ladder of loathsomeness and so needn't fear any further relegation at the hands of that punk, not to mention Samuels and his gang of clients and cronies: more accurate, then, to say he was momentarily immune—best of all to himself (who never tired of abetting the infiltration of those pundits, clients and cronies)—rather than strong.] But here was Joyce imperiously announcing she needed to return to the oncology wing ASAP for her one A.M. half- and quarter-doses. Something in her gaze told him she was a long way from forgiving his smothered outburst (would she ever?) but had elected, in the name of conserving the little of her strength that was left (wild horses couldn't have made her admit she'd been genuinely cowed), to put vengeance on hold. Defiance, however, is addictive (only defiance itself can quash the shame it induces) so all he could make himself do in response to her plea was turn away—defiantly, mumbling that she should go call herself a taxi or have Fred drag her back to the farm (these were the words he used—and instantly regretted using) if she was feeling so damn bad. Through the corner of an eye he could see that, even from the mumble he tried to make as incoherent as possible, she'd managed to decipher his gist and, predictably, was dutifully beginning to do what she did (or thought she did) best, namely, seethe for all she was worth. And he began to— very visibly, he hoped, for once in his life (only why, with a terminal case on his hands, did it have to be now?)—seethe back at the seething. I'm a dying woman, she confirmed piteously (as if to help get all the eggs of his self-hate into one basket), and it's here of all places you choose to bait me—her moan being so wrenching, he actually thought he loved her madly: that's what the hating boiled down to, then, if only for a split second—but once the split second was over what she (or rather, her moan) really seemed to have been saying was, Where do you come off to be seething at my seething over your turning your back on my dying? Let's get something straight, buster: A reaction by me must always be perceived as having preceded and as taking precedence over anything and everything to which it is the semihysterical response. My reactions, however gratuitously sour, however rancorous and irrational, are to be tagged (you have been vouchsafed strontium-soaked vibrissae—in the vicinity of your perineum—for that very purpose)—and well in advance of their capacity to shock or appal—as an undislodgeable given of our shared form of life. The so-called vileness of such reactions is to be factored in as an essential building block—of that life. My right to those reactions, then, is as incontestable as the weather (which, since they have the best interest of all my fellow creatures at heart, is immeasurably improved thereby) so the villain of this piece must be (for protesting against what is so patently part and parcel of our common nature, of things as they are) none other than you for how can he be me inasmuch as I'm no longer me but an undislodgeable shard in the monument of our daily round? He was reprehensible in other words, her piteous moan concluded, not for turning his back (hunch- or sway-, what difference did it make now?) on a poor old lady whose dying was desperately in need of a little personal attention after several lifetimes' dire neglect but rather for—just now, and in the presence, no less, of everybody who was anybody—seething at her seething over his having done so for didn't he know her seething (however haglike in its fetor) was— the life of the planet? Indeed, insofar as it was already common knowledge the commercial must prove a notorious flop on all fronts (so that once again he could look forward to being bounced by El Canonizer's goons and, more to the point, loathed—but as never before—by the prime-time hordes and their mediatizers), Bert should be kissing her ass since thanks to the seething's provocation, inevitability of defeat had been supplanted (and if he had one shred of decency he'd admit as much), at least for a little while, by the infinitely more bracing "*obsession with* inevitability of defeat" which unlike inevitability of defeat pure and simple entailed a bona fide course of action involving, among other things, gritting his buck teeth, returning his key to the soon-to-be-built executive-washroom, putting his house in order, passing on the torch to a far worthier successor, etc. (and big deal that these, supposedly the most practical and hard-line of preparations hung in fact by the merest thread of a belief most magical—most apotropaic—that the minute said defeat got wind of the fact it was already forestalled by such preparations, like any self-respecting creature committed to being original above all and at any cost—in other words, like Bert himself—it would surely elect to pack up instead and go perpetrate inevitability on some victim infinitely less vigilant).

He was shaking his head. Before she could trill, What's wrong, he mumbled, I like my states of affairs straight (no explanations)—but what was that you were saying about a taxi, my dear Joyce?

It was unbearable to be near her because she was still seething, but when he looked around and saw how bloated Fred looked and how disapproving Samuels looked and how happy GreenHurstWood looked (as if he'd just heard something particularly unflattering with regard to Bert's chances of success with the prime-timers—maybe from Flowers, or from Gift whose loyalty was, he should have known by now, a thing of shreds and patches or maybe even from Belle who, having probably mixed plum brandy or Jamaican rum with the most contraindicated of her medications, looked a wee bit woozy) then he found himself eagerly turning back to the seething but still he couldn't stand the sight. So he tried his hand at another look around but when he saw how bleary Belle still looked and how prissy Prissy looked since Gift had definitely dumped her in favor of—yes, Dinka! (they were holding hands, of all things, but then Bert remembered what women routinely said about men of a certain age wanting—and Gift, now that he saw him up close and with no makeup, was closer to an Old fart than a Spring chicken—little more, nor less, than a nurse-maid with plenty of cash) and how self-satisfied Flowers looked and how constricted Samuels looked and how moribund Fred looked he simply couldn't wait to turn back and feast his eyes on Joyce again but this time almost with a feeling of reverent expectation for suddenly Joyce's utter—her bludgeoning—might he even go so far as to say her fabled—indifference to the occasion (what was the occasion, by the way? Oh yes, how silly of him, celebration of the commercial's imminent opening night)—her willed obtuseness about what it was all supposed to mean as a bid for accession to the Best-dressed (so what if only as a scrawny alternate)—had somehow managed to become his very own private weapon. The arrogance of her unyielding self-preoccupation (Where the hell is that taxi? he thought he heard somebody croak, and not necessarily Joyce) had now become his ultimate bulwark against any further willingness to be scalded, degraded, tossed aside, filed away—though certainly not for future reference for who in the future, or elsewhere for that matter, would ever refer to him (tone of psychoanalyst forecasting the erotic fate of middle-aged gal patient's paralyzed perineum: *Who'd be interested in that?*)—just for having put all his artistic eggs in one Flowery basket or was it one Samuelsy basket—it didn't matter: Flowers, Samuels, GHW, they were all his enemies. What did matter—oh meaning, meaning, mean-

ing, how he loved it after all! as long as he got to it before Joyce did—
was that the obtuseness of his greatest enemy handselled protection,
rather like a made-to-order condom guaranteeing henceforth un-
woundable commerce (an oxymoron if ever there was one) with the
workaday world, that is to say, some form of as yet unspecifiable participation in her total indifference to any doings that did not immediately drop everything to defer to her own, terminal and otherwise—
just what the doctor had, in fact, never been smart enough to
order—must become his foothold amid so many shifting sands.
Smelting down his predicament in the white-hot crucible of her indifference, he would—he knew he would!—manage to yank himself up
and out of its—the predicament's—stinking mulch. (Oh thank you,
Joyce; how can I ever begin to repay you?)

Excusing himself in order to be alone with his exultation, he
drifted towards the phones on the lower level. The maître d', who'd
been Johnny-on-the-spot eager-to-please at the time of arrival, now
eyed him oddly. Before he could decide whether or not to take a piss
(a crap was out of the question) Joyce was beside him groaning at the
fact that it was he who would have to pay for the phone call rather
than the establishment itself which should be jumping at the chance
to be able to take care of this detail for the birthday boy or the man of
the hour or whatever the hell he was. But as he waited for a vacant
booth Bert tried to remain absolutely still starting from deep within,
to achieve rigor mortis of the astral body if possible, for every movement inevitably detectable by Joyce, especially in her present condition
though any condition would have done very nicely (and who in any
condition had such an impoverished field for the exercise of her vigilance that the slightest murmur awakened the full force of its facility),
would be all too avidly interpreted as unjustifiable recoil from this, her
rightful insistence on condemning the management hence as a daring

to relapse into the prohibited old devil seething at her own seething when that seething constituted—if she'd told him once she'd told him a thousand times—far too much of the native sap of things as they were and always would be to be localizable—i.e., desecrated—as target of a counterseethe.

The hack's imminent arrival confirmed, they returned to the table where all of the actors (with the exception of Ralph who either knew how to hold his liquor or never touched the stuff) were a little drunk. Samuels stopped by on his way to the men's room and said he was looking forward to the world premiere and, more to the point, that to a man his clients were looking forward to it. What does Green-HurstWood think, Bert couldn't help asking. It doesn't matter, said Samuels, and although Bert could have heard this as a vote of confidence—as a reminder that the boss could be trusted to know his boy without any help from the help—it somehow managed to get itself heard otherwise. He tried to remember how Pudd/Gift was supposed to feel on the way to the gurney but his mind clouded over just in the nick of time maybe because Joyce was sitting across from him with her coat half-off, half-on, ostentatiously closing obstinate eyes against the onslaught of her pain (but in this case wasn't it the pain of observing Samuels pay exclusive attention to Bert of all people?), looking for a moment as she might have looked sunbathing in some old photograph arrayed in the kind of skirted one-piece that, according to Belle at her most fetishizingly filial, they just didn't put on the market any more, and making a great display of what she evidently hoped the few connoisseurs in *our studio audience* would acknowledge to be stoicism at its most exemplary. Belle joining them, Samuels eyed her with interest and stayed his course. Widowed, Belle would certainly, Bert had to admit, make an attractive consort for the gracefully balding Samuels and he suddenly found himself indulging in what clearly had the makings of an old pastime though this was neither the time nor the place: curiosity about what the mythical second husband would turn out to be: as if he could only begin to see her through the filter of another's—a better's—loving and indulgent compassion (*What had he ever really loved but his commercials et al? A mere sum total, with no remainder, of frustration, all along he'd been too rancorously suppressive of any sign of spontaneous life*). Such musings, moreover, were the closest he'd ever get to a full-fledged love affair with another man.

With the prospect of Joyce's departure and the evening's ending, the star of these musings was growing more and more effusive, even going so far as to compliment Priscilla on her vintage feather boa (picked up, as it so happened, en route as a lark just hours before) and to applaud Flowers on his glum-coy and pedantically defiant little beret which the wearer, like all such wearers, clearly regarded as an almost too audacious throwback to a more stouthearted epoch. Bert, however, sensing there was nothing easier than for Joyce to hate said star for much too effusively distracting attention from the killjoy spectacle that she, back by popular demand, was trying singlehandedly to mount yet again—her very own world premiere, as it were—began to counsel Belle against the effusiveness with his knock-knees but now, oddly enough, it was for reasons having nothing to do with Joyce's seething: for one thing he himself was uncomfortably conscious of an inability (before all these people, rabid for false moves!) to match such bouncy, bubbly eagerness to please and be pleased or, humbly, to find plausible habitation inside it. Belle knocked back in unmistakable sign that henceforth she was insensible to knocks and their connotations: tonight, maybe even from this moment on, she would have no further truck with suppressors. It was her evening too, after all: she'd put up with plenty, God knows, during the many weeks of rehearsal so wasn't she entitled to hope all the sacrifice might bear fruit or, better yet, to imagine that it was already doing so here and now. As Joyce howled, Where's that damn cab (Fred alone seemed to be listening and, by staring hard at the speaker, admitting he understood what he heard but only, so it appeared, in order that, now, the pleasurable turning his back in disgusted indifference might be the more telling) Bert wanted to howl back and at the same time to denounce Belle for making herself too accessible to Joyce, and Fred for not making himself accessible enough—she was his consort, after all—and (while he was at it and for the same price) Samuels for not having provided working conditions more ideal than a chilly loft, but (he warned himself as he tried to smile away the waiter's question whether monsieur mightn't like a few more anchovies with his vodka cocktail) this was to petition old modes of thought and he must avoid such retrogressions, especially tonight, whatever tonight turned out to be. He would not let them, the old thoughts, erupt the predictable old chain of heartrending associations about the life he could have had, surely must have had, if only Joyce's disease had never seen fit to arrive on the scene, hot on the heels (how far away it seemed) of the insufferable Albert, and if only GreenHurstWood hadn't taken an immediate and irreversible dislike to him from deep in the gut and if only—if only . . . Instead he would think of crises he'd been forced to weather with Albert but hadn't wanted to (these providing a veritable speculum of memories, and his alone). How often he'd dreaded their time together as time taken away from what really made him unique—work with actors and, to a lesser extent, meetings with Samuels and his crowd to discuss that work. And yet—and yet (though he hated nothing more than such back-door herniations into meaning)—as he caught another glimpse of Joyce her decrepitude seemed to be proclaiming on behalf not just of Albert and of Joyce herself but of all the terminal unwanted the world over that it was those very same crises now constituting the archive of a uniqueness nobody could pillage—for what his uniqueness-mongers so-called, Samuels and Flowers and Priss and the rest, wanted to do above all was to rob him of that uniqueness, not confirm it, and to think that all along he'd believed uniqueness lay as far away as he could get from Albert and Co., and among such . . . bloodsuckers. And so it was poor, dear, desolate Albert (thus continued Joyce's taxiless decrepitude)—and, needless to say, Joyce too—who, by forcing him to live situations not so much inconceivable as irrelevant in their barbarous painfulness, ëd managed to exalt his uniqueness beyond earthly bounds. Once, now that she'd mentioned it, he'd brought Albert or was it Joyce a portion of Belle's apple-betty, or apple-crumble, or apple-crisp—in any event, it was definitely sandwiched between two paper plates, on the back of one of which was scrawled a loving note from Belle who no doubt for the millionth time thereby returned good for evil, in this case the recipient's many years of innuendo-chocked abuse—and, after the toothless consumption of the treat, was making ready to toss both plates into the trash outside the TV room (where Albert/Joyce normally took evening meals) only he/she instantly, fiercely insisted on keeping the one with the writing as it was akin to a greeting card, better than a letter on personalized stationery, and far more thoughtful than the costliest bibelot. (The unique coloring of such an event was his and his alone but, thanks to Joyce's garrulous decrepitude, its noncommunicability no longer frightened but rather thrilled him.)

He looked around—at GreenHurstWood, so sure of himself, so fashionably lean, so certain to be Best-dressed before too long—but he mustn't be re-led, especially now when he was making such progress towards self-acceptance, into the ring of old thoughts about *the life he should have been living*, that is, the life his rivals were reputed to lead, although something about the phrase *the life he should have been living* seemed—in drawing toward it a cornucopia of other thoughts, such as *What gave him the right to think there was any life he should be living*—to annul its own hopelessness.

How had he come to stumble into the ditch of this notion of the ideal conditions of plenary enjoyment forever eluding him yet to which he was sovereignly entitled? Where did he come off thinking that he too should have been a master-enjoyer and not just *a* master-enjoyer but the very master-enjoyer who enjoying all he did not—and would never—enjoy spent his time and the taxpayers' money judging how far he, Bert, fell short of the achievement that might—but only might (since no matter what he ended up achieving or not achieving he'd still be just plain Bert)—have entitled him to master-enjoyership? Why couldn't he enjoy each moment according to his lights rather than, by positing a super-enjoyment contingent on having achieved, *inter alia*, membership in the Flowers' confraternity, be forever annihilating whatever little of joy was available, and from which annihilation already there were only the most temporary of respites: the texture more than the shape of a cloud peeping over the mountains for a glimpse—just a glimpse—of the sea, a seagull's yellow beak plunging into a tiny tub of butter on the too-shiny counter of an outdoor grill, an apiary of oak leaves asizzle in the autumn wind.

Here's what I'll do, he said to Belle as she sashayed by (he had to hold out his arm to stop her progress): Starting now I'm going to let the old thoughts pass through, like gas, without dancing to their gassy old hornpipe since just because they've upsurged once again, these incubi about rivals, I'm under no obligation to honor their willingness to destroy my work (once Belle was gone, however, he discovered they were still very much with him). Impaling some of the uneaten breadsticks with his vodka-cocktail toothpick Joyce, as she pocketed the booty, mumbled something incoherent yet all too comprehensible insofar as it was just the sort of meaningless chatter needed to mask the

312 / MICHAEL BRODSKY

pillage. Even she, then, and even at the height of her illness, must find it a wee bit flagrant to be pocketing gala refuse, hence the actorly effort to undercut the theft's bruteness with a soundtrack. Flowers, seeing Joyce at work without quite seeing her, was emboldened to remark (as if this particular detail represented all too clearly what the commercial sorely lacked) that he had some very nice things to say after all, after some initial very serious—one might even say, dire—reservations, about Bert's finished product but (in a stage whisper) whatever his reservations and whatever his niceties he would stick to his guns regarding the fact that Bert could have told his story far more simply. Bert was just about to let himself feel a conspicuous pang at being lambasted in front of Joyce who surely must make it a practice to lap up these instantiations of his ignoble defeat in order to warehouse them against some future battle where they could be trotted out as weaponry, that is, as the real reasons for his cruelty toward her and neglect of her disease, but somehow the memory of her obtuseness (regarding his own status, however insubstantial, in the theatrical community) as the limit point of the very worst that could happen at the hands of criticasters and, worse, fellow artisans, and itself warehoused by him for just such an occasion, was, in emerging from storage and prompting him to assert with the commanding tone of one who has absolutely nothing to lose: *What makes you think there's a story, Flowers old man, under all this scattershot, eh?* (he instantly regretted not having said, Flowers my boy), much too quick for the pang. As if there is a

Story

here. As if anything worth a damn ever reduces to a story with its neat-as-a-pinafore liquidation of misfortunes. The only story worth a damn is precisely this incessant deviation from the merest whiff of story. And it is not as if the story is available at a moment's notice should I happen to change my mind—it is not as if the story's in fact there, at the tip of my fingertips. Story and I are mutually incompossible. I am, or rather my obsessions are after, Mr. Flowers, a different kind of process. Unfortunately I am not as clever or rather my obsessions are not as clever as those of my rivals—like GreenHurstWood—and I admit it: theirs are constantly aware of just how much of them the story line can tolerate and if the story line can't tolerate them at all then my rivals simply acquire new, more ingratiating—more media-potable—obsessions. But for me there can be no such shifts for I must be true to the process that is Ralph, say, or Priscilla or Gift—or better yet, Priscilla atop Gift's massive shoulders, growing more massive by the moment, even now—which is not to say I haven't been tempted to tell a story, preferably a very very sad story, but routinely I refrain for to give way would be to pander to the craving for story-as-drug so you'll never find me rushing the extinction of those blessed events that refuse to be mightily threatened by a next. (Priscilla's standing erect on Gift's shoulders, for example, going nowhere, having come from nowhere, was the instrument of a force far mightier.)

As there was no telling what effect he was having Bert decided to adopt a more plaintive, coaxingly pouty tone: I thought surely of all people you, Flowers, would have had no trouble appreciating my efforts to steer clear of the usual sheering into the wind of predictability (Flowers smiled but there was no determining what this physiognomic fart intended to convey) but when (as he always ended up doing) he looked at Joyce, who was still spearing breadsticks with other people's toothpicks and secreting them (towards festive adornment of her hospital-room windowsill?), and remembered that at any moment she would be bidding him—them—adieu perhaps for the very last time on earth, Bert, in spite of himself and of the need to respond to Flowers' radiant slur, couldn't help being completely indifferent.

All I'm convinced of, said Flowers, seemingly most for Samuels' benefit who was revisiting them after (judging from the way he fidgeted with his belt) a trip to the men's room, is how skeptical you are of any story, i.e., tale of woe, except your own and I think it all boils down to an obsession with—dare I mention them in the presence of a lady—your rivals (he was now looking directly at Bert's boss, as if to remind him of their common purpose, that is, their common enemy). Before we get on to the subject of my rivals (Bert tried to be casual) I must remind you of a further danger of storytelling: when you tell a story you are necessarily telling somebody else's story and though abstractly on the one hand the somebodies may be blessing you for telling it (thereby allowing them to resume their identity), on the other you must be prepared for violent protests to the effect that you're not getting it right, in fact, nobody could have gotten it wronger, and even if you manage to tell it (the way I tried at first to tell Pudd's story) exactly as it occurred—as you know it must have occurred if it occurred at all—there will be the inevitable growls for the subject's rage at being caught with his pants down must camouflage itself somehow and what better way than as righteous outrage at your failure to have struck the magical balance between precision and enhancement. To become characters people—in our business we just can't escape them no matter how hard we try—tend, if anything, to overemphasize victimization by condemning the well-nigh monumental forces of destruction (forbears, bosses, sweethearts, the CIA) responsible but in fact condemning in the key of overemphasis is but a ploy for aggrandizing said forces even further for without them they're nothing and nobodies, so be prepared never to have gotten those forces right. And that, dearest Flowers, is why I always make it a point to steer clear of stories—they never quite make up their mind whether they want you to tell the story or elide it so whether you do the one or the other or both or neither you can be pretty damn well sure your balls will be lasered off in any case but, to paraphrase Jane Austen, who needs balls?

With an attitude like that it's not hard to understand why your rivals are getting far ahead of you, my boy, said Flowers, with a leering wink—wasted!—at Joyce who was for all intents and purposes dead to gesture: Men like P and T and G. J. not to mention GHW know how to tell a story the right way and it is, let me tell you, no mean pleasure to observe how adeptly those backroom boys scarve opposing life-stances into a plausible whole, at which point Bert decided there was nothing left to do (over voices of protest he couldn't quite identify until he recognized Belle's which was screaming, Then she'll miss the cherry-cheese shortcake and the elderberries jubilee) but escort Joyce to the entrance, cab or no cab. And somehow Joyce's unsmotherable hiss of displeasure at this, her daughter's signature redundant focus on blackberries (sic) when one A.M. administration of the prescribed doses in their correct sequence was the ticket (least of all, however, could she tolerate being referred to as *she'll*), gave Bert the courage to himself scream, over the head of the maître d', once again all attentiveness (everybody suddenly looked like Priscilla atop Gift's shoulders—as if whoever gave way to the folly of gesture must be willing to pay, as at Old Testament high noon, the retail price in instant immobility without term): My rivals are all fools to a man. Then why suck up to them: I've seen him at it—we've all seen you—during those ad hoc meetings? GHW easily screamed back.

Once Joyce, above her shrill protests, was safely planted in the vestibule (on an Adirondack chair) he was able to go right back in and say, Sucking up to them, as you so delicately put it, is just a way of getting closer and the closer I get the better I can observe—firsthand—the lowering of my status. And why, GreenHurstWood snickered with a glass of what looked like bicarbonate in his hand (it hadn't been there a minute ago), do you need to observe that? Because in compensation I acquire something much—infinitely—better than a promotion, namely the sorry state of affairs as component of my . . . edifices—like the one I currently happen to be building (or haven't you mugs noticed?) with the aid of Gift here and Ralph and Prissie and Dinka and which by the way, will go on expanding long after the commercial has been aired to death. Not that when I hurry in to those ad hoc meetings as you call them, knowing all my rivals will be seated in the supreme places of honor on the podium while I myself am consigned to the heel of its loaf, so to shriek, I can necessarily tell whether the urgency that seems to accompanying me everywhere these days—Read panic, sneered GHW giving Flowers an answering look (or maybe Flowers, sneering, was answering GHW's look).—stems from a desire to slobber over my tormentors like the krauts with *their* Hitler and thereby arrest all further invidious comparisons, or rather from the distinct anti-desire to acquire mastery of, qua sum of countable byproducts, this irrepressible will to slobber but in whose irrepressibility of course I don't believe for one moment, or rather, in which I most definitely do believe or, with equal vehemence, don't depending on whether it's my need for a momentary fix of lesions or of edifices that's in the ascendant. I'll let you draw your own conclusions but it would be nice to think that at this very moment and after all I've maintained you were convinced said byproducts subsisted deep—or perhaps not so deep—within the work at hand.

When he looked down it was Belle—not (but how could it have been?) Joyce—clinging to him jealously as if for dear life since her attention had just been completely absorbed (perforce excluding all thought of her mother) by the zigzag of a ferocious-looking blonde. As it was none other than Priscilla in one of her landlady wigs (ultimately scuttled) Bert began to laugh—much harder than he had intended but once embarked how could he stop since the laugh was clearly out to prove at least one among his outputs was not a symptom of the self-hate that made him all too eagerly sick and tired of the desires feeding, and fed on, the hate (its—the laugh's—campaign jingle went something like this: Anybody capable of such a laugh/Is axiomatically *inca*-pable of excoriating himself/For falling short of the achievement/Of his rivals/Let alone slobbering/Before/Them/In celebration of/That falling short/Falling short/Fall/Ing shoooooort). Belle said: You shouldn't laugh. The exact same at-the-drop-of-a-hat trembling when it seems to be a question of your worth as a master director of serial-kill-related TV commercials is what I undergo when my enduring young charms as a woman are at stake. But Belle, he whispered in exasperation (unmanned he wanted to enjoy a prolonged striking back), it's *gotten to the point where* (hey, he liked the clanky finality of this phrase and wondered why he'd never given it more of an airing), everything I do—even a snivelling glance at the woodwork—constitutes denigration of those charms. Belle looked dumbfounded, at a complete loss for words, specifically words like, Well, maybe I've learned the technique from you inasmuch as anything anybody says automatically becomes, my dear Bert, a signal that your very tentative place in Flowers' canon is about to be usurped by another [so what if you already know you'll never be localizable therein and on some bedrock level have no real wish to be for in all that bedrock resides the mother lode of an intuition that you can't be damned by exclusion but only by allowing exclusion to hobble your serial makings hence there mustn't be any such allowing: no big deal—the puniest of (or)deals in fact when you consider the wealth of alternatives huckstered by a world where, ahem, *Arbeit macht frei*].

So will you tell me why (GHW asked, as if Belle had indeed spoken the words she was at a loss for) he manages (sideswiping Samuels with a look-ma-no-hands glance) to go on (I've been watching the

SOB: I know) dreading the moment when I—they—the usurpers—receive the definitive sanction that's his complete annihilation? Because he's a genius where the dread of annihilation is concerned, sneered Flowers: only authentic genii can synthesize the credulity necessary to go on dreading the dread that's essential to their productivity. He never gives up expecting that some rival-related event out there will unselve him completely for he knows (the way Pudd knew from Mama Pudd) this is what the Joyces and Flowerses and GHWs of the world—those strange demons for whom his hatred betrays an even stranger reverence—heartily wish him and so *the comings and goings of rivals end up constituting* (and, indeed, you're so right to think: how sad, how very very sad) *more of an autobiographical moment than his very own doings could ever hope to do.* How sad, how very very sad for him, said GHW, merely to demonstrate, Bert couldn't help suspecting, that in the purest souls compassion easily rises above appal.

Though by the vulpine look of him GHW still had volumes to speak there was no further opportunity for this very minute—would wonders never cease—the taxi had arrived so everybody of course felt obliged to remain silent for as long as it took the patient (without a single word of farewell, much less thank you, changing hands) to get herself escorted (reluctantly by Fred, with Bert, a little less reluctantly, bringing up the rear) into the middle of the back seat. Once within Joyce took a stab at insisting the driver should wait as she made a last, emergency visit to the ladies' room but quickly sensing neither Fred (suffocating within) nor Bert (rewinding his watch at the curb) had any intention of humoring this stall tactic (pun of course intended) gave up. Once she was gone Priscilla, before the company at large, took note of the fact that Bert looked delighted, even delightful. That's because (motioning to the nearest waiter who stood clothespinning the blemishless skin on his slender nape), Priss, when the moment finally arrived for the cabbie to take off (as if West Fifty-fourth was the runway at O'Hare) I felt the way our chaplain must have felt when Pudd was en route to the gurney and finally there was no more room for hope that with just the right mixture of competence and tenacity the sod could still be chalked up as a convert—a feeling positively orgasmic overcame me [like Saint Catherine of Genoa I cried out (1424), *No more world!*] and I suddenly longed for a quiet privy (preferably in the grand ballroom-level men's room of some semiresidential hotel over by the East Seventies) in which to show it—the feeling, not the privy—who was boss. When Flowers drily queried the reference to West Fifty-fourth Samuels (of all people) saw fit, drifting past, to note with astonishment by how much Manhattan distances were shrinking daily— make that hourly: every address was next door to—identical with— every other.

There was no other acknowledgment of Bert's avowal, and that hurt: all the actors and Flowers merely sat down again except for Ralph who, slowly descending upon Samuels and GHW, posted secessionally at a nearby table with their backs half-turned, and bending over with a casual arm around each, appeared to have been dispatched to invite them for a last toast or two. And so Bert looked around for some sign of Belle for never had he felt such a desperate need of her support in the face of things to come—already come (if Gift, Flowers and even Priss's regarding him most oddly was any indication)—or never to come. Gift pouted: Why have you all along been taking that old lady far more seriously than you ever took any one of us? We would have laid down our life for you, Priss added quickly, as if she'd been afraid of missing her cue. I don't understand you, he said in return.

I don't understand you kids, he amended, or rather I don't understand you because I do understand that when one is young one feels infinitely superior to all other beings in their mere particularity (and my brand consists in obsession with the ill-likes of Joyce) precisely because it *is* particularity for being young is nothing if not equidistance from every stance available for use in the world. And the fringe benefit—the perk—is the right to stand by and judge without judging that world as a joust of particularities, one more abject than the next, the next in this case being my enslavement to the old lady (all along I've tried, so her vision of me wouldn't gobble up my own, to make her approve the way the chaplain—you remember the chaplain—tried, in vain, to convert Pudd). But of course inevitably you wake up compelled to claim your own little stance in the sun and (after what now appears to be so much wasted time) ever so desperately at that: suddenly you discover that more than anything you want to be as bounded as the very beings, chock full of particularities, you turned up your nose at in Miss-Prismatic younger and happier days.

This, by the way, is what you, Priscilla my love, discovered (without knowing you'd discovered it) atop Gift's shoulders. At such a height, you no longer wanted to be everyone and no one but, like Joyce, a somebody, a beloved—Gift's, say—even if you might, so potbound, never be able to mold yourself into a lovable stage character again. Up until then, will it or not, smell it or not, to such a character you, Priss (like everybody else before *his* "up until then"), preferred minute-to-minute takeover by the alien, random images (of serial killers, for example) that are forever bombarding us from every direction. Only too gladly do they take our place if we let them, cancelling a doomed quest for selfhood (if we want to think about serial killers we should just—think about them, not wait for things like commercials to provide the fuel of our own meditation, and so what if I'm talking myself out of a job and maybe even out of existence). GHW raised his champagne glass as if to throw it at Bert's head (he was now seated at the Actor's Table, flanked by Priss and the half-dozing Dinka) but, seeming to think better of this grandiloquence, proceeded instead to have Bert know and on no uncertain terms the Board's fondest hope was none other than that its commercial would produce the very minute-to-minute (though but thirty seconds long) usurping effect on prime-time gawkers Bert for one seemed to think so little of and furthermore if those gawkers knew what was good for them they'd burrow as fast as their little sensoriums could carry them into the un-suspected depths of each and every (media) minute in order to achieve all the yea-saying serial-kill visualizations, impossible without such bombardment, required to resuscitate a fast-dying subgenre, so un-justly despised. For it is not true, as Bert suggests, continued Bert's arch-rival, that prime-timers could, any time the spirit moved them, summon up serial killers past and present on their very own steam. The subjects at hand are thinkable only at the precise moment the media fuel such thinkability amid the very greatest number (for never forget it is the prime-timer's subconsciousness of every other prime-timer's having the exact same fuel stashed at the exact same moment down his optic stalk that gives the alien image, soon to be much less alien, its very special force) so Priscilla here (he didn't turn towards her, merely shook his chair a little in sign that her number had just come up yet again) should exult over her participation in this dizzying succession of images. In short, boys and girls, the key event is not just resurrection of the serial killer image but its unanimous resurrection within billions of imaging skulls-souls at one precise moment in time compliments of the media's not-so-gentle prod since no key image event worth its salt is possible without some such (only retrospectively after the imposed image has done the dirty work of mediatizing those skulls does it begin to appear more than likely that the easiest thing in the world would have been to erupt the very same image from one's very own depths on one's very own steam) but you'll better understand what I'm talking about on and following opening night—sorry, I meant Opening Night.

Chapter Nineteen

Bert decided the next day, the day before the premiere, to invite his mother-in-law for a walk in Central Park (surely it was too late to be accused thereby of using her plight as model for the Gift/Pudd march to the gurney) for she was still, with some assistance, strong enough to move. Before Joyce's feet a shrivelled concave plane leaf whose brown-tipped green stem transformed it from crucified palm into ailing rodent nodded back and forth in a total absence of gust but at the very moment when the shadow of the leaves overhanging crowded most populously around its prostrate form the poor thing didn't budge at all, no, not in the least. Only when the turbulence subsided completely did it go back to nodding—and twisting adroitly like a bottlecap—against the gradient nature had produced, or rather, that its own noddings had managed to carve out here in the peaty sand, or so his seeing needed to think inasmuch as the fact that the leaf nodded most turbulently when the air was stillest and was stillest itself when the circumturbulence was at an all-time high—the fact, in

other words, that things didn't evolve as one had been taught to expect—was precisely the sort of bacon one craved to bring home if one
was, as Bert was, the ersatz-artistic type since the more the leaf failed
to conform to expectations the more there was to say about it and the
more there was to say about it, if only to himself (for listening to others had never been the invalid's forte), the greater the probability the
saying would end up a saying about Bert or Joyce or even better the
Bert-Joyce relation. What are you looking at—what's wrong? Joyce
asked, alarmed. She didn't like it when anybody was focused offscreen
even if offscreen was right before her very eyes.

Then out of the blue: I suggested this spot because I thought you'd
like it. I didn't always say so but I *am* grateful for all your attention especially with a daughter like Belle and a husband like Fred though he's
a wee bit more on the ball than Leonard would have been, don't you
agree? and who knows, maybe all my recent tests will turn out negative—every single one of them. She looked hard at his left lapel [in his
case, alas, always (infinitely) less dashing than the right], for final and
definitive confirmation of her devoutest wish though would there
ever be confirmation final and definitive enough to satisfy Joyce or
rather The Likes of Joyce, but even if they both were doomed, he to his
walking papers and a bad press and she to muddy death which is its
own bad press, there simply could not be any allowing himself to
warm to her transient warmth (when he found himself about to weep
at the word *grateful*, realizing that to do so was compatible only with
Joyce's unequivocal resting in peace Bert managed to stop himself just
in the nick of time) knowing as he did how with the inevitability of a
law of thermodynamics it must give way to a counterreacting glower
of insinuation about his—the other's—lack of competence or concern or both—to a catching-up with herself for having shown, if only
for a moment, an unwarranted leniency to one who should have been

made to work harder for it but as this lapse was clearly the epiphe-nomenon of a specific time and place and hence unlayable (or so must run her self-justification) at the doorstep of her own deficiencies as soon as they left the spot every trace would be obliterated.

As they traced their compound kerf through the autumn litter— she seemed to be favoring her left thigh (her Panama hat at any rate, with its moss rose, was most becoming!)—the trees shivered, and Joyce saw to it that they did not escape unnoticed, though her notice was in its own queer way consubstantial with a plotting (with or against them who could, however, begin to say). She asked out of po-liteness, impatience badly camouflaged, how the celebration had ended and if the premiere was imminent—first time she ever heard, come to think of it, of a premiere scheduled for a TV commercial: Was that (meaning, Was he) *normal*? It's tomorrow night, he said, and though every emotion was successfully emptied out of his tone (or at least as much as he could rustle up at a moment's notice for such a purpose) suddenly he couldn't help doubting—not just the success of the world premiere (that, indeed, was no longer a matter for conjec-ture) but the very things he'd begun to fancy might serve as a refuge from the inevitable absence of success—the shivering trees, for exam-ple, and the slueing mousy plane (or was it a cottonwood?) leaf— though what he began to doubt most, of course, was his own existence for Joyce's cloud of shrewdness invoked nothing less than his finally going broke in all planes, spiritual and otherwise—and soon—and having, from direst need, to ask her (of all people!) for a handout since this must be the only conceivable basis of union where Joyce was con-cerned. Bert took a few steps away from the roadway, from Joyce's progress thereon, to try to savor and thereby commemorate his impe-rial self-containment since but a few seconds before rather than wait for the cancer to put an end to his living in her shadow he'd wanted to stifle her last breath yet—miracle of miracles—hadn't succumbed. Even more surprisingly, Joyce started asking the names of some of the shrubs up ahead though he was in no mood to intone *angel's trumpet, dudleya, cotoneaster* et al though once he managed to fork up the merchandise requested she, clearly (and uncharacteristically) entranced, went on repeating the syllables, warmed by them or rather—or rather— or rather—by this newfound license to make use of them as she saw fit in whatever mantra was most appropriate to the occasion, or happily relieved for a moment to impersonate a mere bit player in their stock company. A crow shrieked busily in an alcove of the far-off maples, still reddish-green (what between-seasons was it anyway?) whereupon Joyce, turning around as if she were a moviegoer seated in front of some irritatingly noisy laughers, gave it/them a long puzzled look then, turning back, asked Bert (as if he were their press agent, and as she would have asked if without warning Belle, in the middle of one of her goodwill sallies into caisson-riddled Joyce country, had decided to, say—grabbing for her own pink-and-grey capsules—become vociferously depressed), *What's wrong?*

What's wrong?

What's wrong.

What's wrong

Too late:

too too too late.

If only he had known long before—in the womb, preferably— that Joyce could wax just as outraged, terrified, irascible and exasperated (for she was currently all these things) querying a crow's right to shriek at high noon as impugning his sacrifice of her dying to long hours of rehearsal then he might never have taken her quite so . . . personally. Greater now, much greater, than his present outrage at Joyce's outrageousness was this newfound . . . regret for so many—far too many—flare-ups past. If only he'd known all along—if only he'd been told (but how expect anybody to formulate such a caution though at one time Leonard, or was it Fred? came close)—that Joyce's life-brief was not just against him and Belle, he mightn't have been so cruel. More to the point, mightn't have failed yet again to . . . love when loving at any price (preferably a moribund)—and not just loving but *loving on cue* according to CEO specifications about what directorial tend-encies boded best for the broadest commercial appeal— was very much, *if his memory served him correctly*, the tall order of the day.

What's wrong with what? he asked, testing out his newfound virile playfulness. With the crows, she replied. Why? he resisted. Why are they shrieking like that? You mean, he replied, they're not supposed to. Catching no irony (and even if she did there was the small matter of ensuring that self-absorption—the closest she came to structural integrity—did not altogether disintegrate under irony's seductive stress), she simply shrugged what was left of her shoulders at Bert's refusal to legitimate a modest request—that, in deference to her official business, the world this very instant stop going about its own. Still unfulfilled she died the next day, just before dawn, and Fred survived her only by a few days, maybe a few hours. Bert, on the other hand, was never busier than in the succeeding hours what with finetuning the commercial's heartbreaking final moments and purchasing the appropriately shaped headstone and forfending Belle's cave-in consequential to the vanishment of the (transliterated into prime-timese) *mom* she wasn't permitted to love nor had he ever been wooed so lustily by producer folk from both in and out of town as he was at this crisis (transcontinental word of mouth seemed to be doing quite a number on what he took to referring to privately, now that Joyce was definitively dead, as his little requiem canticle).

Still there were of course moments when he feared the many

years of wishing to be disembarrassed of his mother-in-law must be paid for and heavily but an even bigger fear was that he'd end up, once the commercial was over and done with, making a cult of her memory though all the problems connected with getting the commercial's story told at last should be atonement enough. Bert remembered though that blazing within his commercial was not just the usual plot-twisting story-filled light, alias *she-yesh bo mahshavah*, but—and (burning a hole) straight through it—a story-less (and thought-filled) light, a.k.a. *she-ein bo mahshavah*, which, in being Joycelike—yes, Joycelike!—hence more jealous than Bert himself of his essence qua thought-triggering collisions with the outside world, wanted only the instantaneous resuscitations of that essence (uneclipsed by any story but its own, a non-story if ever there was one) from one collisional thought formation/acquisition to the next. So knowing what he knew about the commercial's inner lighting was it any wonder that at the premiere Bert—though pre-provisional client approval, for what it was worth, had just been achieved and though all the actors to a man clearly knew their places (his last glimpse was of Priss perfectly poised atop Gift's shoulders and Dinka, as the chaplain come to extort a last-minute conversion from the killer en route to the gurney, looking on with nursely pride)—should quickly become unable to endure one more minute of the obligatory waiting for boss, colleague and client reaction (or so he muttered to Belle) and rush away for a whiff of gusty asphalt. It has nothing, he told himself, to do with missing *her*.

As he had all he could do to keep pace with a streetlamp cantering from window to window in an apartment across the street (long before one reflection was completely emptied into the partitioning mullion its successor was already oozing therefrom into the pane adjacent) he didn't, at least at first, devote much thought to whether this unexampled feat of plunging into the autumn drear mightn't in fact be something other than flight from the unendurable—a mobile celebration, say, of more contentment with the present state of the commercial than he'd ever be willing to admit or the compression of what remained of his future into a single moment here and now since such feats would loom impossible once there was no longer a community of actors to buoy him up, an actor in a production by definitional decree being, like an ailing mother-in-law, *one already moved on to bigger and better things even before* preproduction's *begun.*

This night of nights was hazy, soothingly so, yet something was pulling him back to the theater. Approaching the marquee (several news teams seem to be encamping though nothing on the order of the droves who came out for Pudd's parksite capture) he discerns (intermission—so what if the commercial's only thirty seconds long) several figures stretching, schmoozing and smoking, and Belle hanging on the arm of Samuels (!). I hate to say it here and now, says Samuels, as GHW high-steps aside to clear a path for his boss's meandering, but this, I'm afraid, has got to be your very last shot at the title. Why, Bert says limply—too limply. You're doomed, says Flowers: they've put the lid on you, old boy. You—they—haven't put the lid on anything, Mr. Flowers, Belle cries, letting go of Samuels' arm and seizing Bert's. He knows this state of incipient hysteria and normally he fears it but tonight for the first time there's no fear only unalloyed pleasure. We've unmasked him, persists GHW. Belle, her cheeks flushed and temptingly pinchable as after orgasm, insists they haven't. Bert, managing to smile (though the marquee's underbelly bulbs are burning a hole in his hindbrain), says, Oh but they have, Belle dear. I feel it— here (but something prevents him from palpating the flab beneath his rented tux). Belle does not hear or is just too weary after what suddenly seems like several lifetimes to get on with the required ritualistic debunking of his morbid premonition which debunking, as she

knows only too well, he'll immediately repudiate, and just as ritualis-
tically (even if said debunking is the one painkiller that really works),
and Bert has too much pride or rather just enough to keep him, now
that he's detected her reluctance, from rebellowing any more pleas for
reassurance. I've got to go backstage, he announces curtly, though
there is no backstage.

Oddly enough, the performance is warmly received or, at least,
warmly delivered (even Gift seems genuinely transported though nobody in the cast was at any moment quite the favorite Priscilla turned
out to be atop the dome of his doomed shoulders), so in the course of
the small buffet succeeding to the last of the bows Bert tries his hand
(Belle now clings to him for dear life) at forgiving and forgetting just
how hard a nut not merely Gift but the whole *concept* has been to crack
though he can't go quite so far as to start waxing nostalgic, especially
in such ominous proximity to this little claque of investors who seem
to have materialized out of nowhere for no matter what they may
think they're saying about some massive ecoclimatic threat posed to
their particular neck of the woods (West Chest? Greenback Hampton?)
somehow without getting a step closer *he* knows immediately in fact
it's all about privilege and the expansive well-being privilege confers
(yet by the same token being privileged *they* know the best way to peri-
odically rejuvenate that well-being is by peddling a tastefully outraged
version of its ostensible opposite) but before the chatter's sense of being
driven solely by civic outrage can make him weep at having failed to
extract the same shameless conviction from the players themselves
(maybe nothing as vital as said overprivileged well-being was ever at
stake for them) Samuels has extricated himself from his own claque
and come forward to proclaim,

Remember the day I had you sign that short-term contract at
poolside. Yes, says Bert, with a noncommittal nod though instant ret-

rospect replayed it as too-cautious, my father was dying. The day, he too quickly adds (guilty not to have been more active in helping Samuels, who after all isn't getting any younger, over the hurdle of his preliminaries), I picked you up at the heliport—sure I remember. But Samuels now turns on him with disgust, proving he hasn't been the least bit in need of Bert's help—Forget the heliport (what Bert wouldn't give to start the encounter all over again): I'm talking about a goddamn contract and you drag in the fucking heliport. Based on the little I've seen tonight, maybe you're just not ready and if it worries me I know it's going to worry my comrades-in-arms even more (nod at the claque but especially in the direction of GHW who holds a cigar and his drink in one hand and with the other is tracing mad circles above the skull of some tough-looking blonde) for they don't share my soft spot for you. [Bert is about to say (but manages just in time to hold his tongue), Not ready, you mean, no doubt because of Turing and Mildred Pierce and Charley Peirce and Lee Wiley and Marty Heidigger and Larry Hart, not to mention the gigolos and the potted palms and the thought-filled lights of termite art and August Steinberg's giblets and that buttered toast of old Coney, Manny's noumenon.] Now that you mention it (Bert has the uncanny sensation Samuels—the other's hot piss floods his urethra—is about to confront him with everything he's barely managed to leave unsaid) Flowers pointed out not more than a minute ago and GH backed him every step of the way—didn't you, G?—that—I recite verbatim—in contrast to you who begin to take shape only by pretending to resist inclusion in the still life to which you insist on delivering up your own fetishes, the real commercial-maker (someday, somehow, we'll find him), persisting as he does—as he must—in the frenzied moment-to-moment of making, is incessantly transforming *his* (be they palms or termites or floor lamps or dusky puddle quim) into nothing less than tools of the trade, unfetishizable because unfixably one with said making. Now what the hell do you think Flowers meant by all that? But whatever he meant there's just no seeing my way clear to—knowing all I know now thanks to him—keeping you on (I'm running a business after all, not an asylum).

GHW now advances breakneck on them both but—wait: turning again towards the blonde Bert sees he hasn't budged and appears to have no intention whatsoever of doing so. With an impatient wave Flowers (arm in arm with Gift) cries, Good show—he's or rather we're being flown out to the coast ASAP: some new company wants me to direct, and him to star, in the first English-language version ever of that play everybody's talking about—you know the one, Bert (Ralph, nearby, rolls his eyes then, aware Bert's are upon him, modestly bows his head as a sign that even if by contrast he has little enough to look forward to in the way of some such lucky break—outside of another thirty seconds of TV commercial mock-ecstasy—envy is, especially at this late date, simply not going to get the better of him)—and though Bert desperately wants to reply *Of course I know the one—about the big-city squirrel whose starvation-driven gallop invokes, for the practiced mind's eye, a tundraful of gnus in their virile prime. Hell, I've been trying to acquire the rights to that for well over three decades* he knows the very first order of business must be Ralph. Triumph, my boy, he begins in a purposefully pompous tone (like death which it rather frighteningly resembles), never coincides with a flowering nor does defeat memorialize the ultimate withering: so, like men (*like men* makes him suddenly want to weep for it means *This is my very last commercial, brother*), we transform these mere points in time into consummations—puniest contingency as purest predestination—which was exactly what I did when Joyce (my mother-in-law: surely you must remember that lady in question who attended our little gala) finally gave up the ghost at Metropolitan

University General a little less than six hours ago since otherwise we'd have all gone mad, isn't that right, Belle—Belle? (but she was nowhere in sight). Her convulsed collapse (in the preparations for which we'd invested so much of ourselves), painful to talk about, infinitely more painful to witness albeit the only viable issue, simply had to be made to stink of finality even if it persists well beyond death. Ralph, hanging his head, did not answer. Is it (Bert's tempted to inquire, but he doesn't out of respect for the—his—dead and almost-dead, the only ones who matter now) because you're still wet enough behind the jug-ears to think defeat going semipublic is not the least bit pretty? But that's all it is, my friend [he's (even more) tempted to add], that's all it is—pretty.

So why, cries Samuels (adding insult to injury which is all at once his specialty but why shouldn't it be when Bert's deliberately betrayed his investors' trust), couldn't you have done as much for Gift during his last years on stage? How could you allow him to go to his grave— I mean his gurney—unsung? (As if responding to his cue GHW now advances on them for real.) You feel I neglected Pudd, says Bert. Worse! cries GHW, searching out the blonde's approbation with his eyes, which, Bert suddenly realizes, were never really able to sit still for very long under any circumstances, blond or otherwise.

I wasn't interested in beefing it all up, if that's what you mean. I guess I came to believe if I let Pudd sing with his own voice he'd only disappear and that he could be made to sing most eloquently with any voice but his own—the voice, say, of a gigolo or a thought-filled light or a termite or a floor lamp or a Turing machine or a cloud rump or a subway platform sporting a host of tabloid-guzzling straphangers [one per (mirrored) stanchion], among other things, not to mention Joyce—the Voice of Joyce: Joyce and *her* gurneys, Joyce and *her* chaplain, Joyce and *her* towel boys, Len and Fred (to name but a few). What

I mean is I'm naturally skeptical, in other words, jealous, of any woe but my own so naturally I didn't give Our Hero's much of a chance to sing or be sung. No, what I really mean is I hoped to elicit songlike sympathy for Our Hero—that's what I was being paid for, wasn't it?— by showing how the so-called house intermediaries (doctors, lawyers, wardens, chaplains, employment-agency flunkeys) spent all of Pudd's precious time parasitizing the bits and pieces of his doom though personally I have nothing against fleecers since fleecers in the right place at the right time, by fulfilling their obligation to the hilt, reveal cunning to be but raging envy of the fleeced's raw fidelity to the most incandescent spark of his root [long before he's done Bert knows *spark of his root* even minus the too self-serving *incandescent* can mean (hell, weren't sparks what, over egg creams in the Baal Shem Tov Tech campus coffee shop, his old—his oldest—pal, Ikey Luria, always pushed him to get off his ass and uplift), like *like men* before it (though this time he won't weep), only one damn thing]. Wishful thinking, say Samuels and GHW in almost-unison (they aren't buying any last-ditch humanitarianism).

You're right, assents Bert—too readily (at least for his own peace of mind)—it is wishful thinking. I might as well come cleaner. Instead of getting on with The Story of Pudd so as to prevent his—as you put it—going gurneywards unsung (I can't pinpoint the moment when I threw in the towel: such moments are, as you know, unlocalizable), I found I wanted to hide inside him as if he were a (racial) memory come alive [I am sitting with Albert in a cafeteria (the kind they don't make anymore) above Yankee Stadium and just (Odessa) steps away from the Grand Concourse with fried egg oozing out of my plate and the unshaven stranger across (we have to share a table near the men's room because seats are scarce) oozing into our family privacy, albeit a scarred privacy and one subject to further laceration any time of day

335 / CHAPTER NINETEEN

or night compliments of the mood swings of Al's then wife, a. k. a. Mama Pudd, and outside smokestacks are belching against a night sky of bluest black (incidental music by Broadway's Borodin)]—as if he were, in fact, my whole filthy past albeit a past already less filthy now it was to be inscribed in Pudd's very own home movie. But a funny thing happened en route to the movie: I realized said past, filthy or otherwise (of course I never let on to Flowers or any other unfriendly hackpressman), clearly no longer valued the thoroughness and assiduity of my prior strolls, in tormented but always reverential solitude, through its fetid byways in quest of mastery, in quest of enlightenment, and that the precincts were now leased in perpetuity to Pudd—of all people! for what could he possibly know about Yankee Stadium or the Grandest Concourse of Them All? (of course this was his biggest—his only—selling point: that he infernally—glamorously—knew nothing and cared even less). In other words, thanks to Pudd's ravenous expropriation my past became fictional, scrawny, incapable of feeding the dreaded hope of an exhaustively researched catharsis—and I was too damn fat to squeeze back in. On the other hand, as inscribed in Pudd's movie, fried egg-related matters *et al*, so forbiddingly involuted hitherto, suddenly get tantalizingly simple, redolent of a small-town—a frontier America which ought to be dazzled by all the cyberdexterity I've managed to annex between its then and my now. But small-town America ain't interested: it prefers to yield up its riches—rather, the sign of infinite riches to come—to those like Pudd for whom small town A's nothing but a Poverty Row isomer. So here in a nutshell is why I've failed so miserably to sing his gurney-going as it should be sung. Wishful thinking, say Samuels and GHW, their unison now complete.

Suddenly at his side, Belle joins in with, Admit it, Bert [he will admit nothing except that she has every reason in the world to consider herself, like Samuels & Co., fleeced of a birthright (and the kiddies even more so) in exchange for his mess of—dare he so overexalt himself as to call it pottage?], admit it so you and I and our children can start living a halfway normal life again—our marriage hasn't been worth a damn for years: my mother's cancer was the only thing holding it together (Bert was about to say, If only I could have had Priscilla speak lines like those: my fortune would have been made, but stopped himself in time). Samuels grinds his palm into Bert's shoulders: We'll be taking care of you in any case, he murmurs but Bert can't help feeling—or rather he could help it if he cared to only simply or not so simply he doesn't care to—Samuels is less communicating straightforwardly than invoking for GHW's benefit a longstanding private joke.

Bert is making what he must believe is discreetly for the exit (he has no idea if Belle is still at his side and would like to think he doesn't care but knows this is not in the least true) when GHW cries out: Why just look at him fleeing like a bat out of hell, afraid (Bert stops dead in his tracks) he's been canned for good when all you've done by rattling his cage is force him to take stock—and for his own good too, to say nothing of the good of the product bearing his stamp: Bert's problem, boss, if we can speak of a problem—I mean, where Bert is concerned, just *one*—is fear that the commercial will finally take shape. Samuels nods: He thinks shape's a straitjacket. And I can't help asking myself, boys (a half-dozen investors gather round), if this mad rush towards the great outdoors isn't further proof (as if any more were required) of some chronic need for self-avoiding zigzag. Stop him! GHW shouts, pointing to the exit. He's getting away! An investor adds, but far more soberly, Can't be permitted to get away: he's left us with just too many loose ends.

Not knowing quite where to turn Bert stands trembling on the very threshold of night and fog. The shouting stops so he tries to use the lull constructively, seeking out the tip of the feather on Priscilla's shako (another thrift shop find, no doubt) listing within. But wait, isn't this—no it can't be yet indeed it is! . . . Samuels—yes, Samuels!—currently observing him on his threshold and with what appears to be real—rancorless—intriguedness. And as he begins to belt his raincoat against the elements (another gift from the Joyce of days gone by), Samuels is observing more and more closely (no doubt in quest of the straitjacket beneath) and still without the least rancor—indeed, with something almost like admiration but is it for him or for that old threshold?

Unused to such treatment, Bert can no longer focus on his task. He hangs his head, trying to look Ralphlike (so as to expropriate the calm at resignation's heart).

Only it ain't easy to stand resigned on a threshold with Ralphlike, i.e. Berliolike tenement resignedness, and not become (while poised for flight) prey to doubts about, say (as is instantaneously the case here and now), whether or not he, i.e., Bert—no, Pudd—before storming out in triumph, remembered to (even if he *knows for a fact* that he did) turn off stove and kettle and every single faucet in Berlio's apartment; though somebody like Joyce or GHW or Flowers would say (wouldn't they?) that ultimately grasping why he, i.e. Pudd, agonizes here and now over a state of affairs whose nonexistence is so patent must surely undo the even more patent calamities issuing therefrom—If only Pudd's last thoughts could've been polluted with a bit more of just this sort of Schrödinger's cat like perversity! though maybe they were and in consequence the commercial's doomed to be nothing short of an absolute . . . smash? bomb? But whatever its doom there's something about Samuels looming, hovering—no lurking—in the motey middle distance . . .

But don't you find (a sudden look in Samuels' eye never seen before, not even at that spa abounding in annexes) there's a thing or two, boys, about this getaway (what do you mean, which one? the one going on right this minute before our very eyes!)—and not just in terms of the timing and the direction and the speed—that (he's over there by the exit, quick! hurry up or you'll miss it!)—that—that—

Kick him out, kick him out, kick him out, cries a voice ineluctable from the chorus of investors who to a man refuse to follow orders and look where Samuels is looking.

Left to his own devices [Belle, then, has elected not to remain at his side and all the actors, except Ralph (prone) who's allowing himself to be given what appears to be a good talking-to by—Dinka! (stooping), are gone] Bert can only assume the look—Samuels' look—has already begun to wonder whether his getaway isn't about to capture the very spirit of Pudd's last gasp better than anything on display earlier and is thus imploring him at all cost not—never—to let up.

Another, deeper-voiced chorine to the rescue: Kick him *the hell* out. He's a commercial-killer. A commercial-killer with a vengeance, corrects a third.

Indifferent to this ostinato roast Samuels proceeds to get on with the business of looking at its subject/target who's still trying to flee (the fog's never been more saltily, temptingly close) though something keeps drawing him back, to the looking, which (so he—subject—target—Bert—can only further assume) has now realized— definitively and in actual fact—it's his getaway of all things that, however tentative and though just another (albeit the very last) term in the serialization of an endless rehearsal, exactly embodies what Pudd's gurney farewell ought to have been.

Bert catches Belle protesting somewhere within (poor thing's managed to block his looking at the look) that after so much dying and near-dying he's surely entitled to a breather.

Samuels chooses not to hear for now he's busy lamenting (so Bert can, again, only assume since the other never stops looking and looking hard and with eyes that grow ever moister) that this, the purest embodiment of what should have been Pudd's last moment or two on earth (hence he's not going to his grave unsung), will never find its way back into the commercial itself and not because the actors are already en route to other, far more notice-worthy gigs but rather because it is precisely non-transduceable finality that makes for such an embodiment: Bert above all others has been, or so goes the look's death rattle (no doubt in response to some tic Samuels took it into his head to deem annunciatory of the definitive mad dash he still awaits), proving truest to the spirit of the commercial in the very fleeing of its crime scene though he's still no closer to doing so inasmuch as said look, death-rattled or not, is—by suddenly conveying the same entrancement with which during spells of optimism Bert himself (when, for example, Gift was being especially pliant and/or Priscilla especially fetching and/or Flowers especially effaceable) routinely forecontaminated audience response—drawing him already deeper into its force-field.

Belle murmurs, He's just taking a little breather.

Samuels shakes his head dreamily. He won't be back, he tells her even more dreamily—for GHW's taste, far too dreamily: might Gov-'nor Sam actually be toying with the notion that his death-rower merits a stay? But imagine just how nice—

Kick him out, kick him out, kick him out (the ostinato's picked up again): commercial-killer with a vengeance (the Governor remains, as ever, unfazed).

—it would have been for once to—

A last—posthumous—look Bertwards.

—harness all that Vengeance—

(*Exit Bert*)

—to our very own ends.